"At once bittersweet and triumphant, *The Kennedy Debutante* melds history and fiction to stunning effect."

—Sarah-Jane Stratford, international bestselling author of *Radio Girls*

"Bursting with vivid details of America and London during wartime, this is an enthralling tale of a bold woman eager to make her mark on the world."

—*Woman's World*

"A well-paced and engaging novel [that will] appeal to fans of TV's *Downton Abbey*."

—*USA Today*

"Maher's assured debut, set against the backdrop of World War II, explores the life of JFK's younger sister Kathleen 'Kick' Kennedy. . . . This immersive, rich portrait of a complex young woman from one of the world's most famous families will hold readers in thrall."

—*Publishers Weekly*

"An engrossing tale of the importance of family, faith, and love in the life of one remarkable woman."

—*Booklist*

"An engrossing story of forbidden love, World War II, and a legendary family."

—Refinery29

"Maher paints an immersive picture of America and London during wartime, full of remarkably vivid details. . . . Kick emerges as an immensely likable character, and casual readers and history buffs alike will love getting to know her. Her headstrong, lively personality propels the book forward. . . . Maher shows the true cost of war, both for those fighting and those left behind. A romantic and heartbreaking look at an often forgotten American figure."

—*Kirkus Reviews*

"[Maher] vividly captures Kick's spunk and tenacity, and readers will not soon forget Kick and her desire to be her own person, separate from her famous family, even if that means losing her family for love . . . a delight to read."

—Historical Novel Society

THE
KENNEDY
DEBUTANTE

❖ ❖ ❖

KERRI MAHER

BERKLEY
NEW YORK

BERKLEY
An imprint of Penguin Random House LLC
1745 Broadway, New York, NY 10019

Copyright © 2018 by Kerri Maher
Readers guide copyright © 2019 by Kerri Maher
Penguin Random House supports copyright. Copyright fuels creativity, encourages diverse
voices, promotes free speech, and creates a vibrant culture. Thank you for buying an authorized
edition of this book and for complying with copyright laws by not reproducing, scanning, or
distributing any part of it in any form without permission. You are supporting writers and
allowing Penguin Random House to continue to publish books for every reader.

BERKLEY and the BERKLEY & B colophon are registered trademarks of
Penguin Random House LLC.

ISBN: 9780451492050

The Library of Congress has catalogued the Berkley hardcover edition of this book as follows:

Names: Maher, Kerri, author.
Title: The Kennedy debutante / Kerri Maher.
Description: New York: Berkley, 2018.
Identifiers: LCCN 2017058776| ISBN 9780451492043 (hardback) |
ISBN 9780451492067 (ebook)
Subjects: LCSH: Kennedy, Kathleen, 1920–1948—Fiction. | Socialites—United
States—Fiction. | Kennedy family—Fiction. | Aristocracy (Social
class)—Great Britain—Fiction. | Americans—England—London—Fiction. |
Catholics—England—Fiction. | Great Britain—Social life and
customs—20th century—Fiction. | Presidents—United States—Brothers and
sisters—Fiction. | BISAC: FICTION / Historical. | FICTION / Biographical. |
GSAFD: Biographical fiction. | Historical fiction.
Classification: LCC PS3613.A349295 K46 2018 | DDC 813/.6—dc23
LC record available at https://lccn.loc.gov/2017058776

Berkley hardcover edition / October 2018
Berkley trade paperback edition / August 2019

Printed in the United States of America
1 3 5 7 9 10 8 6 4 2

Cover image of woman © Ilina Simeonova/Trevillion Images
Image of London by Sven Hansche/EyeEm/GettyImages
Cover design by Connie Gabbert
Book design by Kelly Lipovich

For Mom and Elena, our second and fourth Kathleens. I love you so much.

Elena—the gum and lollipops you asked for are in chapter 29.

It all seems like a beautiful dream. Thanks a lot, Daddy, for giving me one of the greatest experiences anyone could have had. I know it will have a great effect on everything I do from here in.

—KICK KENNEDY, SEPTEMBER 18, 1939

PART 1

❖ ❖ ❖

SPRING 1938

CHAPTER 1

Presentation day. *Finally*, Kick thought as soon as she opened her eyes that morning. *This is it*, she kept thinking, her heart pounding. *This is it.*

Rising out of damp sheets, Kick stole into the bathroom down the hall and ran steaming water into the tub, then spiked it with a strong dose of lavender oil to cleanse away the sour sweat that had drenched her the night before. Fear had plagued her dreams for weeks, encouraging one of her most embarrassing and least ladylike bodily functions—perspiration—and made daily baths an absolute necessity. Her new friend and fellow debutante Jane Kenyon-Slaney claimed to bathe only a few times a week, and yet she was as groomed and aromatic as the gardens of Hampton Court. Kick blamed her father's insistence on sports for all his children, including the girls. Perhaps if she hadn't exerted herself so often on tennis courts or the harbors of the Cape, she would be as dainty as Jane and the other girls who'd line up with her that day. But then, she thought ruefully to herself almost in her father's voice, she wouldn't have won so many trophies.

Still. Surely even Jane would be nervous in her place. Every photographed move Kick had made since her family's arrival in London two months before had been leading up to the moment when she would lower herself in a meticulously refined curtsy before King George VI and Queen Elizabeth, then drink champagne with the most essential people in England. Kick had always been expected to perform better than anyone else, but here in England she wasn't just Rose and Joe Kennedy's fashionable daughter, eighteen years old and fresh from school, who could keep up with her older brothers when she set her mind to it. She was the daughter of Ambassador Joseph P. Kennedy, the first Irish Catholic ever to be appointed to the coveted post in this most Protestant of countries. This time, she had to succeed. There was more than a trophy on the line.

She'd been waiting for a moment like this forever, through every long mass and from inside every scratchy wool uniform at Sacred Heart. A new life. And now she had a chance at it—in one of her favorite places, thank the good Lord. She'd savored a delicious taste of English society two years before when, on a too-brief break from her year in the convent at Neuilly, she'd attended the Cambridge May Balls in a swirl of music and laughter. Now that she was free of nuns and school, she was ready to embrace it all—but as *Kick*, not just Kathleen Kennedy.

Add to all that the problem of Rosemary, her beautiful older sister who'd be presented with her that morning, whose erratic behavior could make everything impossible, and Kick judged that her fear was well-founded. A long hot soak in a fragrant tub would do her a world of good. Arms suspended in the water, Kick said a solemn Hail Mary and an Our Father before moving on to a short prayer asking God to guide her footsteps that day.

A knock on the door interrupted her. Typical.

"I'm bathing!" she shouted back, assuming it was Bobby, Teddy, or maybe Jean or Pat, one of her littlest siblings, who didn't give a toss about the few moments of privacy she savored in a day. This day especially. As soon as she got out of the tub, she was in for relentless hours of beauty treatments, photo shoots, and then the presentation itself, followed by the most important party of her life.

"It's your mother," said Rose as she opened the door, letting in a gust of cold air.

She was wearing a tweed suit and black pumps, her dark hair sleekly coiffed and her red lipstick recently applied, looking ready for a ladies' luncheon or a visit to one of the children's schools. No one would know that in a few hours, Rose Kennedy would be stepping into a white Molyneux gown designed just for her and the night's grand occasion. "A work of art," she'd said to her favorite designer on the phone.

Now Rose perched on the rim of the white porcelain tub and looked down at her naked daughter. In an effort to look as slender as possible to her petite mother, who'd been monitoring every mouthful of food she ingested on one of her infernal index cards, Kick pulled up her knees, which she thought made her legs look thinner and her belly concave, then she stretched her arms around her knees in an effort to cover some of the rest.

"I know you'll make us proud today, Kathleen," said Rose, her voice sounding higher and tinnier than usual as it pinged off the tile walls and floors. "This presentation is so important for your father. For the whole family. The English have been so accepting of the Kennedy family so far, but today will show them and the world that there is no difference between us and them."

"Of course, Mother," Kick replied, because it was easier than pointing out that more than half of the many articles written about their family had included references to their Catholicism, or Irish descent, or both. It was only with her new friends—Jane, Debo Mitford, Sissy Lloyd-Thomas, and Jean Ogilvy—all of whom would be queuing with her to curtsy before the king and queen, that Kick could sometimes forget who she was.

Rose made an effort to smile, then said, "You've done a wonderful job of keeping your figure, Kathleen. And, after some initial stumbles, of knowing who everyone is and engaging everyone important in conversation. The newspapers love you."

"Thank you, Mother," Kick replied, now shivering in the tub. Her mother had left the door ajar, and a draft was blowing in, cooling the water and giving her goose bumps. It didn't help that Rose kept referring to her "stumble" from a month ago, when Kick had mistaken Lady

Smithson for Lady Winthrop at the opera, a gaffe made worse by the fact that Lady Winthrop was a rotund matron whose husband had expatriated to Paris to live with his French mistress, and Lady Smithson was a statuesque but hardly fat beauty whose husband discreetly kept a French mistress in Bath. Thankfully, Lady Nancy Astor had come to her rescue with her trademark double-edged wit and said to Lady Smithson, "Gretchen, you can hardly expect such a young American to be familiar with the hypocrisies of English society as soon as she steps off the boat. Give her another few weeks and she'll be insulting you without your even knowing it."

It was a profound show of support from Lady Astor, once a belle from Virginia who was now a member of Parliament and one of the most important hostesses in her adopted homeland. When Lady Smithson had huffed off to find her seat, Kick had gushed her thanks to this fellow American, who'd replied with a wave of her hand, "Any opportunity to put that woman in her place is a welcome one, my dear." After that, Kick had made herself a set of flash cards, so that she could study every single name and face that appeared in the papers and magazines, and in the copy of *Burke's Peerage* her mother had given her to study a week before they'd sailed from New York, insisting she *must* know who everyone was. She never got another name wrong.

"I remember how difficult it could be, playing a role like this," her mother went on. "There were times when I wanted to run away from all the duties of being a mayor's daughter. But I'm glad I never did."

"Seems like Grandfather would have made everything fun," Kick said, thinking fondly of her mother's father, Honey Fitz, infamous former Boston mayor and number one grandfather. He never tired of playing on the floor with her and her siblings as children, or taking them to races and dockyards and political meetings as they got older.

"He did," her mother agreed, looking down at her hands, "some of the time. But there is a big difference between being a parent and being a grandparent. He was different with me than he is with you and your brothers and sisters."

"Mother," Kick said, sensing her mother's little pep talk was winding down, and wanting very much to warm back up again, "the water's getting cold."

Rose stood and brought Kick one of the plush American towels she'd immediately ordered from New York when she saw the sad state of English towels, which were, as she'd put it, "little more than dishrags."

Kick stood with a waterfall sound and wrapped herself in the blessedly toasty towel that had been waiting on that most ingenious of English amenities, the warming rack. She loved that the English had found so many weapons to combat the constant chill: warming racks in the bath, hot water bottles in bed, chic scarves from Liberty, steaming tea and sweets at four in the afternoon when it seemed the gray would never dissipate.

Rose looked once more at her daughter, appraisingly, and Kick worried she might say more, but after a beat Rose informed her, "Hair and makeup is at eleven." Then, with that heavy sigh she indulged more and more often when thinking of her oldest daughter, she said, "Now to attend dear Rosie. Thank goodness I can count on you to take care of yourself, Kathleen." Rosie. Rosemary. Her mother's namesake and doted-on darling who was nearly twenty, a year and a half older than Kick herself, who so often acted more like she was ten. Which could be charming—until it wasn't.

Rose left in another puff of cold air. Despite the warm towel, Kick felt chilled down to her toes.

❖ ❖ ❖

At Buckingham Palace, there was a last-minute kerfuffle as Kick and Rosemary were lining up with the other debutantes because Kick's train wasn't properly fastened to the white lace gown that had been hand stitched for the occasion. *Curses*, she thought as a lady-in-waiting pinned it on, stabbing Kick in the side. How typical that Kick had been forgotten with all the attention being paid to Rosemary to ensure that she was perfectly dressed and serene as the Tintoretto Madonna she resembled that morning.

Kick tried to reason that this was correct and necessary given her sister's problems. She told herself not to be jealous, to be a good and patient sister. After all, her mother had employed a genius makeup artist who knew how to coax the bones from Kick's doughy cheeks and make her eyes appear larger and more prominent. Her often unruly auburn waves had been brushed and sprayed into glossy submission, curving smoothly off her forehead and skimming her shoulders. It was surely because of their efforts that the photographers and reporters had fawned over Kick's every move, from the ambassador's house at 14 Prince's Gate to the palace.

Hail Mary, full of grace, please make me graceful today. Just for the next five minutes, at least. And Rosemary, too!

To steady herself, she put her nose to her wrist and inhaled the Vol de Nuit, her first adult perfume, which her mother had bought for her on their last trip to Paris. After an exhausting day of fittings and painful facials, Rosemary had retired to the hotel for a nap, and Rose had strolled with Kick down the Champs-Élysées to the Guerlain store. "It's time you had a woman's scent," she said, handing Kick a square bottle with a propeller design molded into the glass and VOL DE NUIT engraved in a circle at the center. "The name means 'night flight.' It's popular, but not common, bold but still refined. I think it suits you." Kick had lifted the stopper, which produced a pleasing ring as it scraped against the glass, and let a tiny golden drop fall on her wrist. It smelled surprisingly sophisticated, not at all flowery and girlie. "Wonderful, isn't it?" Rose had prompted. Kick nodded eagerly and felt tears needle her eyes. For a moment, she believed her mother had seen her and loved what she saw. And though she didn't say it, Kick relished the idea that *night*, with all its forbidden pleasures and promises, should be so featured on the bottle. Throwing her arms around her mother, she exclaimed, "I love it! Thank you."

Time to fly, she told herself now.

It was almost her turn to curtsy before the king and queen, and her hands were so slick with sweat inside the white gloves, Kick thought for sure she'd lose her grip on the little bouquet she was holding. Meanwhile, Rosemary's eyes were closed and Luella, the family nurse, was running her hand soothingly over Rosemary's arm because Rose herself had to stand in the audience with Joe, the only man in the room not wearing the traditional knee britches because, with characteristic obstinacy, he'd refused on account of his knock-knees. Kick thought her father should have worn the ridiculous short pants anyway, out of respect for the country with which he was supposed to be forming close ties, especially with so many uncertainties brewing in Germany. But she wouldn't have dared tell him so.

Then it was time. As the king's attendant called "Kathleen Agnes Kennedy" in his full-throated bass voice, Kick put one foot in front of the other. When she stood before the monarchs—King George, encrusted in medals, and Queen Elizabeth, encrusted in jewels—she lowered her eyes deferentially as she curtsied, then hurried on. Just as Kick completed her relieved escape, her stiff white gown rustling as if in genteel applause, she heard a thump and a gulp and a whispered, mortified "excuse me," as stifled gasps rose up all around them.

Kick turned back to see that Rosemary had tripped. *In front of the king and queen.*

Her feet suddenly winged, Kick rushed to offer her arm to Rosemary, whose own white hand was on the velvet ground, her long body arched over like a giraffe in a wedding dress. Rosemary smiled gratefully at her sister and miraculously recovered her composure. Then, standing one more unplanned time before the king and queen, Kick lifted her eyes to them and nodded. King George nodded back, and Kick saw a glimmer of understanding in his eye. *Well, why should that be so surprising?* she asked herself. She began to relax, just a little.

Reunited in the receiving room after all the debutantes had been presented, Rose bent over carefully under the weight of Lady Bessborough's diamond-and-platinum tiara, kissed each daughter on the cheek, and simply said, "Marvelous, my darlings. I'm so proud of you both." Their father stood between them and patted each girl on the back, beaming for the flashing cameras with that confidence he always exuded in public, as if he were Laurence Olivier or Errol Flynn. Rosemary appeared unperturbed by the incident, perhaps because their parents had chosen not to mention it and—as usual—to act as if she were nothing less than perfect. In fact, the conspiratorial silence about her sister's fall was so absolute, Kick began to wonder if it had actually happened.

Until later, when her mother clutched the ungloved part of Kick's upper arm a bit too tightly and whispered in her ear without looking her in the eye, "Thank you, Kathleen." Kick blushed hot and red at her mother's gratitude, then saw that her father was there, too, giving Kick a similarly grateful look from behind his round spectacles. She wasn't sure why she felt so much like she wanted to cry, but with the stiff mask of mascara and rouge on her face, there would be no crying that night, that was for sure. She sniffled back the collecting phlegm and coughed out a "You're welcome" just before Lady Astor charged toward her, hands in the air, saying, "There you are!" She was wearing pearls and a green gown, and her copious chestnut mane—which was fading to gray, Kick couldn't help but notice—was pulled gently off her face and secured with pearl combs. She greeted Rose and Joe with kisses on the cheeks, then turned to Kick with a warm smile and effused in her bizarre Anglo-American accent, "Well, if it isn't the most talked-about debutante in London! I am so glad your father did away with that absurd practice of allowing every American tramp with some money to come to court."

Kick glanced at her father, who threw his head back and guffawed at Lady Astor's crass comment. One of his most controversial decisions in office thus far had been to allow only American girls currently living in England to be presented at court. No more could families sail their daughters across the Atlantic for a season of parties and prestige in London.

Suddenly it was Kick's turn to enter into the conversation, and something inside her shifted. She had logged many years practicing the alchemy of spinning nerves into confidence, and pressure—the uncomfortable kind that she'd been feeling for weeks—was a key component of the transformation. How else had she charmed the friends of her whip-smart older brothers? Her parents were depending on her.

Giving Lady Astor's hands a strong clasp, Kick cleared her throat and replied with a conspiratorial smile, "Well. You might not say that if you were his daughter."

"Is it as bad as all that?"

"Let's just say the English press has nothing on the spurned friends from home who've written me infuriated letters," Kick replied.

"Oh, Kathleen, people will be jealous of you your whole life. It's about time you get used to it."

"That would be a welcome state of being," Kick replied. "But I wouldn't want to forget myself or my friends."

Lady Astor laughed. "Oh, my dear, you are so young." Then, turning to Joe and Rose: "Let me have the honor of showing off your lovely daughter."

"Of course," Joe agreed with a generous nod to Lady Astor, and a whispered "Well done" in Kick's ear. Kick knew she would vanish before his very eyes as soon as Joe Jr. and Jack arrived on break from Harvard, so she savored this warm, rare moment with her father, leaning against his broad chest and inhaling his clean scent, the sandalwood notes in his aftershave.

With that, Lady Astor steered Kick away from her parents and deeper into the buzzing room. She patted Kick on the forearm and whispered, "By all accounts, you are a success, my dear, but be on your guard always. The serpents lie in wait." Just as she'd been starting to relax, here was another warning to put the nerves back in her belly. Serpents liked to hide.

As the evening went on, Nancy, as she instructed Kick to call her, laughed and confided benign secrets about this viscount or that duchess, and Kick imparted a few about her debutante friends. Shortly before dinner, Lady Astor released her into the company of Kick's favorite of the other debutantes that year. The youngest of the five Mitford sisters to be presented at court, Deborah—or Debo, as everyone called her—had a relaxed, often hilarious attitude toward the whole procedure. The two had become fast friends, trading quips about the ugly hats worn by ancient matrons at a luncheon weeks before, and they'd been seeing a great deal of each other ever since. Lucky for them, the Mitfords' London house was just around the corner from 14 Prince's Gate. Kick just wished she didn't envy her friend's tiny bones, the delicate arc of her eyebrows, her little nose, and her glistening blond hair, all of which were magnified by the ethereal white dress and dewy makeup she wore that night. Kick knew her own nose was a bit too large and her eyes too deeply set for her to ever be called a great beauty.

"Having a good time in the lion's cage?" Debo inquired.

"The best," Kick replied. "I feel as though I've met the entire cast of Miss Sketch's column. And now I'm famished."

"Only about half of the column," Debo judged. "Here, have a canapé." She flagged down a footman with a silver tray of some sort of mousse on crackers, and Kick wolfed down two, then took a third.

"Is Andrew here?" Kick asked, referring to Andrew Cavendish, the second son of the Duke of Devonshire and their friend Jean Ogilvy's cousin. Debo had liked him as soon as she'd clapped eyes on him at a party in Cambridge. He was handsome and blond and a bit of a gadabout.

"No," Debo lamented and then, deftly shifting the topic, asked, "Did *Grande Dame Astor* introduce you to anyone *fun*?"

"The Duke and Duchess of Kent, the Lancasters, the Grotons . . ."

"Oh, Kent's fun, I've heard," Debo said in a warning tone.

"N-sit?" Kick asked, using one of her favorite London terms, short for "not safe in taxis." It was almost as fabulous as *bloody*.

"Worse," said Debo.

Kick was about to ask for clarification when they were approached by a darkly handsome young man of about Jack's age, who looked like he hadn't smiled all night. He looked familiar, though, and it drove Kick crazy that she couldn't immediately put a name to his face.

"David!" cried Debo warmly, exchanging kisses on each cheek.

Ah yes, David Ormsby-Gore, thought Kick. *Sissy's boyfriend!* She kept a picture of him in a locket in her handbag. *You should have remembered something so simple*, she told herself, hearing her mother's voice.

"David," said Debo, "I'm sure Sissy's told you about our friend Kick Kennedy. Kick, this is David Ormsby-Gore."

Son of the Baron of Harlech, Kick recited to herself, just to prove she wasn't a complete failure.

With a raise of his thick black eyebrows and the twitch of a smile on his lips, David shook Kick's outstretched hand and said, "Miss Kennedy, it's a pleasure to meet you at last. What a relief to see that our press has left you in one piece."

"In dancing shape, in fact," she said, determined to find a way to get this dour young man to laugh. "And please, call me Kick. All my friends call me Kick."

"Does that mean we are friends . . . *Kick*?"

"I don't see why not," she said. "Sissy and I are." *And Sissy's a Catholic, too, so you won't hold that against me*, she didn't add. She countered David's stern gaze and held it. A dare.

Then David Ormsby-Gore shook his head and burst out laughing. "I don't, either, *Kick*. Is it really Kick, as in 'to kick a football'?"

"Or even a soccer ball," she replied.

"Not on our turf," he replied, faking a terrible American accent. Then, back in his normal voice, he asked, "But seriously. How the deuce did you come by such a nickname?"

"None of my younger siblings could say 'Kathleen,'" she told him, not even sure if this was the truth or some sort of Kennedy apocrypha, for she couldn't remember Pat or Jean trying to say "Kathleen" and failing. She'd just always been Kick. Only her mother and the nuns called her Kathleen.

It seemed to satisfy David, though. "Charming," he said, shaking his head in amazement.

Now that the whole coming-out business was done, Kick could admit that she relished conversations like these. Until England, she'd thought only Jack and Joe Jr. and a few of their friends from Choate and then Harvard treated conversation like a blood sport. But it appeared that everyone in society here did, and as she collected laughs and approving nods, she put them down in her mind as points she was scoring in a new and exhilarating game.

They were soon joined by Jane and Sissy, then Robert Cecil and Robin Baring, and it was such a relief to finally talk about Cary Grant and Errol Flynn, and Cole Porter records and dancing the Big Apple at the upcoming balls. She saw that David was something of a leader in this set; his opinion mattered just slightly more than anyone else's. She wondered what it would feel like to be in a position like that, to be more than a middle child in a large family, a Catholic among Protestants, and now an American among the English gentry. To be her own person, worthy of respect on her own terms.

Close to midnight, when the older guests and dignitaries were starting to drift out of the palace, Debo slid her arm around Kick and leaned in close to breathlessly say, "David's offered to give us a lift to the 400 tonight. He said to tell our parents there's a party at Adele Cavendish's. She's agreed to be our cover."

The 400—at last! Kick and Debo had been trying to go there for weeks, but with chaperones and matronly aunts and worried mothers watching the debutantes so closely, neither of them had been able to figure out how to get there.

In fact, when Kick scanned the crowd to find her parents, she saw Adele's husband Charles already chatting with her father. Kick wondered how Charles, not the most handsome or charming of men, had come to marry Fred Astaire's gorgeous and talented sister Adele, who used to perform with Fred until she became a Cavendish.

Kick wandered over to them as casually as she could and said hello, though her heart was hammering holes in her ears. She was used to her brothers doing this sort of thing for her at home. *Time to take care of yourself.*

"Well, well, if it isn't my daughter, the star debutante of the evening, if I do say so myself," said her father.

"You may always speak the truth, sir," said Charles generously, sliding an easy arm around Adele as she joined them.

"You are too kind," Kick said to Charles; then, turning to her father, she teased, "But you are ridiculous to make such a claim with all these beautiful and clearly superior ladies present."

"Such modesty," Joe marveled, still jesting. Then he clapped his hands together and said, "So! I've heard a party is forming."

"Adele and I would be honored to have your daughter back to our house for a late supper and some charades, with some of the other young ladies and gentlemen. I know how difficult it is to wind down after a night like tonight, and we'd be very glad of the opportunity to help her settle."

"May I, Father?" Kick asked, on her tiptoes to meet his eyes as well as she could. She hoped he couldn't tell how flushed she was with antici-pation.

"I don't see why not. You've earned some fun," he said, pressing a meaningful look into her eyes—another reference to helping Rosemary earlier, Kick assumed. Was this the way things worked when you became an older Kennedy? Tit for tat? "And," Joe went on, "your mother's already gone home with Rosemary, so she isn't here to disagree."

Kick threw her arms around him. "Thank you, Daddy!"

And as simple as that, she was in a taxi with Debo, Jane, and Jean heading for the storied nightclub as Big Ben tolled one. *The first hour of a new day*, Kick thought to herself. *And I'm wide-awake to greet it.*

CHAPTER 2

The roar of jazz and tobacco smoke that hit her when she entered the 400 was so powerful, she nearly fell over in her poufy frock. Seeing the slinky, sparkly gowns of the other women, she wished desperately for a different ensemble, but she supposed that her white dress marked her and her friends as special that night. She would only be a debutante once, and this was a night she intended to remember.

David led them to a table with Andrew Cavendish—*Lucky for Debo!*— and three others she'd not yet met. Adele and Charles immediately joined the Duke and Duchess of Kent at another table and blew kisses to Kick and her friends, wishing them a lovely evening and saying they'd see them on the dance floor.

With its shimmering, low light and smooth surfaces, the 400 was the most modern place Kick had been in since leaving New York, and she felt right at home. It reminded her of the clubs Jack and Joe Jr. had smuggled her into uptown in New York, where they would dance well into the night to all the latest tunes by Duke Ellington and their other favorite swing bands.

The men all stood up when the ladies approached the table encircled by a creamy leather booth, and introductions were made: Bertrand Lewis,

James Harris, and Billy Hartington, Andrew's older brother, who was also the heir of the Duke of Devonshire and one of London's most eligible bachelors. She'd read in one column that he was on the list of marriage possibilities for the king's eldest daughter, Elizabeth. Kick had expected him to be more like his brother Andrew, whom she'd met a few times with Debo—outgoing, brash, and entertainingly vulgar at times. But Billy only gave the ladies a half smile as he reclined in the booth.

Though she'd never met most of this group before, everyone already knew who Kick was, and when Bertrand aggressively slurred, "Of course, Kathleen Kennedy! Bringer of biscuits to orphans and American style to stodgy British tea parties," Andrew clapped him on the back and said to Kick, "Don't mind him. His uncle ran off with an American heiress and took the family estate, too."

"It's all the rage," Bertrand ranted. "Even *King* Edward was not immune to the charms of your kind." He puffed on his cigarette and stared Kick down.

She laughed it off. She was no Wallis Simpson, and no spoiled English undergrad was going to ruin her evening. For the first time since arriving in England—since graduating from Sacred Heart, in fact—she felt completely unshackled. Swiping a full flute of champagne off the table, she raised it at Bertrand and said, "You forget I'm a papist, too. *And* Irish. A triple threat." Then she took a long and satisfying drink of champagne.

Everyone howled with laughter, even Billy and Bertrand himself. Sissy was so surprised by Kick's boldness, she covered her mouth and nose to avoid losing her drink in a most unladylike manner.

David stood and held out his hand with an admiring and amused expression. "May I have this first dance, *Kick*?"

Resting her hand gratefully in his, she said, "Thank heaven there are none of those beastly dance cards here! I hate the falseness of it all."

They shimmied onto the dance floor to an up-tempo "Bei Mir Bist Du Schoen" sung by a sultry blonde with a big voice. To Kick's delight, the band never let up. "Nice Work If You Can Get It," "Goodnight, My

Love," and "Sing, Sing, Sing." She danced to every song. Unexpectedly, Bertrand was the best dancer of all the men in their party, and he lifted and twisted her almost as well as if he'd taken lessons at the Cotton Club.

The last to ask her was Billy Hartington. Since she hadn't returned to the table where he'd been sitting for more than an hour, she'd forgotten that he was one of their company altogether. Then suddenly he was there for "Thanks for the Memory," standing an arm's width from her and silently offering his upturned hand, with his other arm genteelly behind his back. She hadn't been able to tell from his posture at the table, but Billy was enormously tall. At least a foot taller than she was, even at a stoop. As soon as he straightened up, she found herself with her face in his chest— and she was wearing her highest-heeled shoes!

It was a slower number, so they moved over the dance floor close together, though Billy kept a firm and respectful three inches between their bodies at all times, which was a good thing because it was already hard enough to crane her neck back in order to look at his face and make small talk. If they'd been any closer, she'd have constantly bumped his chin with the crown of her head. She laughed to herself—they must look absurd together. A few bars of music floated by before he said in a low voice that was almost a hum, "You're a wonderful dancer, Kathleen." He had to drop his head down to say it.

"Kick, please. Call me Kick."

"Ah yes, your nickname. It suits you. And you certainly gave a firm *kick* to Bertrand."

"It doesn't seem to have done him any harm."

"To the contrary. I think he needs many firm kicks a day."

"Are you usually the one to deliver them?"

"I don't see much of him, really. He's more Andrew's friend."

Recalling what she'd read about Billy, and what Debo had gushed about Andrew's family, Kick asked, "You're all at Cambridge together?"

Billy nodded, then said, "We're both at Trinity, though we generally run in different circles. Andrew is more . . ." She could tell he was searching for a way to phrase something that wouldn't offend her, so she helped him out.

"He has more friends who need a good kick?"

He laughed. "That's one way to put it."

"Why are you out tonight with them, then?"

"Sheer boredom," he said, though it sounded a little like a joke. She couldn't quite tell, and that intrigued her. Then he went on, "And my father encouraged me to get out and 'have a look at the debs, William.'"

Kick laughed at his gruff impersonation of his father, the Duke of Devonshire, who she happened to know was one of the few important men in London who had not yet invited her father for any social event, as he was infamously anti-Catholic. She took a private pleasure in knowing how such a father might feel if he knew his son was dancing with a Kennedy.

"Well, I hope no one had to suggest you ask me to dance," said Kick.

"No, no," he replied. "No one would have to do that."

At that, he pulled her the tiniest bit closer, so that she might have rested her cheek on the lapel of his black dinner jacket, had she been so inclined. He smelled of cedar and mint, mixed with a faint yeastiness from the champagne. She was starting to like his height; though it made for somewhat awkward dancing, she felt well supported.

When the song ended he released her, and the bandleader said to the crowd, "I think it's about time for a Big Apple!" There were whoops and crows of appreciation, none louder than Kick's, for the Big Apple was her favorite dance. With everyone in a circle going round and round and in and out, it was easy and buoyant like ring-around-the-rosy, but with a jive. A childhood favorite made adult but without any of adulthood's complications.

After that, panting, she needed to rest.

Around four in the morning, the boys ordered eggs and sausages and toast and coffee, and one final bottle of champagne to mix with orange juice, all of which was "to right the wrongs of the last hours," as Andrew put it. It sounded heavenly to Kick, who'd worked up quite an appetite on the dance floor, but she knew she needed to get home soon. Her mother rarely rose before seven, but Kick didn't want to risk coming in later than six and jeopardize the possibility of another evening like this. She would give herself twenty more minutes.

Thankfully, the food arrived quickly. Their party set upon it like ravenous animals, even refined Jane, and no one said much of anything until Billy accepted a copy of the *Times*. Sissy asked for the society pages, then spread them out among the five girls. Kick flushed when she saw how much text was devoted to her—it was one thing to read these sorts of articles and make comparisons to what they said about your friends in the privacy of your own home, but quite another to do it *with* them. She felt flattered but embarrassed, and didn't know what to say.

But Jean, Debo, and Jane had the good grace not to mention how much of the column was devoted to Kick and Rosemary and their mother, the invading Irish American horde, as Kick sometimes liked to think of her little clan. Instead, she and her friends shared the glory, pointing out complimentary lines about each of them throughout the pages, laughing, and remembering the day before as if it had happened to them all exactly the same way, down to the details about misfastened trains and pinched toes, generous looks from the queen, and toasts made in their honor.

But of course it hadn't happened the same for all of them—*Rosemary!* Kick's heart froze with fear when she remembered her sister's stumble. She stopped twittering with her girlfriends long enough to scan everything for mentions of her sister's blunder. *Nothing*, she thought, and sighed with enormous relief. It did pay to have a father who was a maestro with the press, and she felt so grateful for him in that moment, not just for protecting their family but also for allowing her to go out that evening. She didn't want to disappoint him, and she'd already overstayed her planned twenty minutes by another ten.

Standing up, she brushed a few crumbs from her white dress and said, "It's time I hailed a taxi."

"Me, too," said Debo, rising to join Kick.

Jane, Sissy, and Jean also got up, and Jane said, "Let's make it a five-some. None of us are far from the others."

The boys looked up from their sport and political pages, and Bertrand said, "Tallyho, ladies. Congratulations on becoming the latest batch of royal leeches."

Kick curtsied low. "You are too kind, sir."

Billy smirked, and their eyes met briefly before she and her girlfriends got their coats and went out into the blinding London dawn.

CHAPTER 3

The more she thought about it, the more Bertrand's comments about her bringing biscuits to orphans got under her skin. The season had made it impossible for Kick to do anything but the most cursory of charity work, and if there was one thing the nuns had instilled in her, it was that God loved those who were poor, or who helped the poor. Maybe she couldn't solve any grand problems in the world like her father, but she could at least do her part.

But even resolving to do more good works, and hitting on a possible location for such work after reading in the Catholic bulletin that St. Mary's church near Sloane Square was in need of help, didn't entirely salve the rash left by Bertrand's remark. *Of course, Kathleen Kennedy! Bringer of biscuits to orphans and American style to stodgy British tea parties* . . .

Rising early a few days after her debut, Kick dressed in a simple brown flannel skirt and jacket with a black cloche hat, and presented herself to her mother, who was sitting at her writing desk with a stack of letters to be answered on the fine stationery she'd ordered with the family name engraved at the top. Without her siblings' usual noise, arguing over who got the last roll or whether the Red Sox would win, the house was so quiet, she could hear the tick of the grandfather clock in the hall. Bobby and Teddy had set off for school in a taxi early that morning, Rosemary was at her Montessori teacher academy, and Jean and Pat and Eunice were ensconced in the convent school at Roehampton, a few miles west of the city. Though Eunice was little more than a year younger than Kick, she was happy to be out of the social fray, her debutante season planned for the following year. *We're so different, Euny and I*, thought Kick. At sixteen, she'd have been champing at the bit to get out of the convent and into a ball gown.

While she waited for her mother's attention, Kick again inspected Rose's decor choices. In the two short months since their arrival, Rose had redecorated the drawing room, dining room, library, and several of the bedrooms, banishing the shabby drapes and frayed Queen Anne chairs and bringing in freshly upholstered and refinished antique tables and chairs, and brand-new curtains and works of art. Tactfully, she'd left a few of the paintings and sculptures that had been selected by previous ambassadors and the Morgan family, who'd occupied the house before the American government. Like the editors of *Vogue* and *Harper's* who'd so often lauded her mother's fashion sense in everything from shoes to sofas, Kick admired the chic patina Rose had given 14 Prince's Gate, but occasionally she mourned the genuinely storied quality of the place as they'd found it back in March. She was completely happy for her father's most modern of additions, however: a movie theater downstairs, where he planned to woo the aristocracy with the latest and greatest in Hollywood glamour. "Everyone wants to be in on the next big thing," he'd said.

Kick cleared her throat and waited for her mother to look up. At least a minute ticked by before Rose swiveled around in her seat. "Yes, Kathleen? You're looking rather *plain* this morning."

Exactly, Kick wanted to reply, but thought better of it. "I'd like to do some volunteer work, Mother. Sister Agatha used to say that charity was our work for God on this earth, and I've been feeling . . . disconnected from him lately."

"That's very noble, Kathleen," said Rose approvingly. Kick felt her heart expand a bit in her chest. Her mother went on, "I'm sure I could arrange for you to take more of a role at Brompton Oratory, perhaps organizing a luncheon? Oh!" She snapped her fingers as she thought of it. "I know the perfect thing. Ann de Trafford's mother was looking for someone to assemble an event for Cardinal . . ."

As her mother went on, laying out yet another plan for inserting the Kennedy name into a grand event, Kick felt deflated. This wasn't at all what she had in mind. And not just because hosting a luncheon for the cardinal wasn't exactly good work, but because she could still hear Bertrand's sarcasm echoing in her ears. *Of course, Kathleen Kennedy!* It was too true: *Kathleen Kennedy* would do her mother's bidding and arrange lunch for the cardinal. Just as she had delivered those biscuits and posed for hundreds of cameras in outfits of her mother's impeccable choosing. *Kick* wanted to see what she could do at St. Mary's.

When her mother finished, Kick said, "I had something a bit different in mind."

"Oh?"

"Yes . . . see," she stammered. She never stammered. *Don't be ridiculous*, she told herself, taking a breath and trying to go on with more confidence. "I read that St. Mary's in Sloane Square needed some help, and I thought I'd offer my services."

"What do they need?"

"I . . . I thought I'd go and find out."

Rose sighed heavily. "Kathleen." She shook her head. "Your heart is in the right place, but organizing events for heads of state and heads of the church is really more your style, isn't it? Go ahead and find out what St. Mary's needs—write them a letter, and then I'll send them whatever funds they require."

Kick opened her mouth and then closed it. She wasn't even sure how to reply. *Of course, Kathleen Kennedy!*

"Tell Ann's mother I'd be happy to help with the lunch for the cardinal," Kick said sweetly. As soon as the words were out, she ground her molars together.

Rose smiled and nodded, then turned back to her letters.

Kick grabbed her coat and quietly slipped out the front door. Everything she'd ever done was for the greater glory of God, Joseph and Rose Kennedy, and their sons. Even being a debutante, when it came right down to it. Oh, it was all well and good when something they wanted aligned with something she wanted; then at least she could enjoy the work more than those endless hours of prayer on her knees, or writing essays about the saints. Was it so wrong to want to do something by herself? Without their blessing?

No, she told herself emphatically. But then she recalled her mother's expression a few moments ago and felt a pang of guilt. *Well, what she doesn't know won't hurt her*, she resolved, tugging her gloves down on her hands.

In the damp spring air, she headed for the Underground. She hadn't ridden the tube yet, as her mother and father insisted on taxis, claiming they were far safer, but every time Kick heard the trains vibrate in her ears and chest, it was like they were calling to her. They were such an essential part of London, and she had fallen so hopelessly, madly in love with the city that she was determined to experience as much of it as she could.

Since she'd never been in love before, she hadn't immediately recognized the free-fall sensation whenever she found herself, say, at the base of Big Ben, following with her eyes its spiked, neo-Gothic ascent into a clear blue sky, as Parliament unfurled like a scroll to her left. Or chasing Bobby and Teddy through the Tower of London, occasionally feeling an amazed chill, as if the headless ghost of Anne Boleyn had just shivered through her. Then she began to recognize the way her heart filled with a wanton need for more, more, more of the dizzy— yes, even *ardent*—way the city made her feel.

Despite the reporters that followed her around, jostling each other for the best shots of her and her siblings, it was an intimate romance. She found the accents irresistible, even though she knew Jack and Joe Jr. would tease her mercilessly if she ever admitted it. She might have tripped on the uneven cobblestones at Covent Garden and had to hold her purse close, but she laughed heartily at the ragged performers who entertained clutches of onlookers with scenes from Shakespeare or Cole Porter for a few shillings. And while New York and Boston offered similar distractions, she came to feel that so much of what she'd loved in those cities were mere facsimiles of what had long existed in London. Here was the original, the genuine article. Even what was new and innovative in the big cities of America, like the skyscrapers reaching ever upward, suddenly seemed as though they were trying too hard to compete with everything they could never have.

Not wanting to appear helpless in the tube station, Kick had already studied a colorful Underground map she'd purchased at the newsagent the day before. St. Mary's wasn't far from Knightsbridge, but because of the way the train lines ran, she'd have to travel two sides of a triangle to get there, taking the Piccadilly line to South Kensington, then changing to the Circle or District line one stop to Sloane Square.

As Kick descended the long staircase below the streets, her pulse quickened with excitement. Intermingling with the familiar sound of engines and brakes, male voices called out station names and the shuffle of hundreds of shoes hurried to and fro. The station smelled of damp wool and tobacco smoke. The streams of people thickened as she pressed deeper into the station, and she found she had to brace herself against the rush in order to stand still and read the signs telling her which way to go. By the time she stood on the correct platform, she was out of breath. Gazing down into the wide trough where the tracks lay gave her a zingy thrill of vertigo.

Unlike what her parents had led her to believe, most of her fellow passengers were neatly dressed in tweeds and overcoats, holding leather handbags or briefcases. Reading newspapers. A few schoolchildren ate apples or candy bars as they shuffled impatiently beside their mothers. This was a working crowd, Kick surmised, going about their daily business. *As am I*, she said to herself as she stepped onto the train. There wasn't room to sit, so she grasped a cool metal pole, though she still lost her balance and nearly fell over when the train lurched to a start. She held on tighter, then found herself swaying with the other passengers as the train moved. It was the first time in ages she had felt carried away by something, *part* of something, that had nothing to do with her family, and she loved it.

St. Mary's was far smaller than Brompton Oratory, the grand, domed neoclassical church her parents favored. With its brick facade, peaked roof, and small turret, St. Mary's looked like a chapel from the countryside plunked down in the city. She was too late for the morning mass, which was far earlier than the one offered at the Oratory, and when she arrived, people were filing out of the doors into the warm morning. She entered the cool interior and, after blessing herself with holy water, knelt on a wooden pew under an arch and said three Hail Marys, asking for strength in the back of her mind. By the time she finished, it was silent.

To find someone to speak to, she had to exit the building and walk around the outside to find a door that looked promising. She knocked at a heavy wooden one labeled Rectory.

A plump middle-aged woman with ruddy cheeks answered the door with a frown. "Hello," said Kick. "I read in the bulletin that you're looking for some help in the church?"

The woman huffed and in an Irish accent asked, "Your name, miss?"

"Kathleen," Kick replied, thinking it best to leave off her last name. The other woman didn't seem to have recognized her.

"Come in," she said, standing aside so Kick could enter a tiny room with a rough stone floor and simple wooden furniture. "Have a seat."

Kick perched lightly on a chair and waited, enjoying the shafts of yellow light that filtered dustily into the room and prickled her cheeks and hands with their heat.

Soon she was joined by a gray-haired priest, a slim, wiry man who was younger than her father but much older than her brothers. Maybe forty, she surmised. She smiled at him, feeling a bit shy.

"I hear you'd like to help us at St. Mary's?" he asked. Another Irish accent—but his tone was considerably more friendly than the woman's had been. He held out his hand. "I'm Father O'Flaherty."

Kick shook his hand. "Kathleen," she told him.

He lifted his eyebrows, clearly waiting for her family name as well. "Kennedy," she said, not wanting to begin her relationship with this man of God with a lie.

Instantly, he recognized her—his eyes widened and then narrowed, and Kick felt annoyed. That fight with her mother had been for nothing if she was going to be treated as Kathleen Kennedy no matter what. "Isn't the Oratory your church?" the priest inquired.

"It's my parents' church," she said with a meaningful nod.

"Ah. I see," said Father O'Flaherty in a thoughtful tone that gave her hope. Yes, yes . . . he understood completely; she could see it in his suddenly amused eyes. "Then I won't broadcast your visit to Father Williams without your permission."

"Thank you," she said, beaming a grateful smile. "I came because I saw your ad in the bulletin. I'd like to do what I can, to help."

They discussed possibilities. The church led many charitable projects in the neighborhood, from bringing warm blankets and soup and Communion to elderly parishioners, to assisting nuns in teaching catechisms to local children. But what appealed most to Kick was assembling a quarterly newsletter that would inform the community of all the church's doings and, as Father O'Flaherty gently put it, "to inspire others to help, if not with their time, then with other means they might have at their disposal." He had been looking for someone of good education who could write a page of information in an engaging manner, put it together in an attractive fashion, and then take it to the printer down the road—who, fortunately, was a good Catholic and happy to donate his services and some paper.

"Writing was my best subject in school," said Kick. "I can write to the Mother Superior at Sacred Heart, and she can vouch for my skills."

Father O'Flaherty waved his hand, dismissing this offer. "Thank you," he said, "but I don't think that will be necessary. A young woman of your background is unlikely to have anything less than the right skills. And I am most impressed by your initiative in coming here today. That says more, I think, than your education."

Kick blushed and glanced down at her hands. "I hope to be of some use," she said. And, though she never would have admitted it, she was glad to have discovered some meaningful work that was, well, clean. With all her required engagements, she couldn't afford to get sweaty and soupy before running off to a ball. She almost heard Bertrand's sarcastic voice in protest at her choosiness, but she squelched it. She couldn't completely take the Kennedy out of her nature, could she? She wouldn't even want to. What she wanted was to gain some measure of independence. And she had, with a little rebellion. Why ruin it with pesky details?

She and Father O'Flaherty shook hands to seal their agreement, and when she felt how cool and tiny hers was in his warm, large hand, she was startled to be reminded of dancing with tall, big-handed Billy Cavendish two nights before. She hoped the priest wasn't offended that she pulled her hand away so quickly.

In the tube on her way home, she chose to stand even though there were plenty of seats for her to sit in, because she enjoyed the sensation of being hurled forward, of steadying herself in the tremulous din.

❖ ❖ ❖

The first-class train ride to Blenheim, complete with strawberries and cream in silver bowls in the dining car, couldn't have been more of a contrast to her Underground jaunt to Sloane Square, and she wondered if there was something wrong with her because she enjoyed both trains equally and immensely.

Capability Brown had outdone himself at Blenheim. True to the title Sister Helen had given him in her arts lectures, "His Royal Highness of the Spade," Brown's vision for the estate grounds was fit for kings and queens. The lawns and forests surrounding the enormous palace provided a soft, leafy counterpoint to the imposing baroque architecture and the formal gardens adjoining the house. It didn't surprise Kick that a man as powerful as Winston Churchill hailed from such a place. For this weekend in mid-May, the house was given up to pleasure, with dinners and dances and riding and tennis on the docket, and Kick couldn't wait to participate in everything, despite the fact that she'd be enjoying the festivities under the watchful eyes of her mother and father. Alas, Billy Hartington wouldn't be there. She wasn't sure why she was disappointed by this, and told herself not to be ridiculous. After all, there was never a shortage of other alluring young men.

Most of her friends would be there, including Debo, Jean Ogilvy, and Sissy, whose friendship her mother was aggressively encouraging: "She's a nice *Catholic* girl, who knows young Catholic men of stature. By the way, have you replied to Peter's latest letter?" Rose didn't seem to be aware of Sissy's romance with David, a Protestant, and Kick wasn't about to let her in on the news. And the last person Kick wanted to write to was Peter Grace, her sometimes beau back in New York whose misspoken blunder about wanting to impress "his girl" with his hockey prowess had ensured that she was greeted in England by a maelstrom of tabloid press about being engaged. To Peter Grace! He might have been heir to a major shipping line, but she had no intention of marrying him.

"What a lovely frock," said Debo wistfully of Kick's new lace-edged dress at cocktail hour. A breeze played with its hem as they stood in the Italian garden with its boxwood hedges trimmed into fanciful swoops.

"Thank you," Kick replied, feeling embarrassed by this compliment, which she recognized was also a comment on its newness, so she quickly added, "I love your necklace." It was a sapphire ringed with diamonds on a gold chain, and it lay daintily on her friend's dove-gray gown, one Kick had seen a few times before. It had been something of a shock to discover that so many of the girls from good families here in England didn't have enough money for a season's worth of new outfits. Rose would never dream of letting Kick go somewhere wearing the same dress she'd worn to an event with a similar guest list—though Kick was beginning to wish her mother wasn't so dreadfully aware of such things. She'd have liked to feel a little less conspicuous. *Bringer of American style . . .*

They were soon joined by David and Andrew and Sissy, and a plan emerged to play mixed doubles the next morning. "Best not to have too many of these, then," said David, holding up his gin and tonic.

"Don't be such a damned try-hard," grumbled Andrew, who polished off his own gin and tonic and looked around for another. Debo grinned at him, though Kick noticed he didn't meet her eyes. They still weren't an official couple, and she'd heard gossip that although he had danced with Debo almost exclusively at the 400 the other night, Andrew was often seen in the company of other girls.

Toward dinnertime, Kick found herself with her father, the Duke and Duchess of Kent, and the Duke of Marlborough himself, whom she'd met at the Astors' London house recently at tea. Marlborough was about a decade younger than her father but seemed somehow the same age as her dad—much older than Kent, who was in fact close to Marlborough's age, but because Kent still enjoyed the company of debutantes and undergraduates, he was sometimes part of her own set at parties, frequently without his wife—which was part of the reason, Kick guessed, that Debo had warned her about him.

"Congratulations, Miss Kennedy, on your smashing presentation at court," the Duke of Marlborough said to her with a slight bow of his head. "The king informed me privately that he was most impressed with your composure."

"Why, thank you." Kick smiled and performed a brisk curtsy. She was never sure if people were subtly trying to comment on her cover for Rosemary, whom her parents had decided not to take along on this weekend house party. "And may I say," Kick added, "that Blenheim is absolutely grand this evening. I'm very much looking forward to the sporting events tomorrow."

Joe put a proud arm around Kick's shoulders and said, "You might want to stay away from her and her tennis racket. She's beaten all her sisters and even three of her brothers on occasion."

Oh, Daddy, please don't brag. Kick cringed. The English never bragged. Not so directly, anyway.

"I'll have to put you on my ladies' doubles team," said the Duchess of Kent.

"Goodness, I'll have to set my arms on ice tomorrow afternoon," Kick demurred. "David and Sissy have already claimed me for a match first thing in the morning."

The Duke of Kent raised his mostly finished martini and said, "That's what modern medicine is for."

"Now, now," said Joe, "not too much of that for my daughter. Can't have her leaving England with a taste for gin."

"I'll stick to the fizz, Daddy, not to worry," she giggled, holding up her champagne coupe. She liked the occasional cocktail but preferred the slower build of the softer drinks.

The Duke of Marlborough smiled indulgently at her. Then his face darkened as he turned to Joe and said, "You know my cousin Winston might put in an appearance tomorrow. Or he might not. Difficult to tell with him. He's always been damned mercurial in his social pursuits."

"Not to worry," said Joe, his face ever relaxed even as Kick could feel his posture tighten beside her. "I've seen Winston just recently. We had a fine talk."

"But now, with this situation in Czechoslovakia getting worse," the duke went on, "I must warn you he is working himself into a lather. Thinks Chamberlain's weak, a pushover. When he sees those damned Fascists marching though Hyde Park, I practically have to pry the pistol out of his hand."

Joe laughed it off. "The situation isn't as bad as all that. We're containing Hitler. You can assure Winston of that." Then, after a beat, he added, "I have to agree about the marching in Hyde Park, though."

Kick shivered and looked down at her drink. Two of Debo's sisters, Diana and Unity, had been in those marches. Oswald Mosley, a prominent English Fascist and Diana's husband, had spoken at one. She heard the Duke of Kent sigh exasperatedly and then say, "I don't have any patience for politics at a party, especially one as excellent as this," he said, taking his wife's arm and looping it through his. "If you'll excuse us," he said curtly. He caught Kick's eye and made an inviting expression.

"I think I might follow them," she said, putting a light hand on her father's arm. "And leave you two to save the world."

"Perhaps this new Superman fellow will be able to do that," said the Duke of Marlborough, with an unexpectedly boyish purse of his lips.

It took Kick a second to realize he was referring to the main character of the silly so-called book with all the primary-colored pictures in which Bobby had been morbidly engrossed the other week. She relished the ironic image of this middle-aged English lord doing the same thing.

"Joe, is there any chance," Marlborough went on, "that you might procure for me a copy of the next issue before the rest of the world sees it?"

Joe smiled with genuine surprise. "I might be able to pull a few strings," he said.

"Why, Dukie Wookie," said Kick mirthfully, "we'll make a Yankee out of you yet."

Everyone laughed heartily, no one louder than the Duke of Marlborough himself. The Duke and Duchess of Kent hadn't quite left their little circle, and so Kent offered Kick his other arm with a nod of admiration. When she knelt at her bed that night for her daily prayer, she thanked God for Bobby. *I know I was scornful of his book last week, but I see now that it's another tool to bring the Americans and the English closer together. Like the movies Daddy shows. I hope I am of even small use to Daddy and our country, and if I am, it's all because of the gifts you have given me. For those I am truly thankful. Amen.*

She woke in a fine humor and bounded onto the court for her doubles match with Andrew against Sissy and David the next morning. Lord Wickham, a close friend of the Duke of Devonshire, stumbled over to them during the last set. He had a distinctly old-fashioned air to him, with his spats and outmoded sideburns. As he watched, he drank whiskey and cheered for every good stroke Andrew made. When Kick won the match with an ace serve followed by a smash of a volley at the net, Andrew scooped her up and gave her a bear hug. "I'll always take you for a partner when I have a hangover, Kick! You're better than most of my mates at school."

She beamed and replied, "Wait till you play my brothers." Then she was annoyed at herself for making her brothers sound better than she was. Why couldn't she just accept credit?

Andrew clutched his heart and said, "Oh God, I don't think I could take that."

Everyone laughed and shook hands, and Debo told Kick, "Thanks for bailing me out of that one. I never could have carried the game like you did; then Andrew would have been insufferable all day."

Lord Wickham approached them then, and clapped both David and Andrew on their backs, saying, "That was disgraceful, men." He was trying for a jovial tease, but with the boozy thickness in his voice, the jest fell flat.

Putting on an indulgent smile, David said, "Certainly the ladies deserve most of the credit today." Then he quickly kissed Sissy's hand in appreciation; she had indeed played extremely well.

"How can you let these convent girls show you up, lads? And one a Yank? Even worse!"

Now I see what this is about, thought Kick. Reflexively, she reached for the wit most Englishmen appreciated, and said in a featherlight tone, "You can hardly blame them, Lord Wickham. God's not on their side."

Before anyone could laugh or augment her quip, Wickham narrowed his eyes and jabbed his finger toward Kick as he snarled, "Your time will come, *Kick Kennedy*. These foolish young people may be enamored of your money and fine teeth, but sooner or later they'll see what you and your family *really* are."

"That's enough, John," Andrew said with a clenched jaw.

"Yes, I believe it is," Wickham spat before marching off toward the house.

"Don't listen to that old drunk," David assured Sissy and Kick. Sissy looked close to tears, but Kick stood fuming with her hands clenched into sweaty fists. Wickham may have been drunk, but Kick knew the whiskey had only loosened his tongue to speak what he felt was the truth. *But how many Englishmen did he speak for?* Kick wondered. *Too many*, she suspected moodily, *starting with Billy Hartington's father*. She felt horribly guilty, as if she'd let her parents down, and vowed to step up her efforts on the cardinal's luncheon.

She was still brooding when she got back to London, was sullen and cantankerous all through dinner. Just before bed as she said her prayers, there was a knock on her door and a soft "Kick? It's me, Rosemary."

Kick opened her door to see her sister holding a tray of desserts, smiling like a child who'd gotten away with something big. "I thought you needed some cheering up," she said with hopefully raised eyebrows. "Let me in quickly, so no one sees." *No one* meaning Rose, who wouldn't want to see her two daughters stuffing themselves with sweets.

As the rich, sugary flavors of cream cakes and chocolate éclairs worked their magic on her mood, Kick was grateful that Rosie wasn't asking any questions about *why* she'd been so cranky that evening. Sometimes her older sister was just that—the thoughtful, more mature one who looked out for her younger sister. "Remember when we used to sneak candy bars into our rooms at Hyannis Port and eat them after everyone went to bed?" Kick asked.

Her mouth full of cake, Rosemary smiled and nodded. In the silvery spring moonlight, her sister was exquisite—her skin flawless, the curves of her nose and lips soft and inviting.

"Thanks, Rosie," Kick said. "I needed a treat tonight."

"You'd do the same for me," said Rosemary with a shrug.

I certainly hope so, Kick thought to herself, though she wasn't sure. Her sister's needs were so often beyond what cake could fix. But it felt good to promise she'd try.

CHAPTER 4

Derby Day was nearly ruined by rain, and everyone in the Earl of Derby's box at Epsom Downs was talking about it. Kick was bored to death of all the complaining when Billy Hartington appeared suddenly at her side and said, "Lovely weather, isn't it?"

"Not you, too!" she said, but her voice was merry and not reproachful. She was embarrassingly glad to see him. She wondered again if Andrew or David had told Billy about her quarrel with Lord Wickham, and if it had resonated with him. Instinctively, she closed her lips around the expensively tended teeth Wickham had criticized. Oral hygiene was one of her mother's obsessions, and she took enormous pride in her children's healthy white smiles; all nine children used to travel into New York City to see dental specialists. But Billy appeared so genuinely pleased to see her, she couldn't help but grin again. He was just as good-looking as she remembered—tall, dark, and handsome, the real McCoy.

"Should I not apologize for the perpetually lousy weather of my country, and the resulting dourness of my countrymen?" Billy asked. He was once again stooping over, with the hand that had just shaken hers now pinned behind his back; his other hand held a sweating highball glass containing a gin and tonic. Kick hoped he didn't slouch just because she was so short.

"No one seems dour today," she observed, gesturing around at the buzzing crowd, ladies in their smartest day dresses topped by elaborate feathery hats, and gentlemen in morning suits and top hats. "Nothing like dressing up to lift one's spirits," her mother had said as they left 14 Prince's Gate earlier, her own spirits clearly lifted by her couture linen, weather be damned.

"That's because there is money to be made today," Billy said in a low, confiding voice. "And if there is one thing the English love more than complaining about the weather, it's complaining about winning or losing money."

"Complaining about *winning* money?" she asked.

"Oh yes," interjected Boofie Gore, a cousin of both Billy and David Ormsby-Gore, who had just joined them. "I assume, Hurly Burly, that you are referring to the curious national aversion to actually enjoying one's wealth."

"Exactly," Billy said, "though I do wish, *Boofie*, that you'd toss the moniker."

"Hurly Burly?" asked Kick, confused. Boofie was chuckling.

"Quite apart from the fact that I'm no longer the Earl of *Burl*ington, I'd prefer not to have my name associated with *Macbeth*," Billy said with a shudder.

"Terribly sorry, Billy," said Boofie, without real sincerity, "but I've known you as the Earl of Burlington since you were in knee britches."

Billy rolled his eyes at Kick, and she giggled.

"Oh, and you're so *old*," she said to Boofie, trying to help Billy out. "You're talking like a matronly aunt or something." In fact, Boofie and his boat-racing wife Fiona were only a few years older than she and Billy.

Boofie gave Kick a jokingly stern look and said, "You're hardly one to talk about nicknames, *Kookie Kickie*," referring to her now-infamous comment to the Duke of Marlborough, who'd become one of her champions.

"Hilaaaarious," drawled Kick as the two men laughed companionably now. She was starting to relax; Billy didn't seem to be holding anything against her—her teeth, her family, or her height, for that matter. "Explain to me," she went on, gaining confidence, "because English titles continue to elude me, *why* you were ever the Earl of Burlington?"

"It's arcane," Billy said sympathetically. "But the Duke of Devonshire is the title given to the oldest man in my family. His heir is called the Marquess of Hartington, and the marquess's son is the Earl of Burlington. So when my grandfather died last year, my father became duke, and I became marquess, but I'd had nearly twenty years as the Earl of Burlington, which is why old Boofie here can't get used to it."

"Oh, I can get used to it," said Boofie. "But I still like to associate you with *Macbeth. When the hurlyburly's done, when the battle's lost and won*," he cackled like one of the three witches in Shakespeare's play.

Ignoring this admittedly funny jibe because it obviously bothered Billy, Kick asked, "And yet your family estate is in Derbyshire, not Burlington or Devonshire?"

Billy laughed. "Yes," he said. "I told you it's arcane. I'm sure to an American, it also seems *in*sane."

She shook her head and said with conviction, "Not at all." In fact, she loved these little facts about English life; they were like biting into a chocolate and finding a perfect, crunchy nut inside. Then, remembering that Debo had said she would be in the Duke of Devonshire's box with Andrew that day, Kick asked Billy, "Speaking of dukes, why aren't you in your father's box?"

"Oh, I had to escape," he said conspiratorially. "For one thing, Andrew and Debo can be a bore when they get to flirting, and for another, well, I wanted to get closer to the horses, and this box was on my way. When I saw you in here, I thought, I bet she's never properly seen the Derby."

"So you came to right this wrong, did you?" Her pulse sped to a gallop.

Putting a hand on his heart, he said gravely, "It is my solemn duty as an Englishman."

"Well, I shouldn't like to keep you from such a serious matter," she said. "And look! The weather has decided to cooperate."

The wet outside held steady at a light drizzle. Billy put out his bent elbow for Kick to lace her arm through and said, "Boofie, will you join us?" He did, and on their way out, they collected Robert Cecil, Jean Ogilvy, and Billy's school friend Charles Granby. Sally Norton, who was stuck talking to the Marquess of Blandford, gave their party a sad little wave as she watched them leave. Rumor had it that Sally had a crush on Billy, and Kick couldn't help but be relieved that another of Billy's admirers would not be going on this little excursion.

Billy led Kick purposefully through the crush of damp, noisy racegoers, and their group snaked closer and closer to the track. Though they were outside, all the bodies and the unmoving, humid air made Kick perspire hotly. Her hair stuck uncomfortably to the back of her neck, and by the time they reached their destination, she was fanning herself with her hand. Billy offered her a dry white handkerchief, which she accepted gratefully and used to dab her forehead and neck as daintily as she could.

"Just in time!" shouted Billy, gesturing toward the horses, who were stamping their hooves and shaking their heads in readiness. As the whistles and whoops around them crescendoed, Kick's heart beat faster and her eyes darted between the horses and Billy, whose gaze never wavered from the track.

"How much have you wagered?" she asked him, leaning close to his ear so he could hear.

"Enough," he replied.

Then, suddenly, the horses were thundering down the track. Had there been a shot? If so, Kick hadn't heard it above the crowd. Billy stood still, and so did she, letting her body absorb the vibrations from the ground and the low rumble of six sets of hooves vying for the win. The horses and their jockeys strove forward, and Kick wished she knew which horse Billy had bet on so she could cheer for the right one, but he gave nothing away except his nerves, his knuckles going white as he gripped the railing in front of them. She had no such restraint, and quickly found her own favorite—a chestnut-brown stallion with a streak of white in his tail and a rider in shiny pewter silk, who was just behind the leader but whose progress seemed effortless. This horse managed to glide while the others ran and strained.

"Go!" she shouted, bouncing on her toes and waving Billy's handkerchief above her head. "Go, go, go!"

Two heartbeats before the finish, her horse pulled in front of the leader and won, breezing past the finish line in a glossy brown streak.

Billy turned to her and gave her an unexpected hug, using his own height to pull her effortlessly off the ground. "He won!" Billy shouted.

"Your horse?"

"Yours, too, it appeared. Bois Roussel."

"I didn't want to pick the obvious winner," she said. "I loved the way he sailed through at the end."

Billy laughed and hugged her again. He wasn't stooping now.

In the celebratory moment with Billy—absurdly tall, boyishly charming Billy—Kick had almost forgotten their other friends, but then he set her back down on the ground and offered his hand to Charles, who was frowning. "Sorry, mate. Maybe next time. I'll get you a stiff drink in mere moments."

Back at the Earl of Derby's box, Billy said to Kick, "I'll see you tonight?"

"If you're going to the court ball, you will," she said, hope making her cheeks hot again.

"Be sure to leave a space on your card for me," he said. He paused for just a moment, studying her face intently, as if trying to puzzle something out. Rashly, she wanted to lean up and kiss him on the lips. They looked so soft. But before either of them could say or do anything, he muttered another goodbye and disappeared to find his father's box, leaving Kick utterly winded.

❦ ❦ ❦

She left more than one space for him on her dance card. In fact, she began leaving spaces for him at every party she knew he would attend, and when he started appearing at more and more of them, she wondered whether his presence had anything to do with hers. She certainly looked forward to seeing him. Not only was he an excellent dancer, he was a sparkling conversationalist, so full of interesting historical tidbits about their milieu—like the fact that Parliament always adjourned for Derby Day, and afternoon tea during the season had once been a time for visiting mistresses, or that in 1850, life expectancy in England was only about forty years old, which meant that the debutantes and their suitors would have been practically middle-aged!

But as much as she enjoyed dancing and flirting with him, she kept her distance. If there was one thing she had learned from watching both of her parents in the baffling waltz of their marriage, it was not to give too much of herself to anyone. Her mother's frequent solo travels abroad, and her father's dalliances—it all appeared to keep things interesting between them. Kick had once snooped in her mother's desk back in Bronxville and found a letter from her father, who was working in Washington at the time, and it was radiant with love and admiration for Rose. Kick hoped it might be possible for a couple to share that sort of love and be more together, though the other men she'd observed up close didn't give her much hope. Her gadabout brothers didn't seem prepared for greater togetherness than their father did.

Romance was so complicated—and that was true even for a couple like her parents, who had religion and nationality in common. She couldn't imagine how complicated it must be for a couple like Sissy and David. And she was ever cognizant of Wickham's warning, *Sooner or later they'll see what you and your family really are.* Unlike Bertrand's *Ah, Kathleen Kennedy*, which she felt could be addressed by behaving differently on her own terms, Wickham's words were more insidious, implying that she *and her family* were hiding dark secrets behind a pretty veil of money and hygiene. So, even if she felt a thrilling tightness in her chest each time Billy asked her to dance, Kick decided it was in her own best interests not to think too much about the Duke of Devonshire's oldest son.

Please, Lord God, she prayed more than once beneath the ornate arches of Brompton Oratory, *deliver me from temptation. I don't want to let any-*

one down, especially not Daddy, who's worked so hard to bring us all here, to make sure our family is respected here in England. Show me the right path, and guide me down it without stumbling.

When her mother suggested she step out with Michael Fitzgibbon, then Ralph Heany—both well-to-do Catholic boys on the London social circuit—she went because she assumed each time that this was the course she was supposed to follow. But she found herself in the dark each time. Michael bored her during lunch with his plans for returning to Ireland and starting his own bank, and Ralph kept finding ways to ask if she'd introduce him to her father. She tried to remind herself that the nuns had told her God's will wasn't easy to follow, and she resolved to do better. She just wished London didn't offer so many enticing detours.

CHAPTER 5

"Jack!"

Kick ran down the stairs at 14 Prince's Gate and threw herself on her brother in an enormous hug. It was always a bit of a shock to see him after a long time away, and remember how golden he was, especially in the summer, how tan, how rakish the glint in his blue eyes. Through his rumpled travel suit, she could feel how thin and bony he was—the mysterious afflictions that had tormented his back and lungs since childhood were at work again. Mother would have many choice words about his characteristic lack of concern for his appearance and health when she returned from checking every detail of the Independence Day bash to be held at the embassy that night. But for now, right now, her brother was hers.

"Kick!" he exclaimed, embracing her in return; despite his skinniness, his arms felt strong around her.

She pulled away with a sisterly challenge on her face, and sang, "I said it fi-irst."

"No rest for the weary, I guess," Jack sighed with good humor. "All right, then."

And assuming the familiar waltz position, they began dancing jig-like around the foyer, barking the rhymes with each beat.

"Jack," she began.

"Hack," he followed.

"Black."

"Shack."

"Rack."

"Tack."

"Mack."

"Lack."

"Uh . . . uh . . . track!"

"Knack."

"Stack."

"Thwack."

"Pack."

Jack opened his mouth for another rhyme and instead began to laugh, then cough. He backed away so he could cover his mouth with a hankie. "You win, little sister."

"Are you all right?" she asked, her heart thudding from their dance.

He finished hacking and said, "I'm fine. All that sea air, you know, and now the fog. I hope Mother isn't here to see me." As usual, he didn't sound *worried* that their mother might see him in such a state, but rather annoyed at what her reaction would be if she did.

Kick shook her head. Everyone else in the family had gathered around. Joe Sr. and Joe Jr. had followed Jack into the house, and all the other Kennedy kids plus Luella had rushed down when they heard Kick and Jack's familiar rhyming dance. They hadn't seen their brothers since Christmas, and hadn't seen their father in weeks, since he'd gone to America for his namesake's graduation from Harvard. In fact, the whole clan except for Rose was at that moment standing in the exact same spot, the foyer of Prince's Gate, for the first time in nearly a year, and there was a raucous round of hugs and greetings and tickles and pokes and "Come here, let me show you this!"

Joy filled Kick's heart as she hugged and kissed her father and Joe Jr., who looked handsomer than ever and utterly carefree now that he was finished with college, ready to embark on what he had always referred to as "real life." He was darker than his younger brother, in looks and disposition. Ever the brooder, Joe Jr. had thick cola-colored hair he kept combed back, and his eyes were deeply set like Kick's own. He smiled less easily than Jack, and sometimes Kick thought that made his smiles more precious to win. He smiled at her now, and enveloped her in a hug so much stronger than Jack's that Kick felt more alarmed about her other brother. But the last thing Jack needed was a mother *and* sister nagging him about his health.

As she'd predicted to herself four months before when she arrived in London, Kick became all but invisible to her father with his oldest sons in the room. "Give them some space!" he shouted at the rest of his children, so that he could lead Joe Jr. and Jack on a grand tour of the house. The littler Kennedys trailed behind like eager spaniels, but Kick slipped away to her own room, where she could savor a little privacy before the big events of the day. Perhaps there would be benefits to her new invisibility, but still, she'd begun to get used to her father's compliments and attention in recent months, and this slide back into her brothers' shadow jabbed at her insides.

The next few hours were a chaotic sprint to the Fourth of July dinner at the Dorchester Hotel given by the American Society of London, to be followed by a party for 1,500 hosted by Joe and Rose at the embassy. There was no time for catching up, only bathing and freshening and throwing clothes and footballs down the halls in euphoric excitement. Somehow, under the sheepherder-like guidance of Luella, all nine Kennedy children—Joe Jr., Jack, Rosemary, Kick, Eunice, Pat, Bobby, Jean, and Teddy—all managed to make themselves presentable for the soirees. Together with their parents, they occupied three taxicabs that honked and shoved their way through London toward the festivities.

The Dorchester was festooned with American flags and red, white, and blue swags of every size, shape, and dimension. Sparklers crackled and men attired as minutemen drank ale. As the Kennedys entered, a big brass band wearing white linen jackets, stars-and-stripes bow ties, and white straw hats was playing an up-tempo "When the Saints Go Marching In."

"Is this really England?" laughed Jack.

"Looks more like New Orleans to me," agreed Joe Jr.

The two brothers shook hands and grinned so hard, their cheeks practically eclipsed their eyes, and Kick knew why: they had a running bet for how many women each of them would speak to that night, and likely another for who would bed one first. Kick sighed. Her brothers were NSITs. She didn't like to think what Debo and the others would say about that. Tomorrow, she'd have to give her brothers a stern talking-to about which of her friends were off-limits.

Fortunately, it was mostly Americans that night. The Kennedys were seated with the Rockefellers, who were in town with their son David. Joe Jr. and Jack immediately set about grilling him for his knowledge of local haunts. Because of course Kick's word as a girl wasn't good enough—even though David gave them precisely the same advice about the 400 and Café de Paris that she had in the car on the way over. She rolled her eyes at them.

John Rockefeller had imbibed just enough of the freely flowing "Independence punch" to ask Kick's father, "So, Joe, what are you planning to do about the Jewish problem? You must know from your recent visit stateside that they are very unhappy with the things Hitler is saying. Damned incendiary, I have to agree. Do you believe what he says? Take him seriously?"

"I think we have to," Joe replied, keeping his expression a balanced mix of appreciation for his countryman's concern and stoic belief that he was in the right. Kick watched Jack and Joe watching their father, as if they were memorizing images for a test. "Hitler is many things, and I think so far he is showing himself to be a man of his word. For better and worse. His opinion of the Jews in Germany is . . . unfortunate." Joe frowned, letting just enough emotion onto his face that Kick could tell the subject was painful to him, though she'd heard her father get annoyed at the Jewish journalists over the morning papers many times.

"Rest assured," Joe went on, "Chamberlain and I are working on ways of getting the oppressed out of Germany. But I'm sure you'll agree that *peace* between our nations is the essential thing. No one wants another war."

"Wanting and getting are two different things," warned John. "Be careful, Joe."

"I can't be anything else, can I?" her father replied. Jack nodded subtly.

Then, expertly, before anyone had a chance to utter another word on the uncomfortable subject, Rose swooped in: "I've read such wonderful things about your Sealantic Fund, Mr. Rockefeller. Please tell us all about its first beneficiaries." *Is that the extent of a woman's role in a conversation like this?* Kick wondered. *To make everything pretty again?* If so, her mother had certainly mastered it. But she couldn't help feeling its triviality.

Leaning over, Kick whispered to Jack, "Which oppressed people was Daddy talking about?"

"The Jews," he whispered back. "He wants to get some to America and some here to England."

His answer had come so fast. "How do you know that?"

"We had a lot of time to talk on the boat."

Of course their father had used that time to confide his plans to his sons. To educate and groom them. The last serious conversation Kick had had with her father was about the weekend she'd spent at Hatfield. She'd amused him with the irony that she'd been put in the Oliver Cromwell room to sleep and say her prayers. She had to figure out how to change that.

❧ ❧ ❧

She needn't have worried about her brothers. They fit right in with her new friends and set their less honorable sights on women several years older. In fact, Jack did such a first-rate job of disarming everyone that after one supper at Londonderry House, Debo's mother Muv Mitford told her daughter, "Mark my words, someday that boy will be president of the United States."

This report sent Kick into a fit of giggles. "Jack!?" she said to her friend. "Doesn't she mean Joe? Surely the English of all people believe in primogeniture."

Debo shook her head and said, "But she's very aware that the Kennedys are *not* English. And come on, you must see that Joe's more . . . sullen. Jack has such a light touch with everyone, and gets them to do everything he wants."

"I suppose he does," said Kick, unworried. Her father would likely be president first, anyway. He'd struck some sort of deal with FDR, and this ambassadorship was just a stone on that road.

It was Rosemary she was starting to worry more about.

Kick had just come back from a hot afternoon selling programs with her sister for a Tower Hill improvement cause, and was sitting on her bed massaging her legs, when Rosemary burst into Kick's room, her voice dangerously shrill. "Why can't I go?"

The obvious answer to Rosemary's question was that she wasn't going out that night because she hadn't been *invited* to dine with the Duke and Duchess of Kent, nor had she been invited to attend Sally Norton's ball afterward. But Kick knew that to utter such a truth out loud would be a kind of betrayal of the whole family. Her mother simply didn't admit such oversights—for the same reason that she sent Joe Jr. and Jack to escort Rosemary to every single dance back home that she *was* invited to. *Make sure she dances all night, boys! Kennedys should never be wallflowers.*

"Honestly," Kick said, hoping to distract her sister, "I wish *I* could stay home tonight after all we did this afternoon. I'm sure Bobby and Jean would love to watch a movie with you downstairs in Daddy's theater."

"I've seen all the movies already! I want to go dancing! Why do *you* get all the invitations? Everyone says I'm prettier."

Kick swallowed deliberately and reminded herself not to take Rosemary's slight personally. After all, her disheveled older sister didn't look or sound pretty at the moment.

"You most certainly *are* the prettiest, Rosie," said Kick, rising off the bed and gently approaching her sister to rub her back.

"Don't touch me!"

Rosemary coiled her long fingers into her dark curls and started to tug forcefully, her wide-eyed gaze directed at the ground.

"Rosemary, it's me, Kick. Didn't we have fun together today? Let me take you to Luella and Bobby and talk about a movie. Clark Gable can cure any ill."

"Don't touch me! Don't! Don't!"

Rosemary was yelling and crying now, and Kick heard fast footsteps on the stairs and in the hall outside. She was expecting her mother, but it was her father who cradled Rosemary in his arms, leaning her head against his chest. "There, there, my darling girl. How can Daddy help you?"

Rosemary clung to her father and sobbed into his lapel.

Joe gave Kick a *what happened?* look, and Kick shrugged. *One of those times.*

Her father stood and patted Rosemary's back, then hushed her into submission. No one else was as good at this maneuver as their tall, broad-shouldered father. As she watched him patiently sit with her sister, something cracked open in Kick's chest and she felt like crying herself. She felt like a child. Why should she be jealous of this attention? She certainly didn't want to be like her sister in order to get it.

❖ ❖ ❖

Her mood improved at the Mountbattens' penthouse, where everyone was in the mood to dance, and the feeling in the air was closer to that of a club than one of the staid debutante dances, even though this party was to celebrate Sally Norton's presentation. Maybe the more relaxed atmosphere was because it was a smaller affair in a fashionable apartment looking down on the shimmery London streets. Or because of the Naughty Show-girls, an original and very strong cocktail the Duke of Kent was serving up. Or because the band specialized in swing. Whatever the reason, every-one danced that night. Big Apples, Lindy Hops, and the Charleston.

A little after midnight, Kick was catching her breath with Debo and Jean when Sally Norton dropped into a chair looking happy and flushed, her blond curls bobbing cheerfully at her shoulders.

"The boys are at their best tonight, aren't they?" she asked.

"Indeed!" agreed Jean. "And what a wonderful party, Sally."

"Thank you, darling," she said. "Of course, I had next to nothing to do with it."

"Don't be so modest." Debo waved her hand.

"I may have had some input on the band," Sally said. "After all, I wanted to make sure all my girlfriends got to take plenty of turns with their beaus."

"Speak of the devil," said Jean as Andrew pulled Debo up from her chair and spun her onto the smooth parquet floor to "You're the Top." "I think I might go find James," she added, leaving Kick and Sally alone at the table.

"Too bad about Billy and that Oxford girl," Sally said.

"Pardon?" asked Kick, her stomach giving an unexpected lurch.

Sally looked embarrassed at her gaffe, but Kick wasn't entirely sure it was genuine. Sally elaborated: "Oh, you know, Margaret . . . oh, what's her surname? I can't remember. Anyway, she's reading literature at one of the women's colleges at Oxford. How dull, right? And she's not from an especially good family, so Billy's parents would be absolutely opposed. Still, there was that photo of them in the Oxford paper."

"Well," said Kick, trying to laugh although she felt queasy—and she wasn't sure if her uneasiness was because of the news itself or because of the snaky way it was being revealed to her. *Serpents lie in wait*, Nancy Astor had warned. "It's a good thing Billy and I aren't serious or anything, or I'd be terribly upset."

"Yes," said Sally with a raised eyebrow. "Good thing."

Kick couldn't help adding, "And who reads the college papers anyway?"

Sally didn't have a reply for that.

To her dismay, Kick spent the rest of the evening trying to figure out how to get more information about this Margaret girl without sounding jealous. At last, dancing slowly in Billy's arms, she decided it did not—*should* not—matter. They *weren't* serious. Best to emulate Jack and keep things light.

Then she thought, *Boy, am I in trouble if I have to use Jack as a model in romance.*

CHAPTER 6

It was such a relief to get to St. Mary's, away from all her other obligations and confusions, she almost wept into the tea Mrs. Allen brought her. Kick had finally become friendly with the plump woman who'd first opened the door for her at the rectory, and she now smiled warmly every time Kick arrived. Kick was fairly certain the older woman now knew who she was, because she refused to call her Kick or even Kathleen and always pronounced *Miss Kennedy* with a certain degree of reverence in her brogue. But she never asked anything about her life outside the church in Sloane Square, and Kick was grateful for that kindness.

Kick set to work deciphering Father O'Flaherty's nearly illegible scrawls and translating them into what she hoped was reverent prose on the old typewriter with the *W* that stuck exasperatingly. She was glad when the priest visited her later, both for the break from that *W* and because she had an idea to propose.

After some chitchat about her family, she broached it. "Father, I hope this isn't too completely out of the blue, but . . . I've been reading the papers and listening to my father lately, and from what I understand, the situation of Jewish people in Germany is getting rather oppressive. It sounds like some of them are trying to get out. And I wondered if there is anything we can do to help them."

Father O'Flaherty beamed at her, and she felt for a moment like she was ten and had earned one of Sister Benedict's red-penciled stars on her schoolwork. "What a noble heart you have, Kathleen." But then his face darkened. "I have been wondering the same thing, and I've written numerous letters to cardinals and bishops asking what we could do to help, like opening up Catholic orphanages and homes to any children who might be separated from their families trying to escape as refugees."

"But?" she asked.

"But," he sighed heavily, "many fear drawing Hitler's attention to the church. *Der Führer* doesn't like Catholics much more than he likes Jews. The other problem is that even the more sympathetic priests view it as an opportunity to convert children."

"And you don't agree?" This surprised Kick.

"I don't think the church should convert any child who is separated from their parents of another faith. Adults are free to make such weighty decisions, but not a child of six who feels he has no other choice."

Kick felt instinctually that this was right, and admired Father O'Flaherty's compassion.

"Still," he went on. "Something must be done. Perhaps . . ." Kick knew exactly where the priest was going with his reluctant tone of voice, as she'd heard it so many times before from people who wanted something from her family. This time, though, she'd come prepared to make the offer.

"My father?"

He nodded but said, "I know you want to keep your work here private, and I respect that."

"I think I can put you two in touch and still keep my work private," she said.

"I would be very grateful," he replied, exhaling with relief. "And if I may, Kathleen, I understand how important it must be for a girl in your position to have a private life, something rewarding that you can call your own. But I feel certain your parents would be very proud of what you do here."

"Feeling proud and being supportive are two different things in my family," said Kick, wincing inside.

"I wish that weren't the case," he said. "Especially for a young woman as capable and talented as you are. Have faith in them, Kick. Have faith in yourself."

"Thank you, Father," she replied, glancing down at her tea and blushing. "That means a great deal to me." She hoped that God would be more like Father O'Flaherty, inclined to compassion, rather than like some of the other priests and nuns she'd known, who were inclined to punishment. For she knew her sins were many, and she feared what they might become if she continued to dwell too long on the hands and lips of Billy Hartington.

❦ ❦ ❦

She spent the next few days agonizing over a few pressing problems: Now that she'd said she would, how on earth was she going to tell her father about St. Mary's and ask about helping the Jewish refugees? She felt guilty that she wasn't acting fast enough. There was also the vexation of Billy and that girl from Oxford that Sally Norton had informed her about. On top of all that, Peter Grace had written to say that he would be visiting England soon for the specific purpose of seeing her. She prayed and prayed for guidance, but received no answer.

Then, during the most staggeringly dull sporting event she'd ever attended—a cricket match at Cliveden, the Astors' estate—a sign was presented to her in the unlikely form of Page Huidekoper, her father's ambassadorial assistant. Page was only a year older than Kick, and she'd always assumed it was the other girl's friendship with FDR's son Jimmy that got her the job. To Kick's annoyance, her father was always singing Page's praises and suggesting the two of them get together, but Kick could never see them having a particularly good time. Despite her youth, Page always appeared so competent and stern in her blouses buttoned up to her neck, and her slim skirts, matching jackets, and sensible heels.

That day, though, Page surprised Kick in her fluttery linen dress, with her hair swept up and a deep coral stain on her lips. She handed Kick a glass of ice water with a slice of lemon and observed, "You look like you need some refreshment."

Page looked so relaxed and summery, and Kick was regretting her choice of a raw silk dress; though it was tea length and loose enough, the fabric didn't breathe at all, and the back of her neck and underarms were slick with sweat. She was glad Billy was not there to see her looking so out of sorts.

Grateful for the water, she gushed her thanks to Page. After drinking it down in a few gulps, she ladled on the sarcasm and asked, "What brings you to this most exciting of games?"

Page laughed. "I love baseball back home, and your father thought I might enjoy the English version, so he gave me the afternoon off to attend this game."

"And what do you think? Are you now a cricket enthusiast?"

"Ha. Cricket makes American baseball seem as fast-paced as horse racing."

Kick cackled. "Thank goodness it's not just me. Everyone wants to talk about the finer points of play, and I just want to say, 'Has anything at all happened? Even once?'"

She and Page went back to squinting at the game, trading the occasional jibe about this player or that, when it dawned on Kick that here was *her father's assistant*. Who better to give her advice about her predicament?

But could she trust Page?

She decided she didn't have much choice. It was her moral duty to introduce him to Father O'Flaherty; God wouldn't have given her the idea if it was not.

"I need your advice," Kick began.

Page seemed surprised, but said of course she'd like to help, and then Kick explained her situation with St. Mary's, and about wanting to help the Jews but also wanting to preserve the little bit of independence she'd created for herself. She also explained her mother's posture toward St. Mary's.

"I'm impressed," said Page, which irritated Kick. She made it sound as if she were a decade more mature. "But I'm not sure why you're so worried about your father. He'll be impressed, too."

"You don't think he'll say I have other more important duties, like Mother did?"

"More important than your church? Than helping him with his job?"

"You really think this could help him?"

"I know it can. I heard him on the phone the other day trying to convince an orphanage to open its doors. But that sham of a conference at Évian has made everything harder."

"I know," said Kick. She'd read the papers carefully during the week that representatives from all over the West had met in Switzerland to discuss, then not do nearly enough for, the thousands of Jews who wanted to leave Germany. "It's shameful that the United States in particular should put such a small limit on the number of refugees," Kick said. "The country is enormous!"

"Your father agrees," said Page.

Kick thought for a moment. "Do you think he would mind not telling my mother?"

Page cocked her eyebrow, then said, "Perhaps you are not aware of how much he doesn't share with your mother?"

Kick felt herself flush hotly, though not from naïveté. No, she knew what Page was talking about. But she was red with a mix of relief and anger that this girl, who wasn't even a member of the family, should make such a comment about her father. "Of course I know, Page," Kick replied.

"Well then," said Page, putting out both her hands, palms up. *You have your answer.*

Kick didn't waste more time. While she felt clear about her motives— and also, if she was being honest, a sense that even her father had weaknesses, too, which made *her* feel less alone and somehow stronger—she knocked on Joe's office door at 14 Prince's Gate as soon as she returned from Cliveden.

Though he sounded harried when he shouted "Come in" from the other side of the heavy wood door, his face brightened when Kick entered.

"Hello, darling," he said, kissing her on each cheek before they settled down on the sofa together. "How was the cricket?"

"Hopeless," she said. "Page thought it made baseball look like racing, and I agree."

He laughed and unbuttoned his gray suit jacket as he reclined and crossed his legs. "To what do I owe the pleasure of this visit?"

Kick nearly lost her nerve and said something benign about the upcoming family vacation on the French Riviera. But she managed to say, "I have . . . an . . . opportunity for you."

Then he listened in inscrutable silence while she described her work at St. Mary's and her recent conversation with Father O'Flaherty. She finished by saying, "I hope you don't mind, Daddy, but Page was telling me how much you've struggled with the refugees, and I just thought, here is a priest who wants to help. And maybe together you can."

The eighteenth-century grandfather clock behind her ticked *one, two, three, four, five,* as her father regarded her, again with an expression that was impossible for her to read. As the seconds went by, Kick became more and more alarmed.

He tapped his knee lightly with his fingers, then finally he said, "You've been very busy, haven't you?"

"Yes, Daddy. I hope that pleases you."

"It does, of course it does," he said. "All your siblings have been a great help to our mission here. Of course, I expected much of your older brothers. I didn't think you would want to help in this way."

"You never asked," she said, sticking her chin up and out just a little.

He nodded, and she thought she saw the faintest smile on his lips. "Pardon my mistake," he said.

"So you'll talk to Father O'Flaherty?"

"I will, of course. But I must say, Kick, that I'm not sure how much good it will do. If our own country's leaders, and the church's leaders, whom President Roosevelt himself has written to, haven't responded kindly . . ." He let his voice trail off and waved his hands, as if to imply that the good intentions had already gone up in smoke.

"There must be *something* you can do together," she said. Then she added a bit of flattery to strengthen her cause. "Two smart and resourceful Catholic men."

"I'll try," he promised, "if not for them, then for *you* and your industriousness, which I think should be rewarded."

"Daddy, I don't need a reward. I like to help. But." She paused. This part was risky. She'd never made this kind of request before. "I would like one thing."

Behind his round glasses, her father's eyes went a bit wider with curiosity. "I'm all ears," he said.

"Please don't say anything about this to Mother." Her heart was thudding; her shoulders felt tight.

Then her father burst out in surprised laughter. "But why? She'd be relieved to know that all your time and thought doesn't revolve around a certain Protestant aristocrat. Frankly, so am I."

"Of course it doesn't," she said, too quickly and, she knew immediately, too petulantly. So her parents had noticed—and even discussed—her and Billy. She would have to be more careful. Though she had promised herself to keep it from getting serious, she was finding it difficult when her thoughts strayed toward him in so many idle moments, and when she found herself so flustered by the idea of him with another girl. Not wanting to lose any of the ground she'd gained with her father, she changed her tone and explained as evenly as she could, "I would prefer you not tell Mother because when I first suggested that I work at St. Mary's, she told me not to because she didn't think I'd be able to fulfill my other obligations."

"And you did it anyway?"

Kick nodded.

Joe laughed again. "Well, you're a Kennedy, that's for sure. As if there was ever any doubt about that. When it's important, we stand together. *And* we think for ourselves. And I daresay your *other obligations* have hardly suffered."

"I don't think they have," she agreed earnestly. "Can you put your faith in me to continue as I have been? And not tell her?"

"All right, Kick, you win. This time. Just make sure you can keep it all up. I think this rest in France will be good for you. Best for a young lady not to burn the candle at both ends."

"I'm looking forward to it," she lied. In fact, she was dreading France. She wished she could join her friends in the cooler climes of the Scottish Highlands rather than swim and diet with her family. And she wanted to tell her father that it wasn't just ladies who shouldn't overdo it, but she didn't want to overstep. The fact that she'd gotten what she wanted out of this conversation felt like a huge victory. She walked out of her father's office feeling lighter on her feet than she had in weeks. As light as Jack always appeared. So this was what it felt like to be free.

CHAPTER 7

A note from Peter Grace arrived the morning she was to leave for the Goodwood races and pulled Kick swiftly down from her cloud. On the stationery of the Dorchester Hotel, he'd written in a neat script:

Just arrived. I can't wait another minute to see you. May I take you to dinner tonight? Anywhere you like.

Stealing a glance out the window at the glorious late-July day, all cloudless blue sky and a slight breeze ruffling the green trees, Kick could almost hear the horses thundering in her ears, taste the crisp white wine she and her friends would share at their picnic. It was the final event of the season. *Her* season, as she'd come to think of it. And how could she pass up a chance to stay at Compton Place, Billy's family's home in East-bourne near the south coast?

Prince's Gate was quiet, with her father at the embassy and her mother and half her siblings already in France. With a steady hand she started to reply to Peter's note, then stopped. It would be better if he thought she'd already left and just missed him. Let their butler deliver the bad news. Anyway, she'd be back in a few days. She'd see him soon. Then her mother wouldn't be able to accuse her of ignoring him entirely. And Rose *did* know she was planning to attend the races. Before she'd left, she'd told Kick to have a marvelous time. She just didn't realize that Peter's ship was due to arrive. And how was anyone supposed to know it would be early?

With that thought, Kick put on her hat and gloves and slipped out of the house, feeling very dramatic and alive.

In just a few hours, she was with Debo and Billy and Andrew, piled into one of the Cavendishes' comfortable Austins. There was a long drive to the races, and the traffic was terrible, but the boys kept things lively with bottles of champagne and cartons of cherries. Kick refused when Billy offered to refill her glass, saying, "I don't want to be drunk when I meet your parents!"

"Fair enough," he said. "But *I do*."

She wished she could have convinced him otherwise. With all the other troubles occupying her mind these past few days, she hadn't given much thought to this meeting, but now that she was on her way and it was a reality, all she could think about was Lord Wickham insulting her and Sissy at Blenheim. Billy's father, Edward Cavendish, hated Catholics with an equal or maybe even greater fervor. One of his most well-known statements was that it was a shame he could see Westminster Cathedral from his London house. Billy's mother Mary, whom everyone called Moucher except her children's friends, who were obliged to refer to her as Duchess, was reputed to be much more friendly, with a flair for art and antiques that Andrew shared. Kick hoped to find some common ground with her there.

Soon enough, their party was mingling beneath a sprawling white tent where maids and footmen bustled about making people in top hats and peacock-feathered hats comfortable. It was hard not to reach for every coupe or highball to undo the knots behind her ribs. She'd met plenty of lords and dukes, and was way beyond her flash card days, but her hands felt damp, and she worried she'd put on too much Vol de Nuit. It wasn't even *nuit*, after all. But Billy liked it.

Billy. She could tell he was tipsy, and wondered if his parents could as well.

She timidly sipped some champagne, and then Billy said, "There's Mum and Dad," looking over at the tall couple who were greeting the Marquess of Blandford at the other end of the tent. The duchess, who had a long and elegant neck that was accentuated by wearing her hair up, wore a stylish dress the color of terra-cotta with wide shoulders, and a brown hat with cardinal feathers that matched the duke's red waistcoat. The rest of Billy's father's attire was hardly befitting a duke at the races—his trousers and sleeves were frayed, and Kick was sure there was a moth hole in his jacket. She'd heard that Billy's father was eccentric, but she hadn't expected him to be pauperish as well!

Taking her gently by the elbow, Billy led Kick over to them.

"Mother, Father, this is Kathleen Kennedy," Billy said. "Kathleen, these are my parents, the Duke and Duchess of Devonshire."

Kick shook each dry hand offered to her and smiled, though Billy's father smiled back in the least genuine way possible. The duchess seemed friendly enough. *Just keep smiling*, Kick told herself, but then she remembered—*these foolish young people might be enamored of your money and fine teeth*—and she slid her lips closed.

"Are you enjoying your time in England, Miss Kennedy?" asked the duchess, her voice low and musical like her son's.

"Very much, thank you," Kick replied, clearing her throat. "Billy's made me such a fan of the races, and I'm honored to be here with you today."

"He hasn't corrupted you with betting, I hope," said his father, with a stern look at his son.

Billy chuckled. "Of course not, Dad," he said.

"I wouldn't dream of placing a bet myself," added Kick. Then she remembered something Billy had told her about his father's success in betting and said, "But I enjoy watching Billy. I feel certain he's learned from the best."

The duke was momentarily taken aback by Kick's flattery. "I'll let the horses be the judges of my success," he said.

"They always are," the duchess singsonged in a vaguely reprimanding way.

"The flowers you've chosen for the tent are divine," Kick told her. "The roses have the most delicate scent. My mother also likes arrangements of roses without other flowers mixed in. 'Rare beauty is best left alone,' she always says."

"Why, thank you," said the duchess with a gracious nod.

"Of course, Moucher mostly leaves such details to her staff," added Billy's father.

Perhaps you'd like to add that her flower arranger is a nice Irish girl? Perhaps an immigrant you saved from the clutches of the IRA and made Protestant? Kick straightened her back and was glad of the two inches of height her heels gave her. "Indeed," she said, "you've chosen your staff well, then."

"We're going to be late for our party," said Billy, nodding at his parents and putting a steadying hand on Kick's back. "Please excuse us."

They let the young pair go without hesitation, and Kick flashed as many of her expensively straight, white teeth as possible as she took her leave of the Duke and Duchess of Devonshire, though her knees had begun to feel like custard.

"You know," Debo said quietly to Kick as they unpacked their lunch, "Sally was quite put out that she wasn't invited to come along with us today."

What a relief, Kick wanted to reply. Having Sally *and* Billy's parents to contend with would have been too much for her exposed nerves. Trying to sound casual, she inquired, "Oh? Who left her out, anyway?"

"Andrew doesn't love her. Thinks she stirs up trouble."

"Speaking of stirring up trouble," Kick said, seeing an opportunity to get the information she wanted without bothering Billy, "Sally said something to me at her dance the other night about Billy and some girl at Oxford . . ."

Debo laughed. "Margaret? She's practically a maiden aunt. Some distant relation. She and Billy always got on, but don't worry, she's engaged to a man named Thomas Brown. They're going to run a school together. No, Sally's the one who has her sights set on Billy, so watch out."

"Sally?" said Kick, feeling stupid. But of course it made sense—Sally was trying to make trouble between her and Billy without having to admit what she really wanted. Kick so disliked dishonesty of that sort. She'd have preferred an honest rival.

"Sally's liked Billy since before you set foot on British soil," said Debo.

"Does he . . . ?"

Debo shook her head. "Not since you blew onto the scene."

Kick blushed and felt her belly settle down.

Debo tutted, a smile on her face, a secret discovered. "I see you return the feelings. So . . . has he kissed you yet?"

"Deborah Mitford!"

"What? You might be Catholic, but you're not a *nun*."

"And Billy's not an n-sit."

"He doesn't have to be to kiss you."

"Well, he hasn't. And I appreciate his restraint," Kick said. Kissing would complicate things much more.

"You mean you don't want him to?"

Kick thought of the way she felt when she danced with Billy, and how often she'd wanted to reach up and touch his lips.

She must have taken too long to answer, because Debo said, "I can tell you do! You should see the dreamy look in your eyes."

"Oh, stop," Kick said, looking down at the ground and busying herself with the picnic blanket. "Billy is charming," she said, "but how serious can we possibly be?"

"Look at his uncle with Adele née Astaire," said Debo. "Look at the bloody former king of England, for heaven's sake."

"I'm sure I'm not the sort of woman a man would risk everything for."

"Have you read the papers, Kick? *Everyone's* crazy about you. Even the notoriously reticent English aristocracy. You've cast something of a spell."

Kick was about to reply that she was hardly a witch with supernatural powers, when Billy and Andrew came over and both girls put fingers to their lips at precisely the same moment, then giggled. It seemed a promise that they would talk more later. It was a new opening in their friendship, and Kick was glad.

Later, when Billy's horse won the race and therefore the bet he'd placed on her, he scooped Kick up into the same sort of ecstatic embrace he had at the Derby, and when he set her back down on the ground, he put his hand on her cheek. "You seem to bring me the best of luck," he said. "I didn't win half so often last season."

His hand felt hot and smelled salty, of sweat and the thick rope he'd been clutching while the horses thundered down the final yards of the track. She had the most intense urge to taste his hand, and felt ashamed almost as soon as the thought occurred to her. He bent down, and she thought for a second that she might finally know what his lips would feel like on hers, but he aimed instead for her forehead, where his kiss lingered a little longer than necessary, just long enough for her to confirm the softness of his lips and stir in her the acute desire for more.

❧ ❧ ❧

"What *on earth* were you doing at Goodwood? When you had Peter Grace waiting for you?"

Her mother had made a special long-distance call from France just to yell at her. The phone had rung practically the moment Kick walked in the door. Jack handed Kick the receiver with a whistle of warning. Rose must have seen the picture in the paper of her picnic with Debo and the boys.

"Mother, it's *fine*. I'm going to see Peter soon."

"He's been waiting three days! He didn't come to London to see the sights, Kathleen. You couldn't invite him along to Goodwood?"

Not in a million years! "It was too late for that, Mother. Besides," she lied, "I didn't know when he was going to arrive. He surprised me. Aren't you always saying you prefer it when Daddy makes *plans*?"

"A marriage is quite different. Your father and I need to make plans because of his job and you children. When you're a young lady of marriageable age, you need to think more about the men and what they want."

Rage pulsed from Kick's heart into her intestines, legs, arms, and her reeling brain. Peter was hardly the man she was going to do that for, but she knew there was no way she could say that to her mother. Ever. And anyway, why was Rose giving her such a hard time lately? The lunch she'd planned for the cardinal had been a major success, and all the press about Kick had been positive of late. "I'm going to see him, Mother," she said through clenched teeth. Because she was. She just hadn't figured out the details.

"Where? When?" her mother demanded.

"Tomorrow," Kick said, since that was most likely. Today was already mostly gone. "Lunch," she added, since that, too, was most likely. Dinner felt too romantic.

Her mother was silent for a few seconds, and Kick thought she could hear her breathing fire through her nose. Finally, she said, "I have to go. This is costing a fortune. But *think*, darling. You don't want to ruin your excellent reputation."

Kick slammed down the phone.

The next day, she let Peter Grace take her to one of the liveliest places she could think of for lunch—the Savoy—following a morning trip to the National Portrait Gallery, where he showed a distinct lack of interest in any of the famous people whose pictures hung gorgeously on the walls, except for the heroes on both sides of the Revolutionary War. John Adams, Ethan Allen, even King George and Benedict Arnold—all their ruddy visages deserved praise, he seemed to think. But "Oscar Wilde? How'd *he* make it in here?" Peter gaped. "He's hardly in league with Washington or Wellington." Kick thought it pointless to try to explain. *This, right here, is why I cannot marry you*, she also thought.

She wished she wanted to. Peter wasn't a bad man; on the contrary, he was polite to a fault. He was tall and athletic with dark hair and eyes. Nothing extraordinary—or unexpected like Billy's puckish face juxtaposed with his height—but he was handsome enough. And he was intelligent and successful. There were also the unavoidable facts that he was an upstanding Catholic from a good family with a grand career in the shipping lines in front of him. She wondered if loving Peter, or someone like him, would make her mother softer toward her. Give the two of them more moments like those in Guerlain.

At lunch Peter didn't even wait for the soup to say, "Kick, hear me out."

"Of course," she said, glancing around the large dining room to see if she knew anyone there. The coast was clear, but she was sweating nonetheless. *Please God, don't let him take out a ring here and now.*

"I've missed you, Kick. I'm not afraid to admit it, even though I know you have everyone here wrapped around your little finger. You could have anyone you want."

"Hardly," she said, dismissing his words with a wave of her hand.

"You know it's true. You don't have to be modest with me. I've always liked your forthrightness."

"Thank you," she said. She wasn't being forthright now, though, was she?

"And I hope you'll appreciate my being honest with you, too," he went on.

"Please do," she said, even though every muscle in her body had just cramped with fear. The waiter brought their bouillabaisse, and the scent of the seafood made her want to retch. She only picked up the sterling silver spoon because it was something to do.

"Well, Kick, here it is," said Peter. "I can tell you're not ready to make any promises. You're having a good time over here. And why not, with your dad as ambassador and all. But I know you're a good Catholic girl, and soon you'll have to think about your future. Maybe very soon if Hitler keeps up the way he is."

"Let's hope not," she said, relieved to utter words that didn't feel false, "and not just for my sake."

"But Hitler or no Hitler," Peter said, his brown eyes trained on her, "I'm sure your parents will want you to set up house sooner rather than later. And my house would be more than comfortable. Don't discount the life we could have together," he said.

"I won't," she said, feeling her shoulders and stomach unclench a bit—

this didn't feel like a proposal. She wouldn't have to make a decision immediately. "And I *do* appreciate your honesty," she added.

"I got you something that I hope will help you remember me better while you're over here," he said, and from his inside jacket pocket—a brown linen jacket, all wrong for lunch at the Savoy, where all the other men were in more formal gabardine—he pulled out a long, slim, brown velvet box.

Thank goodness, not a ring. She exhaled as she took it from him across the table.

"I had plenty of time to shop while I was waiting for you to get back," he said pleasantly enough, but she knew it was a reprimand for skipping town as soon as he'd arrived, and it made opening the box a penance.

Inside was a gold link bracelet, simple and unadorned except for a sapphire at the clasp that sparkled when it caught the light.

"It's beautiful," she said, and it was. She only wished it had come from someone else. "I'll think of you every time I wear it," she said with a smile, passing it back to him and offering her wrist for him to fasten it on.

Just as she was pulling her hand back to dutifully admire the gift, Sally Norton came into the dining room with two cousins Kick had heard were visiting.

Taking in the scene, a lunch with wine and an open jewelry box on the table, Sally cocked her perfectly arched blond brow and waved at them. Kick put on her best Kennedy smile and waved back.

Showing no interest in who'd just walked in, Peter picked up his spoon and said, "Just don't wait too long," before diving into the bouillabaisse like a man dying from hunger.

There was no way to see Billy to explain anything before she left for Cannes, because he was already up in Scotland. When she talked to Debo on the phone, her friend promised to set any rumors straight, and Kick got on the train to Dover telling herself that if Billy *did* hear what had happened, it would be God's will, and she would do her best to accept it. But she prayed to the Virgin that it would not be her path.

CHAPTER 8

On the other side of her painted toes, the vast blue of the Mediterranean shimmered out to an almost invisible horizon, so indistinguishable was it from the azure of the sky.

"How perfectly dull," Kick said to Jack, who was lying on the cushioned chaise next to her, dripping from his latest dip in the pool.

"Open your eyes, Kick. We're in *Eden*-Roc."

"*You* are in Eden. I am in Mother's fruit-and-fiber prison."

Jack chuckled. "You are looking very svelte, though."

"I'm starving. And I want to go to the clubs with you and Joe. If I can't be with my friends, I'd like to at least have fun where I am." But her mother was determined to make her lose the pounds she'd put on during the season, and, in her words, *Even dancing can't undo the ravages of too much champagne and cream sauce.*

"Buck up, kid. It'll be over soon."

"In three more weeks!" Meanwhile, Sally Norton was no doubt insinuating herself with Billy.

"Why don't you come with me to Austria?"

"What would we do there?"

"Tour the castles. Hike the mountains. Drink beer. Jimmy's invited me. I'll have to do some fact-finding for Dad, but it shouldn't interfere too much with our fun."

She wondered if she could lose the last four pounds by then. "And what'll we tell Mother?"

"You're coming to keep me in line?" Jack smirked, and Kick knew exactly why. He hadn't shut up about it.

Kick rolled her eyes. "I wish you wouldn't gloat so much."

"She's a *movie star*, Kick. *The* movie star."

"Marlene Dietrich is hardly *the* movie star anymore, Jack. Try Vivien Leigh."

"The younger ones aren't as . . . *experienced* as Marlene. Dad would be proud, don't you think? Chip off the old block?"

"I wish you wouldn't talk about Daddy that way."

"You know it's true, though. I don't believe in protecting you like Mom and Dad do."

Jack smiled widely. She suspected he'd shone that same smile on Marlene Dietrich when he'd bumped into her at the Cap d'Antibes Hotel three days before. No one had ever been able to resist it. Since his little brother had made off with the movie star, Joe Jr. hadn't spoken to Jack; instead he rough-housed with Teddy and Bobby in the surf and read books about Spain, as he'd recently become obsessed with seeing the revolution there in action. Their father had forbidden him to go, however, saying, "I'll be damned if my oldest son goes to the bloodiest place since the Somme, especially when I'm spending all my time trying to avoid another war in the rest of Europe."

Jack closed his eyes and faced the sun. Kick flipped through her magazine, unable to focus on any of the pictures. Maybe some time with her pleasure-seeking brother, away from the rest of the family, was just what she needed.

❧ ❧ ❧

Rose took her five daughters out for a special lunch and shopping excursion in Monte Carlo two days before Kick was to leave for Austria.

"You look wonderful, Kick," said her mother warmly, using her nickname, which she rarely did. They were strolling side by side down a sun-flooded street with Rosemary and Pat ahead of them, arm in arm; and behind them, Jean and Eunice were gossiping about Marlene Dietrich's party at a neighboring resort. *If only they knew*, thought Kick.

Kick did feel lighter. To be exact, she was ten meticulously weighed pounds thinner than when she'd arrived. She also felt light-headed, since the grapefruit and thin slice of dark bread she'd eaten for breakfast had been close to four hours ago. The thousands of dollars her mother had just spent on her in Chanel, then in Lanvin, had not fully distracted her from her hunger, nor from the nagging sense that something more than her size had changed recently. She wanted to bask in her mother's compliment and the shower of new clothes, but inside her empty stomach was some sort of barrier that only let Rose's best intentions permeate so far.

"Didn't I tell you that being closer to God here in France would set us right again?" her mother asked.

"You were right, of course," Kick agreed, though in truth she felt closer to God in St. Mary's with Father O'Flaherty, or praying on her knees before bed.

"It's a pity Peter couldn't see you now, so lithe and tan. But I'm sure he'll visit again, won't he?"

"Are you so anxious for me to get married?" Kick asked.

"Certainly not," her mother laughed in her high voice, sounding like a cartoon ghost on a Halloween movie reel. "But I *do* want you distracted from Billy Hartington and his sort."

"I thought you wanted me to fit in," Kick said, beginning to chew the inside of her lip, a childhood habit she had recently found herself doing again. Sometimes she only realized she'd been at it when she tasted blood.

"Of course I do! But please, don't forget who you are." Rose paused for effect before going on. "If you're not madly in love with Peter Grace, then maybe you'd like Edward Ashcroft? Or John Parkinson? He's certainly handsome, and so industrious! I heard he got a first at Oxford in philosophy and is doing very well for himself in the City."

Ah yes, more rich Catholic Englishmen. "If they ring me, I'll let them take me to lunch. But I can't promise to fall in love with them, Mother." Her lower lip felt ragged when she ran her tongue over it.

"Of course not. Just give them a chance."

Rose looped her bony arm through Kick's and leaned on her daughter, and said in her most lavish, cozy tone, "Shall we stop in to Hermès before lunch?"

Kick would have taken a grilled cheese and soda over Hermès at that point, but she followed her mother into the sumptuous store, wondering what was wrong with her. It wasn't just that she wanted to eat and her mother wanted to shop that bothered Kick; it was the sense that so many of her desires were departing from those of her mother these days. And this scared her. *Who is Kick Kennedy?* she wondered. *What sort of future does she have?*

❖ ❖ ❖

At first, Austria seemed like exactly the right medicine. She and Jack relaxed in a stunning house overlooking the sparkling Wörthersee with Jimmy Foster, hiked the mountains and ate sausages with dark bread— though she was careful not to overindulge, lest her mother regret her decision to let Kick go. One night they met Jack's Harvard friend Paul Baker, and Paul's friend Rudi, at a club ironically named Schloss Armstrong. Far from a castle, this *schloss* was a small, dark bar down a few steps from the street at the end of a long alleyway, then down more steps, where an excellent band played if not a Louis Armstrong tune, then at least a Cole Porter song in perfect harmony.

The place was almost full at ten o'clock, but they managed to secure the last table. Rudi, the son of the former Austrian minister to Rome, and also a Jew, was very nervous that their table was next to one occupied by three young Nazis in uniform who were drinking large steins of beer and playing cards.

He immediately began mopping his brow with a wrinkled handkerchief, whispering earnestly, "Please, no loud references to my father or any other obvious detail."

Jack nodded silently. Kick and Paul did, too. *How awful to have to constantly hide oneself.*

They ordered beer and pretzels, and the fizzy pilsner cooled them off in the hot underground room. Sweat dripped from the noses of the trumpet and trombone players onto their shiny brass instruments, then onto the floor.

"No ventilation down here," said Paul as he shrugged off his jacket and draped it over the back of his chair, then offered Kick his hand for a rendition of Benny Goodman's "Stompin' at the Savoy." *Might as well dance*, Kick thought. *I'm already hot.* Jack, ever fresh in a linen suit, sat and talked with Rudi about recent films.

After a few songs, Paul and Kick shimmied back to the table and stood beside their friends, panting and slugging cold beer. Wet stains were spreading on Paul's shirt, but he didn't seem to mind, nor did Kick mind the drops rolling down her back. Dancing always lifted her mood.

As they drank, one of the Nazis at the neighboring table stood up, pointed at Paul, and said something in aggressive German.

Paul replied, and Kick couldn't tell if he was being confrontational or not; to her ears, German always sounded pushy. From his seat, Rudi's eyes darted between his friend and the tall young man in uniform. Kick thought she could see him trying to melt into his chair and become invisible. The music was still playing, but Kick thought she heard the buzz of the other patrons die down as they turned their ears to the conflict brewing at their table. Her heart sped up nervously.

Jack sat still, and Kick stood unmoving beside Paul.

The Nazi shouted louder at Paul, which fully silenced the other people in the club, though the band played on. *Lord God, please don't let anything terrible happen*, she prayed. She had never been truly *afraid* before, not like this, and she had to suppress an urge to run. Her legs felt tense and ready.

Paul shouted back at the Nazi, and it became absolutely clear that he was in fact being confrontational.

Rudi kneaded his handkerchief. The clenching in Kick's legs spread upward, priming her whole body for escape.

When the Nazi took a few steps toward Paul, his right fist clenched, Jack stood up, threw a wad of German reichsmarks, Austria's new currency, on the table, and clapped his hand on Paul's shoulder. "Time to get my sister home," he said firmly. For once, Kick was grateful to be the feminine reason for ending an evening early. She felt a rush of blood course through her relieved body.

Paul gave one final menacing look at the Nazi, pulled his jacket off the chair with a flourish, and stalked out.

Soaked with perspiration, Kick followed, with Rudi and Jack behind her. They hurried silently into the street, then down two blocks, where they checked to make sure they were alone. Then Rudi exploded at Paul. "Why didn't you just put on your jacket when they asked?"

"Because they need to know they don't own us all," Paul spat. Loathing for the Nazis oozed out of him as profusely as the sweat that ran into his ears.

"What if they had refocused their attentions on me?" Rudi demanded.

"You would have been fine."

"All they would have to do is look at me and ask where I live, and they would know I am a Jew."

"You don't have to tell them. Or you could lie," Paul suggested, daring his friend.

Rudi shook his head, disgusted. "It's so easy for you." Then, after giving his head one final shake, he took Jack's hand and pumped it appreciatively. "Thank you, friend."

"You're welcome," Jack replied, clasping Rudi's hand with both of his.

Rudi turned to Kick and said, "It was a pleasure to meet you, Kathleen. Please enjoy your stay in my country, for I fear it won't be *Austria* much longer."

Kick felt queasy. "I'm sorry we didn't get to dance," she said with as warm a smile as she could muster.

"I'm not much of a dancer anyway," sighed Rudi. "Now, if you'll excuse me, I have to get home."

Without waiting for another reply, Rudi shoved his hands into his trouser pockets and stalked off into the night. Later, Kick couldn't sleep, knowing that no matter how many children her father and Father O'Flaherty might save, neither of them could protect Rudi and the thousands—or was it millions?—like him. At least, they couldn't do it without the fight that Winston Churchill was spoiling for and her father was dead set against.

❧ ❧ ❧

Kick was relieved to get back to Cannes, where there were no swastikas in the street and she could swim cleansing laps in the club's pool. She even felt grateful to get back to the predictability of her mother's regimen of prayer and diet. She wrote Billy and Debo and Jane letters, but mentioned to no one except God what had happened with Rudi. She worried about him daily, what with all the news flooding the radio about Hitler threatening Czechoslovakia and calling up a million German reserve fighters. And Roosevelt didn't make anything feel more stable with his speech saying the United States would defend Canada if Hitler and his ally Mussolini attacked America's neighbor and friend. But the worst of it were the telegrams from their father in London sending his love and also telling them they might "get to return home soon."

Home. Was that New York? Boston? With a war on here in Europe and her friends fighting in it? No American city would feel like home.

Kick's mind swirled as she swam in the Mediterranean on a blue morning in late August, her muscles getting more and more fatigued with each stroke. She'd grown weary of the pool and craved the greater physical challenge of open water. It reminded her of her racing days in Hyannis Port. But she quickly started to feel tired and hungry. Her brothers and sisters were off aquaplaning, and she could just make out their shrieks of delight in the distance. They were far enough away, though, that when she felt herself getting caught up in a current, none of them could see that she was in trouble. She was pummeled by the sea, salty waves whooshing over her head and pushing her body to and fro. She kept trying to swim up and against it, and to shout, but opening her mouth only sent water down her throat.

She began to pray. *Our Father, hear my prayer. Mary! Hail Mary full of grace, send our Lord to me . . . Please! Oh please please please . . .*

Her prayers were heard, and hands on her arms and torso dragged her to shore, where she coughed water and bile onto the beach. Then the white midday sun hit her retinas, and she lost consciousness.

She woke to the sensation of satin sheets against her legs and arms, and she knew she was not in her parents' villa. Rose didn't believe in satin sheets, saying they inhibited the body's ability to breathe in the night. She preferred a finely woven cotton. Not entirely conscious, Kick slid her limbs against the luxurious fabric and some tabloid detail flashed to her mind, something about a movie star who said how much she liked to wake up with her lover, and Kick's mind went straight to Billy—his long body, his cedar scent, his lips. Then she felt a strong tug in a deep part of her body, followed by a series of hot pulses that ricocheted through her, causing her to convulse gently against the slippery sheets.

Kick bolted upright in the bed, and the satin slithered right off of her. Fortunately, she was wearing a nightgown of some sort. Also satin.

"Are you all right, dear?" said an older voice with an American Southern accent. "Bad dream?"

Squinting, Kick glanced around the room till she saw a woman with gray hair wearing a wrinkled white linen dress. She had been doing needlepoint in a rocking chair, but now she crossed the room to sit beside Kick on the large bed.

"Where am I?"

"Maria Sieber's room, dear," said the woman. "She insisted on putting you in her own bed."

Kick narrowed her eyes and then saw the glossy black-and-white photos of Marlene and other stars on the walls, all autographed and addressed to Marlene's daughter Maria. So she was in the Cap D'Antibes Hotel.

"Does my family know I'm here?"

The woman nodded. "Marlene phoned your mother herself. Then she put me in charge and told me to call over there when you felt a bit better."

Kick collapsed back against the pillows, which welcomed her in a feathery embrace. Her head pounded as if she'd drunk too much champagne.

"Would you like anything to eat or drink? You've been asleep for hours, and it's well past lunch."

"Maybe some ginger ale," said Kick.

The woman disappeared and Kick put a hand on the pale violet material that covered her belly. What had just happened in there? It had felt . . . too good. She felt certain it was the sort of pleasure she'd heard references to in movies, and was spoken about less kindly by the nuns. The sort of pleasure that was only supposed to be shared between a husband and wife. What did it mean that the thought of Billy had brought it on so powerfully?

She attempted to distract herself by examining the glossy photographs framed around the room: Clark Gable, Bette Davis, Laurence Olivier . . . So many! *They* would surely know what she'd just experienced, Kick thought. For a moment she wished she could make it happen again, but when she closed her eyes and tried to summon back the moment, she couldn't. She was relieved.

Then the older woman returned with a silver tray that had the ginger ale as well as cucumber and ham sandwiches spread generously with butter, and potato chips. Chips! Kick swooned at the first crunchy bite, then tried not to get greasy crumbs on the perfect sheets.

She felt, suddenly, happy. The unexpected and divine chips, the sandwiches, the sunlit afternoon. The fact that she was still alive. The fact that her body could be abused by the ocean, then give something so wonderful back to her . . . Father O'Flaherty had told her to believe in herself. She was going to try to do more of that from now on. That very morning felt like proof that she was meant to try.

JUNE 1936

*T*oward the end of his last year at Eton, Billy drove off one fragrant June
afternoon with Charles Granby, their white ties and top hats in the boot,
claiming to be spending the weekend at David Ormsby-Gore's house. In fact,
though, they planned to crash the Trinity May Ball. I'll be matriculating in
September, *reasoned Billy.* I'd like to know what it's all about.

He was surprisingly nervous as he dressed himself in a little hotel close to
the college. What if everyone saw he was still just in school? Would they kick
him out? Of just the ball, or the college altogether? Almost all the previous
dukes of Devonshire had gone to Trinity; it would be rather embarrassing if
he were to get expelled before he'd begun.

But that was the fun in this, wasn't it? The risk? He'd taken so few risks
in his life. Foolhardiness, as Billy usually called it, had always been Andrew's
strength. But something about turning eighteen and never having kissed a girl
or pulled off a legendary prank had begun to wear on Billy. He and Charles
had agreed to an extra dare as well: before the night's end, each of them had
to kiss—really kiss, that is—a girl the other boy chose for him. One hundred
pounds and an ego were at stake.

Once the spring sun had descended in the sky, and the college students were *plenty drunk and there were shadows to hide in if necessary, the two school chums set off for adventure. They accepted the first glasses of champagne offered to them and drank them quickly, and were both relieved and disappointed to discover that they were immediately recognized and welcomed by the older boys they knew, the ones who'd graduated Eton the year before. "Look who's here!" "How'd you escape the beaks?" "Got your eye on anyone tonight?" "Have you seen the American bird? Appeared out of nowhere. Who is she?"*

For it was Kick who stole the fame he'd so coveted that night. All eyes were on her. He watched, too, mesmerized. She was so relaxed, despite being completely out of place and hardly the prettiest of the girls there, but her smile was delight itself. She had a charming dimple in her left cheek, and she was a shameless flirt. But wildly successful in her flirting, to judge by the swarm of young men clamoring for her next dance.

"That one," Charles whispered in Billy's ear, making Kick the object of their bet.

"Right," Billy said, feigning confidence, trying not to let his embarrassment show, knowing he'd be saying goodbye to those hundred pounds. There was no way he was up to the task of asking this otherworldly creature to dance, let alone of kissing those animated lips.

Two years later, when he saw her picture in the effusion of press about the arrival of Ambassador Joseph Kennedy and his brood, Billy's heart had stopped for a moment. He'd never dreamed he'd see her again. When he went to the 400 the night of the girls' presentation at court, it hadn't been because his father told him to have a look at the debs. It had been because he thought she might be there, and he was determined not to be such a coward again.

PART 2

❖ ❖ ❖

FALL 1938

CHAPTER 9

Finally—*finally*—she saw him at Cortachy Castle in September. She'd been standing on the front lawn talking to Jane Kenyon-Slaney, and he'd scared her to death by sneaking up on her and covering her eyes from behind.

"Good lord, Billy," she said, panting with surprise as he smirked and Jane giggled.

"I do apologize, Kick, but I couldn't resist."

"Giving me a scare?"

"Raising your pulse."

She blushed. "Surely there are better ways to accomplish that."

"Perhaps," he said, his voice mysterious. "Perhaps."

Thumbing their noses at Hitler, Chamberlain, and the whole mess across the channel, Kick and her friends drank cocktails and danced to the phonograph well into the night. Since the house belonged to Jean Ogilvy's family, cousins of the Cavendishes, all of Kick's favorite people were there—Billy, Andrew, David, Debo, Sissy, Bertrand. Things took a raucous turn after midnight when someone set off the fire hydrant, Nancy Astor's son Jakie spilled whiskey all over the Persian rug, and Bertrand nearly broke his leg during a game of blindfold tag in the damp grass. And still the boys managed to go grouse hunting the next day. "Onward, men!" Billy shouted at Andrew and Bertrand, who looked much the worse for wear.

The next night the world encroached. After a dinner presided over by Jean's father Lord Airlie in his kilt, which he apparently never took off, everyone retired to the drawing room to listen to the news, play cards, and smoke. On the wireless was endless debate about what might and ought to happen. With Mussolini's speech in Trieste officially declaring Italy's support for Germany, and Hitler's ever-tightening grip on Czechoslovakia, it was looking less and less likely that England, France, and the United States' desire for peace would hold.

"Bloody criminal what Chamberlain's allowing," said David during an advertising break.

"Hear, hear," said Billy. This was the first Kick had heard of his politics, and it sounded like he wouldn't much agree with her father. She hadn't fully committed her own opinion yet. On the one hand, she admired her father for wanting to spare her brothers and all the other young men in England and America another fatal war. But on the other hand—how could they *not* stand up to a man who just kept grabbing for land that wasn't his, who was making it so difficult for peaceful Jews to live in his country that they were leaving in droves? She remembered, too, what Father O'Flaherty had said about Hitler not liking the Catholics much better than the Jews. What if people like her were next on the Führer's list?

"Do you honestly want to go to war?" asked Debo, exasperated. Kick had a feeling she was getting an earful on this topic at home, what with her two Fascist-leaning sisters and brother, and Communist sister. Unity had recently joined Hitler himself in Munich.

"Of course not, but we wouldn't have to if Chamberlain were to grow a backbone and tell Hitler where to stuff his sauerkraut," said Bertrand.

Billy sat back in his chair and stared down his long legs, frowning and tapping his thumbs together.

"I'm with Chamberlain if it'll keep you boys out of the trenches," said Jean.

"Trenches?" laughed David. "My dear girl, this war will be fought from the sky. No more brutality in the trenches."

"Ah yes, now there are bombs to pick off whole squadrons, not just a man's legs," said Bertrand.

"And they will drop from the sky like rain," Billy added.

"How poetic," muttered Bertrand. "You'll be a regular Wilfred Owen."

"I hope not," said Billy. "As David said, we need to take a harder line with Hitler. He keeps asking for more and more. We can't just give it to him."

"And now we're back to war," said Bertrand.

"I still believe diplomacy is possible," said David. "Kick, what does your father think?"

"He always speaks his mind in his speeches, so you know as much as I do. He still wants peace," she said, though she wondered irritably what he might say privately to Joe Jr. or Jack.

"With due respect, Kick," said Bertrand, "America is a long way from here. She can afford to plead for peace."

"Maybe," said Kick, feeling insulted, "but *I* am here. *We* are here. The Kennedys. We all want what's best for England *and* America."

Billy smiled at her, but it was a pensive smile, and maybe even a little patronizing. She couldn't quite tell, which just went to show how little she really knew him, she supposed. She bit the inside of her cheek.

"I hope you're right," said David. "And I hope it matters."

"Come on, girls," said Debo, rising from the chaise with sudden conviction. "Someone pick out a record and shut off all this nonsense."

❖ ❖ ❖

Let's escape for lunch. Meet me by the great oak at one?

The handwritten note from Billy arrived on her breakfast tray the next morning, and she must have read it one hundred times as she sipped her tea. The hours couldn't pass fast enough, and when the time came, it was drizzling. She found him under the protective cover of a navy mackintosh and umbrella.

The oak tree was locally famous, and with good reason. It towered over the entrance to the Cortachy estate, and the leaves were turning the loveliest orange color.

"You're frozen," he observed.

"I suppose I am," she said through chattering teeth.

"Can't have that," he said, ushering her into a black Lagonda he'd parked a few yards down the road. As soon as he started the engine, the heavens opened.

"Are you sure you want to drive in this downpour?" asked Kick. The windshield wipers hardly cleared the water long enough to see the road.

"I haven't seen you properly in more than a month, and I'm not going to let a little rain get in the way."

Thankfully, he was a slow and careful driver even in this luxurious sports car that would have been much more fun to drive fast with the top down. They didn't talk much as he drove, but Kick sent up a quick prayer of thanks, since she figured the timing of the rain would make it unlikely that anyone else would head into the village for lunch. The last thing she wanted was to have to welcome anyone else to their table.

By the time they sat, damp and chilled, in the warmest corner of the village pub, Kick was jittery with excitement and dread. Was he planning to bring up Peter Grace? Or would he kiss her? Both?

They ordered a ploughman's lunch to share, along with two bowls of the onion soup, and two ales. It turned out Billy was something of an expert on beer, of all things. Kick was amazed to hear him wax on about the regional differences in ales, lagers, and stouts. He told her that the best ale he'd ever had came from the house of his family's gardener at Church-dale Hall, where he'd grown up.

"You know, my grandfather also loves beer," she told Billy, thinking fondly of Honey Fitz. "He loves nothing more than a stout and a bowl of chowdah"—she pronounced the word in her best Boston accent—"for lunch."

"Sounds like my kind of man," said Billy.

Kick laughed hard. "That's difficult to imagine, I must say."

"Why?"

"Grandpa is just so . . . rough around the edges. But don't tell him I said that."

"Your secret is safe with me," Billy said. Then, after a quiet slurp of soup, avoiding her eyes, he said, "It would appear that you don't go for men with rough edges."

"Are . . ." *Are you asking me about Peter?* But her voice failed her.

Billy set down his spoon and looked her in the eye. "I'm sorry. I don't want to be ridiculous. But I did hear about Mr. Grace," he said. "I've noticed you haven't worn the gift he gave you, here or in the few photos I happened to see of you in France."

"You looked?" This revelation sent her heart straight into her throat.

Billy nodded. "Then I realized I was being absurd, and I should just ask you directly."

"What are you asking, exactly?" There was her heart in her neck again, making it hard to speak normally.

"Are you engaged?"

At this, she had to laugh. "Far from it. As you guessed, the gift was unwanted."

Billy looked relieved—she hadn't realized how much tension he'd been storing in his shoulders until he let them down.

"But," she began. This was a moment for honesty, after all.

"But?"

"My mother wished it wasn't."

"Is that all?"

"She *is* my mother."

"I have one of those, too."

"More to the point, I think, you have a *father*."

"Yes," he agreed. "We each have one difficult parent, haven't we?"

"Mmmm." Kick chased a ribbon of onion around her bowl with her spoon, feeling her pulse throbbing in her neck.

"Let's not worry about them just yet," said Billy. "Can we agree to do that?"

Kick looked up at him. He was so handsome, so . . . *unexpected.* "I'll try," she said.

Billy smiled and raised his hand to her face. His palm covered her entire cheek, and he cupped her jaw, just as he had at Goodwood. This time he used his thumb to gently stroke her temple.

To better absorb his warmth, the clean scent of his white shirtsleeve, she closed her eyes. It was little more than a blink, but in that fragment of a second he kissed her. His lips held to hers and at last she had confirmation that they were as gentle as she had imagined. Even better was the promise, the sensation as he pulled reluctantly away, that more of this exquisite closeness was in store.

❖ ❖ ❖

The next ten days were a bizarre mix of parties and races at which people were either looking for a radio to turn on or trying to avoid news altogether. Debo was firmly in the latter camp, as she didn't want to be reminded of the trouble her older sisters might be getting into, and Kick followed her into it willingly to numb her own worry about what might be happening to Rudi and other innocent people in Hitler's way. One piece of good news came in a letter from Father O'Flaherty: he and her father had convinced another orphanage in Ireland to open its doors to one hundred children. Billy headed back to Trinity for his final year of university while Kick went on to Frances Dawson's house in Balado, where everyone drank too much to calm their nerves.

Since she was also in Scotland, Rose summoned Kick to a golf course clubhouse to have lunch and warn her that they might all have to go back to America if Chamberlain didn't find a way to peace with Hitler. Joe was working around the clock to ensure that wasn't the outcome, but there were no guarantees. Finally, on September 28, Chamberlain took yet another flight to Munich. This time with France's Daladier at his side, his purpose was to sit down with Hitler and Mussolini to sign an agreement that would keep Germany from expanding further. They could have

Czechoslovakia, but no more. Like everyone else, Kick slept restlessly and felt jumpy all day long.

Two mornings later she woke in her bed at 14 Prince's Gate for the first time in a month, to the rowdy whoops of her younger brothers downstairs. In her nightgown and robe, she stood at the entrance to the breakfast room. "Well?" she asked Bobby and Teddy.

"Dad and Chamberlain won!" shouted Bobby.

"Hitler signed the agreement?" she asked.

Teddy threw his stuffed bear in the air, and Bobby said, "Yes! There won't be a war!"

"That's wonderful news," said Kick, heaving a long-held sigh of relief. *Daddy must be so happy*, she thought.

There was celebrating to be done. Even before she'd finished her egg and fruit, the phone rang and it was Debo saying everyone would be at the Café de Paris that night. Kick planned to go to St. Mary's for a few hours in the afternoon, but at the moment she had the strongest urge to get outside. The sun was shining and there was officially no threat of bombs.

"Let's go out," she said to her brothers. "Get a little fresh air, maybe toss a ball around in the park."

Bobby was all for it, but Teddy complained about his throat again. He was angling to get his tonsils out just so he could eat his weight in ice cream. So Teddy stayed with Luella while Kick and Bobby brought their pigskin football with them to Hyde Park.

Kensington Street was jammed with shoppers spending untold sums of money on all the things they had feared they wouldn't be able to afford if wartime austerity had hit. Street vendors sold toys and balloons. Children ran and skipped and played tag, and it seemed that many people—usually so reserved in England—stopped to speak to one another, to shake hands and laugh and talk. Bobby spent some of his own pocket money on a honey cake, and Kick bought an apple, and they breathed in the crisp fall air even as they passed signs reading "Gas attack! How to put on your gas mask," with greenish illustrations of parents and children hidden behind their masks, like actors in some gruesome Saturday matinee. The Kennedys' own masks were ready and waiting in a closet; their father had seen to that. Bobby peeled off one such poster and balled it up. "No need for those now," he said.

In the park, they passed air-raid trenches ringed by enormous piles of brown earth. No one was digging deeper that day, but the trenches were patrolled by armed guards in military uniforms carrying long firearms. They were a blight on Kick's mood. Why were the trenches being protected? Why not let children climb the mounds of dirt, or throw pennies for wishes into the pits? Or fill them back up again? She wished they would just disappear and someone would plant more of that luscious English lawn on top. No one would even remember them come next spring.

Out of sight of the trenches and other signs of war, Kick and Bobby threw their American football back and forth. They were joined by some other boys about Bobby's age who asked why their rugby ball was so large, and Bobby laughed and explained the sport to which their ball belonged. Then some other boys and even a few intrepid girls joined in, and soon a game had begun, a kind of rugby-football hybrid they invented as they went along. It felt good to exert herself, to get dirty and a little scuffed on the knees and elbows. For a moment, Kick almost felt transported to Hyannis Port, to summer, to a time before she knew rugby, knew England, before she'd fallen in love with London and had to fear losing it.

CHAPTER 10

When she learned from Father O'Flaherty that England and France were putting limits on the growing number of refugees, she immediately went to her father. In his office, she found him drinking tea with a confusion of newspapers covering his desk.

"Hello, darling. What a fine day this is!" he exclaimed jubilantly, still on a high from Chamberlain's coup with Hitler.

"It is, Daddy. Everyone is so happy and relieved." How could she bring this up now? "I've just come from St. Mary's," she began.

"How is Father O'Flaherty?" Joe asked, his tone expansive.

"He's . . . concerned. Since Munich, he's gotten even more requests from people hoping to get out."

"We'll do everything we can. You know that, right?"

"Yes, Daddy," she said, wishing she could sound happier about it. But the priest's pessimism haunted her.

Meanwhile, the boys in her set were not at all happy with what had transpired on the continent. They thought it was further evidence of Chamberlain's weakness. Debo, no doubt to protect herself from being reminded of Unity, made the boys promise not to talk more about war until there was a good reason—they agreed, but Kick had a feeling that even this treaty of peace among friends wouldn't hold. And while the tenor of conversations in society had become more pessimistic, the fall season afforded generous distractions. "We must all remain calm. Carrying on in the face of adversity is a great English strength," Dukie Wookie had said at one luncheon raising funds for a new hospital wing. Kick preferred that sentiment to Bertrand's drunken one at the 400: "You know us, too proud to know when we're whipped."

After the Nottingham races, a euphoric Billy, having just won his bet on the second-place horse, practically carried Kick into Churchdale Hall, the charming stone house where he'd grown up. Unlike so many of the large estates she'd visited, Billy's childhood home looked like a house that a person could actually live in, and he made complete sense there. Inside it was lavish with antiques and art, and rows upon rows of the duke's dusty books. Outside it was ringed by simple gardens with acres of lawn and clusters of climbable trees. With its gables and chimneys, it was a solid and stately place, and felt like the sort of home where a boy could run around, where he could be alone when he wanted or play games of cricket or rugby with packs of school friends when the inspiration struck. Which was exactly what they did with David and Sissy and Andrew and Debo—Andrew dug out some croquet mallets and they played a jokingly competitive round.

When the sun set, the cold and darkening night chased them into the house. A crackling fire welcomed them into the spacious drawing room, and the six friends sprawled on the floor and couches, warming their fingers and noses.

"Feels more like November," Debo said, shivering.

"Perfect excuse to break into Dad's whiskey," said Andrew. "Anyone else?"

David asked for a short glass, and Andrew poured two from the heavy crystal decanter. They clinked glasses, then Andrew turned to Debo and declared, "Sorry, darling, but I'm afraid our little pact is finished." Turning to David and Billy he said, "I don't know about you, but I don't know who I want to clock first: Tom Mitford or Chamberlain."

"*Andy,*" reprimanded Debo. The day before, they'd all been at Debo's Oxfordshire house, and her brother Tom had tried sparring with Andrew about Munich. Andrew had valiantly refrained from shouting down Debo's brother, but everyone could hear him grind his molars to avoid it.

"Don't worry, love, it's nothing to do with you," Andrew replied. "But before you rose in the morning, Tom was nattering on and on about how envious he is of Unity for being at the center of things."

Debo rolled her eyes at Sissy and Kick, who replied with sympathetic expressions. Why ruin the perfect mood of the day?

But the boys obviously disagreed; they'd held their tongues as long as they could. Billy shook his head in disgust and answered his brother's question: "I'd knock Chamberlain down first. He'd be worth the bruise on the knuckles."

"He's just stalling, and the worst of it is, he doesn't even realize it," agreed David.

"And we're the ones who will pay for it," said Andrew.

"Yes," said David grimly.

"What about 'this war will be fought from the sky'?" asked Kick, recalling David's statement from a few weeks before.

"It will," David affirmed. "But that doesn't mean there won't be casualties on the ground. I must have been in a particularly optimistic mood that night. Even with air bombs, there'll still be ferocious combat with guns and grenades."

"It will be our duty," said Billy, tapping his fingers restlessly on his leg, then getting up to pour himself a whiskey.

"You'll go willingly, then?" asked Andrew.

Billy drank, then said, "*We* will have no choice."

"The main thing is that the Fascists must be stopped," said David. "If Hitler thinks he can get away with killing Jews and seizing Czechoslovakia and Austria, what's to stop him from taking over France? Killing the Catholics? The intellectuals? Hitler's no friend of gentility, either. He had a hard childhood. Like something out of a Dickens novel. He's not one of us."

If Kick agreed with David before, she fully agreed with him now. *Why doesn't Daddy see it this way?*

"Enough," said Billy, downing the end of his whiskey. "Time to dress for dinner."

Kick was relieved the duke was absent from dinner because he was in London on business. She had hoped Billy's two younger sisters, Elizabeth and Anne, might be home—in the hopes of making them allies—but they were both away at school. Luckily, the duchess kept the conversation light and apolitical. Immersed in her plans for Chatsworth, she was intrigued by Kick's knowledge of certain interior design firms and auction houses in London that worked with houses in New York, dealing in the art of Mondrian, Picasso, and Matisse. *I'll have to thank Mother for this*, Kick thought to herself, knowing that were it not for Rose, she wouldn't have had nearly as much to contribute to the dinner conversation. Andrew was also keen on her knowledge of the American-art-collecting scene, asking many questions to which Kick didn't know the answers, but she tried to offer names of galleries with whom he might correspond. It was the most animated she'd ever seen him.

"I didn't realize you were *this* interested in art," Kick said to him as the fish course dishes were cleared.

"It's always been a hobby of mine," said Andrew.

"He's being modest," said Debo, carefully touching her napkin to her mouth without smudging her red lipstick. "He's also a talented artist himself."

"He used to amuse us at school," said David, "by drawing excellent caricatures of teachers."

"And some of the other boys he didn't favor," added Billy, with a joking, older-brotherly scold.

"I remember a lovely basket of fruit you once painted," said Sissy. "Where is it now?"

"I gave it to Mother for her birthday," Andrew said coldly.

"Yes," the duchess replied, taking a sip of her wine with a mournful expression that reminded Kick of the look her mother sometimes got when regarding Rosemary. It was the first sign of any real sadness in Billy's family life, and she felt her heart and stomach clench a bit at recognizing it. "I wanted to hang it in the library beside the Turner, but your father thought it was better suited to my room. Where, I might add, I enjoy seeing it every day."

"Our father is known around here as Mr. Bell," said Billy, and everyone laughed at the absurdity of the Duke of Devonshire as art critic Clive Bell of the notorious Bloomsbury Group. Andrew's laugh was muted, though, and Kick guessed that the only reason he'd laughed at all was in thanks to his brother for smothering the memory of his father's slight with humor. They reminded her of Jack and Joe Jr. in that moment—partners, secret keepers, and protectors.

Later, Kick and Billy lounged against large red pillows on the floor in front of a fire, alone at last since his mother had retired to bed, David and Sissy were in the library, and Debo and Andrew were who knew where. She wanted to talk about some of her observations from dinner, to feel closer to him that way, but couldn't figure out how to do it without sounding like a nosy American. So she tried to bring up Andrew in as light a way as possible. "I had no idea the Cavendish brothers were so artistic," she observed. "Andrew with his painting, and you as Wilfred Owen—wasn't that was Bertrand called you?"

Billy laughed. "I'd make a rotten poet. I'm a much better reader—and I do admire the Great War poets, like Owen and Sassoon. And my brother, talented though he is, has sworn off painting."

"That's sad."

"We have other duties," said Billy matter-of-factly.

"'Duty' seems to be the word of the evening. And no one's especially happy about it," Kick said.

"Duty's not often compatible with fun. But that doesn't mean we don't willingly do it."

"That's very honorable, I suppose."

"Suppose?"

"It's just that . . ." Kick wasn't sure how to put it, and her shoulders tensed as she considered how honest she ought to be. "It's nice when the call to duty aligns with one's own ideals and hopes," she said, but as soon as the words were out of her mouth, she realized how unrealistic they were for anyone like Billy. Or for anyone like her, for that matter, remembering how torn she'd felt with her mother in France.

"Are we talking about war now? Or more personal duties?"

"Both. But I know it might not be possible," she said with a frown, wishing she knew how to say more, how to get him to say more.

They were quiet for a few moments, and then he said, "How can I put a smile back on that beautiful face of yours?"

Since words had failed, what she really wanted was a kiss, but she couldn't very well ask for *that*, so she rested her head on his shoulder. After a minute, Billy stood and led her by the hand to the stairwell. "Take a step," he whispered, and when she did, they stood face-to-face. "Now we're the same height," he said in her favorite low, secret tone.

The dark silence of the stairwell emboldened her. She slid her arms around his shoulders and felt his arms wrap around her waist so entirely that his fingers touched the sides of her belly, and when he slid his tongue gently over her lower lip, she opened her mouth in a breath of surprised bliss. It felt so delicious, she actually heard herself think, *I don't care if I go to hell for this.*

That thought, more than the kiss itself, made her pull back and draw in a breath.

"Everything all right?" he whispered.

"Yes," she whispered back. "But it's time for bed."

He kissed her again. It was long and tender but he kept his lips closed, and she was sorry she'd stopped him.

She fell asleep that night saying her rosary and asking God for forgiveness and guidance. *What is happening to me?* She racked her brain for an answer, but none came.

❖ ❖ ❖

Before she'd ever laid eyes on William Cavendish, Marquess of Harting-ton, heir to the dukedom of Devonshire, she had read in one of her moth-er's homework assignments that his family's estate at Chatsworth was one of the finest stately homes in all England, and had belonged to the Cav-endish family since the sixteenth century.

It showed. Again thanks to Sister Helen's art and history lessons, Kick could almost see the centuries piled on top of one another, in the shape of the land and on the inside of the house. The enormous rectangular building with its Ionic pilasters and the balustrades that were so promi-nent on the roof were all English baroque, but she knew the original Tudor house was inside there somewhere. Densely forested hills served as a backdrop if you approached the house from the west, which is exactly what Kick and Billy and Andrew and Debo did the next morning on horseback. According to Billy, by horse was "the only way to see" his an-cestral home. "Not only can we see more of the land on horses than on foot," he'd explained at breakfast, "but it's the way the estate is designed to be seen. The Bachelor Duke didn't have a Rolls-Royce."

Surrounding the huge, imposing edifice were layers of Elizabethan, baroque, and Victorian gardens that whispered pieces of English history, like Queen Mary's Bower, where Mary, Queen of Scots, had been allowed to breathe fresh air while she was a prisoner at Chatsworth. Kick tried not to dwell on the fact that Billy's family estate had held one of the last Cath-olic aspirants to the English throne. There were plenty of other monu-ments of bygone days, like the waterfall fountain with its baroque domed Cascade House and the now-dry Emperor Fountain, named for Tsar Nicholas I of Russia. The Bachelor Duke wanted to have the tallest foun-tain in the world to impress the imperial ruler when he visited, but Nich-olas never actually made it to Chatsworth. And the fountain required so much water, no subsequent duke had run it except on special occasions.

"Pity," Billy lamented after telling the story. "But have a look at this."

Their party rode across the green grass, kept short by the industrious chewing of a roving band of hungry sheep, to the Willow Tree Fountain. Atop a large rock was what appeared to be a bare tree, with branches that arched artfully overhead—until they sprayed Kick and Debo with water!

Billy and Andrew, who'd been standing farther away, laughed heartily.

"Is that any way to treat your lady guests?" huffed Debo. "If you're not careful, *you'll* be the next Bachelor Duke."

Hardly, thought Kick, laughing with the boys as she brushed water off her felt coat. She hadn't gotten *that* wet, and she'd enjoyed the prank—as well as the thoroughly amused look it had produced on Billy's face. And anyway, if she let herself get ruffled by every practical joke, she'd never survive her own family—just recently, Bobby had hidden all her right shoes and she'd had to come to dinner barefoot.

"I don't think he was a bachelor because of the way he treated the *ladies*," said Andrew, egging Debo on.

"Have my coat," Billy said, offering Kick his worn brown leather jacket. It felt heavy and warm on her shoulders, and the wool lining smelled of his soap and aftershave.

"Where to next?" she asked, her spirits high.

Billy pointed back toward the house. "Lunch."

"Well, then. On your mark . . . get set," Kick said, tightening her grip on her reins. "Go!"

With a swift kick of her heels into the horse's taut belly, she was off, the glossy brown animal straining beneath her, the wind pushing her hair off her face. She could hear Billy urging his horse on just behind her, and soon he was beside her, and they were both galloping fast. *I could get used to this.*

As the house neared, she pulled the reins and encouraged the horse to a trot. Billy did the same and turned to her with a huge grin. "I had no idea you could ride like that."

"One surprise deserves another," she said.

His smile was reward enough. He'd enjoyed her little stunt, and for that she felt all the more satisfied with herself.

Debo and Andrew caught up and they spread out the lunch they'd brought with them on the lawn right in front of the house, then ate ravenously. When they'd all had their fill of cheese sandwiches and apple tarts, Billy said, "Ready for the tour?"

Inside the house, Kick pulled Billy's warm jacket tighter around her. The place had been shuttered for months and felt very drafty. Paintings of former dukes and duchesses by the likes of Van Dyck and Reynolds and Gainsborough loomed over her head, and large white tarps covered who knew what excellent specimens of Tudor or baroque or Georgian furniture and sculpture. Kick could see why reopening and decorating the estate was such a consuming project for Billy's mother.

Billy and Andrew struck up a game of tag in the main hall, as they must have done when they were small. As their shouts echoed through the dim halls, Kick and Debo found themselves standing beneath a portrait of Georgiana, Duchess of Devonshire, painted by Thomas Gainsborough.

"She was married to a William Cavendish," said Debo, scrutinizing the painting.

"She was a great beauty, it would appear," said Kick. "Though they always are in these portraits, aren't they? Then you read in some history book that she was one of the least desired women of her age."

"Not Georgiana," said Debo. "She was the real thing. But she had a terrible time of it. Her husband was a complete philanderer and hypocrite. He made her life miserable when she finally took a lover of her own, even after she'd done her duty and produced another William Cavendish."

"Typical man," said Kick, knowing with a pang that even her father would be unforgiving if her mother were to stray. She was less sure about Jack. Joe Jr. would most certainly uphold the double standard. And she couldn't help but wonder about Billy—this was his heritage, after all. It was well-known that his father had had the same mistress for years, and there wasn't so much as a whisper that his mother might also have a lover.

"I hope we've come further along since Georgiana," said Debo.

"You mean that in this advanced day and age, men don't cheat, or that men who do cheat are more likely to allow their wives the same liberties?"

Debo looked with surprise at Kick. "Both, I suppose. Though I prefer the former to the latter. Do you think I'm foolish?"

Kick linked her arm through Debo's, and they both looked back up at the duchess. "I wish I knew," she said.

The boys panted back over to them, and the tour continued. As she oohed and aahed over the enormous rooms and their partially covered elegance, Kick couldn't shake the image of Georgiana staring down at her from her elevated position on the wall. *What I wouldn't give to know what you know*, thought Kick.

When the sun began to set, Billy took her hand and squeezed it. For the first time, she stood on her tiptoes and kissed him instead of waiting for him to lean in to her. "Thank you for showing me Chatsworth."

"Wait till you see it unveiled, with all the dustcovers gone," he said.

"I can't wait," she said, and she knew that despite all her questions and doubts, it was true.

CHAPTER 11

London glowed with fall beauty. Orange leaves fell from the trees and swirled around the sidewalks before diving into the Thames. Back were the hot water bottles toasting her sheets, the steaming cups of tea and crackling fires that welcomed her inside from a windy day. And since the sky darkened before five, falling like a sapphire curtain on the trenches and gas mask posters, it was easier to ignore the signs of war that spoiled the streets and parks as she went about her business with charity events and work at St. Mary's, attempting to fill her time as productively as possible with Billy back at Cambridge.

Her father had been in a sulky state ever since his unpopular speech on Trafalgar Day, about how the dictator countries and democratic countries ought to be able to coexist. Plus, Joe and Father O'Flaherty had petitioned Roosevelt and Chamberlain for higher caps on refugees without luck. Joe was uncharacteristically silent at breakfast and rarely present at their few family dinners. Kick didn't dare ask him about his recent misfortunes and risk unleashing his wrath—not just as he was developing some respect for and renewing his interest in her without the boys around. Jack was back at Harvard and Joe Jr. was working with Ambassador Bill Bullitt in Paris.

Her father's mood proved to be a harbinger of more bad news.

On November 10, when she read in the paper about the slaughter of the Jews in Germany and Austria, all that broken glass on the street, almost one hundred killed and thirty thousand forced out of their homes and sent God only knew where, with Hitler speaking ominously about the Jewish "problem," Kick felt sick to her stomach. *Kristallnacht*, they called it. Forgoing her usual careful preparations for the day, she dressed quickly and headed outside, where workers were grimly stacking sandbags in front of whitewashed town houses and pasting fresh posters for air-raid shelters on lampposts. If St. Mary's and the comfort of Father O'Flaherty had been closer, she would have gone there, but her need for immediate prayer steered her to nearby Brompton Oratory.

The pews were full of people, mostly women with gray hair, bent over their clasped hands. Blessing herself with holy water, Kick surveyed the cavernous nave and tried to figure out where to slip in. Amid the scarves and felt cloches, she spotted a smart black hat with a peacock feather atop a very slim figure in a fine black coat. It was her mother, whose gloved fingers were interlaced with a pearl rosary.

Part of Kick wanted to kneel down next to her mother and pray side by side, but another, stronger part of her wanted to be alone to pray for things her mother seemed to care nothing about—Rudi, Billy, her life here in England. She excused herself quietly to the strangers who occupied the last pew as she moved to a seat in a far corner. Kneeling, she took out her own onyx rosary, closed her eyes, and began to pray. She tried to focus on the meaning of every word and phrase, just as the nuns had taught her, to make sure her pleas were as pure and potent as possible. Behind the memorized words, her mind reeled the plea *Show me my path* over and over again.

A few days later, Joe Jr. came home from Paris and the atmosphere at home lifted. Bobby and Teddy roughhoused with their older brother and took the football to Hyde Park every chance they got. Eunice and Pat and Jean were full of questions about French films and chocolates and romance in the street. Even Rosemary, who spent virtually all her time at the Montessori school these days, came home and smiled more with her oldest brother around.

One family dinner to celebrate his return was especially boisterous, with the boys starting a game of throw-the-roll, in which even their father participated, barking tips like a coach from the sidelines—"Raise your elbow, Teddy, there you go!" and "You can throw harder than that, Bob. I'm not raising a sissy"—prompting their mother to shake her head and rub her temples and say, "The things people would think of us if they could see us now," as crumbs showered down on the silver.

As the discussion on the younger side of the table devolved into talk of "yucky" English foods like blood sausage, which none of them had actually tasted, Kick listened to the more adult conversation developing on her left.

"Why don't you tell the press how you feel?" Joe Jr. asked their father.

"The damned Jews in the New York papers have already decided how they feel about me," said their father. "The maliciousness is appalling. There's no middle ground for them. Unless I side with them and send you and all your friends to a front line that doesn't even exist yet, they are not going to take my side."

"Don't you think Hitler *needs* to be stopped?" erupted Kick, letting her fork clatter to her plate. She'd held her tongue too long. And maybe she'd earned enough respect from her father to be able to participate in this conversation now.

Her brother and father stopped and stared at her. Then her father narrowed his eyes and said, "You've been listening to those aristocratic friends of yours too closely."

"Isn't that why you brought me here? To make friends with them?"

"I brought you here, Kathleen, to help make the family look smart—in all senses of the word. And you've done a very fine job. But don't confuse your loyalties."

Kick swallowed down the rage—*You're wrong! Stop treating me like I'm ten!*—but shook her head in frustration and disbelief. She was still just a girl. Maybe a smart one, capable of helping her dad from time to time, but a girl just the same. If she had been a boy, her father would have asked her to elaborate.

"If it's your friend Rudi in Austria you're worried about, Jack wrote me about him, and he's on a list to get out," said her father, his tone a bit softer.

Kick was surprised to discover that while this news gave her some relief, she was still very angry—at her father, at the whole situation, even at Jack for thinking of this when she hadn't. "Good," she said.

"Would you have me send your precious English friends to war?" her father asked. "Is that what you want, Kathleen? For them all to die in a ditch in Germany?"

The whole table was quiet, listening for her reply.

Her eyes felt hot with tears. She blinked them away and swallowed hard.

"No," she said firmly. "But letting Hitler just *have* Austria and Czechoslovakia doesn't show him much backbone, does it?"

Joe Jr. whistled, genuinely impressed. "Well, I'll be damned," he said. "My sister's turned into a regular firebrand."

"If you didn't know already that Kathleen's a fighter," said Rose, her normally shrill voice unusually smooth and low, "then you haven't been paying attention."

Did I hear that correctly? Did Mother just defend me? A fighter . . . she could have said "troublemaker," but she didn't. Kick smiled at her mother, who nodded slightly in reply. Eunice's eyebrows were so high, they practically touched her hairline.

"I raise *all* my children to be fighters," her father said, looking at Kick in a way that said, *But enough's enough.* Then, turning to his namesake, he said, "I want to hear more about what you learned in Paris. But later. This dinner table conversation needs brandy," he said, a knock on Rose's prohibition on alcohol at family dinners without guests.

Kick raised her glass of water to salute herself, then drank it down.

❧❧❧

"Hello, Kick," chirped Page Huidekoper from behind her enormous and extremely tidy desk at the embassy. Her glasses had slipped down to the tip of her nose, and when she looked at Kick, she pushed them back up. Chicly dressed in a wide-legged brown pantsuit, Page glanced down at her diary and said, "I'm afraid I didn't know you were coming in today. And your father is out."

"Oh, I know that," said Kick. "I'm here to see you."

"Me?"

"Do you have time for some lunch? Or even just a cup of tea?"

Page looked at the diary again and then back up at Kick. "I'd need to be back in forty-five minutes."

"Perfect."

Page steered them to a nearby café and they ordered egg and cress sandwiches.

"I need your advice," said Kick. "You were so helpful the last time, and I'm getting . . . worried about the political situation, and concerned that we Kennedys are going to be shipped home if things get worse. Daddy was already threatening to send us all back to the States two months ago before Munich, and with this recent horror in Germany . . . well, I want to make sure that doesn't happen."

"I'm not sure how I can help with that," said Page.

"I need to become . . . more independent. And also, if at all possible, more important to my father. So that he won't want me to leave, and—"

"So that he'll see you can take care of yourself," Page said, completing Kick's thought.

"Yes," Kick said, relieved she'd been fully understood.

"This doesn't have anything to do with the Marquess of Hartington, does it?"

There wasn't much point in lying to Page—not when she was so perceptive, and not when she needed all the facts in order to properly help Kick.

"Billy's part of it," Kick admitted. "But of course Daddy can't know that. The other part is how much I love it here. England, London." She thought of Chatsworth and Blenheim, the races and the Underground, the whole way of life she loved here, and how protective she felt of it—not just for herself but also for her friends and the little island itself. If war did break out, she wanted to stand with her friends *for* England, and against tyranny. Even if that did mean being part of a war her father was trying to avoid at great personal cost. How ironic, she thought, that in order to stay and do what she wanted to do, she would have to make herself more indispensable to her father than ever.

"I can understand that," said Page. Kick could see from her increasingly daring fashion alone that Page had come into herself here just as much as Kick had. Page checked her slim gold watch, then went on: "I have one or two ideas. Since you'll never be allowed to get a job like mine, you'll need to find meaningful work in other ways. *Work* is the key to all this. If you do it well, you'll prove yourself in many ways."

"Like the work at St. Mary's?"

"Writing for St. Mary's is fine, but for your plan to succeed, you need to write something with a byline. Something that makes your father look good and spreads goodwill about the Kennedys."

Kick frowned, remembering the impression her honest opinion had made on her father. She told Page, "Do you think that's wise? I'm not willing to say something in print that I don't really think just because it flatters Daddy."

"Ah yes," Page said, "I heard something about a disagreement with your father. You thought he wasn't showing enough backbone?"

"He told you about that?"

"No, I heard him tell Mr. Roosevelt on the phone that even his eighteen-year-old daughter and her friends didn't think America was showing Hitler enough backbone, and that he ought to be more honest with Joe in the future if he wanted America to look more authoritative on this side of the ocean."

"He did?" Kick was bewildered. Her father had used something *she* had said to make a point to *the president*.

"Don't let it go to your head," said Page, amused. "Let me look into a few possibilities and make a few phone calls. Can you come back on Friday? Your father will be out again that day."

"Yes," said Kick. "And thank you."

"In the meantime, start helping out Eunice with her coming-out next year. I know your father likes to see you children be helpful to each other."

Kick nodded. Then, emboldened by their little chat, she asked, "What about you? Have you met anyone special here?"

Page looked down at that gold watch, which she twisted around her left wrist with her right hand. "No," she said, "no one new."

Kick thought she knew what that meant, and though it made her feel squirmy, she appreciated Page's discretion. Also, it wasn't like the watch was proof of anything. The Huidekopers had money of their own, after all; it might have been a gift from her parents, like Kick's own Cartier watch.

In the following weeks, Kick sent off three letters, and even though each of the jobs was very like the luncheon for the cardinal that her mother had been so eager for Kick to organize months before, the fact that Kick was choosing these herself made them feel different to her. She was especially excited about the one to the *League of Catholic Women Bulletin* in Boston, asking if they needed a European correspondent—a genius idea, Kick thought, since it would soothe her mother to know Kick was prominently displaying her Catholic identity, and her father would appreciate having the Kennedy name printed sympathetically for once. She sent another to the American Women's Club in London, asking if they needed assistance with future events; and another to the British Museum, asking if she might help raise funds for any new acquisitions. If Jane Kenyon-Slaney could do it, so could she. Yes, Kick told herself, she'd do well to emulate a girl who'd been raised since birth to be an indispensable woman in English society, very likely the wife of an important viscount or—dare she think it?—duke.

CHAPTER 12

Christmastime, with its twinkling strings of white lights and lush red and green decorations, just barely managed to distract Kick from the halted but still haunting war preparations marring the streets. Billy wore the amethyst cufflinks she'd given him for his twenty-first birthday to every soiree of the holidays. The two of them were becoming expert at stealing kisses all over the city—the dark corner beside the stage entrance at the Café de Paris, in the powder rooms of the finest town houses in London, and behind enormous holiday displays of toys and clothes at Harrods, where she'd also glimpsed a stack of satin sheets, and the memory of Maria Sieber's bed sent an extra volt of electricity through their embrace.

She wished all the kissing didn't weigh so heavily on her conscience, however. There was no way she could lighten the burden by confessing to Father O'Flaherty or any other priest! She couldn't even admit to herself what was happening between her and Billy, except in French: *baisers amoureux* was the perfect obfuscating description.

In the ladies' lounge at the 400, Sissy observed, "You and Billy certainly seem to be more serious. He hasn't taken his eyes or hands off you."

"Goodness! Can't keep his hands off me? That sounds so *sordid*," Kick laughed.

"Hardly. Billy is the perfect gentleman. And notoriously shy. He stepped out with a French girl a while back, and she lost patience with him! I wouldn't be surprised if he hadn't even kissed you yet."

"Well . . ." Kick began, using a coy tone.

"Oh! Do tell!"

"I actually have a question about . . . kissing," said Kick in a hushed voice, seeing an opportunity to at last confess her sins to a Catholic friend, at least.

Sissy appeared to be stifling laughter as she said, "Yeeeeesss? It's not difficult."

"I know that!"

"So what's the problem?"

"Every nun I ever had for school is screaming at me in my head."

"Oh, that," said Sissy, waving her hand. "That will pass."

"Even if the kisses are . . ."

"Excellent?"

"Better."

"Well, the nuns in my head eventually shut up. And I had quite a few items on my guilty conscience. While David might appear to be rather an old-fashioned bloke, believe me when I say he is full of surprises." Sissy snapped her handbag shut as if to punctuate her statement.

"My, my," said Kick, suddenly giddy at being part of this hitherto se-cret league of women who knew about kissing and satin sheets and what it felt like to rebel against their upbringings in this marvelously forbid-den way.

"Listen, Kick," said Sissy, "of course the nuns tell us not to do things we might enjoy. Look at the life they've chosen for themselves."

"I doubt my mother would approve, either, and she has nine children."

"As long as you know where to draw the line with Billy, I say enjoy yourself." Sissy paused, then said carefully, "You do . . . know where the line is, don't you?"

"Of course!" Kick exclaimed, grateful that Sister Kit, one of the younger, more outspoken nuns at Sacred Heart whom Kick had always suspected of nursing a broken heart, had given some of the girls in her class a clandestine lesson, complete with a tome called *Gray's Anatomy*. Some of Kick's classmates had blanched when it came to the reproductive part, but Sister Kit had been adamant that the girls leave the convent "with some accurate knowledge of your bodies and those of your future husbands. To protect yourselves." Kick had listened intently, but it was only recently that she'd begun to understand what Sister Kit had meant about protecting herself. *Drawing the line.*

"So, you've never mentioned David in confession?" Kick pressed, feeling a little shy about asking but needing the answer nonetheless.

Sissy laughed. "Why should I?"

"*Impure thoughts* and all that."

"I don't believe in that nonsense. I believe actions are more important than thoughts."

Kick felt this was right, even if it did go against some of the stricter rules she'd been taught. She badly wanted to push her conversation with Sissy further, and ask if she planned to request that David convert to Catholicism. It was already pretty clear that the two of them would marry. But Kick sensed she'd asked enough for one night.

She linked her arm through Sissy's and said, "Thank you."

Sissy leaned her glossy ebony head against Kick's auburn one and sympathized, "Poor Kick. We English seem to be corrupting *you* rather than the other way round."

"Who'd have thought?" Kick laughed. Her friend had no idea just how welcome that influence had been.

❖ ❖ ❖

Right up until she had to leave for the family Christmas in Switzerland, Kick's days were full of productive engagements. Her name had begun to circulate as a result of the inquiries she'd sent, and now she was invited to hospitals and galleries and schools, and asked to organize book donations for underprivileged children and to speak at benefit luncheons. It gave her a real sense of accomplishment—people were asking for her, Kick Kennedy, without going through her mother first, because they wanted Kick for her own skills and talents.

Five days before Christmas it snowed, which sent a fizzy happiness through Kick when she met Billy on Bond Street for some shopping. At noon, it felt like dusk with the sky a tumultuous dark gray, but the shops lit up the street, and fluffy white flakes melted on their shoulders and stuck in their eyelashes. They ambled in and out of stores, making purchases for family and friends, their arms becoming heavy with bags containing crisply wrapped little boxes of joy. Late in the afternoon, Billy delivered her home, and even though they had plans to meet later at Ciro's, she wanted to prolong their afternoon and invited him in for tea. As soon as they'd taken off their coats, she heard the screams.

Billy looked at her, all concern, and asked, "Is something wrong?"

Before Kick could answer but not before her heart rose into her throat, Rosemary ran down the stairs in her slip and stockings, red lipstick smeared all over her mouth.

"Kick!" she exclaimed, running over to her sister, oblivious to the fact that a young man was standing right there as well. Her eyes never fell on him once, so focused was she on Kick. "You have to save me from Mother! She's trying to put me in the closet."

Kick took hold of Rosemary's shoulders and tried to find her sister's eyes with her own, but they were shut tight. "Rosemary," she said as soothingly as she could, "Rosemary, darling, look at me. Look at me."

When her sister didn't look at her but instead moaned and shivered and clenched her fists, Kick glanced upstairs. Her mother was nowhere in sight, though Jean and Teddy peered out from behind a bedroom door. Kick couldn't imagine Rosemary was telling the truth about Rose threatening to put her in the closet that night, since their mother stopped using that particular punishment right around each child's tenth year, but *something* had set Rosemary off. And Kick was mortified that this detail of her childhood had been spoken aloud in Billy's presence—though his expression was only one of brow-knitted worry, not surprise or disgust.

Turning away from him, Kick tried putting her arm around Rosemary's waist, but Rosemary twisted violently away, shouting "No!" and struck out with her clenched hand. Kick ducked, and her sister's fist nearly missed her right temple.

Count to ten. One, two, three . . . Oh, I don't have time for that now! Kick mustered all her compassion and composure to squelch the anger now boiling in her own body, and said, "Let's just sit down together. On the couch. You're shivering. Let's get a blanket and play fort. Hide from Mother." She tried to sound enticing, make it a game like they used to play, the kind that had once reliably snapped Rosemary out of any bad mood.

"You can't trap me, either! No! You're never around anymore! Why are you here now if it's not to help *her*?" Rosemary howled and slumped to the floor.

Then Billy, like a statue made magically animate, knelt before Rosemary and held out his hand. Speaking in the most soothing low tones, he said, "Rosemary? Do you remember me? I'm Billy Hartington, and we danced together several times last season. You're a wonderful dancer. May I help you back up to your room now?"

Rosemary lifted her wet eyes to Billy and searched his face—for what, Kick wasn't sure. Recognition? Trust? Whatever it was, she must have found it, because she put her hand in his, just as she did with their father.

Billy used his other hand to help lift Rosemary off the floor, and Kick hurried to lead them upstairs to Rosemary's room, which was in complete disarray, the bedsheets and duvet on the floor, shoes and stockings and girdles and skirts and blouses everywhere. Billy tried to step on the patches of carpet and successfully led Rosemary to sit on her bed. Kick followed.

Then Rosemary looked up at Billy and said, "Will we dance again?"

"Of course." Billy smiled.

Rosemary lay down on her bed and curled into a ball, and Kick tucked some sheets gently around her. Then she and Billy left the room, closing the door quietly behind them.

Back down in the foyer, she said, "I'm so, so sorry you had to see that."

She was so *angry* at her sister right now—she'd probably single-handedly ruined her relationship with Billy. Her chest felt tight, her breath short.

"I had no idea," he replied, his voice steady.

"Few people do," Kick said.

"I mean, I heard she'd tripped at the ceremony, but . . ."

"No one really understands what's wrong with her. And my parents . . ." *Ignore it? Don't help?* It was so hard to explain, the way they loved and doted on their eldest daughter, protecting her in some ways but also pushing her to be just like the rest of them. Kick's head hurt. All the joy of the day had drained out of her.

"You know," said Billy, "two of the queen's nieces are hidden away somewhere because of . . . difficulties."

Kick nodded. "I've heard that. But Mother and Daddy like to pretend that Rosemary's fine."

"I'm sorry, Kick," he said, and he reached forward to lace his fingers between hers. Her heart sped up—was it possible he wasn't leaving? That he'd helped her sister and now wanted to help her?

"Don't be," she said, sniffling back the threatening tears. "I am very grateful for your help today, but I'm just . . . sorry you saw it."

"Don't be," he said, echoing her. All she wanted was to dissolve into him, to feel his strength and height and make them her own. She felt cracked and fragile, as if those truths that Wickham had referred to were beginning to leak out.

They were quiet together, standing awkwardly with their fingers still intertwined. Until Billy said, "I'll tell you a secret, too."

Kick looked at him with wide eyes. "The Cavendishes have secrets?"

Billy smirked and said, "More than most families, I'd imagine. And this one should have the dual purpose of also amusing you. Right. Well, my father is a great angler. Loves nothing more than to catch salmon up in Scotland. And he is rather obsessed with tying little flies as bait for his line." Billy shook his head, as if he couldn't imagine anything more dull than this hobby of his father's. "Anyway," he continued, "the way he likes to test his flies is to lie in a full bathtub pretending *he* is a salmon, dangling the bait above him in the water. If the bait is appealing, he keeps it. If it's not, it goes in the bin."

"He pretends he's a salmon?" Kick said.

Billy nodded. "His poor attire is hardly his only eccentricity." Kick remembered the duke's fraying sleeves at Goodwood. So.

Then she burst out laughing. "Thank you, Billy. I didn't think anyone could amaze me today, but you just have. *The Duke of Devonshire, a fish.*"

"You're now in on a secret that only the residents of Churchdale Hall know."

"I'm honored," she said, her hand on her heart.

Billy gently tapped his forehead against hers. "So am I," he replied.

After a quick glance to see if anyone was nearby, which they were not, Billy bent down and gave Kick a tender kiss on the lips. "I'll see you later," he whispered.

Before she went upstairs to change, Kick found Rose with a glass of whiskey, slouching at the dining room table. "There you are," Kick said.

Her mother raised her red-rimmed eyes to Kick and said, "How dare you bring that boy in unannounced!"

"We bring friends home all the time, Mother."

"You've never brought home a *boy*, a *stranger*, not without warning." Her mother laughed, an exhausted, cynical cackle. "The Duke of Devonshire's son, Kathleen! He has so much more power than you."

"If you'd bothered to come out and help your own daughter, Mother, you'd have seen that Billy was the hero just now."

"Not after she hit me," said Rose tightly, touching her left cheek, which Kick could now see was redder than the other one, and not from rouge. Then she noticed the bag of cold peas sitting next to the glass. "I heard the whole thing, of course. Billy was . . . well, he was your knight in shining armor, wasn't he?"

Then why can't you sound happier for me? But there was no point in asking that particular question. Instead Kick asked: "What happened before we got home?"

Rose shrugged. "What ever happens? I asked her to take a bath, and get ready for a dinner event at the Oratory. She didn't want to go."

"She said you tried to put her in the closet."

"I might have reminded her that when my children misbehave, there are consequences."

Kick rolled her eyes. "She's twenty!"

"Then why doesn't she *act* like it?" Rose whispered fiercely. Kick always marveled at this, the way her mother's love, especially for her precious Rosemary, could transform into revulsion.

The question hung between them. Neither of them knew the answer, not any more than her doctors and teachers had known.

"Speaking of misbehaving," Rose said, straightening her posture, "I heard *you* canceled a date with Robin Baring the other day?"

"How on earth did you hear that?" For the first time, Kick didn't feel guilt at being caught in a lie and a disobedience. Rather, she felt annoyed, like Jack usually sounded in the same position.

Rose acted as though she hadn't heard Kick's question, and instead continued her own interrogation. "Was it to be with Billy?"

"Yes." There was no point in lying, not when her mother was so clearly in possession of the facts. And part of her wanted her mother to know the truth, to dare her to react.

Rose finished the whiskey, set the glass on the table, and left the room. It felt like a small but essential fragment of her soul followed her mother out, leaving Kick feeling unsteady on her own two feet.

CHAPTER 13

Winter passed slowly, in a damp fog of work at St. Mary's and a few high-profile engagements, like giving her first official public speech at the Foyles bookstore luncheon for children in need. Most of her friends were in a funk about the bad weather, and Billy was back at Cambridge for his last term. Joe Jr. finally made a break for Spain, leaving only a letter to his father saying he had to see the end of the civil war, and that was that.

At first, Joe Sr. was furious that his oldest son had disobeyed him so thoroughly, but in letters and phone calls, Jack managed to convince him to be proud that his namesake was a crisis hunter who wanted to make his own name. "When he runs for president, you don't want the Republicans to say he's only a puppet, do you?" Unsurprisingly, Jack was convincing. Joe began using his term "crisis hunter" when colleagues asked where Joe Jr. had gone.

Then Rose left for a long holiday in Greece, and Kick was suddenly on her own, making completely independent decisions about how to spend her days and nights. Craving some physical exertion when everyone else seemed content inside, she took long walks through London and explored neighborhoods like Islington, Richmond, and Greenwich, then rewarded herself with a half-pint of ale, wondering if Billy would like it.

The only truly auspicious moment in those months was the Valentine's Day wedding of Ann de Trafford and Derek Parker-Bowles. The pair were a few years older than Kick and her friends, and their wedding was the first of their set. It was even more important for being between Ann, a Catholic, and Derek, a Protestant. The ceremony was a grand affair at Brompton Oratory, and it was well-known that Derek had agreed to let their children be raised Catholic. Since Derek was a cousin—not a first cousin, but still a relation—of Billy's, and the Cavendish family attended the wedding in good cheer, the whole frothy affair gave Kick hope for the future. Until she overhead Lady Astor, who never could tone down her feelings about the Catholic Church regardless of her fond feelings for individual Catholics like Kick or Joe, saying, "Well, at least the de Traffords are a good English family, even if they are papists. But still, I wish Derek hadn't capitulated. How can England survive if it moves backward to the ways before Henry the Eighth?"

Instantly, the effervescence of the day fizzled, and Kick once again felt her profound disadvantage in this country she illogically continued to love. *Why should I love it here so much if I am not wholly welcome?* She wondered whether England—and Billy—was somehow for her what Marlene Dietrich was for Jack: a nearly impossible challenge. The problem was, she'd been raised to tackle impossible challenges. She found them irresistible.

A few days later, she must have seemed especially mopey at St. Mary's, because Father O'Flaherty asked what was wrong.

"A man," she blurted out. "Well, he's not a *man*, like you or my father. He's close to my age. He just turned twenty-one." She looked for signs that Father O'Flaherty might already know whom she was talking about, but he maintained his open expression, betraying nothing.

"But he's not Catholic," she said.

"Church of England?" Father clarified.

"Yes."

"I assume, because you have such fond feelings for him, that he is a good and kind young man."

"Yes, Father."

"Have you discussed the possibility of him converting to Catholicism?"

"No." She shook her head. "I'm not . . . we're not . . . neither of us has made any promises or declarations. Yet. But I sense that we might, soon."

"I see," the priest said, and his face took on a grave expression. "Then perhaps he *might* convert."

Kick looked down at her hands and admitted the truth at last. "I doubt it, Father."

"Would you consider converting to Anglicanism?"

Kick jerked up her head and looked at Father O'Flaherty in dumbfounded surprise. "Wouldn't that damn me to hell forever?"

"The archbishop of Canterbury certainly wouldn't think so."

Was she really hearing this from a Catholic priest?

"In school," Father O'Flaherty went on, "one of my closest friends was Protestant. He and I used to have endless debates about religion, and none of them ended our friendship. When I finished at the seminary, he took me to lunch and gave me an excellent bottle of whiskey. I'm the godfather of his first child. I don't tell many people this, but I refuse to believe he is going to hell because of his faith. He is a good Christian man. In fact, he's been helping your father and me petition families and schools we wouldn't otherwise have access to, to accept Jewish children. *Jewish* children. I don't want anyone to suffer, in this life or the next."

Kick opened her mouth to reply but couldn't.

"If you love this man, and he returns your affections—and I hope he does, for I can see in your eyes how deeply you care for him," Father O'Flaherty went on, making his tone as kind as she'd ever heard it, "you will be faced with a difficult choice, between your church and your heart. I don't envy you that. But I also respect you too much not to tell you the truth."

"Do you know of the marriage between Ann de Trafford and Derek Parker-Bowles?"

"I do."

"They didn't seem to have to choose. She is remaining Catholic, and he is remaining Protestant, and their children will be raised Catholic."

"True." Father O'Flaherty nodded. "And that sort of arrangement is a possibility for a couple in their position. However . . ."

"Yes?" she asked eagerly, not sure why his voice had trailed off.

"The de Traffords are an old English family, very established in society. They are recusant Catholics, part of a minority in the nobility who dissented from the Reformation. I have colleagues in the clergy from similar families, and I can tell you that they are treated very differently from Irish Catholics like me."

"Or me," Kick added, seeing with depressing clarity where he was heading with this little history lesson. "So you're saying that Derek's and Ann's families were more likely to reach an agreement like that than, say, the son of an important English Protestant family and the daughter of an upstart Catholic American of Irish descent?"

"Very precisely put," he said grimly.

Kick pursed her ragged lips. "It's not fair," she said, knowing she sounded like a petulant child, and not caring.

"It is not," Father O'Flaherty agreed, and she nearly burst into tears, she was so grateful for his compassion. "Just remember, you have choices."

"My heart or my church," she repeated his words, her voice wet and embarrassing. She cleared her throat and went on, "But I should add 'my heart or my family,' because my mother is the strictest Catholic I know."

"I'm sorry to hear that," he said, and again she felt close to tears. At least Father O'Flaherty seemed to think that her choice was a worthy one, not to be dismissed as the fantasy of some deluded girl.

"Thank you," she told him.

He rose from his chair, patted her hand, and said, "You can talk to me anytime."

Then he left and the tears came.

❖ ❖ ❖

If God was trying to remind her of the power of her own faith, he certainly sent her a strong message in March, when she traveled to Rome with her father and siblings for the coronation of the new pope, which she'd also be writing about for the *League of Catholic Women Bulletin* in Boston—her first byline! She wasn't happy to leave Billy behind, but the promise of Italy's beauty, her article, and the front-row seat she'd have at the coronation were more than adequate compensation.

As a bonus, Jack would be there, too. Just a few weeks before, he'd proposed to Frances Ann Cannon, a Protestant girl he'd been seeing, only to have her parents instruct her to turn him down. Then they sent her on a long cruise to get her as far away as possible from Joe Kennedy's boy. Jack had been so heartbroken, he'd dropped out of Harvard for a semester and come to London to spend the spring working for their father. Kick kept trying to ask her brother for more details, but the only thing he'd say on the subject was, "Don't make the same mistake."

Kick wondered which mistake he meant—falling in love with a Protestant or trying to marry one. She'd already made the first, despite her best attempts not to. But she was determined to make sure that the second, if it came to that, would *not* be a mistake. Jack always rushed into things without thinking them through. She, at least, was taking plenty of time with Billy. And Father O'Flaherty had faith in her.

Rose, tan and rejuvenated from her travels in Greece, was waiting for her husband and children at their palatial hotel suite in Rome. Jean and Teddy threw themselves into her lap and talked over each other in their bids for her attention. She laughed happily, and hugged and tickled them. It was always the most intimate she ever was with her children—right after a long trip away. Then things would return to normal. The older siblings knew the pattern and, instead of soaking up the short-lived attention, went to the marble table where wrapped gifts were spread out, to try to guess what was inside.

Rose gave Kick an ancient vase. Small but heavy in her hands, it had a dark brown background and creamy maidens in long, rigid dresses with heads bent in reverence.

"Do you like it, Kathleen?" Rose asked Kick with a proud smile. "I went to some trouble with the dealer for it."

"It's very pretty, Mother, thank you," she replied, though she felt no affection for the vase—it wasn't especially beautiful, and she hadn't gone on the trip with her mother to give it any meaning. She knew it was meant for her trousseau, to bespeak her worldliness. Someday, she was supposed to place it on a mantel and explain to admiring guests how her shrewd connoisseur of a mother had procured it for her. It was no Vol de Nuit, though its value on paper was much greater.

After gifts, the family descended to the hotel's well-known restaurant for a seven-course Italian meal. Jack, who sat next to Kick, said to her after the fourth course, a divine pasta dish with mushrooms and cream, "Kill me now," with a hand on his still-concave belly.

"I want to hear about all of *you*," Rose said to her children after regaling them with stories of her travels. She pushed away a barely nibbled plate of tender lamb in glistening amber gravy. "Tell me, Kathleen, how is our next debutante coming along?"

Kick smiled at Eunice and replied, "She's going to dazzle everyone. Her curtsy is flawless, and she passed the flash card test of Who's Who in London."

"Kick's been a huge help," gushed Eunice. "I don't know what I would have done without her."

"Kathleen was also quite the star at Foyles," added their father. "I believe the *Mail* called her speech 'charming and intelligent.'"

"I have no doubt that it was," said Rose. "And you've kept your figure, too. My, my, but I might have some competition on my hands!" Her mother laughed, but Kick sensed a certain seriousness in her tone, confirmed by Jack's brief eyebrow raise.

I'm not trying to compete with you, Mother. For heaven's sake. Though I am the one who made the preparations to get the family to Italy, all while also helping Daddy host two dinners at the embassy. At least her father seemed to appreciate her.

At every site to which her parents herded the family on their tour of Rome, there was evidence of the strength of the Kennedys' faith, almost as if Rose and Joe were trying to drive home to their errant children who'd lately entangled themselves with Protestants what it really meant to be Catholic. There was the vast stone Colosseum, where the early followers of Christ had succumbed to hungry lions; churches and basilicas dedicated to early martyrs and saints; and of course the sprawling, domed Vatican itself, where Pope Pius XII was crowned in a ceremony awash in so much scarlet, Kick couldn't help but think of all those bloody beginnings for Catholicism in pagan Rome.

Writing about the coronation proved harder than anything she'd done in a long while. Everything she wrote felt trite and schoolgirlish, as if she were writing a report for the nuns—which she supposed she was, in a way. The Catholic matrons of Boston were devout and exacting, and they expected certain things of anyone with the Kennedy name. And because Kick was half-Kennedy and half-Fitzgerald, anything she wrote would be doubly scrutinized. She tried not to think about them as she wrote three drafts in longhand. By the fourth typed draft, she was feeling braver, finding something that sounded more like her voice. After a long description of the events and the sensation of peace and unity in Christianity that she'd shared with so many millions that day, she concluded, "The enthusiasm for Christ's Vicar was mightier, more spontaneous, than any number of 'Heils' from a drilled populace. Here there were no commands, issued by authority, for waving and cheering. Here it was only the command of the heart."

The political message surprised even her as she reread it. But it felt right to position Christianity—not just Catholicism—against the Reich, to pit the command of those in power against the will of those commanded, the multitude who possessed voices of their own and wanted more than anything to use them.

Just a few years before, the man who was then Cardinal Pacelli and now Pope Pius XII had visited the Kennedys' home in Bronxville. Rose had been so honored that she'd roped off the chair on which he'd rested his derriere, as if the seat belonged in a museum. Somehow she had known the man would become even more holy than he already was. Despite that, Kick's mother decided to skip the family's private audience with the new pope in order to keep her fitting with Molyneux in Paris. "I wish I could take you, Kathleen," she'd said mournfully before kissing her daughter on the cheek the night before her train left for France.

"I'd rather stay," Kick replied. The only place she'd *rather* have been was in Scotland, where her friends had gathered for a shooting holiday. But going with her mother on an errand for clothes, instead of meeting the the pope face-to-face? No. She marveled at how her father, who was so proud to be the United States' representative at the coronation, who'd written so many letters to win this private audience, merely kissed his wife goodbye with a hug and a smile. Was unfettered independence part of the arrangement of their marriage? If it was, then she thought she'd be willing to trade some independence for more . . . passion, more tenderness and devotion.

When Pius laid his knotty, cool hands on her head as she knelt in a quiet tapestried chamber in the Vatican, Kick wanted to feel blessed, to feel the profundity of the moment in her heart. She closed her eyes and willed it to be so. But she couldn't clear her mind, and found that her dearest wish wasn't to feel God in her soul but to feel Billy's arm once more on her shoulder.

❖ ❖ ❖

Two days after her family's meeting with the pope, Hitler moved his troops into the territories of Czechoslovakia that were supposed to be off-limits, effectively sending the Munich agreement up in flames. Joe was on the first train to Paris to meet with Bill Bullitt at the embassy there, have dinner with Rose, and then head back to London. Kick and the rest of the family went straight to England. On her journey, she read all the newspapers she could, even muddling through the French ones. The debate for and against war was more heated than ever. The only thing on which both sides agreed was that Hitler was not to be trusted.

Then, on April 1, Franco declared that the war in Spain was over. Everyone Kick knew other than Teddy, who simply hoped this supposed victory meant his oldest and favorite brother would soon be back in London, sensed that this was a serious blow to democracy in Europe.

Thus, the season of 1939 began under a dark, hazy cloud of uncertainty and mistrust. Her father still worked for peace, though despondently, as he was increasingly referred to as ineffectual and redundant. Roosevelt felt war was inevitable, and Joe suspected he was colluding with Winston Churchill behind his back. Surprisingly, though, despite the general feeling about Kick's father's policies, her family was invited to just as many parties and events as last season. When her friends used dirty words like *isolationism* and *spinelessness*, they were careful not to apply them to her father specifically but to American policies more generally, which she took to be a sign that they cared about her and her feelings, as much as they did about Debo's, whom they'd known for years, when they tiptoed around the subject of English Fascism.

Until the worst happened, even because the worst might happen, Kick was determined to enjoy her second season in English society, for it felt in many ways like a stolen season. Races and dances, dinners and cocktails, charity and church work gave her a sense of purpose, an anchor, as the rest of the world spun wildly, veering ever more out of control. "Do you ever wonder," Kick asked Debo as they leaned on each other, shoulder to bare shoulder, in a taxi at the end of another late night, "if we ought to be, I don't know, taking things more seriously with all that's going on?"

Languidly covering her yawning lips with the crook of her arm, Debo replied, "And how would *that* charm the Cavendish brothers?"

Kick laughed. "Good point," she agreed, but inside, her stomach twisted. None of this would last long, but there was nothing she or any of them could do but talk and debate and wring their hands until a decision was made somewhere way above their heads.

In a few quiet moments, she let herself picture her life as Billy's wife at Chatsworth: it would be much the same busy, full life it was now, though she'd be more of a leader, *giving* the parties and *heading* the charity work of her choosing, as she raised her own brood of happy . . . *Catholic? Protestant?* children. And there the fantasy would end, as she attempted to assemble a picture of her future family on the bright green lawn of the estate, their youngest child in a glowingly white christening gown.

But as spring gave way to summer, Kick began to wonder whether she and Billy would ever speak seriously about their relationship again, as they had last fall in Scotland. She'd felt some urgency to do so after Ann and Derek's wedding, but then she'd gone to Rome and more time had passed. She hardly felt she could complain, after all—he sought her out, found reasons to kiss her every chance he could, and never took out other girls. But here they were again with war looming, and the very real possibility of having to go back to America before her. Billy and David and Andrew even registered with the army. When she let her mind drift in the wrong direction, it went to violent images, grotesque sounds, a frightening collage from war movies, books, paintings. Gunfire from the air, from the ground. Grenades. Gurgles, blood in the throat. It all seemed suddenly, horribly real. On her knees by her bed, even in the small hours of the morning when she returned after nights of dining and dancing, she prayed for something specific to happen with her and Billy, something to make things plain between them at last.

CHAPTER 14

The July weekend at Blenheim should have rolled out before Kick as a vast expanse of pleasure, all verdant lawn and croquet games, rooms bedecked with flowers and champagne fountains. Both Jack and Joe Jr. would be there, as they'd returned from the continent for the Fourth of July celebrations a few days before, and her parents were likely to be so engrossed in their own intrigues that they wouldn't pay much attention to her comings and goings. But instead of looking forward to the festivities, Kick was dreading having to tell Billy that she could not attend his huge coming-of-age celebration at Chatsworth in August, since she was due to leave for France in fewer than three weeks.

Ever since her mother had dreamily announced the plan over breakfast the previous week, Kick had been alternately scheming, shouting, praying, and crying to herself. The best solution had come from Debo, who'd offered to let Kick stay with the Mitfords, but when she presented that idea to her father behind the safely closed door of his office, he'd laughed. *Laughed!* "Kick," he'd said, "no young woman in her right mind would pass up an opportunity to swim, shop, and sun in unlimited quantities on the French Riviera."

It was a delicate game she was playing—she didn't want to give away how much Billy's party meant to her. So she'd replied, as calmly as she could, "Daddy, I have important commitments here, with the league, and Father O'Flaherty, and I thought I would register to work with the Red Cross as well. I don't want to let anyone down just to go shopping."

"This wouldn't have anything to do with Billy's party, would it?" Her father leaned forward on his desk.

Kick set her jaw and swallowed. "I'd like to go to that, of course," she conceded, as to deny it would give the lie to her plan. But she wanted to downplay it. "Everyone is going. It's to be the culmination of the entire season. Frankly," she added, "I'm surprised you and Mother don't want to go."

"Going to that party would be tantamount to admitting you and Billy will become engaged," he said.

This idea thrilled her in the deepest, most elemental way. But she laughed off his suggestion. "Hardly, Daddy," she replied.

"You don't seem aware enough of the consequences of your actions," he said. "I've been asked on more than one occasion how I feel about my daughter marrying a Protestant."

"You have?" Kick's eyes widened. "But we're not engaged! We haven't even discussed it. Whoever asked you that couldn't have known very much about me and Billy."

"It's no use pretending, Kick. I may be your father, but I know what love looks like. It's time to cool things off. You *will* go to France."

Kick bit down hard on the inside of her cheek, drawing blood, to squelch her immediate reply—*Is that a dare?* "If you think it's best," she just muttered.

At her next meeting with Father O'Flaherty, the priest listened patiently while she paced and pleaded for guidance in the little office where she usually worked in contented silence.

"The time might have arrived for you to ask Billy how he thinks you both should proceed. What compromises he is willing to make. What compromises you might be willing to make," he replied.

Kick thought back to Father O'Flaherty's anecdote about his boyhood friend. If she could strike a bargain with Billy that satisfied her, that felt true to her life and faith in God, she had a feeling this priest would support her when it came time to stand up to her family.

The question was *what* bargain. *What* compromises. What would Billy give? It was hard to know what she would give, could give, without knowing first if he returned her affections. Her love.

It was time for some answers.

◇ ◇ ◇

Dukie Wookie had outdone himself in honor of his debutante daughter Sarah Spencer-Churchill, transforming his sizable ballroom into a Garden of Eden with tropical flowers, fountains of a fizzy pink punch, and a superb American jazz band. In the peachy twilight of the first night, Kick and Jack stood among the playful topiary animals in Blenheim's Italian Garden, sipping glasses of the famed local mineral water, which she needed. She'd already drunk two glasses of champagne too quickly to settle her nerves, and now her legs felt leaden and her head like a hot-air balloon. She had yet to see Billy.

"Sometimes, here in old Blighty," mused Jack, "I feel like I've stepped into a time machine. At this moment, I could be standing in Marie Antoinette's Versailles."

"Except this is England, and the music is Benny Goodman's," observed Kick.

"Details, details," he said airily. Then, tapping his glass to hers, he strolled toward the ballroom, where a Technicolor rainbow of gowns shifted between pillars of black. Her brother seemed to have recovered from his broken heart. Or he was hiding it well. Impossible to tell. She assumed the consolation of the Duke of Kent's continental mistress, a Romanian princess with whom Jack had been photographed in Germany, had helped.

Kick took a few deep breaths and told herself tonight was *not* the night for a serious discussion with Billy, and this calmed her stomach a bit. Tonight was for dancing the Big Apple and making sure Billy thought as highly of her as possible before she gave him the news. She'd worn her slinkiest fuchsia dress just for this purpose. Tomorrow they'd take a long walk alone and she'd broach it.

Feeling too cool with a breeze tickling her exposed back, Kick headed inside and found Billy on her way.

"Are you ignoring your dance card, Miss Kennedy?" Billy said in mock horror.

She laughed. "You know how I feel about those horrid things."

"Undemocratic."

"Precisely. The enemy of spontaneity."

"Bastards."

"Such language!"

"I'm a soldier now. I can swear with impunity."

"Sounds like dangerous logic."

He moved close to her, put his hands on her waist, and swayed her gently to the music drifting out of the house. She put her hands on his chest and felt his heart beating, so she put her ear on her fingers to see if she could hear it as well but, alas, no.

"Soon you'll see Chatsworth as you've seen all these other estates, restored and ready for glamour once more," he said.

His birthday party. *Holy Mother, why is he saying this now? I can't very well* lie *to him.*

"Billy," she said, her voice uneven as she pushed him slightly away so she could look up into his face. "I have some bad news about the party."

Billy didn't say anything, but looked expectantly at her.

She'd thought a lot about how to phrase this, and her rehearsed words came out of her mouth maybe too smoothly. "My parents want me to come on our annual family vacation to France. In August."

Billy took a step back from her. "I see," he said.

Tell me you don't want me to go. That you couldn't imagine the weekend without me. That it's time to defy our parents.

"I'm just distraught," she said. "I . . ." She couldn't very well *ask* him to declare his feelings, could she? Yet she could see the hurt on his face.

Say something.

"Are you saying that your parents are trying to keep us apart?" he asked.

Answering this question truthfully felt too painful, so she dodged it as best she could. "I assume your parents also want us apart? They hardly speak to me when they see me." She'd seen them at numerous events in the last few months, and they rarely engaged her in conversation. Occasionally his mother would inquire about Kick's charitable engagements, which she'd read about in the papers, but it was all rather *bland*, and his father just said nothing at all.

"They are . . . avoiding the issue," Billy admitted. "Waiting, I assume."

"For what?" *Say it*, she pleaded. *Say "waiting for me to declare my feelings." Let's not wait any more.*

"For you to disappear, presumably, in the same puff of magic in which you arrived," he said with a heavy sigh.

"Puff of magic? What are you talking about?" She could feel her pulse chugging in her neck.

"Kick, we're going to war," he said regretfully, taking her hands in his. "I feel it in my bones. I know we all joke about it, because, well, that's what we do. And when England goes to war, it seems likely that you and your countrymen will go home. Especially since your father is dead set against war. He won't want you in harm's way."

"But I don't have to go," she said. "I could stay. Joe Jr. went to Spain without Daddy's permission." Her heart was hammering a hole in her chest, her throat, her brain. *Please, please, give me a reason to stay.*

Billy looked at her, the corners of his mouth downturned. "I know what you want me to say, Kick. And I can say part of it, which is that I love you. I love your wit and your passion and your boldness. I love how you lean on me when we dance, and I love that you hate dance cards because they are *the enemy of spontaneity*. I love your tiny hands, because they belie the size of your character," he said mournfully, looking down at their four hands folded together between their bodies. Kick's heart wanted to break through her chest and fly away with delight at his words, but she knew the other part, the part he'd implied he *couldn't* or *shouldn't say*, was still coming.

She decided it was worth the risk to interrupt, so she put two fingers to his lips and said, "Before you go on, I want to tell you that I return your feelings. In my *soul*, I love you. I love your loyalty and your humor. I love that you read poetry, and that you prefer your gardener's ale to the French wines served at parties like this one. I love your height, how *safe* I feel when I'm with you. I love *you*, Billy Hartington."

Instead of kissing her, he squeezed her hands and took another step back.

"But," he said.

He didn't immediately go on, so she rushed in, "Billy, I feel certain we can figure the rest of it out."

"The rest of it? Are four hundred years of history so easy to sort out? When a major war is about to break out?"

"We don't have to bring our churches together, Billy. We have to bring *us* together. You and me. We won't be the first couple that's managed it."

"Have I mentioned that I also love your optimism?" His smile was sad, though.

"But you don't share it," she said.

"When I'm dead on a field in Italy, you'll be glad you didn't defy your church and family for a man who was only going to die."

She withdrew her hands from his and balled them into fists. "Don't tell me how I would feel."

"I'm sorry," he said, and she could tell he meant it. But sorry for what, exactly? For loving her, or for his cowardice?

"When were you planning to tell me all this?" she demanded.

"I'd hoped . . . I'd hoped we would have more time."

"Time for *what*? For you to ruin my reputation?" Anger had flared in her chest, and she couldn't contain it.

"Kick, if there wasn't going to be a war . . ."

"Don't bring the war into this. This is about religion and heritage, your *birthright*."

"Partly," he agreed. "But for me, it *is* also about the war. I didn't understand it myself until I put on the uniform."

"I'll make it easy for you, then," she said. She curtsied, then stood as tall as her frame would allow and turned her back to him to face the looming facade of Blenheim, lit up for revelry but looking to Kick's eyes like a house on fire. Before she could change her mind, or Billy could say more, she walked forward with every intention of losing herself in the decadent flame.

❖ ❖ ❖

When Joe Jr. proposed she visit Spain with him and Hugh Fraser to, in his words, "get off this blasted little island," Kick immediately accepted his invitation and thanked God for the opportunity to run away. How ironic that she should want to leave as quickly as possible when just days before she'd been looking for any reason to stay. As soon as she set foot in Barcelona, she was grateful for the profound differences between Spain and England, for the possibility that this Catholic country decimated by civil war might rescue her from her memories of opulence in Billy's Protestant homeland.

From an elderly peddler in a northern village, who smelled of garlic and urine and had only three teeth, Kick bought herself a new wooden rosary, and she carried it with her everywhere in her purse so that it would be handy when she entered a chapel, some of which were still being pieced back together. She said countless Our Fathers and Hail Marys as trickles of sweat rolled down her thighs and lower back, for the midsummer heat in Spain was relentless. She prayed ardently and deeply, asking God for forgiveness and mercy and deliverance from Billy's insistent grip on her heart.

Kick let her brother lead her around and show her his Spain, a place of stark contrasts where children played soccer in little more than slippers on patches of brown grass or dust while men and women lugged rocks and carted away rubble to repair their villages; where older devout Catholics prayed dutifully every morning though they ate dinner as late as eleven o'clock and the young people promenaded on plazas till midnight or later; where ancient synagogues had been transformed into mosques and churches, in a style of architecture Kick had never seen before, decorated by mosaics composed of millions of shards of colorful glass and pottery, as gorgeous as any stained glass window she'd ever seen.

In Madrid, after the fierce sun had set and the cooler evening air had rolled in, Joe Jr., Kick, and Hugh met with Joe's friends Mateo and Pedro, and Pedro's fiancée Gabrielle. A light wind played with the hem of Kick's cotton dress as two old men strummed guitars and sang by a fountain with no water in it. Their little group walked at a leisurely pace with the locals, and Kick listened while the others talked about the changes in the city since the war had ended. The three Spaniards were her brother's age, and so a few years older than Kick, but their paths in life had been dramatically altered by the war. Though they were from well-off families who prized education and made sure their children learned English, Mateo and Pedro had put off college to fight, and Pedro walked with a deep limp. They spoke freely of their lost friends, of how Mateo's sister Leona grieved for her dead fiancé every day, praying for hours and lighting countless candles on a shrine in her bedroom that their parents had to extinguish when she either left the house or fell into a stupor, for fear of setting the house on fire. "And we are among the lucky ones," Mateo said.

After an hour of walking, Hugh admitted to feeling hungry, but since no restaurant was open as early as nine at night, they found a bar with four round tables that was just opening a few blocks off the Plaza Mayor. They sat and ordered two bottles of cava and a few plates of tortas and olives. "But no more," counseled Pedro. "You must save your appetites for later."

Gabrielle turned her attention to Kick and asked if she was enjoying Spain so far. She had long black hair done in a thick braid down her back, and the most remarkable eyelashes Kick had seen on any woman. Her rolling, husky accent was robust and amorous, and Kick felt young and ugly next to her.

"Spain is beautiful," Kick replied, aware as she said the words that they were thoroughly inadequate. "It's also sad," she tried again. "We've seen so much ruined by the war. But what remains is just beautiful. And the care people take in putting it all back together again is also beautiful."

Gabrielle nodded. "You should have seen it five years ago, before Franco." She spat out the name of her country's new ruler, as if it were a piece of grizzled meat. "I was probably your age," she added.

"Did you know Pedro then?"

Gabrielle nodded. "I wanted to become engaged when the war started. I begged him to marry me and make me pregnant so that if he died, I would at least have his baby."

Kick was shocked by the intimacy of this disclosure. Was it the difference in their cultures that made this other woman so bold, or was it the war? Looking at Spain, Kick saw that war had most definitely *exposed* things, laid them bare.

"But he said no," Gabrielle went on, before taking a sip of wine. "And now we will be married in one month."

"That's wonderful." Kick smiled, but it was hard to be truly excited for her new friend since she didn't seem elated herself. She was far from a bride-to-be in America, who went about waving her ring finger and gushing about trousseaux and honeymoons.

Gabrielle nodded and agreed, "It is wonderful, yes. But now it might be difficult for us to have a baby." She looked past Kick toward the bar behind her, her eyes glazed over. Then she added, "War *takes* things, things you don't expect."

Kick couldn't understand what might get in the way of their ability to have children. Sister Kit hadn't covered that in her *Gray's Anatomy* lessons. Maybe it had something do to with his limp. She prayed for the couple the next day in the dark, chilly nave of San Isidro el Real, but her mind kept straying to Billy. Was Gabrielle's willingness to marry Pedro, knowing their marriage might be childless, so different from Kick's recent willingness to pledge herself to Billy knowing he didn't share her faith? Had she really been willing to do such a thing?

She thought she might have been, had he told her that night at Blenheim that he loved her *and* wanted her with him forever. She'd have done anything that night to keep him. But she certainly would not now. She felt resolve within her, not as a hardening or straightening of her body, but as a kind of clearing, a relaxation of her shoulders and chest and legs.

Gracias, Madre Maria.

Thank you for showing me the way.

CHAPTER 15

Many letters greeted her when she arrived at the Domaine de Ranguin, the chateau her mother had rented on a hilltop just outside Cannes, the opulence of which blinded her after the rubble of Spain. Set up on a bluff, the house was massive, with green shutters and awnings at each of the many windows that overlooked the Mediterranean. Most of the letters were from correspondents she could predict—Debo, Father O'Flaherty, Jean Ogilvy, Sissy, and even long-suffering Peter Grace—but two were from Billy.

"I had to snatch them from the butler before Mother saw them!" a tan and relaxed Eunice told her sister triumphantly. "She would have thrown them out, I'm sure. Or at least read them first."

"Thank you," said Kick, though she wasn't sure if she really was thankful. It was true that, despite everything she'd seen and felt in Spain, part of her had been hoping for *something* from Billy when she arrived. But another part of her had been hoping he would stay silent and confirm her worst suspicions about him.

In her white, sun-flooded bedroom, Kick sat at a little desk as lace curtains fluttered in the breeze. She set aside the two letters from Billy and started with the others, which were full of the usual reports and gossip; she was so distracted by the presence of Billy's letters, she barely comprehended them. By the time she finished the last one, the anticipation of opening Billy's had practically winded her.

The sound of the thick, creamy envelope ripping open reverberated in her ears, and she began to read the letter with the earlier postmark.

Dear Kick,

I feel I must apologize for our discussion at Blenheim. It's been an agony knowing I've caused you any pain, when you don't deserve anything other than the purest happiness. And especially when I treasure the memory of every moment we've spent together. In fact, I cannot stop bringing them to mind, and dwelling on them, which only brings me more distress. If I go on now, I'll only embarrass myself further. Please know I will ever be your

Billy

Kick inhaled again, this time with her eyes open. *You should be sorry,* she said to the letter. What could he possibly have had to add to that? The second letter was postmarked the next day.

Darling Kick,

I almost committed a crime yesterday by breaking into the post office, so great was my desire to retrieve that last letter, because it only tried to excuse me and beg your pardon. What I ought to have written, and will endeavour to write now, is that you were correct. We should be able to work out the differences that keep us apart. I love you, and these last days of being without you have shown me that I was a fool for ever thinking I could lead a happy life without you. It's true that there are four hundred years of history separating us, and I cannot promise that it will be easy for us to find our solution, but I would like to try. Surely if we can overcome these obstacles, the trials of marriage will look like

nothing in comparison. All this is possible only if you will forgive my
wretched behavior of the other night. You'll be amused to discover I've
gone to Westminster Cathedral, whose spires so annoy Father, and lit a
candle for you every day since you left. (In my mind, I hear you laugh
as you read that line, and I hope I am right.) I've been worried about
you in Spain, as I've heard it's still not safe there. Even if your answer
to me is no, please set my mind at ease by telling me you've arrived at
the sea in a single piece. Waiting on pins and needles, I am forever your

Billy

By the time her eyes got to his name, she was crying and laughing so
hard (for she'd started laughing on top of the crying in exactly the place
he'd predicted), she also gave herself the hiccups.

There was a quiet knock on her door, then Rosemary popped her head
in. On seeing Kick with a red, wet face, she rushed over to her sister, saying, "Oh no, what's wrong?"

"N-n-nothing," Kick hiccupped, smearing the tears off her face with
the back of her hand. A few drops bled into Billy's letter.

Rosemary looked dubious. "This is not nothing," she said.

Kick hugged her sister tightly. "You're right, it's not nothing. But I'm
all right. I promise."

After their embrace, Rosemary looked at her sister with a confused
smile. "Well . . . if you say so. Mother wants me to tell you that dinner's
in an hour."

"Thank you, Rosie," said Kick. "I'll clean myself up."

Rosemary nodded and turned to leave, but at the door she paused with
her large, supple hand on the brass knob. "Kick?" she asked.

"Yes?"

"Were those letters from Billy?"

Kick looked at the desk strewn with letters. The two from Billy were
in her sweaty hand. "Yes," she replied.

"I'm glad," Rosemary said with a sigh. "I know Mother thinks he's not right for you, but he's the only person who's ever been able to calm me down, other than Daddy. And that must mean something, right?"

Kick felt her heart swell to a dangerous size in her chest. "Yes," she whispered hoarsely. "I think it does."

After dinner, Kick turned down Joe Jr. and Jack's offers to go to a local cabaret, because she wanted to slip upstairs and write her reply to Billy. As the moon changed places with the sun outside her window, she went through four drafts blackened with scribbles and doodles, until she was finally satisfied. She would reread it in the morning to be sure.

She tossed and turned all night, dipping in and out of dreams about Billy, and others about rough ocean waves rushing over her head. In the nightmare that finally woke her up, a wicked harlequin on a unicycle chased her off the grounds of Chatsworth. It took a rosary and two cups of coffee before she was ready to look at her letter again, and she made one small but important strike at the end:

Dearest Billy,

When I read your second letter, I was able to breathe again for the first time since we last spoke. Spain was not as dangerous as you've been told, and though everything beautiful and delicious about it should have taken my mind completely off you, it could not succeed. I am sorry, again, that I cannot be with you at Chatsworth on your special day, but I am overjoyed to know that when I return we can begin again, with love as our primum mobile. (Have I also made you laugh, as you correctly guessed you made me laugh, at my blasphemous use of Ptolemy?) I shall miss you every moment until then and will be in my heart, mind, and prayers, your

Kick

She'd taken out the sentence that had been her final line, and instead made it a promise to herself: *Be warned, however: my brothers have always found me a tenacious sparring partner, and when it comes to the matters we must discuss, I should warn you I shan't be a pushover.* What was the point of such a wounding remark? She thought the word *prayers* was a sufficient reminder that her prayers were of a different sort from his and she wasn't likely to give them up. Not after Spain.

Until then, she intended to enjoy the sun and the tan that would make all her friends swoon with envy when she returned to London. There had to be a silver lining to her absence from Chatsworth somewhere.

❖ ❖ ❖

When Jane Kenyon-Slaney arrived to stay for a week at the end of August, Kick couldn't contain herself any longer. She'd planned to remain quiet about Billy's letters and his reply to hers in which he pronounced himself "the happiest man in England," but she burst like an overblown balloon when she and Jane were alone in Kick's room after a day of sun and swimming, a jazz record spinning to muffle their voices. Jane was the catalyst. "I haven't wanted to bring it up," she said, "since you seem so happy, but I don't think I'd be much of a friend if I didn't at least say that if you wanted to talk to me about what happened with Billy, I'm happy to listen."

"We're working on finding a compromise," Kick blurted out. "A middle way, between our religions."

Jane raised her eyebrows. "Has he *proposed*?"

"No, no," said Kick, lowering her voice and sitting closer to Jane on the bed. "In fact, I don't think it's any secret that Billy and I had a fight and basically ended things at Blenheim."

"Yes, and he was miserable after that, especially when you disappeared to Spain without any warning, or even saying goodbye to anyone."

"I'm sorry about that," Kick said, picking at a knot on the white bedspread. "But it was just too painful to talk about. I didn't want people asking me questions I'd have to answer. Then Joe had this idea about Spain, and all I really had time to do was pack."

"I understand," said Jane, putting a hand on Kick's. "I wouldn't have wanted to talk about it, either. No one blames you, you know. We were more worried than anything else."

"Thank you," said Kick, with a sigh of relief. "Anyway . . . when I arrived here after an amazing time in Spain, just about ready to forget Billy and move on, I opened the most romantic letter from him. Saying he wanted to 'work out the differences that keep us apart.'"

"That's wonderful, Kick!"

The girls looked into one another's eyes, and Kick could see that Jane was really and truly happy for her, which in turn made Kick's eyes well with gratitude. "But, Jane, this is all top secret," Kick added in a grave tone. "It's possible I'll go back to London and we won't be able to work anything out, and then . . . well, I don't want to be a laughingstock," she concluded, borrowing the angry word her father had used at breakfast the other day. *Franklin's made me a damn laughingstock.*

"That you could never be," Jane assured her.

"You can never be too sure," Kick pointed out. After all, when her father arrived in England just a year and a half ago, he was the opposite.

"I'd place a bet on it," said Jane. "And on things working out with Billy. Truly, Kick, he was a mess after you'd gone. Taking brooding walks and rides on his horse, turning down invitations, losing weight. He just kept saying he was ill, but no one believed him. I'm glad he came to his senses. I wasn't sure, at his birthday party, if his smile was genuine or forced for his parents' sake, but given the timing you describe, it must have been the real thing."

"I wish I could have been there," complained Kick.

"Oh, don't," Jane said, waving her hand in a pooh-pooh motion. "It was more fun for the small children, who enjoyed the elephants and other circus animals. It was all a goodwill gesture, really, the new generation of Cavendishes now inhabiting Chatsworth inviting the servants and villagers to the big house. Billy's birthday was just a good excuse."

"I think it's nice," Kick said. "And I still wish I could have been there."

"I'm glad all of our traditions are so quaint to you, otherwise you'd be bored to tears like the rest of us. You are just what Chatsworth needs, I suspect," said Jane. Then, emphatically changing the subject, she went on, "What do I have to do to get the attention of that handsome brother of yours, the one Debo's mother expects to be president someday?"

❖ ❖ ❖

Thankfully, the boys left to help their father, who'd flown back to London on a rumor about Germany and Russia, since a romance between proper Jane and playboy Jack would have ruined the halcyon perfection of those waning August days. Kick and her friend waterskied in the morning and drank cold champagne with lunches in hilltop towns, then napped in the shade of huge umbrellas on the beach. They slept too late to bother reading the papers, and chose cabarets and, once, the gaming glitz of Monte Carlo over the news on the radio every night.

Beneath the radiant southern sun, as the salty blue Mediterranean licked her toes, Kick looked forward to seeing Billy again and beginning their life together. She thought maybe this was the happiest she'd ever been.

"Kathleen! Kathleen," came the shrieks. Her mother was yelling and waving a scarf from the deck of *la maison*.

Kick turned, shading her face with her hand. "Yes, Mother?" she shouted over her shoulder.

"Come quickly!"

Kick sighed heavily—*What could possibly be so urgent?* Jane was asleep on a chaise, a paperback of *Murder on the Orient Express* facedown on her long, slim legs. Reluctantly stepping out of the cool water, Kick walked up to meet her mother.

"Is the sky falling?" she asked teasingly, fully expecting her mother to say something like *The market had no fruit, what shall we do about dessert?*

"Your father called. We have to leave. Now."

"What? *Why?*"

"Germany's signed a treaty with Russia. Your father has issued a statement advising Americans to leave England, and he just told me it's worse to be here in France. Pack only what's necessary for a few days' travel. I'll have the rest shipped. Probably to New York."

Between waking Jane and throwing travel clothes into her large Boston bag, then standing in line in the intolerably crowded, confused train station and wishing she'd bathed that morning, Kick hardly had time to reflect on what was actually happening. She felt a leaden dread in the pit of her stomach in those hurried hours before finally collapsing in a first-class cabin that was stuffed to the gills with her, Jane, Eunice, Pat, and all their luggage, enduring a sauna-like heat that even the air rushing in through the open window could not assuage.

Once there was nothing to do but wait until Paris, she felt that dread erupt, pumping a lava of fear through her veins. There were so many things to be afraid of, and for, and they all competed for attention as she gnawed on her ragged lips: Hitler's erect and aggressive minions swarming Europe, perhaps soon to even march on her beloved London; Rudi, wherever he was; barefoot children speaking languages she couldn't comprehend, missing the parents they'd been separated from; young men she loved putting on uniforms and fighting—*killing*. But most of all, Billy being forced to march off with his regiment before she even arrived to say goodbye, let alone begin their promised discussions.

"Excuse me," she said, clambering over the sweaty legs of her sisters to get to the bathroom in time. She hadn't been sick from nervous tension since school, but in the train's tiny box of a water closet, all her anxiety poured out of her bodily. Mortified by her own weakness and filth, she wobbled back to her cabin and fell into a deep sleep.

When she woke, it was nearly dark, and most of her travel companions were taking their own turns snoozing; only Eunice was awake, reading Jane's Agatha Christie novel. Silently, Kick lifted her head, which felt like an anvil on her sleep-sore neck. The train had stopped at some quiet provincial outpost. Breathing shallowly in the thick, humid air, she felt her empty stomach rumble and prayed that she wouldn't be sick again. Staring out the window at the fuzzy orange horizon, she swallowed and felt a trickle of saliva burn her dry throat. She was so thirsty, and she reeked of old, curdled sweat.

Another train pulled up beside hers, and through her open window she saw six men packed together in a plain metal car without curtains or other signs of passenger comfort. They were dressed in brown military uniforms like those she'd seen in London, and she could tell at a glance that the men—boys, really, closer to Jack's age and hardly older than Bobby—were French, not English. Two of them were reading, three were sleeping, and one was staring blankly out his window. From beneath sleepy lids, his eyes roved over Kick's car, and when they came to her face, they stopped. She and the soldier regarded one another without speaking long enough for Kick to wonder whom he'd left behind. Where he was heading. And what he'd face when he arrived.

Cracking open the silence, the engine of her own train chugged and whistled to life, and as it pulled slowly away, she said to the unknown soldier, "*Merci*."

He nodded slightly in reply.

CHAPTER 16

The specter of war had descended like a shroud on her city. Her first glimpses of London from the incongruous cradle-like rocking of the train made her heart sink lower than she'd thought possible. Virtually every man in the street, and many women as well, wore a uniform of some sort, either military or civilian. Brown, gray, and white figures moved through the relatively empty streets like parts on one of Henry Ford's assembly lines, swift, purposeful, and cold. Sandbags were stacked high in front of houses and official buildings. Fresh posters for gas masks, enlisting, and war bonds papered sooty brick walls. She wondered how many Americans had already left. Thankfully, her father hadn't yet set a date for their family to evacuate. More so, she was grateful that Billy had not left the city.

Almost as soon as she arrived, she rang him and they arranged to meet the following night at the Spanish restaurant where, just six months before, she'd drunkenly convinced him that it was a great American tradition to steal ashtrays from restaurants, and he'd done it just to humor her. At least the hours until she was to see him were full—no time for morose daydreaming. All the Kennedy children were required to go through their clothing and other belongings and set aside what they wanted to bring with them to America, and what they could do without for a few weeks.

They had to try on the gas masks their father had ordered for them months ago, with the help of a constable trained to fit them properly. Teddy and Jean, who'd grown the most, needed new masks. Then there were the letters to write to the organizations Kick worked with, explaining that she was back in the city but unsure what was the best course of action in light of recent events. To Father O'Flaherty she simply wrote on a note card, "Returned. Hope to be in this week."

Once they realized it, all her siblings could talk about was the fact that 14 Prince's Gate didn't have an air-raid shelter.

"Mother," said Bobby, his voice suddenly low enough to make him sound masculine and nearly adult, "is there anything I can do to get one built?"

Rose, who stood at the window fiddling idly with the pearls at her neck, replied, "If the ambassador couldn't get one built, I doubt the ambassador's son could, but you are more than welcome to try."

"I'll speak with Page," he said resolutely.

The nearness of danger had the effect of honing everything down to its sharpest state. When she saw Billy's face illuminate with boyish delight the moment he saw her, Kick felt her own longing for him like a blade. He ushered her into a small private room at the back of the restaurant, behind the cover of a heavy curtain.

"I had no idea this was back here," she marveled, looking around the small room with the candles and olives and wine on the table. "What *would* people think?" she joked.

"I don't care," he murmured, pulling the curtain closed and swooping her into his arms in one smooth gesture. When he kissed her hello, every inch of her tingled with goose bumps, a ticklish feeling that made her fear she might burst into giggles. Not for long. As their kiss deepened and he pressed her body against his, the sensation changed to an intense, nearly painful ache. She curled her arms around his neck and wove her fingers through his fine brown hair.

"I've missed you, too," she said when they separated.

"I made sure to come hungry for food so I wouldn't want to devour *you*," Billy said, taking a step back and sighing regretfully, still holding her hands.

"How gallant of you," she replied.

But even the deliciously piquant meal wasn't up to the task. They ate and talked until they were satisfied in one way and more ravenous in the other. During the main course, Billy put his hand on her leg just above her knee, and though it gave him some trouble to eat without his left hand, he never removed it. She wanted so much to bring up their letters, and their promised discussions, but she'd vowed to herself that she would *not* at this reunion. She wanted him to remember why he'd written those letters in the first place.

After coffee and pears poached in wine, Billy said, "I can't let you go yet."

"And *I* can't run the risk of being home too late," Kick said. "Not while things are so volatile, and my parents are on high alert."

Billy nodded, then looked down at his watch. "It's almost midnight," he told her.

"It is?" She had no idea. "I have to get home," she moaned.

Billy frowned. "We have much to discuss."

She nodded solemnly.

"Thank you for . . . *not* . . . tonight."

"Soon, I hope," she said.

"Very," he agreed.

And she heard the clock strike up again in her mind.

❖ ❖ ❖

Kick padded downstairs the next morning to the sound of a radio crackling up from the dining room. Everyone who wasn't away at school or abroad, which meant Bobby, Teddy, Eunice, Mother, and Daddy, sat in varying states of shock at breakfast—her mother with her fingers on her temples, her father with his fist at his mouth, Eunice slouched on the table, and Bobby and Teddy with shoulders up to their ears. The voice on the wireless was narrating an invasion of Poland by Hitler's army.

Kick sat, unacknowledged, and listened.

Rose began to pray quietly, and Joe stood up and shouted, *"Damn it!"* before leaving the room.

It's happening, Kick thought, this time without the sickening panic that had engulfed her on the train to Paris and instead with the same focus she'd learned to apply to races and tennis matches. *Help me, Blessed Virgin*, she begged as she began to calculate her next moves.

The single-mindedness was difficult to maintain in the next forty-eight hours. Joe Jr. and Jack arrived home immediately and almost magically, swooping into 14 Prince's Gate like foul-smelling heroes. On September 2, following a defeated speech by Prime Minister Chamberlain, London heard its first air-raid sirens and the Kennedys underwent their first drill. Their butler, who'd served in the last war, brought order to the chaos with everyone running to and fro throughout the house. A few of the servants thought that real bombs were about to start falling. In the huddled, dark silence while sirens wailed outside, a frightened Teddy tried to cross the room to sit with Joe Jr. but tripped over Jean, managing in the process to sprain *her* ankle and rip the blackout shade covering the sitting room window. Rose shouted at him about what a stupid thing that was to do, and did he want to get them all killed? Teddy ran to his room in tears, and Luella followed while Joe Jr., who'd gotten a bit of medical training in Spain, gently inspected Jean's swollen ankle.

The next day, Kick went with her mother and two older brothers to meet their father at Parliament, to hear Chamberlain speak. It was a foregone conclusion, though. England and France were at war with Germany, because Germany had at last refused to capitulate or compromise, finally showing itself to be the unyielding force so many had feared. The prime minister's speech was complete in fewer than five minutes. *Surely there's more to say*, thought Kick, *when the world has started spinning a thousand times faster.*

When she emerged into the streets, flanked by her older brothers, pandemonium reigned. Kick covered her eyes with her hand after a photographer's flashbulb popped loudly. "What do you three think?" "Mr.

Kennedy! What does your father say?" "Have any thoughts on the ambassador's failed policies?" "Miss Kennedy! Will there be a rush to the altar?" The reporters shouted and sneered.

While Joe Jr. and Jack stayed to answer questions, Kick fled and spent the rest of the miserable afternoon poring over the classified sections of every newspaper in the house, looking at rooms, bedsits, and apartments for rent all over the city, becoming increasingly more discouraged with every depressingly spare listing, every neighborhood she didn't recognize and assumed was poor and dangerous, every shared bathroom. Was she prepared to live in a tenement to stay in London? But then she realized how absurd that question was—because unless her parents felt confident about her residence, she wouldn't be allowed to stay, and that was the goal of this entire project.

God—or more likely the Holy Mother—must have taken some pity on her, because that evening Luella rapped tentatively on Kick's door and proposed that the two of them get a flat together and suggest the plan to Joe.

Kick's eyes went wide.

Luella explained, "You see, I have an English beau as well. He's wonderful, and his whole family is, too, and . . . well, I have as much reason to stay as you."

"Luella! You darling dear!" Kick exclaimed, jumping up to hug the family nurse. This woman who'd been with them for years, who was only a few years older than Kick herself, who—Kick was ashamed to realize in that moment—had been invisible to Kick all year, had descended like an angel in her hour of need.

This had to be a sign. Everything would be all right.

"Let's talk to him tomorrow," Kick said, the sick feeling in her belly salved at last.

Things went a little more her way when she was able to convince Jack to take her to the 400. Then, just before she was to go out, there was another knock on her door. It was Eunice, frowning, playing with the grosgrain on her cardigan sweater.

"You don't have the radio on," her sister observed.

"I've had enough bad news for one day," said Kick, turning down the Glenn Miller record she'd put on instead.

"I have more of it," said Eunice.

Kick sighed so heavily, her chest inflated and her shoulders went up, then slowly down. "Well, let's have it, then."

"Unity Mitford was found in a garden in Munich, bleeding at the head," Eunice said.

"No," Kick whispered, even though she believed it. The word was more of a talisman, a wish, a defiance. *Poor Debo!* She couldn't even go around the corner to comfort her friend, since she was with her family in Inch Kenneth.

"But she's not dead," Eunice went on. "At least, that's what the report said. Attempted suicide. Failed."

Kick instinctively hugged her sister. Tight enough to feel Eunice's ribs against hers, her sister's sharp chin resting on the softer flesh of her own shoulder, and tight enough to find comfort in her sister's slim arms as she reciprocated her searching embrace.

❖ ❖ ❖

After a maudlin night at the 400 with everyone depressed for Debo, whom no one including Andrew had been able to reach, Billy convinced Kick to take a circuitous taxi ride back to 14 Prince's Gate, where they would drop her off a block away so as not to be seen together by anyone in her household. "It'll give us a chance to talk," he said.

"What an irony that taxis are now our refuge to *talk* instead of . . . you know," she said, blushing.

"Mmm," Billy agreed, his voice rough and serious.

Inside the large black car with its cracked leather seats, the lingering odor of too many perfumes in the air, Kick and Billy were silent for a few minutes. Outside, the city was black; all the twinkling lights that had once made London appear enchanted were snuffed out. In the dark, it was difficult to tell one building from another, and Kick marveled at the leveling effect this had, making a corner apothecary the same as a Swiss watchmaker's shop.

"Kick," Billy said, his voice nearly a whisper.

Turning her eyes to him, seeing his somber face as a perfect and terrible complement to what was outside, she wanted to smother him with kisses and plead to get married right away, to do something that would bring light back into their little world. She thought about Gabrielle and Pedro—the Virgin had sent Kick a powerful sign in their story, one she hadn't fully understood until now. She wanted to wring every drop of happiness out of her time with Billy, not to wait and see what waste the war would lay.

"Billy, I . . ."

Shushing her tenderly, Billy adjusted his long limbs on the cramped seat and turned toward her, taking both her hands in his. "Kick . . . I . . . I love you. And—"

"As I love you," she interrupted. It felt good to say it out loud and see the happiness it brought to his face. Their interwoven hands in Kick's lap were hot, but his were shaking as if they were cold.

"But," he went on slowly, deliberately, and her heart clenched. She knew what he was about to say, and the confusion she'd felt a moment ago tightened into panic. "Loving you makes me *fear* for you," he said, "for your safety and health. I've gone over and over this in my mind, and now that the war is here, it's real and not a hypothesis, I want to protect you."

Then bring me to Chatsworth. How could I be safer than I would be surrounded by four centuries of stone? But, she had time to counter herself, *at what cost?*

"Before I leave," he went on, "I also want to establish an understanding between us . . ." How her heart thrilled to that Jane Austen–like word, *understanding*! She moved her hands so that her little still ones covered his larger trembling ones.

"Billy, can we speak more plainly? We don't have much time."

He laughed. "You're right. I know I can go on. It's just that I fear your reaction to what I want to propose."

What I want to propose. That didn't sound like a proposal.

"Just say it, Billy."

"All right. What I said before, at Blenheim, about the war, is still true. I do not want you to compromise everything you hold dear by asking you to change yourself and hurt your family, when it's possible I might not return. What sort of man would I be if I stranded you on this war-torn island like that?"

"The sort who loves me," she said.

He smiled in a sad way she'd never seen before. "I am too English, too much a product of the Cavendish family, to let love make me reckless. I'm sorry."

"Don't be sorry," she said quickly, not sure if she meant it. She wanted to be reckless.

"Then may I ask for time?" he asked in earnest. "For the time to be in love, to pledge ourselves to one another and the promise of a future together? Time to think and talk about what we want to do about our religions and families?"

"But how, Billy? It's been much harder for me to find a way to stay here than I thought it would be. And it's only a matter of time before Father sends us all back to America."

"And you'll be far safer there," he said.

"But it will be impossible for you to visit, impossible for us to see each other. All we'll have is letters. Paper and ink. It's not the same as *this*," she said, shaking his hands with hers.

"This is the part I'm sorry for. I can't change the way I feel about keeping you out of harm's way. And I cannot marry you before we've established what it would mean for our churches, and our . . . children."

"You've thought about them, too?"

"Of course I have," he said quietly.

Hot tears flushed her eyes. She knew she ought to be glad of his love, his desire to keep her safe. "But . . ."

"What?"

How could she say it? That he was a *man*, as well as the noble Marquess of Hartington? That even if he wasn't like Jack or her own father, she knew it was unrealistic for him to wait for her for the length of an entire war?

"I've never seen you at a loss for words," he observed, amused.

"I'm glad you could bring a bit of humor to this conversation," she said, reaching for the easy, familiar sarcasm.

"Kick, what is it? *Speak plainly.*"

"It's just that . . . well, you're a man. You won't wait for a wife forever."

At this, he laughed heartily, actually throwing his head back with the roll of it.

"Is the sacred vow that men and women are supposed to bring to marriage such a funny thing?" she asked, finally letting something of her feelings on sacraments into the discussion.

"No, of course not," he said. "And I don't mean to make fun of you or of marriage. I take both very seriously. But . . . I hardly think we'd be waiting forever. Maybe a year? We'll write fervent, romantic letters in which we also negotiate about God, which I think would amuse him greatly," he smirked. She couldn't help smiling back, relieved that he was finally presenting a plan.

"And if all goes well, and a German tank hasn't taken off my legs, then we will figure out how to get you back here. Have no fear that the baser needs of my sex will lead me astray."

"They better not," she countered.

"If we are going to marry someday, you'll have to put more faith in me than *that*."

He was right. She kissed him to show it. Just as she felt herself untether from the difficulties they'd been discussing and lose herself in the warmth of his lips and arms, the taxi stopped, and the driver said, "Ten Prince's Gate!"

And deliver us from temptation, she couldn't help thinking to herself as her heart plummeted. *Once again.*

CHAPTER 17

Her father laughed—*laughed!*—when Kick and Luella suggested the two of them get a flat together and enlist their services with the Red Cross.

"Nice try, you two," he said. "But you can help the war efforts from the safety of American soil." Turning to Luella, he said pointedly, "When I brought you here, you were a nice single girl, and I intend to bring you home to your family in the same state." To Kick, he said, "I won't tell your mother about this little request." Then, turning his eyes to heaven, he said, "Is this your idea of a joke? I work myself into an early grave to avoid war, and now three of my oldest want to rush into it?"

It was pointless to explain that it wasn't just Billy she wanted to stay for, that Billy had in fact told her to go back to America. Even though she knew England would change, she wanted to stay, to have the privilege of reminiscing about the last prewar season with the only friends who would ever be able to understand. She wanted to help care for London in its hour of need, and she wanted to be in her city when the lights came back on.

In despair, as Jack went to play boy hero in Scotland on Daddy's orders, to rescue the survivors of the torpedoed *Athenia*, Kick went to the Red Cross to inquire about the shared homes for women who volunteered as nurses. Maybe if she had meaningful work to do, her father would change his mind—or she'd make just enough salary to allow her to stay anyway. After standing in line for close to two hours, she came face-to-face with a harsh-looking woman not much older than she was, with wind-scrubbed cheeks and an accent Kick could barely understand.

"I hardly need to ask *your* name, do I?" the woman snorted. "I'd rather ask what a fine Kennedy lady is doing looking for work of *this* sort. Bed-pans and blood."

Kick smiled as kindly as she could. She hadn't imagined she'd encounter hostility like this for wanting to help, and she realized how foolish she'd been for not considering the possibility that she'd be recognized—*Of course these girls read the society pages! It's a national pastime.* "I want to do my part," Kick offered.

"Don't suppose you'll be needing the form for accommodations, then," the woman sneered, handing Kick a white sheet of paper with blanks to fill in, volunteering her hands in the service of king and country. Fearing the newspaper maelstrom of speculative gossip if this young woman went to the press with her information—*Ambassador's daughter looks for anonymous digs in London*—and the betrayal her parents would surely feel when the news broke, Kick did not ask for the other form.

When she returned to 14 Prince's Gate, she found her travel trunks stacked in her room. All the desperation she'd been trying to channel productively unleashed like a storm inside her. She tore down the hall. Her mother was the first person she saw, in her own bedroom, sorting jewelry.

"Have you set a date?" Kick demanded.

Rose turned around and looked surprised to see Kick standing at the entrance to her room. "As soon as your father can arrange it," her mother replied.

"Two days? Ten?" Kick was yelling, her voice hysterical. Though Billy was due to leave in five days to join the Coldstream Guards, it was thankfully only for training, so he would still be in England, where she'd be able to visit him.

"I don't know, Kathleen." Rose stood, and her calm demeanor made Kick even more irate.

"*How* will we know? *When* will we know?"

"We need to live as if we might leave the next day," Rose replied. "Which is why you must pack immediately. Where have you been all morning? Eunice and Pat and Jean have finished already."

"And Rosemary?"

Rose sighed and looked fleetingly away from Kick. Then she set her small brown eyes on her daughter and said, "Rosemary's staying to complete her Montessori training."

"*What?*"

"Kathleen, I can't discuss this with you until you've calmed down."

"I *am* calm!" she shrieked. She felt sick, though not like she had on the train from Cannes. This was worse—a vertiginous nausea had set in. She felt dizzy and queasy, like she was at the edge of a great and terrible precipice, staring down into certain doom.

Rose stood and walked slowly to the door, and stopped inches from Kick. "Ask the cook to make you some tea, and calm yourself. Then pack. We'll discuss this later."

Without waiting for her daughter to respond, Rose closed her door. If Kick had leaned forward even a centimeter, her nose would have touched the fine wood panel. She might as well have been in the closet in Bronxville, six years old again. All this time, she'd been seeking her parents' approval, looking for ways to get what she wanted with their blessing. But she saw now that she wasn't going to get what she wanted that way. She was going to have to summon the courage to go after it alone. She hoped God would help. Instead of packing, she found her wooden rosary and started to pray.

❖ ❖ ❖

It embarrassed her to realize that she lacked the courage to defy her parents in the way she would have to in order to stay in London. She turned once more to the want ads, and even went to visit some of the bedsits, most of which were in unfamiliar parts of the city where getting to any of her favorite haunts would have required nearly an hour on the tube. In two apartments she heard mice in the walls, and in one, she saw large black insects scuttling around the single cupboard of the so-called kitchen. All the money in the bank with *Kathleen Kennedy* written on it wasn't going to help her if she was going to stay in London against her parents' wishes. Standing in a fifth and final apartment—this one at least in central London, a few precious blocks from Covent Garden—barely big enough for a small bed, desk, and wardrobe, she was embarrassed at how frightened she felt at the prospect of actually living there. The thought of tea and digestive biscuits for dinner depressed her. *At least I'd be as thin as Mother always wanted me to be*, she thought bitterly.

On her way home, she literally ran into Bertrand—her bowed head bonked right into his chest. "Whoa, whoa, there," he said, taking her upper arms in his hands and holding her out for inspection.

"I'm so sorry," she said, for once doing a rotten job of faking levity.

"I know I'm not Billy, but is it so bad to see me?" he asked.

She shook her head and opened her mouth to reply, but her throat was so clogged with strangled tears that she couldn't speak.

"Kick," Bertrand said more seriously. "Are you all right? Can I help?"

She shook her head again, wrapping her arms around her body and shivering.

Bertrand led her into a nearby pub, ordered her a shandy, and sat her down at a discreet corner table.

"Drink this, then decide if you want to talk," he told her, pushing the half-pint glass toward her.

She did as she was told, guzzling the sweet combination of lemonade and beer. Bertrand always knew just what to order.

"Thanks," she said. Then a burp escaped, and she blushed deeply and put her hand to her mouth.

"There's my girl," said Bertrand. They laughed together, drily.

"So," he said, "you can tell me what's wrong, or we can get drunk together. Both are good enough medicine."

What did she have to lose at this point? If she didn't speak up, she stood to lose everything. "I don't suppose you have an attic to stow me away in when the rest of my family leaves for America?"

"Ah," he said, and she knew he had immediately understood. "I don't, as it happens. My matronly aunt in Liverpool might, but then you'd have to live in *Liverpool*."

"Maybe only temporarily?"

"I'm afraid there is no escaping the north," he said in an exaggerated northern accent.

She chuckled half-heartedly, then both of them were quiet before he jumped up suddenly, went to the bar, and came back with a full pint of ale. "Drink," he told her.

"I already feel drunk," she said, pushing the glass away. She hadn't eaten in hours and the shandy had affected her quickly.

"I'll feel better if you have three more sips before I tell you what I feel it my duty to tell you," he said.

She raised an eyebrow, then followed his instructions, and immediately she felt more relaxed, even though she sensed that what he wanted to tell her was not something she wanted to hear.

"Go home," he told her.

"Pardon?"

"Go home."

"Can you elaborate, please?"

"Gladly," he said, crossing his legs and sitting back in his chair. "It's going to get messy here in England. I know you want to help, and believe me—we, by which I mean all your real friends here, know you want to stay in England for noble reasons: love of king, of country, and of a certain marquess, heir to one of the greatest dukedoms in the land. And we love you all the more for not loving him just for his lands and title. Because lord knows, you don't need any of that."

She opened her mouth to say something about his vulgarity, but he held up a finger and said, "Let me finish. If there was ever a time for bald honesty, this it is. Now." He drew a breath, then went on. "What's more,

Billy knows you love him, and he knows you love him for the right reasons. But I've come to know Billy well, and I believe he will love you *more* if you remain unsullied by the filth and degradation that's to come. Get on a boat and let him pine for you. Let him remember you in one of your fine Parisian frocks dancing with abandon, while every other Englishman wished he had you. Believe me, he will dwell at length on that image while he is stewing in his own sweat."

"It just feels like such a risk," she said.

"What's your alternative? Staying here alone because he hasn't proposed, and being the desperate American girl who waits around for the English aristocrat to make her an honest woman? No. That plot is beneath you."

Her eyes went wide. She'd never considered the possibility that her staying might appear that way. She'd been so overwhelmed by her desire to stay, she hadn't thought about it from every angle as a Kennedy should, as she'd been trained to do. Maybe she still needed more training. The thought was comforting, but also maddening, in the same way as looking at pictures of her hero brother in the newspapers every day.

"When would you suggest I come back?"

"When Billy gives you a reason," he said.

"A proposal."

"Very likely."

Bertrand's advice bore a striking resemblance to Billy's own plea, but Bertrand had only her interests in mind. "Thank you," she said, feeling a bit like a scolded child who knew she was in the wrong.

"You are most welcome," he said. "Now if only there was room in your bag so *I* could stow away to America with *you* and avoid fighting in this god-awful mess."

Maybe she was luckier than she'd thought.

❖ ❖ ❖

The sense of luck was fleeting. The next week, her final week in England, was as confused as it was confusing. She had to rummage around in her packed trunks every morning to find something to wear, and in the evening when she went out to meet her friends, they had to grope their way through darkened streets, often on foot because too many taxi drivers feared drawing attention to themselves with headlights. So she and her friends arranged to meet at houses where pockets of them lived. Debo showed up to one party before Kick left, on the night before Billy left to join his regiment.

Andrew, Debo, David, Sissy, Billy, Kick, and a handful of others were gathered in the Cavendishes' London home for dinner and dancing, courtesy of one of the 400's most popular bands, whom the boys had hired for the occasion. Were it not for the reason they were all coming together, the party had the makings of a perfect evening. Even Sally Norton wasn't present, and Billy and Andrew had banished their parents to Chatsworth for the weekend. "I told them that this wasn't the way they wanted to remember their son," Andrew had said, ever the jokester. But that night, Kick saw great tenderness in the kind and gentle way he tended to Debo, drinking very little so that he could dance with her and remain alert, constantly asking if she needed anything, and keeping his hand protectively on her back.

Debo put on a good face, and for once she was the one to drink too much. Kick could hardly blame her; she'd have wanted to use the evening to forget her tragedy, too. Before she could say anything comforting to her friend, to whom she'd already written a heartfelt letter saying she wanted to help in any way she could, Debo said to Kick, "I don't want to talk about Unity, Hitler, or anything to do with anyone who has ever caused me pain. So don't even try to offer your sympathies."

To which Kick replied, "I won't. And me, either."

Throughout the night, Kick kept Bertrand's advice in mind and attempted to be her most lively, likable self. She wore an emerald-green bias-cut silk dress that Billy had once said he liked, and she laughed and joked relentlessly. But dancing with Billy was physically painful. When he held her close and she felt the satisfying way her cheek rested on his chest, the crown of her head nestled in the curve of his neck, her heart hurt with sadness and longing.

At last he pulled her away from the others, into the downstairs kitchen of all places, where it appeared they were alone—all the servants must have gone to their own quarters, as it was close to one in the morning. There, they kissed. And kissed and kissed. The open mouth that had once shocked her on that dark stairwell was now a familiar, welcome force, his large hands moving deftly over curves and hollows on her body she'd never have dreamed a man would touch only a year ago. Now she welcomed Billy's hands, and wished, *wished*, they were in a position to enjoy more.

Both of them sensed when it was time to pull away. He picked her up by her waist and set her down on the rectangular wooden table in the center of the room, which gave her a little more height, enough so that he could touch his forehead to hers without having to stoop too much.

"I miss you already," he whispered.

"I miss you, too."

"If I asked you to marry me tonight, in Westminster Abbey, by the archbishop of Canterbury . . . would you?"

"Is that even possible?" *Is it?* She couldn't think clearly with so much blood coursing noisily through her ears.

"If it was?" His eyes were closed, like a boy wishing on birthday candles.

So many things came to Kick's mind . . . Father O'Flaherty's kindness, Wickham's and even Lady Astor's prejudices, her mother's door in her face, her father's pride in her London accomplishments, Gabrielle's childless future with the man she loved, the majesty of the new pope riding on his crimson throne into the Vatican, her imagined photo of herself with Billy on the lawn of Chatsworth, their children in white christening clothes.

No, she realized. *Not tonight.*

"I'd hardly be the woman you've fallen in love with if I just said yes without question, would I?" she asked, closing her own eyes and wishing herself.

She heard him inhale and hold his breath. *One . . . two . . . three . . . four . . .* Then he kissed her fiercely and quickly.

"No," he said, pulling his head back and looking into her eyes, which she had opened at the same time. "No, you would not. And I fear I love you all the more for it," he said.

"Good," she said. "Race you to the first letter."

"I've already started mine." He grinned.

"Then I have some catching up to do," she said.

"Hurry," he said quietly. *"Hurry."*

BELGIUM, JUNE 1940

His hands were so afflicted with palsy, he could barely open the door of the car. But there it was, a Baby Austin, an improbably English car in a country God had forsaken. An end to his searching. When he'd seen it from the other side of the field, he thought it was a mirage. He had been seeing and smelling all sorts of things that weren't there—the end of a rifle around the corner of a barn, yeasty bread hot from an oven, Kick's stride in that of a faraway country girl—so he'd begun to doubt his senses. But there it was, this vehicle that could get him out of hell.

If he could get it to turn on. There were no keys. One of his men had taught him to start an engine by sparking a few wires together. Jonathan. A coarse young man from Essex who'd obviously had plenty of experience in the art of starting cars without keys. "Society man like you," he'd said to Billy, with a sniff of arrogance, "may have a thing or two to teach me about the ladies, but you never know when you're gon'to need a skill like this. Now listen up, mate." A month later, he was shot in the gut when he'd run toward the Huns, screaming, "For England!" He'd been one of the few soldiers who hadn't turned tail on those fateful, fearfully given orders when the German tanks rolled into their camp. Their supposedly unapproachable camp on the *other side of the supposedly impregnable Maginot Line. That false security had made cowards of them all, except the rare man who understood what war really was.*

Billy's first attempt at the wires was unsuccessful. His hands were shaking too much. Steady, steady, he told himself. He sat on his hands to warm them, not that they were especially cold on the damp, temperate morning, but he hoped the extra heat might relax the muscles enough to help his fingers do what they needed to do. He looked furtively around. It was quiet here, only cows on the horizon, but that didn't mean there wasn't danger. There had been danger everywhere.

Not danger like the chaos of bullets and grenades and gurgling and cursing following the terrifying sound of the tanks defiling the earth beneath their tracks, or worse, the danger he could hear in the silence when the tanks stopped. That danger he'd escaped. Without a compass or map or any other guide, he'd been on his feet for days and days since then. Two weeks was his best guess. Part of the time, he'd been with other English and French men, and together they'd intruded on the hospitality of farmers, innkeepers, barmaids, and grandmothers, all of whom were only too happy to give them a cup of wine and a hunk of bread and listen with shaking heads to the soldiers' firsthand confirmations of the horrors they'd read about in the papers. "Are we German now?" one little boy had asked his father. "Never," his father growled.

One by one, the other men began to disappear. Billy would wake in the morning on a bed of straw and find another one had taken his rucksack and left. They had discussed where to go and what to do, but none of them knew how to get to safety alive, and none of the locals they spoke to had any promising intelligence.

Billy knew, though, that the main reason he was alone now, so long after the event, was that he was ashamed. He was ashamed of his country and its leaders for not seeing this coming, for depending on a fortification they hadn't built themselves, for once again not predicting that Hitler would find a way to surprise them all. But mainly, he was ashamed of himself for not being Jonathan.

When he thought his hands were ready, he tried to do what Jonathan had taught him. Maybe, *he thought to himself as he fumbled with the wires,* I was given this little auto lesson for a reason. Kick would certainly think so. I'm meant to live, and to apply what I've learned. I'm meant to be part of the solution.

At last he got the wires to spark, the engine to fire up. He put his right foot on the gas, his left on the clutch, and gripped the steering wheel and gear stick, which steadied his hands. The vibration from the engine shook the car to life and filled his body with hope for the first time in weeks. He made a vow as he drove out of the field and onto a dirt road: When I come back here, it will be to kill or be killed. Maybe both. I'll never run again.

PART 3

❖ ❖ ❖

SUMMER 1941

CHAPTER 18

Even two years later, she woke up some mornings and thought for a few glorious moments before she opened her eyes that she was in her bed at 14 Prince's Gate. In that hazy, half-sentient state, the pillow would feel the same and her body would be heavy with that after-party languor she used to shake off with a few cups of tea and a slice of toast before heading out into the mercurial London elements. Then she would open her eyes to find herself in Hyannis Port or Bronxville or Palm Beach, and now Washington, DC, and the reality of her situation would flood her with the now-familiar dread. Another day in exile.

Her beloved London had been blitzed, and in his letters Billy's sole concern had become when he would return to the continent "to crush the Huns." She had tried once, gently, to turn his attentions back to their time before the war, when they had made those hopeful, hushed promises to each other, but that had been a huge mistake. He'd told her that he couldn't possibly think about anything so weighty with the fate of England hanging in the balance. *I cling to the hope that we can begin again, if you can find a way back here,* he'd also written. So. She'd been right all along. *I should have stayed.* Had she been there, she could have *shown* Billy how much she, too, cared for England. She could have been part of his quest. Instead, she found herself defending the embattled island to American friends who saw it as weak and in need of assistance. No one understood.

The last two years had gone down a drain of lackluster parties and half-hearted attempts to study antiques at Finch while her girlfriends in England were getting married: Sissy and David. Jane and Peter. Debo and Andrew. Kick had been so paralyzed with longing after reading the columns about Debo's wedding in Muv and Farve's London town house right around the corner from where she had lived her happiest life that she'd barely gotten out of bed for a week. If they weren't getting married and having babies and giving their soldier husbands a reason to fight and live, her other former debutante friends were working as nurses or in factories. Sally Norton was working in a code-breaking facility, for Pete's sake. With Billy's determination to defeat Germany, Kick could only imagine how admirable Sally's new profession would seem to him. And how Sally would use that admiration to her advantage, with Kick out of the way, across the bloody Atlantic Ocean.

Kick had almost forgotten what it felt like to live a life of purpose, like Sally and the rest of them. Nothing she'd done these past two years had appealed to her, and Kick feared she was getting brittle with a too-early old age. She caught herself snapping at Jean and Pat, sounding just like Rose. *How could you not know Katherine Porter was in town? Surely you could do something better with your time than read that drivel.* She'd actually been relieved when Daddy had told her sternly one morning after breakfast in Palm Beach that she either had to get herself into a real college or get a paying job.

Kick picked up the phone and called Page Huidekoper, who'd been living in DC and working at the *Washington Times-Herald* as a reporter. With a sweaty hand clutching the slick receiver, Kick listened as Page, the architect of her last partially successful transformation, spoke of an open secretarial position on the paper.

"It's not terribly glamorous, I'll be honest, but people move around on the paper all the time. You could be doing something more interesting in no time. And Washington's not a bad place to be these days. Full of characters. I think you'll like it."

Something about being in a totally new environment appealed to Kick and made her heart beat faster for the first time in she couldn't remember how long. A change of scenery and pace. And best of all, she'd be living completely on her own for the first time, away from the worried gaze of her parents. She hung up the phone and started packing her bags.

Her interview with Frank Waldrop, the handsome and youthful editor in chief who spoke with a genteel Southern accent that explained everything about the conservative bent of his paper, went swimmingly. Though she didn't agree with the isolationist politics he shared with her father, she was well practiced in setting aside her own beliefs to get what she wanted. She even hid her real identity. Kathleen Kennedy was a common enough Irish name, and Waldrop didn't recognize her, so rooted was he in everything south of the Mason-Dixon Line.

But then, during her second week of answering his phones, Frank came back from a lunch mildly tipsy and leaned against Kick's tidy wooden desk.

"Kathleen *Kennedy*, eh?" Frank drawled. "Why didn't you tell me?"

"Same reason I keep my mink in this bag under my desk," Kick said, pointing to the softly rumpled brown paper bag rolled up at the top to keep the contents hidden. She barely had time to wonder how he'd found out before she came up with the answer herself: her father was in town. She was supposed to meet him for dinner, but now she could see whom Joe Kennedy had made a point of bumping into first.

Frank raised his head to survey the large room Kick shared with twenty or so reporters with small desks and big ambitions. He nodded, patted her on the shoulder with something like appreciation, and said, "Then I expect you won't be sitting *here* very long, if what I know of your family has any basis in reality."

He started walking away, then stopped and turned back to Kick. "I thought you were married to some English lord of the manor," he said, half in question and half in jest.

Why did Waldrop have to go bringing Billy's sweet face into this place that had been mercifully devoid of any memory of him, where the hustle and bustle of reporters and the hammering clack of typewriters were vigorous enough to keep her mind present *here*, and not floating off in some cloudy memory-fantasy. *Shake it off*, she told herself. "I should think the editor of a newspaper would be better informed than that," she replied with her most winning *dare me* smile.

Frank's ears turned red for a second before he guffawed with laughter. "I can see I'm going to have my hands full with *you*," he said.

"I'll see to it, sir."

It felt good, mouthing off like that to her new boss. She'd forgotten how thrilling that kind of risk could be. Still, it was hard to lose the image he'd brought to her mind, of Billy heading out to dinner in London on his night off, without her.

❖ ❖ ❖

"He's crazy about you, you know," said Inga Arvad on a sultry late-July morning on their way to work. Kick and the stunning Danish journalist had become friends at a party given by one of the *Times-Herald*'s beat reporters in his cramped studio apartment a few weeks before. She was referring to John White, one of the paper's star journalists, who had also been at the party. He and Kick had argued heatedly about birth control, of all things: he thought it was essential for the modern family "who didn't have as many resources as Pa Kennedy to raise a noisy brood, to say nothing of the modern man and woman who want to fully enjoy one another's company," and Kick believed what the church had taught her, which is that it wasn't man's place to stand in the way of God's will.

He'd been hounding Kick ever since, which was nothing short of remarkable, since he might have been going after Inga, like everyone else. Her social views were more liberal, like his—in fact, she was still married to filmmaker Paul Fejos, but he was in Peru working on a documentary series, and his memory never gave her pause about taking lovers. Plus, she had that glossy blond hair, exotic accent, and tantalizingly mysterious continental past, which included a brief flirtation with Adolf Hitler. But Inga was no Unity Mitford: she was too confident to be sycophantic, and too worldly to be in thrall to such a monster. If Inga was like anyone, it was Marlene Dietrich.

"John's such a big bag of wind," Kick said dismissively, though secretly she was flattered. John White reminded her of Bertrand—a whip-smart iconoclast who wasn't afraid to say anything. But John was pure American, more vulgar without the British sense of propriety to temper him. He had a gruffness, a very masculine appeal. Kick could imagine him as a boxer or football player, always tan, fit, and a little disheveled.

"Be careful, *ma chérie*. John is handsome and can be very charming," Inga warned in that auntly tone she sometimes took, the only thing that irritated Kick about her new friend. She was merely seven years older, twenty-eight to her twenty-one, and Kick had traveled just as much as Inga—though she knew she lacked the experience with men that twice-married Inga had. Still, Kick had been in love. And had likely lost him for good. Didn't that count for something in the realm of experience?

"I'll be fine, *Madame Bovary*," Kick joked. "I know how to watch out for myself."

Inga laughed gently and linked her arm through Kick's. "I am sure you do, *Isabel Archer*."

"Well, at least we both have ignominious ends in common," Kick quipped, glad that Sister Kit, the same nun who had educated her about her body, had also lent her copies of these otherwise verboten novels.

Soon she'd situated herself at her desk with a cup of the horrible black stuff from the staff room everyone politely called coffee; at least it woke her up, so she drank it to be part of the team. The phone rang off the hook that morning, and she took pages of messages for Frank, who stayed behind his closed door. Inga was across the room, alternately resting her feet in their chic shoes on the desk as she talked on the phone or sitting with elegantly straight posture as she typed on her Royal with a furrowed brow. Page was a few desks away from Inga, as buttoned-up and serious as ever despite her red nails and lips.

A bit before noon, John breezed past Kick's desk on his way into Frank's office, and without looking at her, he dropped a sealed envelope on her desk. There was something small and round inside, and she couldn't for the life of her figure out what it was, but something told her this was a prank. If there was one thing a Kennedy could sniff out, it was a prank. The thing to do was be ready to strike back. With that thought in mind, she drew in a fortifying breath and opened the envelope. Inside was a folded piece of paper with John's handwriting on it, and when she unfolded it, a little disk of rubber fell onto her desk. It looked a little like a deflated balloon that had been rolled up, and it had a vaguely chemical smell, similar to what she sometimes inhaled when a car was being filled with gasoline. Perhaps the note would provide a clue.

> *Moonlighting at a gentlemen's magazine for extra cash, doing an article on these little gems. Even the military promotes them in adverts to our boys. "Put it on before you put it in," the slogan goes.*

Kick felt her cheeks flame up. This was one of those things that men . . . she couldn't even think of it. Quickly wrapping the disk back in the paper and stuffing it into the envelope, Kick looked around to see if anyone had noticed what she'd been reading and touching. As she sat at her desk, drumming her fingers on the blotter and considering how she could *possibly* retaliate, her phone rang. It was Rose.

"Mother, I'm not supposed to receive personal calls at work," Kick said, her irritation sharper for having just been made a fool of in so private and intimate a fashion.

"I know, Kathleen, and I'm sorry, but this is business, in a way."

"Oh?" She could hardly concentrate with that *thing* on her desk. And she hated all the more that John had succeeded in distracting her this way.

"Yes, you see, your father's heard about a procedure that might help our dear Rosemary." *Of course. Of course you're calling about Rosemary. Not to see how I'm doing. Not that I'd tell you the truth right at this of all moments.*

"Procedure?" she repeated, trying mightily to focus.

"There is a Dr. Walter Freeman, at Saint Elizabeths Hospital right there where you are in Washington, and he has been getting some apparently excellent results with a sort of new brain surgery. Your father and I read an article about it in the *Times*, and he's been curious about it ever since. As you know, Rosemary has been having . . . more trouble lately." Kick knew. Her older sister was in a convent just a few minutes away from her own apartment, but she'd been sneaking out when the last lights were turned off, then wandering the streets until either she got scared or someone caught her and called the Mother Superior.

Unlike with John and his little roll of rubber, Kick knew exactly what her mother was asking her to do. "You want me to use my press card to make some inquiries about Dr. Freeman?" Kick asked her mother. She wouldn't have to go far, as it happened—John White had recently embarked on a series of articles about the hospital. But *why* did it have to be *John*?

Rose sighed with relief at not having to actually make the request in so many words. "Yes. Could you? I'd be so very grateful."

It was amazing how solicitous her mother had become since their return from England. Kick couldn't quite bask in it the way she wanted to, though, knowing that she couldn't share with her mother her heart's greatest desire.

But their interests were aligned here, at least: Kick did care what happened to Rosemary, so she replied, "Of course, Mother. I'd be happy to."

"Thank you, Kathleen. Bless you. Now, what about you? Do you have everything you need? I'm going to Saks tomorrow and could pick something up for you."

There were a few things she needed, but she didn't feel like using now as the time to make such requests. "No, thanks, Mother. I'm fine."

As soon as she hung up, John appeared at Kick's desk.

"What did you think?" he smirked.

"Of?" Kick replied innocently. It was a pity she didn't find him less attractive. That frequently unshaved jaw and those big shoulders stirred something in her. It was different from what chivalrous, fine-featured Billy evoked, that pure, girlish longing. John infuriated her, but the fury was tinged with pleasure. It was difficult to describe, it was so unfamiliar. Perhaps it was exactly what she needed.

But first there was the matter of the "little gem" in her desk. She wasn't about to let him have the satisfaction of knowing he'd rattled her.

John crossed his arms over his chest and stared down at Kick, who sat, trying to look as naive as possible.

"You inscrutable little kitten," he finally said.

"Someone told me once I had a good poker face," she said. "Too bad I hate playing cards."

"Cards are for people who don't know how to play real games," he said.

"My brother Joe would disagree with you," she said, standing up and grabbing her handbag from the floor. "Hot Shoppes?" she asked breezily, referring to the diner so many of them frequented for lunch. "I want to pick your brain about a few things." No time like the present to start working on her mother's request.

"Can't today," he said, sounding genuinely regretful. "Have a meeting with a source."

"So clandestine," she said in an exaggerated tone.

John waggled his eyebrows and took off, leaving Kick short of breath and confused. Slipping out of the office and into the searing August noon, Kick shaded her eyes as she trotted around the corner to a deli, where she bought a tuna salad sandwich and a cold bottle of Coca-Cola, which she pressed against her forehead as she crossed the wide boulevards to get to a bench in the shady, green respite of Franklin Square. Even sitting under the generous branches of a leafy cherry tree, Kick was hot. Like she was in one of the steam rooms of the spas her mother sometimes took her to. The cold soda helped, until it was gone. Soupy Boston had nothing on Washington's humidity.

She squinted against the powerful sun. From her bench, she could see the arching white dome of the Capitol, the immensely tall Washington Monument piercing the blue sky, and even a bit of the Doric splendor of the Lincoln Memorial, though she couldn't see the great president enthroned behind the columns. It was a sight to behold, and she understood why all those buildings' clean, white lines appealed to patriots and immigrants alike, speaking as they did to the rigor and order of life in the United States. Occasionally, especially at night when the cruel sun had dipped below the horizon and streetlights and spotlights began to illuminate the city, Kick could feel a surge of pride in her chest at the sight of these buildings.

Then she would recall what it had felt like to stand at the base of Big Ben, or St. Paul's, or to look out a window from the houses of Parliament down into the rushing Thames, and for a precious second or two she could feel in her bones how those buildings had changed her. But that sensation was hard to hold on to. And if it was getting hard for her to remember what it had felt like to be in London, she could imagine how hard it must be for Billy to remember being with her, especially after all that had happened. London itself was changed. Though he had traveled across the channel only once in two years, *he* was in the new and exciting place, having new and exciting adventures, not her.

When the Blitz began, her friends invented a whole new way of going out in the evenings. First, everyone who was on leave and in town would check in at the Ritz or Savoy—before it was bombed and had to close, it was the Café de Paris. Some nights, a few of them would stay long enough to gather a larger group that would move on to one of the other nightclubs, always leaving word of the next destination with the maître d', who passed along the intelligence to anyone allowed to have it. There was something so deliciously clandestine about it all, and so admirable in the way they worked all day and then danced so much of the night, only to get up the next morning and do it all again. "It's our only way to thumb our noses at Hitler now," Debo had written her. "We carry on, to show him he hasn't gotten the better of us." How Kick wished that she, too, could be at the center of things, even as the bombs fell, even if it meant having to pick her way through rubble to get back home. All that danger, the huddled togetherness of drinking and dancing while sirens wailed outside, sounded vastly more thrilling than moving to Washington, DC, to live the independent life she'd craved for so long.

Kick finished her sandwich, then crumpled its wax paper cover and gripped it in one fist while she held the now-warm Coke bottle in the other. Only proximity would mend the rift between her and Billy; of that much she was sure. *How can I get back?* It had been her nightly prayer of the past two years, always going unanswered.

CHAPTER 19

Her prayers at last received an answer in the unlikely form of Carmel Offie, a friend of her father's who worked in the State Department. She made a passing remark that DC "is great, but no London," and he'd replied, "You know, you could parlay that job at the *Times-Herald* into a press visa to get to London, though your father would kill me for suggesting it." The rest of the lunch had been consumed with plans for making it happen, starting with a well-placed phone call Offie promised to make to Ambassador Anthony Biddle, who was stationed in London working with Poland and other countries currently occupied by the Nazis.

To celebrate her bright, shiny secret, she'd gone out with Inga and John and some of the other reporters and had quite a gay evening, though she regretted it the next morning when her head was pounding and her stomach churning. "If you're going to keep up, you'll need to learn to pick yourself up the next day," John told her at work before taking her to lunch at a tiny restaurant called Betty's. "Best thing about this place is that you can get eggs any time of day. And eggs and bacon are exactly what you need."

The coffee was good, too. "I hate to admit it," said Kick, starting to feel human again halfway through her breakfast for lunch, "but you're right."

"Why is it so hard for you to give in?"

"Kennedy curse," Kick said.

"You joke, but it appears to be true. It's what got your father in that mess in England."

"Let's not talk about Daddy," Kick said. *Or England—I don't want to jinx my chances of getting back.*

"Can't talk about Brother, or Father," John said, stroking his chin as if in deep thought. "What *can* we talk about? The only Kennedy lady I'm interested in is you."

Kick felt her face flush and drank some cool water to restore herself.

"How about Dr. Freeman over at Saint Elizabeths?" she asked as casually as she could. "I read your first article about him. Sounds interesting."

Asking John about his writing was like flipping a switch in his brain—Kick was convinced it was part of his arrogant streak that he liked discussing subjects he knew more about than anyone else. But she also liked to see the way his work animated him, the way it ultimately took him outside himself and his own immediate concerns and desires. "It *is* interesting," said John, leaning both arms on the table. He had such a tightly wound body, the heat from it just wafted off of him. She leaned back in her seat to stay cool.

"The hospital's been in that huge Gothic building for almost a century, and few journalists have ever really looked into it. Did you know that Carl Jung worked there? And Ezra Pound was a patient? It's the nerve center of psychiatric work in this country, if you'll forgive the metaphor." He went on to describe the hospital's state-of-the-art medical equipment and the new "truth serums" they were beginning to test on patients.

"Is that what Dr. Freeman is studying?"

"No, no," said John, lighting a cigarette. "Dr. Freeman is testing lobotomies."

"What're those?"

"Brutality, if you ask me. He's scraping out people's brains in the hopes of curing them of a whole host of mental disorders. Which it does, in a manner of speaking. It can make hyperactive patients calm. Too calm."

Kick shivered. "What do you mean?"

"I mean, you look into their eyes and it's like looking through a window. A clear glass pane."

"But you said it calms them down?" She wanted him to say something more . . . hopeful. Something that might validate any shred of what her father seemed to believe.

"Who'd want to be calm at the expense of everything else? Drinking too much and falling in love and having eggs and bacon on a Wednesday at lunchtime when you ought to be pounding away on your typewriter?" John grinned at Kick. It was his best smile, the kind and solicitous one that made her feel beautiful and necessary. She only hoped he meant that part about falling in love generally. Not specifically about her.

"So you disagree with these articles in the *New York Times* that seem to suggest Dr. Freeman's a genius?"

John inhaled deeply on his cigarette and blew the smoke out so it just tickled Kick's right ear. "Oh, he's a genius all right. But so's Adolf Hitler."

She nodded, understanding exactly and shivering again at the foreboding goose bumps on her spine.

"And now for a happier subject," he declared. "My sister Patsy is dying to meet you."

"Me?" Kick's head was still in the discussion about Dr. Freeman, and she felt conversational whiplash.

"She can't imagine anyone as smart as I've said you are believing in all that Catholic nonsense."

"Not this again!" Kick moaned.

"I'd leave you alone for a kiss," he countered.

She laughed off his offer, and said, "I suppose I'll have to find a way to cope, then."

John looked put out, but Kick ignored it. Surely he knew that a girl like her would take more courting than a few lunches and an invitation to meet his sister? American boys had no clue. She thought of Peter Grace and his years-long patience, which had finally come to an end. Just a few months ago he'd married mousy Margaret Fennelly, of all people. *Well*, Kick had thought when she learned the news, *if he's going to be happy with Margaret, then his pursuit of me was completely misguided.*

I know what love can be, and I'm not going to settle.

❖ ❖ ❖

It was torture waiting for word from Offie and Biddle, but lunch with Nancy Astor's niece Dinah Brand went a long way toward reassuring her that she was on the right path. Dinah blew into Washington on a cloud of Penhaligon's perfume, armed with a packet of letters she handed Kick as soon as they sat down.

"These are all from your friends, begging you to come back and save Billy from that parvenue."

Kick laughed at the flattery.

"I'm working on it," Kick said, still not wanting to mention the press visa. "I have a plan, but I don't want to say too much about it yet. It's almost impossible for Americans to get over there."

Dinah waved her long fingers, and said, "Pish. You're a *Kennedy*."

Kick looked at the letters and opened the one on top from Debo and Andrew that began, "Dearest Kick, Billy still loves you. You! Sally is only second-best, and he'll be ruined if he marries her. Even the duchess doesn't like her . . ."

Kick felt her heart swell, her stomach riot. So things had gotten that serious between Sally and Billy? Just a few months ago, it only sounded as though they'd been seen together in the groups that roved from club to club over London. Now, it appeared, much more was at stake. Kick swallowed and realized her throat was parched. Her precious press visa— maybe she was too late. "I haven't heard from Billy himself in weeks and weeks," she admitted to Dinah. "I worry that I might not . . . make a difference."

Dinah looked at Kick as if she'd suddenly sprung a third eye. "Darling, none of us has ever seen Billy so smitten with anyone as he was with you.

His heart is yours, forever. He's just that sort of man. Of course he hasn't written you lately because he doesn't want to remind himself of you when he's on this absurd collision course with Sally. He's only with her because he's lonely and doesn't want to go back to the war a bachelor. God forbid a virgin. He'll drop her like a hot potato if you arrive back on the scene."

From your mouth to God's ears, thought Kick, though Debo's letter sat like a bad omen on the white tablecloth.

The next day, there was a letter from Billy waiting for her after work. The sight of his nearly illegible scrawl on the Compton Place stationery sent a convulsion of excitement through her. Maybe their friends had succeeded in talking him out of it already. Maybe he'd come to his senses all on his own, and in her reply she'd be able to write the wonderful news that she was just waiting on a visa for the next boat to him. Maybe God had sent Dinah to prepare her for this news.

Her eyes moved over his words so fast she hardly understood them, especially as the tears rushed in. "I finally had to give up hope of our ever marrying . . . 400 years of history . . . I respect your position on the religion question . . . I respect you too much to ask . . . I must return to the war . . . Sally's been a great comfort to me . . . I've made up my mind . . . duty . . ."

Curses on the passenger boats! It had taken longer for Dinah and her packet of pleas to sail across the ocean than it had taken Billy's letter in one of the new airmail carriers. When Dinah had boarded her ship in London, there had been hope. Now there was none. He was engaged to Sally, code breaker extraordinaire.

And curses on Billy! Hiding behind what he thought *she* wanted. Behind propriety and those four centuries of history.

She crumpled the letter and threw it into her closet before screaming into her pillow. Then she was seized by an overwhelming need to *move*. Run, swim, jump—do *anything* other than sit in her wretched little apartment. But where would she go? This wasn't Cannes or Hyannis Port or Palm Beach, where there were wide-open spaces in which she could exhaust herself in water or on a court. So she screamed and screamed and screamed, until the cotton pillowcase was hot and wet, pulverized with her grief.

❖ ❖ ❖

"Kick!" Jack shouted jubilantly.

"*Rats*," she cursed on seeing her brother in the foyer of the Gothic *Times-Herald* building. "You saw me first." But really she was thrilled that he wanted to play their old game during the busy lunch hour. They bumped riotously into many people, some of whom stopped to watch while they jigged in a tight circle, calling out their rhymes:

"*Trick,*" she said, with emphasis.

"Lick."

"Prick."

"Stick."

"Chick."

"Flick."

"Brick."

"Crick."

"Thick."

"*Mick.*"

"*Hick.*"

"Shtick."

"Knick."

"Yick."

"Yick?"

"Another form of yuck," he said as both of them cackled and the small crowd who'd been watching applauded and then went about their business.

"Sounds like a party foul to me," observed John White, who thrust out his hand to shake Jack's. Kick introduced them.

"This must be the famous John Fitzgerald Kennedy? Hero and best-selling writer?" came Inga's sultry voice from behind Kick.

The moment Jack laid eyes on Inga, Kick knew where the two of them were headed. Her brother kept his cool in the face of the older European beauty, shaking her hand almost as if she were a man and saying, "I don't know about the hero part," but Kick could tell from the way his blue eyes lingered just a little too long on Inga's fine, creamy features that he would be single-minded in his pursuit of her. Inga was harder to read. No blushing or stuttering gave *her* away. But when she breezily gave her regrets, saying she couldn't join them for lunch because she had other mysterious plans, Kick was pretty sure her friend was already playing hard to get. And there seemed to be a subtle, but still extra, swish to her step as she clicked away in her Italian heels.

Kick and John and Jack made their way to Hot Shoppes, which was jam-packed with reporters and junior statesmen looking for a fast and decent lunch on the cheap. Kick always ordered the grilled cheese sandwich with tomato and a Coke. If she was especially hungry, she'd add fries to her order and say a little prayer of thanks that her mother wasn't within one hundred miles to see how low living alone had brought her daughter, dietetically—though with all the walking she was doing hither and yon, she was maintaining her figure without much of a problem. Taxis were a luxury on her salary, on which she was proudly living. John always ordered the Reuben and coleslaw, frequently with a root beer float. That day, skinny Jack ordered something called the Lumberjack Special: chicken-fried steak, mashed potatoes with gravy, and maple syrup carrots. Plus a chocolate shake.

"Will all that fit in there?" John asked dubiously, scrutinizing Jack's frame, which was about half the size of his own.

"Just you wait," said Kick. Like her mother, she'd learned to be glad when Jack *could* eat, when one or another of his ailments wasn't stealing his appetite.

"Far cry from what our friends across the pond are eating these days," said Jack, referring to the tinned meat and dry toast even their finer English friends were suffering. The friends she was avoiding writing to in the wake of Billy's bad news. She wanted to kick her brother under the table for bringing them up but didn't want to have to explain why.

"Well, enjoy it while it lasts," said John.

"Killjoy," grumbled Kick.

"Come on, sis, I thought you were Roosevelt's number one fan these days?"

"Just like my *bestselling* brother?" Kick asked with a raised eyebrow, referring to what she and her brother both knew was his last-minute reversal of thesis for the bestselling book Inga had mentioned, *Why England Slept*, prompted almost unbelievably by their father, who wanted to ensure his son didn't make the same political mistakes he had. *Just make Roosevelt look good*, he'd told Jack.

"Dad says to tell you he's sending a few dead mice for you in case you get hungry, Hawk Lady," Jack jibed.

"Caw, caw," Kick crowed in a flat voice. Jack chuckled the way he always did when he knew he'd gotten her goat.

"You, a hawk?" John said to Kick. "I wouldn't have guessed you're for the war."

"Shows how little you really understand me," Kick said, suddenly annoyed.

"You're right," John said. "I especially can't understand how a woman of such intelligence could waste her mind on a religion that oppresses women."

Jack whistled and Kick groaned, "Here we go again."

"Again?" Jack asked John.

"I've made it my mission to disabuse Kick of Catholicism. Surely *you're* not in favor of the tenets of your faith that keep women barefoot and pregnant," John ventured to Jack as their food arrived. "I saw the way you looked at Inga back there. If she were a good Catholic girl, she'd hardly be so desirable at twenty-eight."

Kick couldn't help but be glad that John's castigating eye knew no boundaries.

But typically, Jack didn't let anything ruffle him. He laughed, dug into his mashed potatoes, and washed it down with a long swig of shake before replying, "John, my friend, there is Saturday night, and there is Sunday morning. Never the twain shall meet."

Kick smirked as John shook his head in disbelief. Though Kick didn't love the truth behind her brother's retort, she was mighty glad he'd put John White in his place. God had sent her broken heart one small consolation, it appeared. Washington was about to get a lot better with her favorite brother stationed in the Office of Naval Intelligence.

CHAPTER 20

Her telephone rang in the middle of the night. When she rubbed her eyes and focused on the alarm clock beside her bed, she saw it was just after two in the morning.

"Hello?" she said sleepily. It was cold standing in her kitchen in her cotton nightgown, and she began to shiver.

"Kathleen! I'm sorry to trouble you in the middle of the night, but I couldn't reach Jack, and I simply had to talk with someone who could help. I wasn't going to be able to sleep until I did." Rose was practically hysterical, having trouble getting enough air between shallow breaths.

"What is it?" Kick asked, though she knew. There was only one person who could transform her mother into this kind of mess.

"Rosemary's been out on one of her walks," Rose said, with all that implied.

"Where was she this time?" Kick asked, pulling an afghan off the couch and wrapping herself in it to warm up. The last time Rosemary went out, she'd been in a bar, smoking and drinking and flirting with a man old enough to have voted for Honey Fitz. She'd gotten very worked up when he'd proposed taking her back to his house. The bartender had been the one to call that night. The previous time, she'd been sitting on the lap of a young navy officer near the Washington Monument when a passing police officer, an Irishman with great national pride, recognized her and pulled her away. "Can't have treasures like the Kennedy girls getting into this sort of trouble," he'd told her father, who'd swiftly had the young man promoted to sergeant.

"The same place as last time," her mother gasped.

"What do you want me to do?"

"Visit her later today. Please try to talk some sense into her. And ask Jack to come, too."

"I doubt she'll listen to either of us, Mother. She's dying for some independence." Which, honestly, Kick could understand. When her parents had shut down her life in London, she'd lost everything. In some ways, she was glad Rosemary was showing her parents the dangers of locking their children away.

"Please try, Kick."

"Why don't you come down?"

"I'm booked solid with closing up the house in Bronxville and a thousand charity events."

Of course.

"And if what you say is true," Rose went on, "and Rosemary is angry with her lack of freedom, then she's more likely to listen to her siblings than her parents."

"All right, Mother."

Rose sighed with anxious relief and said, "Bless you. Please do try to get Jack to come with you. Oh, and, Kathleen? Have you learned anything about this procedure of Dr. Freeman's?"

"Yes," Kick said. She'd been dreading this conversation. She wasn't sure what her mother really wanted with regard to Rosemary and this procedure, but she had a feeling her mother was on a different side from her father. Kick didn't want to cause either of her parents more pain, especially her father, who'd suffered so badly these past two years.

"I knew you would," sighed Rose. "I've been praying for it."

"Well, I hope you'll still feel that way after I explain what I've found," began Kick as her whole body tensed. "It sounds like most of Dr. Freeman's patients are really quite disturbed. Nothing like our Rosemary. And when he has performed the lobotomy, the patients might become less disturbed, but they are less *aware* as well. My friend John White, who's been researching the hospital and its doctors, says that looking at the patients is like looking through a glass window. There's nothing *there* anymore, if you know what I mean. That's not what we want for Rosemary, is it?"

Kick was surprised to find herself breathing heavily at the end of this speech, her heart pounding rapidly in her chest.

"Oh, Kathleen," Rose said, her voice small. "That is what I feared you might discover."

"Is Daddy convinced otherwise?" Kick asked.

"Not entirely. Not yet," said Rose. "But now that you have given me real information, I am armed with some arguments."

Soon she was off the phone but unable to get back to sleep. So she was wide-awake by the time she headed to the office, having already consumed two cups of strong, hot tea with toast. Inga joined her as she walked to work, and Kick was glad not to be alone with her thoughts.

"How is your brother getting along in our fair city?" Inga inquired.

"He's busy," Kick replied. So. Inga was curious about Jack. And he hadn't shut up about wanting to bump into her again.

"I haven't been dancing in ages," Inga said transparently. "How about a group of us get together tonight or tomorrow? I heard the new singer at the Tahitian is supposed to be excellent."

"Sounds like a plan," said Kick, because dancing at an American club, the antithesis of the 400, was probably just what she needed.

❧ ❧ ❧

The convent where Rosemary was living had high stone walls like all the Sacred Hearts in which the Kennedy girls had lived and studied, walls that made everything inside cold, echoey, and damp. The familiarity of it made Kick feel small and intimidated just as she had when she was eleven. At least this building had a garden at the back, full of climbing roses and patches of vegetables, with two wrought iron tables and chairs nestled into the greenery. Kick and Jack sat and waited there until the Mother Superior brought Rosemary out.

Their sister looked pudgier than usual, and not just in her hips and arms, where she usually carried her weight—this time, her face seemed bloated, her eyes smaller. Her gray dress seemed to be made of sackcloth. Kick wondered what she put on when she snuck out.

"Rosemary," said the nun with a solicitous smile, "your brother and sister have made a special trip to see you."

"They live here," Rosemary said flatly, to the ground more than to any one of the three people standing around her. She didn't smile.

Kick took a few steps forward and gave her sister a hug, which she didn't reciprocate. Jack went next, and he crouched down and tried to get his sister to look into his eyes. "I've missed you, Rosie!" He smiled that Jack smile, and for a second Rosemary smiled back.

Taking that as her cue, the Mother Superior said, "I'll leave you three to visit. There's a bell on the table should you need anything."

She can't leave fast enough.

"It's gorgeous here," said Jack. "Have you helped with the planting? I always suspected you'd have a green thumb."

"Everything was planted when I arrived," said Rosemary. "I just do the watering and pruning."

"Well, that's quite a lot," said Kick. "Pruning isn't easy! I'm terrible with flowers. Remember that flower arranging class Mother made all us girls take? I failed miserably."

"I liked it," Rosemary said wistfully. Then, her face brightening a bit, she asked, "How is Mother?"

Jack and Kick exchanged nervous glances. "Worried," Kick blurted out. She felt so unbalanced here.

A few bees buzzed around the garden.

Jack took Rosemary's hands in his and led her over to the table, where they sat at last.

"We're worried, too," he said.

At this, Rosemary laughed—a hard, almost cynical laugh. "Worried? I'm not doing anything *you* don't do."

The fact that she said this to Jack and not Kick was alarming. Just what *was* she up to at night?

Unbothered as usual, Jack chuckled. "Now, Rosie, you know that it's different for girls. I understand as much as the next person how important it is to have someone special in your life, but sneaking around isn't the way to find a man. Certainly not a man worthy of you."

"How am I going to meet that man?" Rosemary demanded. "I'm not invited anywhere!"

"Rosie, darling," Kick said, trying to adopt something like the soothing tone her father used when his oldest daughter became recalcitrant, "You must focus on your health first. You know how Mother goes away to drink the mineral waters at special spas, and prays to heal herself."

"This is a *prison*, Kathleen," Rosemary hissed, "not a *spa*."

"I'm sure it's not as bad as all that," Kick said, though she knew from experience that it almost certainly was that bad, and hated herself for the dishonest words she'd just spoken.

"Let's make a deal," interjected Jack, tapping Rosemary's soft white hand with his freckled, knuckly finger. "When I've gained ten pounds, and you've lost the same number, and if the Jail Warden"—he tilted his head toward the convent to indicate the Mother Superior—"gives her blessing, I'll take you out for a night on the town. I know plenty of gentlemen who'd be honored to dance with you."

Bluffer, Kick thought. *No wonder you beat everyone at cards.* She realized she was gnawing on her lower lip and stopped.

But Jack's deal worked. Rosemary suddenly looked like a child who'd opened exactly the right present on Christmas morning. "You will?" she gushed.

Jack raised his left hand and put his right over his heart. "I swear."

Rosemary gave Kick a petulant *so there* look that would have been complete had she also stuck out her tongue. Kick just barely kept herself from rolling her eyes. Once again, her brother had saved the day. Mother would be pleased.

On her way home to change for her own night on the town with Inga and Jack and John, she stopped into a small church in her neighborhood, St. Catherine's. Though she hadn't found another parish or priest to compare to St. Mary's or Father O'Flaherty, she was comforted by the simple wood carvings in St. Catherine's and the constant flicker of candles lit by other faithful men and women who needed help. That day, she put a dollar in the donation box and lit one herself, then kneeled in the last row and prayed a rosary for her sister. And for her father, so that he might make the right decision.

Later, as John moved Kick effortlessly among the bamboo and palm trees surrounding the dance floor of the Tahitian, and Inga and Jack became increasingly entranced with each other over another round of rum cocktails, Kick wished she could lose herself the way she once had with Billy. This thought brought the familiar heat to her eyes, and when "Moonlight Serenade" finished, John asked her if everything was all right.

"I'm just exhausted," she said, rubbing her eyes as if she were throwing off sleep and not sadness.

John offered to take her home, but what was waiting for her there? She stayed for another few drinks so that when he did take her home, she could fall into her bed and a deep, dreamless sleep.

❖ ❖ ❖

John's sister Patsy White had married Henry Field, a renowned anthropologist who had worked on the Chicago World's Fair and the excavation of the ancient Mesopotamian city of Kish. He and Patsy had recently moved from Chicago to Washington because President Roosevelt had invited him to be part of a secret research project. All he or his wife could say about it was that it had to do with "migration patterns." Every Sunday, Patsy and Henry hosted a party in which everyone who was anyone in Washington could drop in for a plate of spaghetti and a glass of rough red wine, all consumed while sitting cross-legged on the oriental rugs that covered the floors of the Fields' cozy bohemian house, which was crammed full of books and South American pottery and oddly shaped furniture like something called a Thai axe pillow, on which Lord Halifax, the new English ambassador, regularly reclined.

Kick's first time there, she and John arrived late because John had been so busy nervously explaining who Henry was, and the others who were likely to be there.

"You're being ridiculous, John. I already know Halifax and Jimmy Roosevelt and David Rockefeller and all that lot."

"I just want you to feel comfortable."

"Don't you worry about me," she said, patting him on the shoulder. Nothing could compare to the nerves she'd felt those first months in England when she'd had everything to prove and everything to lose. What could she possibly lose now? "Honestly, I'm more worried about *you*," she added. John was a mess, with his hands shaking and a dribble of sweat rolling down his right temple.

"I just want it to go well."

"I'll be fine. Let's *go*."

When they arrived, late because of John's dithering, about twenty people were there, and most of the spaghetti was gone. "Good thing I'm not hungry," she sang, though she was actually famished.

"I'll make it up to you later," he whispered.

She sniffed at him and filled a glass with wine, at which point a parade of people began greeting her.

Lord Halifax was first, setting his empty plate on an intricately carved side table. "Kathleen! I didn't realize you were in Washington!"

"I've been hiding," she said in a conspiratorial voice. Though it wasn't altogether false. She still hid her fancier clothes at work so that her co-workers wouldn't think she was a rich girl who couldn't cut it on the paper. And she hadn't yet reached out to some of her friends and acquaintances in town because she didn't want the word to get out too

fast. She had a feeling her appearance here would put an end to her ano-
nymity.

"Well, don't hide too long," he said with an appreciative smile. "I saw
your father just recently. He seems . . . better."

"He is," Kick agreed. At least he'd gained back a few of the fifteen
pounds he'd lost in England before returning home in disgrace; his mood,
however, remained morose. Halifax, who'd shifted his politics away from
appeasement in 1939, was faring far better than Joe. Churchill must have
felt he could rely on him in Washington, unlike Roosevelt, who'd re-
placed her father with John Winant. The thought set her teeth grinding.

"I'm sure you've gathered that the mood in Washington is with your
old chums these days," Halifax said.

Had John just flinched at the mention of her English friends? "Yes,
well," she said, "it's not easy to watch any nation with whom we share a
language and so much culture be bombed like England's been bombed."

Halifax frowned. "Indeed," he said.

David Rockefeller and then Arthur Krock of the *New York Times* and
the attorney general were next to say hello to Kick, and since John had
never met these last two, she introduced them. This annoyed him greatly,
much to her delight. At last, Patsy herself broke away from the intense
conversation she'd been having with Henry Wallace, Roosevelt's rumored
choice as vice president for his third term as president, to come over and
hug her brother and meet Kick. "I've seen out of the corner of my eye that
I didn't need to play hostess for you at all, Kathleen. But *welcome*."

"Please, call me Kick," she told Patsy, a tall woman nearly ten years her
senior with short brown hair and a kind, plain face decorated by dangling
turquoise earrings and a thick silver choker. "And thank you for having me."

"I can't believe John hasn't brought you before," Patsy said in a reprimanding tone with a cocked eyebrow at her brother.

"Oh, I'm sure he's been bringing his other women," Kick joked, but
she could see from the way Patsy blushed that she'd hit a nerve. *What a*

relief, she thought. *I don't want him pining uselessly for me.* As she eyed him and noted with satisfaction his embarrassment at being called out so easily, she once again regretted that she found him so attractive. Good thing he was also so disagreeable.

Then Patsy's husband Henry Field joined them, and the four of them spoke a bit about the increasingly shrill speeches coming out of Charles Lindbergh's America First Committee.

"I hardly need articulate how I feel about *Lucky Lindy,*" said Henry disdainfully. His slightly English accent tugged at Kick's heart. *That's right,* she thought, remembering what John had told her. *He studied at Oxford.*

"I take it he hasn't been lucky enough to be invited here?" said Kick.

Patsy laughed and put a gentle hand on her husband's arm. "I've tried to convince Henry to invite him in the spirit of openness and conversation, but I'm afraid that if Mr. Lindbergh did come, he and Henry would wind up fighting a duel in the garden!"

"It is a pity a national hero like Charles Lindbergh has gone so far to the right," Kick said. "He does sound terribly *angry* when he speaks."

"I'm relieved to hear that straight from your mouth," said Henry.

"Haven't you heard? Our former ambassador has no sway over his fourth child, at least in terms of politics. Don't get her started on religion, though!" John needled.

Kick looked with exaggerated sympathy at Patsy. "Has he always been like this?"

Patsy leaned forward and said in a low tone, "He used to be much worse." And the two women laughed.

John spoke remarkably little that afternoon, but he kept his eyes uncomfortably on Kick the whole time. When the two of them were alone again, she said, "I feel rather like I'm under a microscope, or taking a test."

"Don't be absurd."

"Is it absurd to think that the most vociferous person I know would be quiet here, where talking is prized, unless he had a better project in mind?"

"And what would that better project be?" he said in an amused tone.

"Making sure I'm presentable. Which is patently ridiculous, since *I* should be subjecting *you* to that test."

"Yes, I'm beginning to see that," he grumbled, draining the last of his glass. "Don't I owe you some food? Want to get out of here?"

"Oh, I'm way past hunger now," she said with a smile. "At some point, words replace food for me."

But the party was winding down anyway. As guests began drifting off into the chilled air, Kick and John shook hands and exchanged continental kisses with Patsy and Henry.

"Next time," said Patsy warmly, "feel free to bring whomever you like."

"Except Unlucky Lindy," Kick quipped.

"Or anyone you haven't cleared with *me* first," added John.

"Don't listen to him," said Patsy with a wave of her hand.

The following weekend, Kick invited Jack and Inga without "clearing" it with John, and thoroughly enjoyed the annoyed look he threw her from across the crowded living room when her brother arrived with the Danish beauty queen, both smelling fresh from a bath. Kick lifted her full plate of spaghetti at John. *Cheers.*

Kick began calling Patsy's weekly event the Spaghetti Salon, and she looked forward to it like nothing else in her Washington life. Despite Halifax and Henry's Oxford-educated inflections, everything else about the gatherings was profoundly American, which had the effect of helping her forget Billy and all the rest. Unlike Rose and most of the English hostesses she'd observed, who believed in executing the smallest details with painstaking correctness, Patsy was casual but no less effective. The spaghetti she served every Sunday was genius. It was delicious, but it didn't get in the way. Not only did her guests understand from her simple menu that the gathering was more for serious talk than for cuisine or posturing about cuisine or any other trappings of setting, the fact that it was easy to prepare (or so Patsy said—Kick was still having trouble with omelets, which so many women claimed were easy to make) freed Patsy to tend to other things. She didn't have a full staff of servants, and so this was essential. "If I was making boeuf bourguignon," she told Kick, "or slicing endless tomatoes for a fresh salad, I'd never have time to read all the newspapers before my guests arrived." Also, the fact that she did actually make the spaghetti on her chef's day off lent that personal touch that hostesses were always nattering on about.

Kick sat down to write Debo a letter about it, to explain how *happy* she was in her *new life*, but she couldn't quite wrap words around these almost-truths without the sense that she was betraying her old friends. Which was ridiculous. Billy was the one who'd betrayed her.

Instead she began a letter to Father O'Flaherty, who was in France working in an orphanage for children whose parents had been dragged away before their eyes. She inquired after his work and told him about the *Times-Herald* and the Fields. For a few minutes as her pen glided over the paper, she fooled herself into believing that she and the priest were still fighting the same fight, that what she was doing mattered at all.

CHAPTER 21

Once word got out that Kick was in town, the invitations for luncheons and teas and cocktail parties started pouring in. Her life began to feel a little bit like it had in London, full of events and similar sets of people mixing and remixing for common ends. Except that instead of the purpose of it all being society and the traditional pursuit of leisure and charity, the purpose of it all in Washington was politics. Instead of attending a benefit for something cultural like the British Museum or Royal Albert Hall, Kick attended dinners and dances raising money for candidates and their causes, like farmworkers' rights or the Women's Army Corps. Even when an event was raising money for the Smithsonian or the National Symphony Orchestra, it was hosted by a senator or congressman and his wife, and there was always a speech before the dessert course.

There was the sense, everywhere, that war was inevitable. That it was only a matter of time before the butter and sugar that Americans still enjoyed in abundance would soon become scarce, and the rationing and state-imposed spending coupons that had become commonplace in England were upon them. Some of the drinking and dancing had an undercurrent of desperation that was markedly different from the defeatism among her friends in 1939. Perhaps it was due to the different national characters of the English and Americans, but while the English had an attitude of pursuing life as usual—parties included—in the face of great adversity, of keeping to traditions because they were a source of strength, Americans were animated more by fear, a profound dread of hardship that made them want to soak up every liquid ounce of pleasure while there was still time.

"Do you get the feeling that people are girding themselves for the worst?" Kick asked Jack one afternoon at the Chevy Chase Club. Two-thirds of the room was drunk already, and the other third was on its way. Inga was fetching their first cocktails, and John was at home and cranky, working on an overdue article. Joe Sr. was also at the club, but he'd shown up with a blond woman not much older than Kick, and she'd known immediately it was not a good time to bring up Rosemary. She hated seeing her father appear places with other women, something he'd begun doing more frequently lately. Kick was perfecting her *what woman?* expression. More card games.

"Of course they are," Jack replied, squinting his eyes at the fire. His skin was still brown from the summer, and Kick wondered if he sat out in the daytime sun to make up for the fact that his body refused to put on any weight. She wondered what voluptuous Inga thought of Jack's protruding ribs. "Roosevelt's just looking for an excuse to send our men over to help your friends."

"Why is it always *my* friends? You made friends in England, too," Kick pointed out.

"True enough. David and I saw eye to eye, and I can see us staying friends a long time. But no one like Lem or Torby." LeMoyne Billings and Torbert Macdonald had been friends of Jack's for as long as Kick could remember; their friendship was a high bar.

Kick rubbed her lips together. "Does Inga make you want to stay here in DC?"

He didn't answer right away and instead closed his eyes. Then, dreamily, he said, "Yeah, she does." Kick had never seen him distracted, even a little dopey, over a woman before. She wondered if he'd been like this with Frances Ann Cannon, and if he had been, did that mean Inga would receive his next proposal? Assuming she ever divorced Paul Fejos.

"What about you and John White?" Jack asked, smirking now. "Has he helped you forget the great Billy Hartington?"

"Ha ha," Kick said.

"Well, for two years, you've been moping around criticizing everything because it doesn't compare to your precious London, and since you met John, you've been more your feisty self," he observed.

"I still don't feel like myself," said Kick, wishing Inga would rescue her from this conversation with those drinks.

"Maybe not, but people can change. Maybe you're growing up, little sister. Figuring out that life isn't one big party."

"It's not?" she asked, gesturing at the crowd around them at that very moment.

"This isn't a party," said Jack with a laugh. "It's a serious meeting of heads of state."

"Oh, right, of course; how could I miss that?"

"Listen, Kick, all I'm saying is that to me you seem more yourself. You're going out, talking to people, living in the present. That's good. Keep it up."

"I'll take that under advisement."

"For what it's worth, though? Don't get too serious about John."

"You must know that such a warning is likely to drive me straight into his arms," she said.

"Go ahead and go into his arms, but don't let him in *here*," he warned, tapping his chest with his index finger.

"Why not?" Kick asked.

"Because he's not just not Catholic, sis; he's *anti*-Catholic. He'd give Mom a heart attack. And . . ." His voice trailed off.

"What?"

Reluctantly, Jack added, "I just don't think he's good enough for you in the long term. He's fine for a good time, but he's no son-in-law for Dad and Mom."

"Is Inga a better daughter-in-law?"

Jack shrugged noncommittally. "The thought hadn't even occurred to me," he said, just as Inga sashayed over in her orange dress and red shoes, with three cold cocktails.

"Sorry for the wait," she apologized. "I was practically attacked by the director of the National Theater about their next production."

Jack took his drink in one hand and slid his other down Inga's curved back. She leaned toward him, and they kissed. It all looked like one fluid, natural movement, the harmony of a couple who knew each other intimately.

Did she even want that with John? Such dazzling moments all seemed to lead to heartache. For Jack and Frances, for her mother, and for her and Billy. What was the point?

❦ ❦ ❦

On Saturday evening, Kick made herself a fortifying cup of tea and called her mother. "How are things in Bronxville?" she asked, feeling suddenly nostalgic for the comforts of that sprawling home. Her two-room apartment was cramped, even for one person.

Her mother sighed. "I love this house. You and the children grew up here."

"It will be sad when it's gone," agreed Kick. "But we still have Hyannis Port and Palm Beach. I have many fond memories from both those houses."

"Yes," her mother said distractedly, and Kick wondered what her mother was actually thinking about. Best to get to the point.

"Mother?"

"Yes?"

How could she say this, exactly? It was such a delicate matter. "Jack was very good with Rosemary the other day, and—"

"Yes, she told me," Rose interrupted, using that reverent tone she always did when talking about her sons.

"Well, it got me thinking about how Daddy has always been good with Rosemary as well. And Billy . . . I know you don't like to remember that time, but she responded well to Billy, too." Kick paused to draw in a breath, and take a sip of her tea, before continuing. "And her recent . . . wanderings . . . all seem to be in quest of . . . male company."

"Where's all this going, Kathleen?" her mother asked impatiently.

"I hate to sound too . . . I don't know . . . *medieval* . . . but couldn't we find some nice man who wants a pretty wife who's good with children, to marry her?"

Rose laughed. It was almost a cackle, but at least it was brief. Then she said, "I'm not laughing at you, Kathleen. It's an idea I have suggested to your father many times. But he is reluctant. I'm laughing because I'd rather not cry, which I've also done, that her sister and mother should know what's best for her and not her father."

"What if I also suggest it to Daddy?"

"Be my guest," said Rose. "But be sure you make it clear it wasn't an idea of mine that I put into your head."

"I will," Kick replied, thinking with confidence of the way her father had treated her opinion back in London. He'd give her ideas some credit now, especially when they pertained to their family, wouldn't he?

"But, Kathleen," her mother warned, not even bothering to conceal the bitterness in her voice, "don't be surprised if he does laugh at you. He's become very adept at throwing away good advice lately."

Kick wondered what advice of her mother's her father had been discarding in his depressed state.

"I'll let you know what he says," she told Rose.

❖ ❖ ❖

The next evening, after the Spaghetti Salon and a movie with John, Kick came home to a fragrant spray of lily and hydrangea blooms waiting for her in the dim hallway beside her apartment.

"Secret admirer?" John asked petulantly. She'd invited him up to her place on a whim, not wanting to be alone.

Kick laughed as she stooped to pick up the arrangement, and said,

"Who knows?" Her heart gave a little flutter. *Could they be from . . . ?* She tried not to smile at the thought, for fear of what John might say.

After a struggle with her purse and keys and the unexpected flowers, Kick stepped into her apartment, which still smelled like the toast she'd made that morning. She went to open all three of the windows before she came back to the flowers sitting on her table to read the card. John stared at them menacingly.

"They won't bite you," she said.

To brighten your day, as you did mine. Love, Mother.

Kick's chest filled with wet emotion at reading the words on the florist's card. So, not from Billy. Of course not. The memory of his engagement to Sally, which she'd been shoveling out of her mind like dirty wet snow, overcame her, and her knees felt momentarily wobbly.

"From your mother, eh?" John said with relief.

"Are you reading my *private* note over my shoulder?" she demanded.

"You're standing right next to me," he said.

"Don't read my mail," she snapped peevishly.

After a bit of banging around in the kitchen, she said with an exasperated sigh, "No vase."

"I suppose I should find that comforting," said John.

"Why? Because it means I don't have scores of admirers sending me expensive flowers?"

"Yes," he said.

"I'm not the one bringing other women to my sister's house," she said.

"I haven't brought anyone else since I brought you."

"But you see them on other nights. Don't deny it." She knew it was true, since he virtually ignored her three mornings a week at the office.

"Maybe I wouldn't if you'd let me kiss you. Just on the cheek."

"Ha," she said sarcastically.

"Try me."

"I don't want to kiss you, John."

"You just want to argue with me?"

"Isn't that enough?"

"No."

"Fine," she said. "Suit yourself." She folded her arms over her chest and stared at him through narrowed eyes.

She felt unrecognizable to herself: angry, sad, and itching for a fight. All the time, she realized. Talking to John—or rather, quarreling with John—was the only way she'd found to release some of the pressure.

In response to her dare, John put on his hat and left in silence.

As the sun set and her apartment cooled, Kick managed to arrange the many stems of her mother's flowers in cups and jars, setting them all over her apartment. The only cup she didn't use was the one for her tea in the morning. When she was finished, her little home looked bright and colorful for the first time. But it was so dense with scent, Kick started to sneeze. And then to cry.

Before bed, she set all the flowers outside her door, and slowly the sneezing and tears subsided. The next morning, she tied the bouquets with string and set them on a few coworkers' desks.

Inga asked, "What's the occasion?"

"Oh, nothing," Kick replied. "My mother sent them to me but they made me sneeze, so I thought I'd give them away."

Inga smiled and took a drowsy sniff of lily. Then she set her translucent blue irises on Kick. "It's wonderful to receive flowers from a girlfriend," she said. "No expectations."

"I'll tell Jack not to send you any flowers, then," Kick joked, but she found herself annoyed at Inga's comment. When, for that glorious half a moment the day before, she'd thought these flowers might have been from Billy, she knew she could have coped with those expectations. Then again . . . had they been from John . . . well there, Kick could see Inga's point, and this annoyed her, too.

CHAPTER 22

She met her father for supper at the Tabard Inn, a quiet place that fashioned itself after a Federal drawing room. He looked better than he had in ages, with color in his cheeks and filling out a trim suit. His smile was genuine and relaxed, and his eyes had gained back a little of that twinkle they used to have behind his round glasses.

"Kick! How terrific to see you *after work*. No more long lunches for my girl," he said proudly. Once they were seated in the leather chairs, he added, "Frank tells me you're doing wonderfully. And don't tell him I let the cat out of the bag, but he'll be giving you a real assignment soon. He knows your talents are wasted on secretarial work."

"That would be great, Daddy." Kick beamed, not caring if it was her father who'd gotten Frank to give her a serious writing assignment. She was sick of the phones and needed a challenge.

Kick and her father ordered, and then chatted about her siblings over old-fashioneds. Bobby was doing well at Milton Academy; Eunice was contemplating a move from Manhattanville College to Stanford, where her recent ailments might be eased by the California sunshine; Jean and Pat were doing well in school; and Teddy missed his older brothers terribly but was happy being his mother's pet. "It's almost like he's an only child," Joe remarked with a laugh.

"And Joe Jr. is off to a marvelous start," he added with confidence. Kick had been exchanging letters with her eldest brother and so knew that there was a part of him that was anxious for America to go to war so that he could distinguish himself as a navy pilot and finally break out of Jack's shadow. He'd never forgiven Jack for hogging the spotlight in the *Athenia* disaster those last weeks they were in England, then for publishing his Harvard thesis as a book to such great acclaim—especially after their father had never been able to get his own dispatches from Spain published. Kick knew that Jack had done none of it on purpose, and in fact supported Joe Jr. wholeheartedly, going so far as to say he was relieved their parents poured all their political ambitions into his older brother. But Joe Jr. still felt threatened. "Every paper I open, there's Jack's smiling face," he'd said in one recent letter to Kick.

Kick had to bring up Rosemary herself. "Jack and I went to visit Rosie the other day," she said.

Immediately her father's face darkened, and he ground his molars together before saying, "I spoke with the Mother Superior this morning, and it sounds like she has been a bit better since she saw you both."

"You don't look encouraged, though," Kick observed, feeling unsteady and less hungry. She set her spoon down without finishing her vichyssoise.

"Believe me, Kick, I'd like to think that the influence of her siblings could make a difference, but it never has in the past. Except temporarily."

"Daddy, I've been thinking a great deal about her lately, especially with the . . . trouble . . . she's been having, and I wondered if maybe getting married might help her? She is such a beautiful girl, and so tender with children. And men have always been able to set her right—you, Jack, and Joe, for instance. I'm not surprised that in a convent full of women she isn't thriving." There, she'd said it. She held her breath.

Joe set down his spoon. "Your mother and I have discussed that possibility. But I can't in good conscience pair her with a man until she's under control. Can you imagine what would happen if I gave my blessing to a match and then she embarrassed herself and the family?" He shook his head, then said gravely, "That would be a sin."

"I don't think that would be likely to happen, do you?" Kick pressed, feeling braver since he hadn't dismissed her suggestion. "If the courtship went well, that is? Wouldn't we see signs beforehand if it wasn't the right choice? Can't we try?"

"I'll tell you what I'd like to try," her father said, his expression changing from melancholy defeatism to spry hope as he sang the praises of Dr. Freeman, with whom he'd actually met twice on this trip to Washington. *Mother will be beside herself,* Kick thought as her stomach dropped a few inches.

"I know a bit about Dr. Freeman myself," Kick said carefully, not wanting to give her mother and their colluding away. "My friend John White on the paper has been writing a series about Saint Elizabeths Hospital." For once she was glad to be able to use a man's name to help her case.

"Oh?" Her father appeared ready to listen, so Kick explained to him the same facts she'd already relayed to her mother.

"Journalists are paid to doubt, of course," was her father's first shrugging reply. "And those extreme cases that he describes are in keeping with what Dr. Freeman has explained to me as well. The results are in proportion to the problem."

"Has he dealt with a . . . *mild* case like Rosemary's before?"

"Honestly, Kathleen, I don't like being interrogated by my own daughter. There are some things best left to parents."

Then I hope you talk to Mother, she thought forcefully, pushing her bowl away. This was just like her father these days. *I should have known.* She only hoped that the carrot Jack had dangled before Rosemary would be temptation enough to help her sister control herself and help their father see the right course of action for his oldest daughter. She would pray a rosary for it that night.

❖ ❖ ❖

Soon enough, the assignment from Frank came through, and she was industriously working on an article about the expansion of a library. It was a dull subject, but Kick enjoyed the work, piecing quotes together with

facts culled from town records and her own descriptions of the facility.
She was reminded of why she'd chosen Father O'Flaherty's newsletter and
the bulletin as methods of gaining independence in London. Those first
attempts at journalism seemed so silly compared to what she was learning
now, though, especially when John sat her down after reading a draft
before she handed it in to Frank, and said, "This isn't an essay for school.
You're not trying to impress a nun with your flowery language."

"I know." She winced.

"Then why did you write it this way? With all the adjectives? 'Beautiful'—which, by the way, you say thirteen times in eight hundred words—
and not just 'dusty books' but 'ancient, dusty volumes' and 'educational
and edifying.' I could go on."

"Please don't," Kick said, feeling her cheeks burn and wishing she'd
given the draft to Inga.

John let the paper flutter down to her desk and said, "Cut this in half
by getting rid of extra words, then add more quotes, and you'll be on the
right track."

She took his advice and found that despite her irritation at his manner,
his guidance had improved the article. And Frank must have agreed because another assignment soon followed. In a few weeks, her secretarial
desk had been taken by a younger, blonder girl, and she'd moved across
the room, two desks away from Inga and one from Page. Neither of the
other two women were around much, though, as both of them were
deeply involved with men not on the paper staff, and they used research
and reporting duties as excuses for not being at their desks. Page's beau
was Frazer Dougherty, and Kick couldn't figure out the attraction. He
was handsome enough, she supposed, but he was nobody—not from a
great family, or on his way to greatness in some other way.

"I'm glad for an escape from all that," Page told Kick when they met
up for a drink after work one night. "Working for your father was glamorous and all, but it was dangerous, too. So many egos at stake."

Kick nodded like she understood, but she didn't really—*Maybe I like
a little danger*, she considered, and the thought surprised her. Inga and

Jack she understood much better. And when she let herself, she felt wretchedly jealous of them, too. Not only was Inga getting the best of Jack these days, when that part of him used to belong to Kick—the dancing and sparring with her witty brother at parties and other engagements—the other woman was balancing the impossible: a husband, a lover, and a career that earned her respect from men, even men who didn't want to sleep with her. In fact, from men who probably wouldn't sleep with her *because* of her career.

One windy autumn night, Kick and John and Jack and Inga were at one of their favorite haunts, a former speakeasy near Logan Circle that served whiskey from the same distillery that had made it illegally in 1925. It nabbed some of the best jazz singers that blew through town, shuttling between New Orleans and New York City, and the four of them loved heading there after dinner at the Old Ebbitt Grill. That night they were waiting for Evelyn Dall to take the stage.

"She sang at Buckingham Palace," said Kick nostalgically. "It was hilarious, actually. Chamberlain was appalled when this platinum blonde American in a slinky dress took the stage. Apparently, he hadn't known what 'crooner' meant, so when his advisors asked him if they should get a great crooner to perform at the palace, he'd thought it was some sort of instrument." She laughed, recalling the absurdity of it, and the way the prime minister's face had blanched.

"He really didn't know what 'crooner' meant?" John asked with no small amount of derision.

Inga said, "You must understand the English sensibility. They are much too imperial to think they don't know everything, and much too polite to inquire when they aren't sure."

"It's not true for *all* English people," Kick said, feeling defensive, "but it was certainly true of Chamberlain."

John shook his head and finished his second whiskey. "No wonder," he muttered into his glass.

And off they went, arguing again while Jack and Inga retreated into their own little sphere.

"Why can't we be more like them?" John said later, nodding over at their companions. Jack's arm was quietly draped over Inga's shoulder, and as she smoked, he drank. A moment ago, they had kissed, and her red lipstick was still on Jack's lips.

"John, I'm just not . . . going to be with you the way you want me to," Kick finally said.

He sighed, exasperated. "Don't bring the nuns into this."

"I'm not. You are. Why do you keep coming back for more if you're not getting what you really want?"

"Because I like you," he said, sounding like the most miserable man alive.

"Don't look so happy about it," she said sarcastically.

"Have pity on me," he said.

He looked worthy of pity, she had to admit. And he was loyal, if not faithful, exactly. There were still other girls.

Brushing a lock of hair off his forehead, she felt a tug of desire. But instead of sensing the welcome pleasure of Maria Sieber's sheets, she felt the shove of the cold, salty waves that had brought her to that bed in the first place.

She was up late that night, and so it was hard to drag herself to mass the following morning. But it was worth the somnolent walk to church. The leaves were changing color, and though they weren't as vibrant as what she might have seen in Boston or on the Cape a few weeks ago, the reds and oranges reached into her heart and wrung some of the sadness out. There was a new priest at the altar that morning, and he did not speak of sacrifice. He spoke of hope and perseverance. Using Jesus's parable of the mustard seed from the Gospel of Mark, he explained how even the smallest of efforts could lead to the mightiest of ends, how kindness to our neighbor could be the seed that grows into a great, shady tree that provides shelter to others from the harsh rays of the sun.

Full of his message, she walked to the convent, where she asked to see her sister. It took a while for Rosemary to emerge, and by the time she did, Kick had become chilled sitting at the tables among the browning stems and fallen blooms of the autumnal garden. True to her promise to Jack, Rosie looked slimmer, and almost girlish in her excitement.

"Oh, Kick, thank you for coming!" she said, grasping her sister's hands. "I only wish you'd been here for mass this morning. It was all about Job and his doubting, and how very important it is to stay confident that our Lord in heaven knows what's best for us even if we doubt it at the time."

Kick laughed. "I heard a wonderful sermon this morning, too," she said. "Though with a different message."

"Tell me," said Rosemary, and Kick did. The sisters sat together as the sun warmed their shoulders. It felt so strange, exchanging observations on two sermons, as if they were speaking to their mother or one of their instructors at Sacred Heart in a more innocent time, before England, before the war. As that conversation faded and Kick tried to think of how to bring up the future, Rosemary preempted her.

"Daddy came to see me yesterday."

"He did?" Kick was surprised. She hadn't realized he was in town again; he hadn't rung her yet, and he always did, first thing if he hadn't done so before he boarded his plane.

"He has such wonderful news," Rosemary gushed. "He's found a doctor who can help me . . . relax. Not get so upset all the time. You know I hate it, don't you, Kick? I hate being the way I am, always causing trouble all the time."

"Rosie, darling," Kick said urgently, putting her hands on her sister's. "You're *not* trouble. You get angry, yes. But don't we all? Doesn't Mother? And Daddy's not one to talk. He's been in a *state* ever since getting back from England."

Rosemary shook her head, her clean brown curls bouncing around her face and making her look so young. "It's different for me. You know it is."

Kick opened her mouth to protest again, but couldn't.

"And Daddy says that if I'm good, and follow the doctor's instructions, I'll be able to have what I've always wanted. Children and a home of my own." Rosemary beamed. Kick began sweating in the cool autumn air.

Maybe John was wrong, she thought desperately. *He's not a doctor, after all. Dr. Freeman is the doctor, and Daddy wouldn't do something bad for any of us. And he has spoken with Dr. Freeman personally, while John hasn't. And the* New York Times *praises him to the sky.* Kick wished that she had been the one to hear the sermon about Job that morning.

Drawing in a shaky breath, Kick asked, "Are you sure that this is what *you* want?"

Rosemary nodded her head vigorously.

Kick squeezed her sister's hands and said, "That's what's important, then."

CHAPTER 23

Though it shamed her to even think it, Pearl Harbor was a relief. It gave her something to pray about other than her lost sister, lost love, aimless life, and the profound, insidious anger she was constantly strangling in her throat. On December 7, she'd been out, having a lazy Sunday lunch with John and Patsy, digging into a slice of roast beef with gravy *and* mashed potatoes because she hadn't eaten any breakfast that morning, so hard had it been to get out of bed at all, when all of a sudden someone turned a radio up to its top volume, and the whole place went silent while the announcer stated with disturbing calm that President Roosevelt had just confirmed a Japanese attack on Pearl Harbor in Hawaii.

Thirty seconds before, John and Patsy had been discussing a Christmas party to try to cheer Kick up, though they had no idea why she'd become so sad lately. Kick suspected John might know it had something to do with Rosemary, but he seemed to respect that there were some questions he could not ask. And anyway, he was enjoying some of the benefits of her distress. In the week after she discovered that Rosie's procedure had "not gone as planned," in her father's words, and that she couldn't so much as see her sister—indeed, would not be able to see her for quite some time, while she "recovered"—Kick hadn't been able to sleep a wink.

After watching her nod off at her desk, John had taken her home after a bowl of some sort of Chinese soup whose powers he swore by, and rubbed her shoulders while they sat on her couch. In minutes, she'd fallen into a deep sleep. He must have carried her to her bed, because she woke up ten hours later in her clothes, with only the afghan from the couch covering her. Since then, he'd put her to sleep several times a week, though she'd begun getting into her longest, thickest flannel nightgown in preparation, and she was certain from the occasional sigh of pleasure that escaped his lips that he relished the feel of her skin and bones under his fingers, just below the layer of cotton. She even let him kiss her goodnight before she nodded off.

Now nothing could seem so frivolous as a holiday party, no matter what the reasons. The radio stayed on quite some time as CBS tried to make contact with Honolulu and got only an eerie, crackling silence in reply. The only other sounds were the filling of coffee cups and the sub-dued scrapes and clinks of forks and spoons on plates. Kick and her friends finished their lunch, paid their bill, and then went out into the street and saw smoke billowing into the sky from a building many blocks up the wide, straight conduit of Massachusetts Avenue. "Something's happening at the embassy," John said, his voice rough. They discovered later that the Japanese were busy burning all the papers in their building.

That night, huddled in the tent of her nightgown while John used his thumbs to undo a tight knot in her right shoulder, Kick asked, "Will you sign up?"

"Not yet," he said. "I think I might be able to do more good as a journalist than a soldier, at least for now."

Kick's heart sank at this, and she wasn't sure if it was because John's patriotism and sense of duty were no match for Billy's and all her English friends' when war became inevitable, or because it meant John would be staying in DC, putting her to bed and presenting her with harder and harder choices.

❖❖❖

A week after America at last joined the Allies, Kick received her first letter from Billy in months.

Dearest Kick,

I write to you from Eastbourne, where I am enjoying a few days of leave with Andrew and Debo. It's not the same without you, even now.

News of your country's misfortune has made me think of you ever more intensely. I know you are farther away from Hawaii than you are from London, but somehow knowing there's been an attack on America has made me fear for you as much as I did when you were still here on those fateful days in 1939. They seem like yesterday and one hundred years ago, both, at once. Goodness, I am rambling, becoming more like my father, I fear.

I suppose I just want you to know I am thinking of you. Despite what keeps us apart, I do wish the very best for you and your family. I wouldn't wish war on anyone, let alone someone so dear to me.

Am, as ever, your
Billy

She wondered if Sally was also at Eastbourne. In the next few days, Kick reread his letter so often that the stiff paper began to soften. She wasn't sure how to reply and began to wonder for the first time in a long time if perhaps she could get to England after all . . . could it make a difference as Dinah and her friends had told her it would, despite the finality of Billy's previous letter explaining his engagement? And even if she could get there, what then? Recalling Father O'Flaherty's story about his Protestant friend, she asked herself what the differences really were between the Catholic Church and the Church of England. If she converted, and believed ardently in that conversion, her soul would be safe. Wouldn't it?

But converting would make her another lost daughter. How could she do that to her crippled family?

❖ ❖ ❖

The last Spaghetti Salon before Jack and Kick were to depart for Palm Beach for the holidays doubled as the Christmas party Patsy and John had been discussing when the news of Pearl Harbor broke. The Fields had trimmed a tall tree with white lights and ornaments from their travels, like little straw hats, pottery stars, and carved wooden animals. The living room was fragrant with swags of pine and holly on the mantel and across the doorways. Kick was relieved not to see any mistletoe. In honor of the occasion, Patsy had only added garlic bread, a green salad, and a few precious bottles of champagne to the table. Other guests had brought desserts.

"I'm sorry I'm not much of a cook," Kick told Patsy, "otherwise I'd have brought something sweet."

"Not to worry," said her hostess, who'd lately become her friend. "Tell me all about this trip to Florida."

"There's not much to tell, really," Kick said. "We'll swim, play tennis, and go to mass, and eat the one indulgent meal Mother allows at holidays. Then it'll be time to come home."

"You make the beach sound like a funeral!" Patsy said with surprise.

That's not far off the mark, thought Kick, *since Rosie won't be there, and her joy in Christmas was always infectious.* For Patsy, though, she shrugged and said, "Not a funeral. Just the usual Kennedy thing. Nothing new. Sorry, I know that sounds so jaded."

Patsy eyed Kick a little too long, just long enough to make her feel uncomfortably inspected before her friend said, "You know you can talk to me if anything is troubling you. I don't have to share it with my brother."

Hot tears rushed to Kick's eyes. She just managed to blink them back.

After clearing the dampness in her throat, she replied, "That's nice to know."

When Kick didn't rush in to confess anything, Patsy nudged her and said in a girlish tone as she nodded toward Jack and Inga, "How about those two? Will they survive the time apart?"

Her brother and his lover were sitting hip to hip on the oriental rug, legs crossed with plates of food balanced above their knees. They were laughing with Frank Waldrop and Jimmy Roosevelt.

"You mean the Danish spy?" Kick asked sarcastically, relieved to be able to inject a little levity, referring to the ridiculous speculations about Inga's possible relationship to Hitler.

Patsy laughed. "It's all so absurd, isn't it?"

Kick shook her head. "Absurd," she agreed. "I wish Page had let sleeping dogs lie." Her father's former aide had found a photograph of Inga with Hitler at the 1936 Olympics in the archives of the paper while researching a different article. After consulting with Frank *and* Inga, Page said she felt it was her duty to show the FBI what she had found. Inga always laughed it off, saying that stories about her and Hitler had circulated for years, but always died off because there was no truth to them. The only truth was that she'd posed as a reporter before she actually was one to get a story on Hermann Göring's wedding, which she'd done successfully, thereby launching her very real career in journalism. And since Hitler enjoyed surrounding himself with attractive blond women, especially for photo opportunities during that show of German strength in 1936, he had invited Inga to watch the Olympics with him. "Simple as that," Inga had said, with a pouty shrug of her shoulders.

"What are you two birds twittering about?" John asked, suddenly beside Kick and putting an arm around her shoulders.

Patsy whistled like a chickadee, and Kick added drily, "Tweet, tweet."

"Oh, I see how it is," John said. Then, he whispered to Kick, "Almost ready to go home, sleepy girl?"

Kick felt desire yank at her core. *Why John? Why this temptation? Now?* She didn't want him, not in the way she'd wanted Billy, and yet her body was betraying her. What she wanted from John was base, forbidden, and she felt ashamed at her own weakness. Stealing another glance at Jack and Inga, she flooded with rage. Her faith, her love for her family, stopped her from behaving as they did. But Jack didn't have to choose between loyalty and lust. What would it feel like to give in? she wondered. Where would that path lead her?

Look where it led Rosemary. Kick knew there were big differences between her and her sister, but what they had in common was more important than all of them: they were both Kennedy girls.

Laughing off John's question, Kick said, "I'm not tired at all. Fancy a dance? Last chance of 1941."

As the gramophone filled the room with Paula Kelly's honeyed voice singing "I Know Why (And So Do You)," John took Kick's hand, pulled her close, and began swaying her to the ballad, inspiring other couples to set aside their cups and plates to join them. It was lovely, and Kick wished ardently that it were enough.

❖ ❖ ❖

Kick made Eunice her pet project in Palm Beach. Her sister had become so thin and pale, she looked sick. Her cheeks were drawn, and her arms looked like two sticks joined with a hinge. *I haven't let this happen to me, and I'm not going to let it happen to my next closest sister, either*, she told herself.

"Come now, Euny, even Jack isn't this far gone," Kick said, setting about opening the shades in her sister's room and letting in the light early one morning. Eunice drew in a painful breath and squinched her eyes shut.

"That's because what afflicts Jack is merely physical," said Eunice, pulling the covers up over her head.

"And what afflicts you is . . . ?" Kick asked impatiently.

Eunice sighed with exasperation and threw off the covers with a flourish. "Spiritual, I suppose. *Existential.*"

"I seriously doubt you've done anything to endanger your soul," said Kick impatiently, thinking, *Honestly, you're only a year younger than I am and you sound like an anxious teenager.* She shoved open a second window to let in some fresh air. The room had a funky smell that wouldn't help anyone who needed mending.

"One's soul can suffer from more than just sin, you know."

Kick sat on her sister's unmade bed and looked at her directly. "What's this all about?"

"Where's Rosie?" Eunice said. It was more of a statement than a question.

"Recovering," said Kick, though she knew what her younger sister was really asking. What good would it do to discuss it, though? It wouldn't change a thing.

Eunice shook her head, disgusted. "You're as bad as they are."

"Who?"

"Mother and Daddy."

Kick sighed and looked away. "Listen, Eunice, what can we do? The only thing we can do is pray that Rosie gets better soon."

"Don't you think it's strange that no one is talking about her? It's like she never existed. She's just . . . gone."

Kick had noticed this same thing since arriving the day before. No one had mentioned Rosemary, not even their parents, and she was sure a few of the photographs of her had disappeared from dusted and polished mantels and tables around the house, though Kick hadn't kept any sort of catalog of such pictures, so she couldn't be sure. It was just a sense that she had. Also conspicuous was the door to Rosemary's room, which was closed. It must have been shut completely, curtains closed and all, because even when the sun shone on that side of the house in the afternoon, no light crept into the hall as it did from all the other children's rooms. The only sign that something was amiss was a new chill between her parents, who'd hardly spoken to each other at dinner the night before.

Yes, Kick knew exactly what Eunice was talking about. And she herself was just barely keeping from erupting in fury at her father, *What have you done! I warned you!*

"Let's make a deal," Kick said, putting her hand on her sister's long, outstretched legs. "*We* won't let her go. She'll never be gone for us."

Eunice drew in a shaky breath. "All right," she agreed quietly.

"Now let's go swimming," Kick said.

Every day after that, Kick cajoled Eunice into some outdoor activity that was as far away from their parents as she could get—golf, tennis, sailing, swimming. Their siblings were in silent cahoots, often following the now-eldest sister out the door and into the sun. Eunice even laughed at a joke Joe Jr. made during a round of golf, and Kick took that as a major victory. One morning, she caught Eunice tickling Teddy on the beach. Meanwhile, her mother practically force-fed Eunice piles of potatoes and chicken and roast beef, washed down with tall glasses of whole milk. Eunice complained of stomachaches and refused dessert, but after a week she'd begun to put on weight and her skin began to look healthy again.

On Christmas Eve, her family dressed in something more like their Easter best. The Florida weather was warm and distinctly un-Christmassy, nothing like the wonderful cold she'd have been banishing with roaring fires and hot buttered rums in London. After a feast replete with cookies *and* cakes, to Teddy's utter delight, all the Kennedys piled into a caravan of cars that took them to midnight mass, as was their tradition. They had celebrated Christ's birth in so many places over the years, but this was the one constant. Midnight mass. As a child, Kick had loved getting to break the bedtime rules and gathering with so many others in a warm and brightly lit church, sharing in the exultation of the holiday. Kick searched herself for this same expansive joy as she stood and sang "Silent Night" beneath the arches of the little cathedral, but found only a tightness in her chest, her heart straining to beat.

She looked over at her father as the priest read jubilantly from Luke, "And the angel said to them, 'Do not be afraid; for behold, I bring you good news of great joy which will be for all people; for today in the city of David there has been born a savior,'" and saw Joe Sr. brush something off his cheek, just under his glasses. A tear, Kick had to assume. Then he rubbed his lips together, and Kick thought for sure her father was trying to keep from breaking down in front of the congregation.

This must be his penance. Every time he was reminded of the happiness a child could bring, he would remember his first daughter and the happiness he must have felt when she'd arrived. Her father had lost so much. True, much of it had been his own pigheaded fault. But Kick knew in her heart that her father always did what he thought was right. He'd believed Dr. Freeman could fix Rosemary, just as he'd believed peace was right for England.

For the first time in weeks, Kick felt the knot in her chest loosen. She took a breath and it filled her lungs fully. *Glory to God in the highest. And peace to his people on earth.*

When the whole family had dragged themselves up to their rooms to sleep, Rose knocked quietly on Kick's door. She'd just put on her nightgown and gotten into bed with a book. A few dry, dull biographies had been her replacement for John's back rubs since arriving in Florida. Usually, she succeeded in boring herself to sleep, but twice she'd been awake when the sun rose, then nodded off by the pool in the afternoon.

Still dressed in the red felt suit she'd worn to church, Rose sat on Kick's bed and said, "Thank you for helping Eunice. It's the best Christmas present you could have given the family."

Kick shrugged, embarrassed. "She's my sister," she said. "Of course I want to help."

Rose looked away and pressed a hand to her chest, and Kick could tell that her mother was struggling to contain her emotions just as her father had in church. *They can't comfort each other*, she thought. *How awful.*

Kick listened as the clock in her room ticked, waiting for her mother to respond. At last she stood and looked down at Kick with a sad smile. "I'll miss you when you're gone."

"I'll only be in DC," Kick said, trying to lighten the mood.

"For now," Rose said. "Only for now. Someday you'll be gone, too. I just hope you'll be as happy as you deserve to be."

"Merry Christmas, Mother."

"Merry Christmas, Kathleen, and God bless you."

CHAPTER 24

No sooner had 1942 begun than Kick received a cable from Nancy Astor saying,

```
THE ENGAGEMENT IS OFF LETTER TO FOLLOW
WITH DETAILS PACK YOUR BAGS
```

Kick could scarcely stop herself from picking up the phone and calling Debo for insider family intelligence, but the cost would be prohibitive, and she knew her friend was still grieving the loss of her first baby—a boy she and Andrew had named Mark, who'd arrived prematurely in November when she was sick with E. coli. "There's no joy for me this holiday season. I mope about like a ghost," Debo had written Kick at the end of the year. Calling her friend to gossip seemed in bad taste, even if she would be asking for vital information pertaining to an outcome both girls wanted.

Instead she called Carmel Offie and asked if there was any way to pick up their stalled plans for the press visa to London. Her chances now were surely improved, since she was an honest-to-goodness reporter with regular bylines at the *Times-Herald*, and Frank was about to promote her to arts columnist. Then, toward the end of January, she got to move into

Jack's large apartment at the Dorchester, because he'd been transferred to a desk job in Charleston, South Carolina. The official reason for the move was that the position would be better for his ailing back, but Jack suspected the hand of their father in the sudden move, since the rumors about Inga and Hitler refused to die. "Can't have his younger son involved with a Fascist if his oldest son's gonna be president someday," Jack had remarked wryly over whiskey, cardboard boxes, and suitcases the night before he left.

"I remember when the plan was for *Daddy* to be president someday," Kick replied.

"Some dreams are like those Fabergé eggs," he said. "Gorgeous, but just begging to be shattered."

If his affair with Inga was that kind of dream, Jack certainly didn't treat it that way. Once he left, she was always slipping down to Charleston, though no one was aware of it except Kick and John, who observed, "You Kennedys are just gluttons for punishment."

Meanwhile, Kick settled into her new digs with Betty Coxe, the girlfriend of Jack's friend Chuck Spalding. Betty was a nice girl if a bit aimless—more so than Kick herself, and even Kick had to admit that was something. She was doing a course in the foreign service, but her heart wasn't in it. Kick was relieved that the other girl's presence put a damper on what she'd begun to think of as John's sleep therapy. When Betty was in the apartment, sometimes both girls would get into their nightgowns while John had a nightcap, but the back rub days were over. Until one unusually warm night in late winter, when he up and kissed her on the lips, hard, right at the door to the building.

Wrenching herself away, she looked at him in disbelief. "John!"

"I'm sick of this, Kick. We've been seeing each other for how long now? Six months? More? A man needs a little encouragement if he's going to stick around."

Panic filled her. She longed to say, *Then don't stick around.* But she found she couldn't. Billy hadn't yet written to her himself about the end of his engagement. What if it never worked out? She still needed John and the

Spaghetti Salons and all the established rhythms of her life in Washington to keep her steady and sane. *He's still seeing other girls*, she told herself.

"All right, John, I'll try," she said, and her stomach churned. Leaning up on her tiptoes, she kissed him tenderly on the cheek.

"Was that so hard?" he asked.

She did it again just to avoid answering the question out loud.

At last, a letter from Billy arrived, and she savored every word.

Dearest Kick,

I hope it isn't presumptuous of me to use "dearest," for I fear I have brutally abused my own affection for you, and yours for me. I cling to the hope that you care for me even a tiny fraction of the amount I still care for you. The engagement to Sally was a terrible mistake. I won't trouble you with my more morose thoughts on life and death and war and marriage and children, but suffice it to say that the tragedies of Pearl Harbor and my nephew's premature death wrenched me out of a fog. It wasn't fair to Sally to embark on a life with her when those days at the end of 1941 made me want to hold you and not her. Even if you and I cannot find a way to be together, perhaps someday I will find someone else who brings me as much pleasure as you once did. If I'm lucky.

And if I'm lucky, I'll soon have a chance to stand with my countrymen and punish the Huns for what they have done to us and their own people. Surely the fact that England remains strong in the face of the Blitz and countless other onslaughts proves we are not the decadent people your brother Jack once derided us as. I am glad America will have a chance to prove itself soon as well. It brings me joy that our two countries now stand together in this war, even if you and I cannot.

With love,
Billy

After a few drafts, this time she came up with a reply that felt just honest and brave enough, though she was not at all ready to use the word *love* yet, not on paper.

Dearest Billy,

> *You are not presumptuous in the slightest. I'll admit to being disappointed by your engagement to Sally, particularly since I have been putting off my own suitors because the memory of you makes them pale in comparison. There, I've said it. I am glad, very glad, of your renewed bachelorhood. I suppose it's no use our talking about the religion question unless we can first figure out the problem of my being an ocean away.*
>
> *But I have news along those lines as well. Kathleen Kennedy is now the byline for the Times-Herald's arts column! I see all the movies and plays that come out, and since my boss doesn't want to demote me back to secretary (he has a blonder model now), he doesn't mind if I sleep in and type my stories at home after I've been out late reviewing something for the paper. There've been some real humdingers. Wait till you see Carole Lombard and Jack Benny in To Be or Not to Be.*
>
> *I have put in motion plans to use my skills on your fair island. I've been asking around, and things are looking promising for me to lay my hands on a press visa. What would you say to that? I'd love to see you and Andy, and Debo and Sissy and David and Bertrand and everyone again. I miss everyone every day. A piece of my heart got left behind in 1939, and I fear I shall never be fully happy till I am reunited with it.*
>
> > *With greatest affection,*
> > *Kick*

A week later, she received a telegram:

```
WHAT WOULD I SAY SOUNDS GRAND JUST SAY WHEN
LOVE BILLY
```

Instead of putting it into her scrapbook, Kick set the telegram in the drawer of the bedside table, so she could read it every night before bed. Then, she did what she was least skilled at in all the world: wait. She waited for answers, and she wrote and wrote and wrote for the paper, hoping that something she'd written might get noticed by the right person. She developed a favorite fantasy, in which she was sitting at her desk at the *Times-Herald* completing another review when the phone rang.

"Kathleen Kennedy?" an unfamiliar Etonian voice would say.

"Speaking," she'd say, palms beginning to sweat in anticipation.

"This is Tony Wilson of the *London Observer*, and I just spoke with my old chum Arthur Krock. Seems you're brave enough to offer your skills in the service of West End theater?"

"Indeed I am!"

"Excellent, excellent. Then let's work out some details . . ."

Of course, she knew the call wouldn't go *exactly* like that, but surely it was close enough. The point was, all her work would finally be getting her somewhere in life. And not just somewhere, but exactly where she wanted to be.

Her fights with John ratcheted up during those weeks, which she found she relished.

"Why would you want to go there?" he demanded irritably. She'd just revealed her plan to live and write in England over lunch at Hot Shoppes.

"Because it's the only place on earth I've ever truly loved."

"I thought you weren't capable of love."

"Shows how much you know."

"Why would someone like you, made and minted in America, want to go to some sinking island and drink tea?"

"It's excellent tea," she joked. She was determined not to let him get to her.

"This is just like your religion," he said. "It's all nostalgia for some bygone age."

"What's wrong with nostalgia? If that is what it is, and I'm not conceding it is."

"If artists were content with nostalgia, we wouldn't have Picasso. Or Matisse. Or that guy Mondrian I saw on exhibit in New York."

"Mondrian?" Kick laughed. She'd seen that exhibit, too, on her last trip to Manhattan. You couldn't not see it, since everyone was talking about it. "I suppose he's very forward thinking," she said, "but I'd rather have a Turner hanging in my home. Or a Van Dyck or a Gainsborough. And anyway, respecting and appreciating the past doesn't have to keep you from moving into the future, you know."

"That *could* be true, but for many people—you included, I'd argue— nostalgia is much more than a respect for the past. It's a yearning for things to be the way they were. Like *Gone with the Wind*."

"Oh goodness, not this again."

"It was rot, and you know it. All that glorification of slavery. *Yessum* this and *yessum* that. Like the negroes weren't risking their lives to *escape* Tara. In real life, that is."

"I never disputed that," Kick replied, feeling prickly and thrilled like she often did in debate with John. "I only defended the movie for artistic reasons."

"And you *are* the film critic," he said sarcastically. "I'm just glad it came out in thirty-nine, before you had a chance to review it in print."

"Now, now, no reason to get personal."

"But it's always personal with us, isn't it?" His face went soft with this question.

"Partly," she admitted.

"Don't go," he said, his voice low and hoarse.

"I'm not gone yet."

"I'll have to find a way to convince you, then."

Was it so wrong that she enjoyed his attempts? What if Billy wasn't waiting for her, pining? Debo's last letter mentioned Sally still hanging around. At least Kick now had a job on par with Sally's, so that nagging feeling of being inadequate was less than it had been before; she might not have been breaking codes in some top-secret bunker, but she was helping to shape public opinion about movies and plays. And everyone—private citizens and soldiers alike—were going in droves to those distractions like never before.

❧ ❧ ❧

Then everything began to turn sour. First, Jack broke it off with Inga: finally and really and officially. The Monday morning after one of her weekend jaunts down to South Carolina, Inga met Kick at the front entry of the Dorchester so they could walk to work; she looked puffy in the face, especially around the eyes.

"Allergic to all these lovely blooming trees?" Kick had chirped at her friend, not realizing anything was wrong. After all, the cherry and apple blossoms had burst into pink and white life, hovering over multicolored tulips and sunny daffodils all around the city. A number of Patsy's guests had been complaining of itchy eyes because of the springtime pollens.

"Jack and I are . . . no longer," Inga replied, her voice hoarse and damp.

"Oh, Inga," Kick sighed, taking a step forward to wrap her arms around her friend.

But Inga backed up and said, "No, no, not before work. Or I'll cry again. Let's talk about the Nazis instead."

Kick nodded and obliged. Later that week, Inga had wept and ranted at Kick's kitchen table close to midnight, after hours of champagne and dancing. "This is where it all began, you know," Inga said, her eyes pooling as she spoke the words and pointed to the couch. "Though when we met, your brother was too timid to seduce *me*."

Kick considered the implications of this statement. A score of other nights rushed up from her memory to the front of her mind—nights on which she was sure Jack himself had been the seducer. But then, things with Inga had always been different. Perhaps he had been unsure enough of his advantage with this older, glamorous beauty not to make the first move. Maybe he'd been besotted from the beginning. Which made it all the more stunning that he'd broken up with her.

Unsure how to respond, Kick sat down at the table with Inga and said, "I'm sorry it had to end."

"The Kennedy men," Inga seethed. "I should have known that I would be a passing fancy to your brother."

"To be honest," Kick ventured, "I always figured it was the other way around. I've never seen Jack so smitten, and you've been married twice, after all. Also, he kept seeing you even after he got transferred."

"Your father hadn't made his point clear enough with the transfer."

"His point?"

"That some women are for fun, and others for marriage."

And I know which kind I am, Kick immediately thought with both relief and pride, but also the familiar envy. The freedom Inga enjoyed, to be with whomever she chose, was too often the right of men. Part of Kick wondered what it would be like to be as independent as Inga, and felt indignant that women in general were not allowed to do what they wanted, but most of her was happier being a precious, wrapped little box, waiting to be given to the right man. It would save her the kind of acute heartache her friend was suffering right now.

Not long after that, Kick received a letter from Jack that opened, "After reading the papers, I would advise strongly against any voyages to England to marry any Englishman. For I have come to the reluctant conclusion that it has come time to write the obituary of the British Empire."

Oh for crying out loud, Kick thought angrily at the letter. *Don't take your heartache out on me.* But a moment later, she swallowed a rising lump in her throat. Jack's letter droned on about the end of England as she loved it, sounding more and more like their father, who'd been spewing similar nonsense about the end of democracy and greatness in England ever since being forced off the island. With her father, she'd put it down to understandable sour grapes, and blamed Roosevelt and Churchill, who'd gone around him one too many times. How was it possible for Jack to side with their father so soon after that same father had destroyed his happiness with Inga?

Being a Kennedy always meant keeping your own heart private, revealed to only a few. The rest was a performance. But why should Jack pretend with her, his favorite sister?

Unless he wasn't performing anymore.

CHAPTER 25

For five glorious days, Kick thought she might be in London by mid-June. She even wrote Billy to tell him. Frank had gotten wind of a research position at the London *Times* for someone to gather facts and information for the new gossip columnist on staff. But then the position was filled by some other girl, one of the many young society women who'd been cheated out of a debutante ball by the war. Arthur Krock told her father that his contacts said there were too many foreign correspondents in London already, and reporters were being shipped out; no one new was being brought in. While her letter to Billy relaying this terrible news was en route across the ocean, she received a telegram from him:

> LETTER JUST ARRIVED WONDERFUL NEWS GET
> LEAVE JUNE 22 LONGING TO SEE YOU WRITING
> LOVE BILLY HARTINGTON

She felt doomed. She prayed and prayed—in church, on her knees by her bed at night—asking for guidance and help. *Virgin Mother, please hear my prayer. I don't know what else to do. There must be another way. Show me that way—soon!*

She missed Rosemary, and prayed for her, too, that she might be back for Easter, or at least next Christmas. But then Easter came and went and again her parents didn't mention Rosie. Not even during the church egg hunt, which used to be her sister's favorite event; she always volunteered to help hide the eggs and found such glee in giving the five-year-olds hints.

Then the men around her began leaving to fight. No more desk posts. The trainings were finishing up. It was time for real combat. Joe Jr. was itching to use his new pilot license to "bomb some Japs," and Jack, whose back was better, would be leaving soon for Chicago to learn to captain a torpedo boat. Even John enlisted in the navy. The son of an old friend of the family, George Mead, had quite a send-off party at his family's estate in South Carolina before he departed with his marine unit for the Solomon Islands. Kick went with her roommate Betty, and Jack was there, too. Nancy Astor made a surprise appearance. She'd been in Virginia visiting family, and when she'd heard that some of her "favorite young Americans" would be congregating, she decided to book a first-class ticket and say hello. Nancy was like a mirage, and Kick fell on her in a hysterical hug as if she were a chimerical oasis in a desert. "You're here! How did you get here? Why didn't you warn me?"

"You have to leave me some surprises in life, Kick," Nancy said with a wag of her finger and another embrace. "Anyway, the important questions don't concern me; they concern you. When are you coming back *home*, my dear? To London? Anglo-American relations need to be repaired, no matter what the papers say now that we're so-called allies. There's too much distrust, and I don't blame the English for it. Roosevelt took too long to get into the war. There was so much hope after—forgive me, Kick—your father left his post, and it still it took Pearl Harbor to galvanize the country."

"You won't hear any disagreements from me," said Kick, though she did marvel a bit at Nancy's selective memory—for a long time she, too, had been against war just like Joe Kennedy.

"What England needs is to remember why they loved the Kennedys, and by extension, America. Who better to make that case than you?"

Kick blushed, and felt embarrassed by Nancy's compliments even though she could have listened to them all day. It had been ages since anyone had flattered her.

"And there is the matter of a certain marquess," Nancy said, hissing the *ss* in *marquess*, "who will make another Bachelor Duke of Devonshire if you don't hurry back."

"I've tried!" Kick blurted out, all the desperation and disappointment of three years burbling up in her. "I tried to get over as a reporter. When I first came back to America, I looked into training as a nurse, but they weren't taking American nurses abroad. England isn't letting anyone in!"

"You'll have to try harder," said Nancy firmly. "The Kennedys are nothing if not resourceful. Leave no stone unturned."

Kick nodded, frowning.

Seeing how distraught her young companion had become, Nancy put her bejeweled arm around Kick's body and gripped her shoulder. "You'll figure it out," she said. "Aunt Nancy has complete confidence in you."

I wish I still had some in myself.

❖ ❖ ❖

Almost as soon as he'd left, George was killed. News of the bullet reached Kick one sweltering August morning as she sat in front of the desk fan Inga had left for her before running off to New York City with a new beau, an obvious rebound from the nearly simultaneous ends of her relationship with Jack and her marriage to Paul Fejos.

"Oh, Kathleen," her mother said on the other end of the line, "I'm sorry to bother you at work, but I thought you would want to hear the news from family first, before it came over the press wire or something."

"What is it?" Impossibly, Kick began to perspire more. *Was someone hurt? If it was Jack or Joe Jr., my mother would be sobbing—wouldn't she? Is it someone from England? Billy?!*

"It's George Mead. He's been killed in action."

Kick released the breath she'd been holding. "George? Oh no, his poor parents." Kick recalled their proud faces, toasting their brave son with that lovely, fizzy champagne just a few months before. "Poor George," she said quietly. It felt like something was clutching her heart in her chest. It wasn't unlike the feeling she'd had on the beach in France when her mother told her they would be leaving not just their vacation but Europe altogether. When she'd raced back to London to see Billy one last time.

"Are you all right, darling?" Rose asked.

A tear slipped down Kick's cheek and joined the beads of sweat on her chin.

"I'm sad, Mother. But thank you for calling to tell me."

"I just know how important it is to get some kinds of news from loved ones. Though of course I know how much you love your work. You know, I once wanted to be a writer."

"That must be where I get it, then. Any talent I have, I mean."

"Thank you for saying that." Rose heaved a sigh on the other end of the line. "I grew up in the wrong era, I suppose."

"It's not too late, Mother, you know. You could start writing things for the Catholic papers in Boston."

"No, no. Your father would never approve."

Maybe George's death had loosened her tongue, or maybe it was the months away from home, or the influence of her debates with John White, but Kick said, "Mother, you *can* do things Daddy doesn't approve of. It would be good for your other daughters to see you being a little more . . . independent. Your sons, too, for that matter." She knew that *independent* was the wrong word, because of course her mother did plenty of things without her father, completely on her own. *Rebellious* would have been a more appropriate word, but it wasn't one she could quite apply to her mother, even in the form of a wish. Still, Kick had a feeling her mother knew what she'd really meant.

"We all have our roles to play, darling. God has not revealed that to be mine. I'll be praying for the Meads."

"So will I," Kick said. And she did pray, earnestly, though it did little to relieve her sense of imbalance and apprehension about nearly everything swirling in her mind—Billy, John, her parents, Rosemary, the war,

England, her friends nearby and far away, the newspaper. *What is my role? What part should I play?* Her knees became bruised from the pews she knelt upon asking these questions, over and over.

She wrote a maudlin letter to Father O'Flaherty about her predicament, her pining for England and Billy, and now her deep sadness about the death of an old family friend. "Some lives are short," she wrote, "and I increasingly feel that it's essential to live the life it's in one's soul to live." She posted it on her way to the airport, where she boarded a plane and flew up to New York City to see John, where he was stationed at the Brooklyn Navy Yard, awaiting orders to go abroad. She wasn't entirely sure why she was going, except that John had become a habit that was impossible to break. She'd missed a few planned visits with him because she was sick or feeling lazy, but that late-summer day she felt lonelier than ever, and so she went.

"I still can't believe you finally decided to sign up," she said to him as they lunched in a tiny restaurant in Chinatown that served steaming, fragrant bowls of soup with long white noodles she pulled out with chopsticks.

"Better than waiting for them to draft me," he said.

"How chivalrous of you," she said, struck again by the profound difference between him and Billy. And yet, she liked sitting with him in this little noodle shop. John was adventurous. She could imagine running to catch a train in Bangkok or Buenos Aires with John, but not with Billy.

"I'm nothing if not a gentleman," said John with a sly laugh.

The rest of the weekend was wonderful, in a fragile, ephemeral way. In the late-summer heat, the air shimmered and swayed up from the city's sidewalks, and the cumulative noise from the efforts of thousands of burdened feet and blaring taxi horns obliterated any other sound from Kick's head. She was one hundred percent present for once, not imagining herself somewhere else, with someone else. Even Jones Beach, where they went to cool off, vibrated with life—glistening, coconut-scented oils on the backs and bellies of countless men and women, the smoke and smell of grilled hot dogs, men with guitars strumming melodies, children screeching with delight or crying from exhaustion. When Kick and John found a space just barely large enough for one beach towel, she stripped off the sundress she wore over her most modest bathing costume, a navy one-piece that tied at the nape of her neck and went low on her hips. John dropped his linen shirt on her dress, and the two of them chased each other to the water, dodging inflated balls and buckets full of beer and soda and melted ice as they ran.

The water was warm but still refreshing, and Kick enjoyed splashing around with John and showing off the clean, fine strokes she'd perfected over many summers at Hyannis Port. She laughed when he couldn't catch up.

"You better work on your open-water swimming in case you get sent west. Wouldn't want you to drown," she said.

"Aw, I'm flattered you're worried about me," he replied, pulling her close. His feet were anchored in the soft sand, but since she was so much shorter, her feet dangled in the water. She put her hands on his large shoulders and felt the heat from the sun that had penetrated his skin. He was closer to her now than any man had been since Billy, and even Billy she'd never seen or touched without his shirt on. John pulled her body to his, and the movement toward him was so powerful and natural, she didn't pull away. So she was all the more surprised when he put his other arm under her legs and then playfully threw her with a huge splash, shouting, "Bet you can't do *that!*"

Later, sitting cross-legged on their towel, after sating their hunger with hot dogs loaded with relish and mustard and ketchup washed down with a lukewarm Coca-Cola, John leaned over and kissed Kick. Fully, with his lips open. For a second, she closed her eyes and parted her own lips as well, but just as his tongue gently grazed her teeth, she pulled back and froze. "John!" she said, mortified that it sounded more like a whine than a warning.

"I can't help it," he said. "I love you, Kick."

"I love you, too," she said. The words came quickly, because she supposed they were true in a manner of speaking, but also because she knew he would be gone soon. And she didn't want to spoil the weekend with the argument that would surely ensue if she rebuked him. She didn't have the strength for that fight.

With a ridiculous smile, he leaned over and kissed her once more, this time on the cheek. Her gamble had worked like a charm. Apparently satisfied with her words, he made do with holding her hand and stealing one more real kiss the rest of the weekend. Before she left for Washington, they stopped in to see Inga in her new apartment, where she lived with her boyfriend Nils Block, who was so much Jack's opposite in everything from his arrogant demeanor to his black hair that it was painfully obvious she was running from the memory of her former lover. Unsuccessfully. After three gin and tonics, Inga had gotten Kick alone in the tiny, stuffy kitchen, and said, "How's Jack? I miss him terribly."

"He's fine," Kick said, thinking it best to remain vague. "He's in Chicago with the navy."

"I still love him," Inga said in a strangled tone.

Kick put an arm around her friend. "He loves you, too," she said, amazed at the way that word—*love*—was falling from her tongue that weekend.

"He loves his *duty* more," Inga said, the old bitterness creeping back in.

From the other room, John and Nils laughed the languid laugh of men who've drunk too much cold beer on a hot summer afternoon. Inga stiffened and brushed the tears from her cheek with perfectly lacquered fingertips, straightened up, then joined the men and tried to pretend that nothing had ever happened.

❖ ❖ ❖

Her first night back at the Dorchester, Kick found herself lying awake at one in the morning, recalling in minute detail every second of her weekend with John, especially the kiss and the proclamation of love.

What was I thinking?

Though she'd said an entire rosary and begged God and the Virgin for peace, her sheets were wet with nervous sweat, and her stomach was perilously close to rejecting the supper of saltines, peanut butter, and milk she'd consumed while standing at the kitchen counter after her late-night return.

She rolled over on her side, exposing her clammy back to the night air, and opened the little drawer of her nightstand, then took out the soft, worn telegram.

```
WHAT WOULD I SAY SOUNDS GRAND JUST SAY WHEN
LOVE BILLY
```

Please wait. I'll figure it out. Just, please. Wait.

Recalling the magnetic sensation of John's body in the salty beach water, the effect it had on her despite everything, she was certain that only physical proximity could mediate the differences between her and Billy. Four hundred years of history could not be addressed in letters. And she didn't have much time left, especially when he was so keen to fight.

She vowed to make getting back to England her sole purpose in life. She'd allowed herself to be detained and distracted too long. It was time.

WINTER 1941

He and Andrew didn't talk much. Never had. They were thick as thieves, of course, in cahoots, mates for life and all that, always in opposition to the same foes—their father, school, drudgery. If there was ever a tree to climb or a relation to trick, it was Andrew who led the charge and Billy who calculated the risk. But once his brother finally decided to marry Debo, his allegiances changed. She calculated his risks now, and he—amazingly but gladly—submitted.

For a long time this turn of events made Billy feel lonely and angry. Coming back from France, licking the wounds inflicted by the Huns, it had almost destroyed him to see his little brother so rewarded with beautiful, thoughtful Debo. Kick's friend. They'd been a tremendous foursome, and Billy hated the fact that Kick's absence had not diminished them as it had him.

When their first son died almost as soon as he was born, Andrew endured a grief of which Billy wouldn't have thought his devil-may-care brother capable. He watched as Andrew and Debo cared for each other in handkerchiefs and cups of tea and gentle teasing, totally united in their sorrow and commitment to not letting it undo them entirely.

A month after it happened, Billy was out with Sally in London. Pearl

Harbor had been bombed the week before, and Christmas was also upon them. Billy could never escape the memory of the one youthful holiday season he'd spent with Kick and the snow-globe-like perfection of it.

They were at the Ritz, already on their second bottle. He drank much more with Sally than he ever had with Kick. She offered him a cigarette from her varnished fingertips, and he took it though he didn't really enjoy smoking. It was more a way to keep his hands and mouth occupied.

"How's Andrew holding up?" Sally asked as she blew a puff of smoke so that it just grazed his right temple, a maneuver that until recently had made him stiff with desire from head to toe. She was a beautiful girl, after all. And she meant well. They'd had some real fun together these last months.

But he looked at her next to him that night, in her black evening dress and blond locks and the velvety skin that had given him feverish dreams just a few months before, and he realized that he couldn't see the two of them surviving what Andrew and Debo appeared to be surviving.

"He seems to be coming out of the fog," Billy replied.

"Good." Sally nodded. "That has to be the first step."

Toward what, Billy still couldn't see. But he intended to find out.

PART 4

◈ ◈ ◈

SUMMER 1943

CHAPTER 26

"Sissy!" Kick cried, flinging herself into her friend's arms as soon as she opened the door of the Edwardian town house where she lived with David and their two children.

"Kick? Could that really be you?" Sissy said, blinking and staring at her American friend as if she were a ghost or some other conjured apparition.

"It is! I'm here with the Red Cross!" Kick gestured to her knee-length brown uniform, then to the supplies sitting in a haphazard heap on the pavement behind her. It had all been so organized when she boarded the *Queen Mary* in New York that obscenely hot morning a week before—now the tin helmet, the canteen and first aid kit, the mackintosh and woolen uniforms, the gas mask, and so many other indicators of her changed circumstances were all bundled together as best she could bundle them for the tube ride from St. Pancras station.

"Goodness! Well, come in already," said Sissy, calling for their one servant to come and help with Kick's luggage.

"The children are napping," Sissy explained as she set about making a pot of tea in her large, subterranean kitchen. Kick marveled at her friend's efficiency in boiling the water in a kettle on the enormous iron stove, steeping the tea in the incongruously dainty china teapot, and carrying it with two cups, milk, and sugar on a tray out the back steps to the little garden. Four years ago, someone like Sissy never would have performed these tasks herself.

"Can I help?" Kick asked.

"Grab that tin of biscuits," Sissy said, nodding at a metal McVitie's box on the disorderly kitchen table, where baby bottles, spilled milk, and crusts of bread lay all about.

Outside, the late-June sun shone down on them from a clear blue sky. Sissy's roses and hollyhocks were in full bloom, and hungry bumblebees buzzed from one pink blossom to another.

"So!" Sissy said as she poured tea into their cups. "Am I the first to know of your return?"

"You are indeed," said Kick. Sissy was of course one of her dearest friends, but this had also been a strategic choice. Debo was away in the north to be close to Andrew while he trained with his regiment, and Kick needed to be in London while she waited for her assignment from the Red Cross. Also, she was eager to be in the company of her one good friend in London who was also Catholic, who'd successfully navigated the problems Kick assumed—*hoped*—she'd soon be facing with Billy.

"I'm honored," said Sissy. "David's away, I'm afraid. Flight training in Hatfield. But I'm sure I can convince him to come visit. I'll tell him I have the most lovely surprise waiting for him."

"I hope I'm a lovely surprise. I know the Kennedy name isn't the most popular in England these days."

"Everyone knows you're not your father, Kick. I wouldn't worry," Sissy said with a wave of her hand. "And I know at least one other Englishman who will be thrilled to hear of your return."

Kick blushed. "I hope so," she said. "I thought I'd get over here a year ago with the press, and I wrote him about it right away, but then both of us were so let down when it didn't work out. I didn't want to get anyone's hopes up again until I was actually standing here. At last."

"Yes," said Sissy, "I heard something about that disappointment. But at least it didn't drive Billy back to Sally. You were wise this time." Then, clapping her hands with excitement, she changed the subject. "Now, tell me all about this work you've come over to do! As the mother of two young children without the sort of help mothers had in *the old days*, I have to live vicariously through my young single friends. Will you be one of the girls making donuts on those lorries that go around to the American bases?"

Kick laughed, and explained that no, thankfully, she would not be a Clubmobiler. "I don't think I could manage being out on the road all day like that." Instead, she would be a Red Cross girl at one of the clubs, "hopefully in London," she said with both sets of middle and index fingers crossed. "I'll still be making donuts and coffee, I'm sure, and also dancing and playing gin rummy, and reading letters from home, and that sort of thing. Keeping morale up, and generally making the boys feel like the girls from home appreciate all the sacrifices they're making to be here, in harm's way." She didn't add that while she'd convinced Page Huidekoper to sign the waiver swearing that Kick wasn't signing up with the Red Cross in order to reunite with a loved one, she had certainly made her preference to be stationed in London known on the other forms. She didn't feel she could press the point without arousing suspicion, but she was on pins and needles waiting and hoping.

She'd even dropped the hint to her father before she left that it would be useful for the family if she were stationed in London. At lunch in Washington before she left for training in Virginia, he'd told her, "I'm proud that you're doing this, you know. Even though I ruined my own future to keep you kids *out* of war, now that it's here, I feel it's our duty to do what we can. I'm very glad you're going to support American troops, though of course I know you'll be spending just as much time with your old friends."

"I want to bring everyone together, Daddy. You taught me that that's possible. And I want people to think well of the Kennedys again."

Joe smiled fleetingly. "If anyone can do that, it's you, Kick."

"I'm glad you feel that way," she said, then added, "But of course, I can't really do that from some backwater in the country. Which is why I'm so hoping to be in London."

"I'm sure it will work out," he said, and her heart fluttered at this assurance. "But your mother will be heartbroken you're leaving."

She had avoided speaking with her mother about any of her plans, not wanting to argue. "You'll break it to her gently, won't you?" Kick asked her father in as sweet a tone as she could muster, knowing in the churning floor of her stomach that she was using her father's affection for her, and his remorse about Rosemary, to her advantage. But she'd made herself the promise, and once she was close to her goal of getting back to London, and Billy, she was going to play every card she had.

❖ ❖ ❖

Her other English friends proved as excited about her return as Sissy, and Kick collected their expressions of ecstatic surprise like a child picking up shells on a beach. She only wished she could have seen Billy's face when he read the telegram she sent from Boofie and Fiona Gore's charming brick house in Kings Langley, just outside London in Hertfordshire, where she spent a lazy afternoon with Sissy and the children.

GUESS WHERE I AM BOOFIE AND FIONA SEND
THEIR LOVE KICK

His reply hours later was almost as good as seeing his face.

OVERJOYED AND IN SHOCK WILL GET LEAVE AS
SOON AS POSSIBLE LOVE BILLY

In her first days back, while she continued waiting on the Red Cross, and on news of Billy's leave, she spent as much time catching up with friends as possible. Debo was in Yorkshire with her newborn Emma, but promised to get down to London as soon as she could, and so Kick passed some lovely hours with Jane and Sissy and Fiona Gore during the day, then adding Bertrand, David, and Boofie in the evening. Bertrand's greeting, "I see you had the good sense to ignore my advice when it came down to it," almost made her weep with relief. Instead, she laughed so hard inside his tight embrace, the tears that came to her eyes seemed an extension of her happiness.

She took long walks to soak up as much of London as her pores could absorb, and was surprised to find her city much as it had been four years before. The wreckage and rubble photographed for the papers after the Blitz had been cleared away in the last two years. The West End was virtually untouched anyway, and most of what she saw looked the same except for the fact that everything closed earlier and there was a blackout every night. St. Paul's and Westminster Abbey and Brompton Oratory all looked nearly as they had before the bombs fell, though the neighborhood around St. Paul's had been decimated, and so the church looked eerily alone with the wreckage carted away and no new buildings yet to replace the old; some stood partially opened like wounds. But everyone in town walked through the empty space, past the gaping structures, with such a sense of purpose and calm, it was impossible not to follow their lead. If the locals weren't going to let such sights get to them, neither was she. St. Mary's church, too, was still standing, but it didn't pull Kick in as strongly as it had without her favorite priest presiding over it. She wrote to Father O'Flaherty of how much she missed him, and how much she hoped God might bring them together soon.

Taxis were still difficult to come by, but the fear that had haunted the city in 1939 had gone. There had been so many air-raid drills, no one paid attention to them anymore. Kick reveled in this jaded English nonchalance. The one thing everyone allowed themselves to lament was the cruel fate of dessert because of the limited butter and sugar, and she made a note to herself to ask for candy from home. Though alcohol was harder to come by and a bottle of champagne was precious because so little was getting out of France or making it across the channel, there was plenty of local ale and spirits to be had, and no one was sober after eleven p.m. when the pubs closed. She even had steak for dinner at the Gargoyle Club after an honest-to-goodness cocktail at the Savoy, where she encountered her first round of anti-Kennedyism in the form of Aneurin Bevan, MP for Wales, who told her that her father was a reactionary Catholic, typical of the American State Department. But when Kick asked him to name even one more typical reactionary, he couldn't.

Her first night back at the 400 on July 5, she was almost glad Billy wasn't there with her because she might actually have expired from the rapture, or at the very least made an emotional fool of herself in front of him. Free from the rules and prohibitions imposed by her parents, truly independent in London for the first time in her life, she felt relief and joy bubble up inside her like the champagne fountains of the prewar years. She felt positively effervescent.

"Golly," said Johnny Williams, her navy escort that evening. "I've never seen a girl dance like you, Miss Kennedy." Admiral Stark's fresh-faced blond aide refused to call her Kick despite the many times she'd corrected him that evening, starting with their dinner at Quaglino's. She'd met Johnny at the Red Cross offices a few days before; he was there with Admiral Stark himself, the commander of the entire United States Navy in Europe. "Betty" Stark was a tall, severe-looking man with a head of white hair, but as soon as he smiled at you, you knew he'd be fun at a party. He'd introduced himself to Kick right away, saying with a hearty handshake, "I knew your father years ago when he was in Washington with the SEC. He's a good man. Misguided much of the time, but a good man."

"I completely agree, Admiral," said Kick, which he found amusing.

Then he'd introduced his aide, saying, "Johnny here's been sampling the city's many delights, and would be glad to escort you around safely. You're not just any Red Cross girl, after all."

"Shhhhh," breathed Kick with a finger to her lips. "I don't want anyone to think I'm asking for special treatment."

The 400 and the streets around it looked and felt the same as they had before the war, though she knew there had been bombings right nearby. A few years before, Billy had written to her about being trapped inside for a few hours starting around two in the morning, "the only time the music's ever stopped there, God bless it." The music had long since picked back up, and that night the jazz orchestra was blaring all the most popular tunes, like "Stormy Weather" and "Pistol Packin' Mama." They had a front man who was a dead ringer for Bing Crosby, with his dark good looks and smooth voice. No one was dancing the Big Apple anymore, and Kick pined for that toward the end of all her jitterbugging and jiving. But she wasn't surprised—she hadn't joined in one of those euphoric circles in quite some time, even in the States. The war had made it feel insincere somehow, and it had faded from fashion.

It was a good thing she didn't have to work the earlier shift, since she didn't fall into bed until five in the morning, with her feet and head throbbing. It was almost as if she'd tried to cram four years of dancing into one night.

Thus far, the only blight on her homecoming had been a ranting letter from John White, written from California, where he was stationed with the navy, saying what a fool she was for going to England and chasing after some lord who'd never have her, and when would she finally learn her place? *That's rich*, she thought, after *his* arrogance had gotten him clamped into prison for taking pictures of British destroyers while he'd been stationed in Ireland. Her final reply to him had included the condom he'd set on her desk at the start of her Washington adventure; she'd unrolled it and put a note inside saying, "Full of sound and fury, signifying nothing."

At least the letters from her mother had been cordial, full of the usual news about friends and family and shopping and plays and church. Once Kick had finally fessed up and told her mother that she was going to London with the Red Cross, Rose had pursed her lips and looked down at her hands. Then she'd looked at Kick and said, to her daughter's astonishment, "I'm going to miss you. I hope . . . I hope you find what you're looking for. But remember that if you don't, I'll always be here, as will God."

❧ ❧ ❧

Before meeting Debo—at last!—at Fortnum's for lunch, she discovered that she was to be placed at the Hans Crescent Club, right around the corner from Harrods in her old neighborhood. Fourteen Prince's Gate would be a five-minute walk from her new home. The club itself was a gloomy, severe Victorian building, a former hotel, but that concern faded completely in light of her dearest wish being granted: a post in London, and in Knightsbridge at that!

Thank you, Daddy, she thought gleefully. *And thank you, Lord Father*, she added.

"Debo!" she exclaimed as she hugged her dear friend, not caring how loud she was in the subdued atmosphere of Fortnum & Mason. "I feel like my homecoming is complete now that I'm here with you, just like the old days."

Despite having delivered a healthy baby three months before, Debo looked as lithe and lovely as ever. "Where's little Emma?" Kick asked. "I thought maybe she'd join us."

"I forced her to leave the tyke with the nurse, so she could enjoy herself," said Fiona, casting a stern eye at Debo, who sighed.

"I miss her," she said forlornly.

Kick knew, but didn't want to mention at such an otherwise happy moment, that she understood perfectly why Debo should feel that way about her new baby daughter after having lost her first child. Instead she hugged her friend again, this time more gently, rubbing a few consoling circles on her back. When she pulled away, she suggested some of their old favorites: "Darjeeling and currant scones, and some of those funny little ham sandwiches?" Debo's eyes went shiny with tears. But she valiantly blinked them back and replied, "What else? Though I suspect it'll be tinned ham today."

Though it was indeed tinned ham in their sandwiches, and there was no little pot of butter served alongside the scones, it was all delicious and Debo relaxed with every bite.

"I start work tomorrow," Kick said with an excited smile.

"You sound so plucky about it," Fiona observed, "and all you're doing is serving coffee and dancing with a lot of GIs."

Debo laughed and said, "Surely you know the *real* reason she's over here."

"I am here to do my patriotic duty," said Kick solemnly with a hand on her heart, "and if anyone asks you, I hope you'll tell them the same or I'll be shipped back to New York on the first boat!"

"Oh, my lips are sealed," Debo said, pretending to lock up her pale lips.

"Besides," continued Kick, looking at Fiona, "not everyone can be an artist *and* a speedboat racer."

Fiona waved her hand, dismissing Kick's compliment. "The war makes boating impossible," Fiona said. "All waters are dangerous."

"It won't be forever," said Kick with conviction. "And you've had more time to devote to your paintings, which are gorgeous." Fiona's latest project was a series of outdoor watercolors of her garden in Hempstead, which Kick had seen a few days before. The pictures were as lush and colorful as the flowers themselves.

Fiona waved this off as well, and asked Kick to tell them all about writing for the *Washington Times-Herald*. Back in 1939, Fiona had seemed part of a different world, since she was two years older and already married. But now that Kick's own debutante set was mostly married, and everyone was involved in some way with the war, those formerly significant differences had become inconsequential. The fact that she herself was not yet married occasionally made Kick feel self-conscious, but she tried to remind herself that she had been enjoying what many other women might envy as genuine freedom. She could travel and pursue activities as she pleased, which were not things Debo or Sissy could do anymore. And while Jane hadn't had any children yet, she was pining for her husband Peter Lindsay and using her prodigious organizational and preparatory skills, once devoted to parties and charity events, to arrange to be with him where he was stationed in India.

As Kick regaled her friends with stories about her life at the *Times-Herald*, complete with nearly missed deadlines for plays and movies she had to review mere hours after having seen them, she thought, *To them, I probably sound more like Inga Arvad than their old friend.* The thought made Kick giggle to herself.

As they were saying their goodbyes, Debo whispered in Kick's ear, "Billy's beside himself that you're here. Go easy on him."

This was unexpected. Though Kick replied, "I have every intention of it," what she really wanted to ask was *why*. It appeared that her once-staunchest ally was now more concerned for her brother-in-law. Why else deliver such a warning?

The next afternoon she had lunch with the Astors at the House of Lords. "Kathleen, darling, I knew you'd figure it out!" Nancy said when she greeted Kick in the dining room, where paintings of monarchs and PMs hung from the damasked walls. "How wonderful to see you in England, alone at last."

Nancy and Waldorf were unreservedly thrilled to see her, and before she'd even had a chance to sit in her burgundy leather chair, at least a dozen MPs she'd known from the embassy days had come over to say hello and to welcome her back. Even Aneurin Bevan, who'd been so downbeat at the Savoy, kissed her on both cheeks and gave her a wide smile. Nancy beamed as if *she* had brought Kick back personally. Kick supposed that Nancy had played an important role in getting her back to England, but in truth Kick was very proud of how hard she'd worked to finally make this happen by herself—the applications, the interviews, the letters, the training. It hadn't been easy, and she'd done most of it before even telling her parents.

Once the three of them were alone at the table with their first course of consommé, Nancy said, "I know you haven't seen Billy yet, because I haven't read about it in the papers."

"Goodness, she's only just arrived!" Waldorf said with good humor. "And William is doing his duty to his country."

"Thankfully not on the front," said Nancy. "And you'll be such a help to him when his run for Parliament gets under way."

"Yes, he's written that he'll be glad to have my writing skills for speeches," said Kick. "But surely he won't need much help. Isn't he going for a seat the Cavendishes have occupied for ages?"

Waldorf shrugged. "There's some socialist unrest out in the counties. This man Charles White is agitating for a seat his own father stole from the Cavendish family in 1918, and managed to hold for five years. He might give Billy a run for his money."

Nancy put a hand on her husband's and said, "Let's not talk of anything unpleasant today. And Charles White is certainly that. I want to hear all about your plans and your work, Kick. Start at the beginning."

She had no idea what the *beginning* could possibly be, but Kick was happy to oblige, and simply started with the heat in New York on the day she boarded the *Queen Mary*, just two weeks before. *Unbelievable*, she thought. *Two weeks and a lifetime ago.* When she first arrived, she'd sat in Sissy and David's kitchen and written in her crisp new diary, "First day back in London and I still can't believe I'm really here. It all seems like a dream from which I shall awaken very soon."

Please, God, not yet.

CHAPTER 27

All through her second official day of work on Friday, she kept the latest telegram from Billy in her white apron pocket so she could feel it near her, and so she could take it out to read whenever possible, not that she had many spare moments between serving the infamous coffee and donuts, sitting at the bedsides of injured soldiers, reading books till they nodded off, and playing cards with the healthy ones on their precious leave days. But each time she read or remembered his words—REACH LONDON 7.15 SATURDAY STAYING AT MAYFAIR CAN YOU KEEP SUNDAY FREE BILLY—she knew all her efforts were worth it. And effort it was. Despite its foreboding exterior, the Hans Crescent was one of the most popular and busiest of all the Red Cross Clubs in London. American soldiers of every rank came for beds, meals, drinks, dances, healing, and company. The Red Cross girls who worked there were occupied every minute of their ten-hour shifts and only got one and a half days off each week—and those days off were not supposed to be weekends. *Doesn't leave much time to see my friends*, Kick thought when she first heard her schedule. Fortunately, pretty English girls were more than welcome in the club, so many of her friends could visit with her there. The other good thing was that she'd been assigned a later shift, which meant she could head out to the 400 or another club after work ended, sleep in, and still be fresh for work the next day.

Mr. Scroggins was her boss, and he looked just as his name sounded: *scrogginly*. Though he was American, his tonsure of curly gray hair and round, ruddy face atop an equally round body made him the perfect overlord of this Dickensian structure. Determined to win him over, she kept her best smile plastered on at all times and did exactly as she was instructed tout de suite. Following Billy's telegram, though, she used her short break Friday afternoon to ask if she could have a private word with him. In his office, which was a bare place with stacks of paper on an under-used desk, he said, "Make it quick, Miss Kennedy."

"First, sir, I want you to know how thrilled I am to be here, and how much I want to help the boys who come through our doors."

"But?" he said with a frown. He wasn't going to have any of her usual coquettishness; she could tell.

"Well, sir . . ." she stammered, knowing she just had to come out with it. Employing a small, well-rehearsed lie, she said, "The assignment to start work came a bit earlier than I was expecting, and I had already made plans with a family friend who's visiting on Sunday. I know the rules, sir, and they are good ones, of course, because I know how much the boys need us girls here on the busy weekends, but it would mean a great deal to me if I could have just this one Sunday off. I can give up my day off next week if it would help."

She held her breath, watching his frown carve ever-deeper lines in his face.

At last he drew a breath and said, "You may have it. But consider this your first favor wasted. I hope he's worth it."

He knows. How could he know? Still, though she'd been caught in a lie, relief flooded her, and she smiled widely and gratefully at Mr. Scroggins.

"Thank you, thank you, sir."

"Get back out there, Miss Kennedy."

She went about the rest of her duties with an incurable smirk of anticipation on her face. In the afternoon, she offered coffee and cigarettes to groups of boys sitting around wooden tables doing puzzles and crosswords or hurling vulgar insults at one another. Jeff, a curly-haired farm boy from Nebraska, said, "Why, thank you, Miss Kennedy," after she'd refilled his cup.

"My pleasure," she said. "And please, call me Kick."

Jeff laughed. "Kick's no name for a girl as pretty as you, if you don't mind my saying. My mother'd have my hide if she heard me calling a girl by her first name anyway."

"Dare I point out that your mother's not here?" Kick said flirtatiously.

"She may not be, but believe me when I say that she'd know anyways."

At this, the other boy who'd been sharing his table while reading a Dashiell Hammett novel lifted his glacial blue eyes to her. He was about Jack's age, and deeply tanned like her brother, but his hair was shaved so short, Kick couldn't even tell what color it was. He interrupted, "You can take a boy off the farm . . ."

"Where are you from, then, Mr. . . . ?" she asked, deciding to take the empty seat between the two boys for a few minutes. This was the sort of informal chatting the girls were encouraged to interrupt chores to do. Anything that made the soldiers' lives seem more normal, more entertaining—within reason, of course.

"*Mr.* Thompson is my father," he replied. "You can call me Tim, *Kick*."

She thrust out her hand and shook Tim's hard, calloused one. "Pleased to meet you, Tim. Where are you from?"

"New York City," he replied.

"City boys never know their manners," teased Jeff.

"And farm boys never get the girls," Tim teased back, though there was a sharpness to his jibe, and Jeff clearly felt its point.

Focusing completely on Kick, Tim said, "So how'd you get suckered into coming over here? You know you'll be homesick in less than a month."

"I've lived in London before," Kick reassured him. "I like it here."

Tim's eyes widened, and he said with a whistle, "I knew I'd seen you before! You're one of *those* Kennedys. Hot damn."

Already? She felt exasperated at being recognized so soon, but tried to laugh it off. "I'm just the same as anyone else," she said.

Poor Jeff looked confused. Kick assumed society columns, especially from abroad, didn't penetrate into his part of the country. And anyway, he was probably two or three years younger than she was. Tim took the liberty of explaining: "Her dad was the *ambassador*, Farm Boy. At least, he was before it all went to hell in a handbasket." Then he turned those eyes on Kick and said, "You're hardly the same as anyone else."

Kick put up her chin and replied, "I'm working, aren't I? Same as Ginnie from Atlanta and Betsy from Albany. Both my older brothers are off fighting just the same as you two."

Tim shrugged. "We'll see, I guess, won't we?" Then he went back to his novel, as if to say, *Conversation over.*

He reminded her so much of John White, she wanted to scream.

Jeff, on the other hand, was pure nice. "Don't listen to him, Miss Kennedy. And pleased to make your acquaintance. You just never know who you're gonna meet over here. If I make it back, the stories I'll have to tell!"

Kick beamed a smile back into his, and said, "I'm sure you'll make it back."

He raised his cup of coffee. "Well, I mean to have fun on my way."

"I'll save a dance for you tonight," she said.

"I look forward to it," he said, and something in his earnestness made her heart break a little.

❖ ❖ ❖

Saturday night when her shift ended, she gave herself a little sponge bath at the tiny sink in the bedroom she shared with Ginnie from Atlanta, with whom she'd barely exchanged ten words yet. Ginnie had as busy a social life as Kick, though she never saw her bunkmate at any of the places she frequented, so she had no idea where the other girl went. It was hardly the leisurely, rose-scented bath Kick would have given herself before past meetings with Billy, but it would have to do. Then she changed out of her itchy uniform and into one of the very few party dresses she'd brought with her, a knee-length black crepe de chine with lace around the neck and on the sleeves. How she wished for a floor-length gown to cover her sore and swollen legs! She'd written her family already asking for some of the other clothes she'd set aside before she left, as well as her Vol de Nuit and the candy to share with her sweets-starved friends. She'd only been able to bring over a bare minimum of cosmetics because of space limitations on the ship, but she wanted to smell nice at the end of the day more than anything, and wished she'd thought about this ahead of time. A bit of rouge and mascara, and a touch of precious red on her lips, did make her feel a bit more like herself. Sissy and Debo had been melting down the stubs of old lipsticks and making pots of lip stains—she was lucky not to have to do that yet. And she had a few packs of nylons to work through. She chose a black pair that night, in the hopes they might do her legs some favors. Then she had to dash.

The May Fair Hotel was as it had always been, a bastion of perfectly appointed luxury. They hadn't even taken down the crystal chandeliers— or if they had during the Blitz, they'd put them back up again. A few of the debutante balls had been given there in 1938 and '39, and many out-of-town relatives stayed there when a family's town house wasn't large enough to host everyone. It felt thrillingly illicit for Billy to be staying there, almost as if he were a husband checked in to meet his mistress— even though she had no intention of actually going up to his room, and even though she knew he had to stay at a hotel because the Cavendishes' London house had been bombed. His parents and sisters split their time between Eastbourne and Churchdale Hall, what with Chatsworth let to Penrhos College for the duration of the war, since his father preferred to have women staying in the house rather than soldiers, as was the choice of the great houses during wartime.

Kick followed the sound of a piano playing a medley from *The Wizard of Oz* through the busy lobby, where Waterford vases overflowing with roses and lilies perfumed the room and made her feel she'd stepped back in time—except instead of feeling light with youthful anticipation, she felt so nervous that she had to focus on every step she took, for fear of falling. Her eyes darted around; she hoped she wouldn't run into Billy unexpectedly. They'd agreed to meet in the bar, and she planned to stop just outside the entry to smooth her dress, check her lipstick, and take a few calming breaths before making her entrance.

So much for plans.

Billy was leaning against the bar, looking right at the large open entrance as she approached. Tall, slim, beautiful Billy, out of uniform and sporting a trim gray suit. There was no place to hide and check anything. There was only that boyish smile of his that filled his eyes with joy, exactly as she'd remembered it. *Better.* At that point, she had to stop herself from running into his arms.

Steady, she told herself as she walked toward him, clutching her black purse in a sweaty hand and returning his smile.

When at last she was standing inches away from him, she had no idea what to say. Hadn't she rehearsed something about how he looked the same? Which it turned out he didn't, not quite, anyway—he looked like a man now, more sculpted, the softness gone from his cheeks. No more stoop. He was even more attractive now, if that was at all possible. He kissed her cheek, which promptly burst into flames. "Good God, I've missed you," he said quietly, just in her ear. The warmth of his breath and the musical depth of his voice nearly made her faint.

"Well," she said, clearing her throat and sliding onto a high red velvet chair. "I think this calls for champagne, don't you?" At that moment, she'd have paid any amount of money for the relaxation those bubbles would bring.

"I've already ordered one," he replied. "It's waiting at our table."

With a smile, she said, "I knew there was a reason I'd missed you, too."

Billy smirked, and Kick began to feel her legs beneath her again.

As he had at their favorite Spanish restaurant years before, Billy had thought ahead—and while he hadn't reserved a private room, he had secured a secluded table off in a dark corner, out of view of the parade of people walking into and out of the restaurant. A bottle of Veuve Clicquot was chilling in a gleaming silver stand beside the small round table, set with white linens, sterling, and cut crystal glasses. Again, Kick had the mischievous feeling that she was about to misbehave with this handsome, forbidden man, and it gave her the strongest craving to run her fingers through his hair and kiss him properly.

They busied themselves with the formalities of ordering and complimenting those first sips of champagne—"What a lovely treat" and "You wouldn't believe the rubbish they called wine on the Maginot Line. A disgrace to anyone who calls himself a Frenchman, if you ask me"— before enduring their first really awkward moment. They looked at each other, each with their mouths open to speak, but words didn't come out. It was as if each was waiting for the other to speak first. After a few seconds, it was clear that both of them were inadequate to the task. Billy laughed, and Kick sighed with a sort of relief. "I suppose we shouldn't pretend that four years haven't passed," she said.

Billy reached under the table and took her hand in his, which was warm and dry and calloused in the palm where it had been soft before. "It's true, yes, it's been four years. And much has happened. But when I look at you, I feel all those same feelings from before. More so, in fact."

"I do, too," Kick said, hoping her tone would convey just enough of what she felt and wanted, but not quite all—since inside, she felt utterly molten with lust and relief. She ran her thumb gently over the rough spots below his fingers.

Had they been alone, he would have kissed her on the lips—she was sure of it. But they were not. Instead, he released her hand, cleared his throat, and said, "Then perhaps tonight we should concentrate on catching up in the way the letters cannot?"

Kick nodded. Billy went first, and talked about his elation at becoming an uncle to his first niece a few months ago. "I'm afraid I rather spoil her," he admitted, "and it surprises me as much as it does Debo, who assumed—along with me, I'm afraid—that I'd be a somewhat detached uncle. Have you met darling Emma yet?"

Kick shook her head.

"Well, wait till you do," Billy gushed. "Wait till she wraps her little hands around your finger and sighs. Goodness. I had no idea. And listen to me, sounding like a nanny."

Kick laughed. "I haven't experienced aunthood yet, but I can imagine I will deeply love Joe and Jack's children."

Billy laughed. "How *is* Jack? Other than a writer-playboy, that is?"

Kick filled Billy in on the thwarted romance between her brother and Inga, and on both her brothers' intense desires to make a difference in the war. "No one wants to fight more than Joe," said Kick. "In fact, he might actually get sent over here soon. I'd love to have him with me in London."

"I might rival him in my desire to fight," said Billy moodily. "But," he said, obviously not wanting to dwell on that subject, "it would be very good to see him again. I always had the highest respect for Joe's sense of duty."

Duty. That was a topic Kick wanted to avoid tonight.

Billy went on and filled Kick in on the comings and goings of his younger sisters Anne and Elizabeth, whom Kick hadn't known well before the war because they were six and seven years younger than she was, and away at school most of the time. Last year, Elizabeth had had a small coming-out party, as was the fashion and necessity these days, and Anne was preparing for hers. Kick filled Billy in on the doings of her other siblings, too, though she avoided Rosemary, and she was relieved that their dinner finished before he could ask about her. She assumed he was just as eager to avoid mentioning Sally Norton, and she'd already decided that since the other girl was no longer a threat, there was no real point in bringing her up. No doubt they'd run into her somewhere. Kick was resigned to the prospect.

"Fancy a dance at the 400?" he asked when they'd finished their meal.

"I'd like nothing better," she said.

As their taxi wound its way through the dark streets of blackout London, they were at last able to reach for each other the way they'd both wanted to the moment she walked into the May Fair. His kisses were an intoxicating mix of nostalgia and discovery, of remembering and feeling anew how he smelled of soap and cedar, how large his hands felt on her back, how tiny she felt in his embrace, and how startlingly soft and insistent his lips felt on hers. There was a new sureness in the way he moved with her, though, a confidence in his own body that she found deeply alluring. It was something John had possessed, which had pulled her toward him against her better judgment. She had feared Billy might lack it, and that her attraction to him wouldn't be as strong as it had been before. She only hoped her own touch pleased him as much as his pleased her. His growl of annoyance when the taxi driver stopped the car was a good sign, she thought, and buoyed her heart in her chest.

The familiar roar of music and laughter greeted them at their favorite old haunt, and as Billy led her by the hand to a table with Bertrand, Tony Rosslyn, Jane, Boofie, and Fiona, Kick saw virtually every other head in the place swivel to watch them. As soon as people saw them, hand in hand and aglow from their taxi ride, the whispering began. Everyone noticed.

"Thank goodness you've given everyone something new to talk about," said Boofie when they sat down at the table.

"I should start taking bets on when you'll announce it," said Bertrand. "I'd make enough to retire at twenty-six."

Kick followed Billy's lead and laughed off the teasing, but suddenly her body felt tight with nerves. This was what she'd come back for, wasn't it? Then why the sense that everything was about to slip completely out of her control?

❧ ❧ ❧

The next day, nursing hangovers by the fireplace while the rain came down in sheets outside Boofie and Fiona's house in Kings Langley, Kick and Billy drank tea and played cards and talked with their hosts about the changes the war had brought.

"The worst isn't the lack of sugar and meat," said Fiona. "It's the way it's narrowed all our worlds. Everyone is so bored without the weekend house parties, or the ability to travel freely, they've taken to spreading terrible rumors about each other."

"How sad," said Kick. "Well, I have no use for gossips, either. They were the end of Jack's relationship with my friend Inga Arvad."

"Oh yes, we heard about that over here. *The German spy?*" Fiona teased.

"Exactly," Kick said drily. *But even my father caved to the rumors about her.*

Later, while Boofie dozed on the divan and Fiona tended to the children in the nursery, Kick and Billy stretched out their legs on the enormous faded Persian rug and leaned against a couch with a navy fleur-de-lis pattern, listening to the crackle and hiss of the new log on the fire.

"Oh, how I've missed fires in July," Kick joked.

Billy chuckled and kissed her on the mouth, then turned back contentedly to the fire.

"So when is the run for Parliament?" asked Kick, feeling uncomfortable with the silence.

Billy sighed. "The election's in February, but I'll have to start campaigning just at the start of the new year. In the meantime, my parents are doing some preparatory work."

"You don't sound very excited about it."

"I'm not," Billy said. "I think I should stay in the war till it's finished, but Father's bound and determined for me to take my place. At least I've gotten him to agree to let me back into the war once the election's done, win or lose."

"But you won't lose," said Kick, trying to sound supportive even though she hated the idea that Billy was determined to go to the front no matter what. "Why do you have to run now, anyway?"

"Well, Henry Hunloke is the representative now, and since Dad's Under Secretary for the Colonies, he's not about to step down to MP, and it's really the seat for the Marquess of Hartington. Anyway, Henry's married to Dad's sister Anne, so the seat's still controlled by the family. He's just been holding it for me, really. But things aren't well between him and Anne, and it looks as though the marriage might end. So Dad's convinced Henry to give up the seat at the by-elections in February."

"I see now. So it should be a simple run?" she asked, not wanting to be the one to bring up the White character Nancy Astor had mentioned the other day.

Billy heaved a sigh. "It ought to be. By-elections during wartime are supposed to be unopposed, and since Henry is a Conservative, it should go to me as the Conservative candidate. But this war's turned everything upside down, especially since it's following a long depression in the countryside. People are angry. They want more for their lives. I can't say I blame them."

"Can't your campaign promise some changes?"

Billy smiled at her. "That's precisely what I want to do, though Dad isn't keen on the idea. I'll need your support and American ideas."

"I'll do what I can," she promised, though the idea of being in further opposition to Billy's father didn't exactly thrill her. They weren't married, and she didn't want to give his parents more reasons to oppose them becoming so.

Billy kissed her again, and as he did, Boofie's snores crescendoed into a choke and woke him up. They all laughed, then Fiona called them into the kitchen for an early supper.

Under the brick arches of King's Cross station, Kick and Billy stole one last kiss before he boarded his train back up to Scotland. He was in the brown uniform she'd seen him wear a few times in 1939. He'd grown into it. Laying her hands on the pockets on his chest, she said, "This fits you so well now. You look like a hero."

"That means the world to me, coming from you," he said, kissing her on the forehead. "I'll see you soon."

"Very soon?" she asked, feeling her breath catch in her throat. *Don't cry, you ninny. It was a perfect weekend.*

"Very. We have a considerable amount of making up for lost time to do."

He hugged her once more, lifting her off the platform for a few glorious seconds before setting her down gently, kissing her cheek, and turning from her at last to find his seat on the train.

CHAPTER 28

What a relief work was—it kept her so busy, she hardly had time to pine. Also, two of her parents' friends got in touch and began filling her evenings with ever more plans: Marie Bruce, an effusively friendly woman of about forty who was living on her own in a chic apartment in the Mayfair neighborhood, and Ambassador Tony Biddle, who was very apologetic about the press visa debacle of a year ago. "The papers didn't know what they were missing, not letting you in," he said to her, "but I'm not at all surprised that you found another way." He and his wife Mary invited Kick to a party where the meal was absolutely delicious, but unfortunately gave her such terrible food poisoning, she had to stay in bed for several filthy days in a kind of delirium. The only good things to come of that experience were not having to face Scroggins for a few days and getting to meet Billy's aunt Lady Cranborne. She was working as a nurse, moving between various facilities in the city, and happened to tend to Kick at the height of her sickness. Kick had met the woman only once before and didn't recognize her. But she recognized Kick.

"We can't have my nephew's favorite so unwell," she said as she laid a cool, wet cloth on Kick's forehead and nestled a metal bowl by her pillow.

"Nephew?" Kick eked out through dry, cracked lips.

"Billy, darling," the statuesque woman replied with a smile. "He'd never forgive me if you didn't make it to Eastbourne next week."

Kick smiled, then threw up again in the bowl.

"I advise against the rich sauces, dear. These days you never know about the milk," Lady Cranborne said.

Just as Kick was feeling better, a letter arrived from her father, which she read under some freshly bleached sheets on her bed at the Hans Crescent. He warned her not to let it bother her if any of her—or his—former friends were angry with him for his "anti-British" actions. He preferred to think he had been "pro-American," and if that meant he was perceived as "anti-British," then so be it. But the line she treasured most was "I don't care what they say, so don't let it bother you. You have your own life to live."

My own life to live. Three years before, he wouldn't have written a line like that, let alone meant it, and it filled her with pride and hope for the future. If her years in exile from England, working and living by herself in Washington, had finally earned her some respect from her father, well then, maybe they'd been worth it.

Her first day back at work after recovering from the food poisoning, Tim called to her across the room just as she steered a trolley of donuts and coffee toward the tables. "Homesick yet?"

Grinning, Kick took one of the donuts, held it up as if in a toast, and took a big bite. Crumbly and barely sweet, a little savory from the oil in the fryer, it was the best thing she'd tasted in weeks. Tim laughed and nodded.

When the second post arrived during her dinner break, it contained a fat envelope from France with the return address of the parish where Father O'Flaherty had been working. In the little room with the old leather chairs where the girls liked to get away and smoke cigarettes and relax during their hours off, Kick sat at one of the small tables. Sweat rushed to her palms and under her arms, and her fingers shook as she fumbled with the envelope. Her last two letters to the priest had been returned, unopened, wrapped in a handwritten note:

Dear Miss Kennedy,

It pains me to be the one to deliver this news to you, since I know how fond you and Father O'Flaherty were of one another, but I am afraid I must report that he was killed in late May. A Nazi troupe invaded our village, and we hid the children (I dare not write where), and he died because he would not tell where they were.

These are barbaric times we live in, and Father O'Flaherty was always a beacon of civilization and calm for my fellow brothers and sisters in God, and for the children whom he treated with such kindness one would have thought they were his own. It is a great loss to us, and to the church, but we try to speak with him daily, in prayer. I find it helps. Please know that your letters brought him singular joy. Nothing else could bring that particular smile to his face. I think he was proud of you in the way a favorite uncle might be, or a godfather. I have no doubt he continues to watch over you and all those he loved.

> *I am yours, in sorrow and sympathy,*
> *Brother Dufour*

Kick reread the letter so much, she completely lost track of time. Suddenly, Scroggins was behind her, snarling, "The Flying Yanks are here." In an hour, she hadn't eaten or done anything else—not that she was hungry—but when she lifted her face to Scroggins, he immediately changed his own expression, going from his usual surly frown to something like compassion. "Everything all right?" he asked gruffly.

Kick drew a deep breath in through her nose and tried to straighten her back, but her attempt at strength failed for once and she burst into tears. "I'm sorry, Mr. Scroggins," she said.

With a glance at the letters on the table, he said kindly, "Take another hour or so, then come back for the dance. Work always helps."

She nodded, mortified and not trusting her voice.

This was by far the worst news of the war so far. The best man she'd ever known had been murdered for protecting children. It was literally unbelievable, preposterous. How could a selfish, wheedling person like Unity Mitford be spared and not good, kind Father O'Flaherty? The harshness of that thought shocked her, and she told herself, *Don't let this make you unkind. Father O'Flaherty would hate that.* But it was hard. This was so deeply unfair.

She felt a fierce pride in all the boys who were putting themselves in mortal danger to fight this great evil, and at the same time a vertiginous fear of that danger. Her brothers, her friends . . . *Billy.* She couldn't protect any of them. She cried more, feeling helpless.

At some point, the Flying Yanks, a favorite aviator band that played all the Red Cross Clubs, began their first set, and the bright, brassy sound of trumpets and trombones filled the building and rattled the floor beneath Kick's feet. *If those boys can play music like that, then the least I can do is dance to it.*

Kick stood up and splashed some cold water from the sink on her face, and checked the mirror to make sure her eyes weren't too puffy. She reminded herself of her father's letter to her, and of the day she'd soon spend with Billy in Eastbourne. Then she allowed herself to remember Father O'Flaherty's kind face, the way he'd listened to her and given her such sage counsel. She felt the tears heat up her eye sockets again, and told them *no.*

She blew her nose one last time on the monogrammed handkerchief she kept neatly folded in her uniform pocket, then went downstairs to dance and laugh, trade insults and pour drinks, and in general show the boys how much they had to live for.

✦ ✦ ✦

Near Billy's family estate at Eastbourne there was the most lovely, fragrant peach orchard. When Billy picked her up at the train station the morning of her precious day off, he took her there first, saying, "I want to show you one of my favorite spots in all England." She'd started to notice that he used the word *England* more than he ever used to, and in a tone that implied he was speaking of a beloved, fragile thing—a child, maybe, or an aging maiden aunt, someone in need of protecting.

They strolled through the orchard quietly, hand in hand, listening to the seagulls in the near distance and smelling the heavy, sugary scent of the peaches.

"The sea air is supposed to be good for the fruit," said Billy as they bought a crate of them to take back to the house.

"Listen to you, sounding like a gentleman farmer," she laughed, plucking a ripe peach off one of the trees and sinking her teeth into it. It was warm and soft, just as sweet as the perfumed air had promised. "Yummm," she said.

When she'd finished and thrown the pit into the shade of one of the trees, Billy kissed her sticky lips. They walked hand in hand a little longer, and the peace of it was the first real balm on her heart after the news about Father O'Flaherty.

"Are you ready to head to the house?" Billy said after a while.

Kick knew what this really meant. Was she ready to see his parents?

"Are you?" she countered.

"Anne and Elizabeth are beside themselves with excitement to meet you again. You're practically a celebrity to them."

Kick laughed. "I hope you've set them straight."

"Oh yes, I've informed them that you're nothing special, nothing at all," he joked.

"Ha ha," she said wryly.

"Kathleen Kennedy, do I detect some nerves?"

"Not about your sisters." *Why must I always perspire at moments like this?* She felt so clammy.

"My parents have promised to be on their best behavior."

"Is that what they promised about Sally, too?" Kick bit her tongue hard and drew blood. She hadn't meant for that to come out.

"I've been wondering when that might come up," he said.

"I'm sorry, I didn't mean for it to," she said, blushing and looking down at the tufty green grass and feeling too hot under the bright yellow sun.

Billy put a finger under her chin and lifted her face so that she was looking at him, then took both her hands in his. "That was all a mistake. I missed you, *terribly*, and she was . . . well, she was fun, and she was there. And at first she reminded me a bit of you. This sounds wretched, doesn't it? I'm afraid I didn't behave very honorably toward her. As the years went by, though, I assumed you weren't coming back, that everything was against us, and I was so depressed about the war. I just . . . I wasn't myself. But I meant what I wrote to you, that she was always second-best, and when I finally realized that wasn't fair to either of us, I broke it off. I'm so glad I saw it in time."

"I heard that your parents helped to put a stop to it," Kick said, holding her breath.

"My parents," Billy sighed, "did not love the match, it's true. My father wants me to find someone who's *worthy*, to use a horrible word that's nonetheless true for him. And my mother . . . well, would it surprise you to hear that she told me she knew I didn't love Sally as I'd loved you? And that she wanted her son to marry a woman he loved, first and foremost?"

Kick opened and closed her mouth. "Yes, I am surprised," she finally said. "But then, why should I be surprised? I hardly know your mother. I shouldn't judge her."

"I look forward to your getting to know her better," said Billy. "She's fond of you, you know."

Kick recalled their past conversations about art, about Andrew's art in particular, and the way she'd always admired the older woman's sense of style and decorum. "I look forward to it, too."

"And my father—" Billy paused. "Well, he's not *fond* of anyone, really."

Kick smiled sadly. The truth was, she didn't want Billy asking about *her* parents, because the answers would embarrass her—her mother's farewell to her had been so conditional. *I'll always be here if you don't find what you're looking for* . . . It occurred to Kick, fleetingly, that perhaps Billy should be asking about her parents, but she had too much on her mind to dwell on that now.

He kissed her forehead. "Anyway, it'll all be well and good if my parents are fond of my future wife, but the main thing is that *I* am fond of her." Then he put an arm around her and steered her toward the car.

Future wife? Had he really just said that? She couldn't think on the choice of words long, though, because in minutes they were standing in the spacious entry of Compton Place.

The duchess greeted Kick with a kiss on each cheek and a genuinely happy "Kick! We are so glad to see you back in England!" As Kick replied in kind, she stole a glance at Billy, who gave her a raised eyebrow and a *see, I told you* look. Then Anne and Elizabeth ran out to meet her. Both girls and their mother were so much taller than Kick, she felt conspicuously short, but paradoxically large-featured in comparison to the other girls, who had such fine noses and weak chins complemented by thick manes of brown hair. They were more giggly than Pat and Jean, who were close to their ages, and also more reticent than her American sisters would have been with a "celebrity" in their midst. Kick was the one to break the ice with questions for them, and a suggestion they all go for a ride since it was such a beautiful afternoon. On horseback, both girls loosened up and began asking Kick more about what her life was like at the Hans Crescent, and what it had been like to write for a newspaper in Washington, DC. Elizabeth even said, "But I just don't understand why you'd leave such a wonderful place and position to come *here*," at which the slightly more worldly Anne burst into laughter, pointed a thumb at their brother, and said, "Don't be daft, Lizzy."

Elizabeth turned the color of an apple and bit her lip.

Inspired to stick up for the embarrassed girl, and for herself as well, Kick said to Anne, "England has much to recommend itself in addition to your handsome brother, I must say. Someday you'll have to come to America to see what I mean."

Elizabeth was quick to say, "Oh, I'd like nothing more than to travel. And New York sounds just absolutely grand."

"Someday we'll go," Kick assured her, and it felt as natural as assuring Pat of something, which she took to be a good sign.

As she changed for dinner in the same dark wood-paneled room where she'd stayed before the war, the weekend of the Goodwood races, an unexpected knock on the door gave her heart a lurch. It couldn't be Billy, could it?

She opened the door nervously, and saw Debo standing in the hall. The two girls embraced.

"What a wonderful surprise!" Kick said.

"I couldn't let you have dinner here for the first time unprotected," said Debo.

"It's all gone well so far," said Kick, feeling slightly defensive. She could take care of herself. But still, she was thrilled to see her friend and glad to have another familiar face at dinner.

"I'm sure it has," said Debo. "And if I'm being totally honest, I needed a bit of a break from cooking and nappy changing myself."

"Did you bring Emma?"

Debo nodded. "And she is blissfully asleep in the nursery, so I can enjoy myself."

"Excellent," said Kick, offering her old friend her arm and setting off through the gallery hallway, hung with portraits of departed Cavendishes and paintings of the local landscapes that testified to the fact that the trees and lawns were the same now as they had been in the eighteenth century. In the well-lit library, gin and tonics were served on a silver tray by a footman, only the second she'd seen in England since arriving. The first had been at Cliveden, when she'd visited Nancy for a day. "Can't let the war make us heathens," Nancy had said, though in truth even the Astors were operating with a much-reduced staff, with so many young men preparing for the promised invasion of France.

Kick had to admit that it felt like the most precious form of flattery that Billy's family would welcome her in this manner. She knew from Debo that they dined like this only on special occasions these days. And even though she wasn't the only guest—his parents had used her visit as an excuse to have over their old friends Lord and Lady Graham and their daughter Mildred, who was Anne's age—Kick was honored to be the reason for the small fete.

This was the first she'd seen of the duke all day. His long form was folded on the large sofa, one leg over the other, his dinner jacket as rumpled as ever. His mustache looked neatly trimmed, and his gray hair wet. "I heard he had an excellent day fishing," Debo whispered to Kick, "which always puts him in a better mood."

"Shall I go over and talk to him?" asked Kick. She didn't want to interrupt, as he seemed deep in conversation with Lord Graham.

"I'd wait till he comes to you," advised Debo.

It took a while. Kick sipped her cocktail slowly so she didn't get too tipsy on her empty stomach, though it was tempting. Billy was also in a good mood, all smiles and laughs, with a casual hand on her back much of the time. Apparently their couplehood was no longer a secret, and Kick was relieved to know she wasn't hiding anything anymore. Just before it was time to go into the dining room, the duke approached Kick as she stood chatting with Billy and Debo.

"Debo," he said, with a nod at his daughter-in-law. "Glad you could join us tonight."

"You know me," said Debo, in an easy manner Kick envied, "any excuse for a fine dinner and a bit of sunlight. I'm taking Emma to the beach tomorrow."

"I wish I could join you," said Kick, thinking of the train back to London she'd be on instead.

"And, Kick, it's good to see you as well," said the duke, as if he'd seen her just the other week. She found it comforting, if a bit surprising, that both Billy's parents were now addressing her by her nickname. She, of course, still had to address them as Duke and Duchess. Even Debo did. "I must admit, I hope your presence inspires Billy here to take more of an interest in his campaign. You Kennedys seem to have politics in your blood."

Kick grinned at Billy, who smiled sheepishly back at her. He clearly took his father's comment as something of a reprimand, and Kick remembered what Billy had told her about the differences he had with his father about the seat in West Derbyshire. She didn't think Billy would mind her taking his father's side under the present circumstances, so she replied, "I'm happy to do everything I can to help."

"Excellent," he said. Then, "I believe it's time for dinner."

Kick let out a long, slow breath as she followed everyone into the dining room, where she was relieved to be sitting between Debo and Billy, on the opposite end of the table from the duke. Still, she thought, they'd made a promising start during the cocktails. She began to relax and enjoy herself.

The next morning, as she relished a breakfast tray in bed and tried not to think about the fact that in four hours she'd be serving coffee at the Hans Crescent, there was another knock on her door. It sounded too firm to be Debo. Feeling playful, she didn't bother getting up and called in a singsong voice, "Come in!"

Billy, already in his uniform, for he, too, was heading back to work that day, quickly stepped into the room and closed the door behind him. With a pleased smile, he crossed the room to sit on the edge of her bed. "I like seeing you here like this."

"I like being here like this," she replied.

"I thought things went well last night, didn't you?"

She nodded. Five years before, he'd been so reticent to discuss things like meetings with his parents, and now he brought them up on his own. She liked this more take-charge Billy.

"My father actually said, 'That girl would charm a snake out of its skin.'"

Kick shivered. "And that's a compliment?"

"From my father? Yes," he said with a chuckle. "He has a sideways way of saying everything. He once told Andrew that Debo was like salmon to a bear."

"Coming from an angler, that sounds rather like a more straight-forward compliment."

"Trust me, Kick, if you were willing to convert to the Church of England this afternoon, they'd welcome you with open arms."

Had he really just said that? So casually? Boiling blood pumped through her veins. "I suppose that's where the snake part of his *compliment* came from," she said. Surely after four years of pining, Billy wasn't going to ask her to convert.

"Kick, don't be angry," he said, putting a hand on her knee, which was more than concealed beneath layers of fine cotton blankets.

"It's *who I am*, Billy."

"I know," he reassured her. Then he drew in a breath and said, "I'm sorry I brought it up that way."

"You mean the subject of those four hundred years of history?" It was all coming back to her, like she was standing at Blenheim again. Running away to Spain and France, then sitting through the horrific train ride back to London. Reading the miserable letters that had really ended things and led to his engagement to someone else.

"Kick, you came back," he said. "You must be willing to make *some* compromise."

It hadn't occurred to her until that moment that he might have been making some of the same assumptions about her that she'd been making about him. After all, she had been the one to get on the boat. How stupid and naive she felt. John White's last chastising letter came back to her, and her stomach churned.

"Are *you* willing to make compromises?" she asked.

"I'm not asking you to convert, am I?"

"No, you cloaked that request in your father's wish."

"I already apologized for that." Billy looked away for a moment, think-ing. "This isn't the note I want you to leave on, darling."

"Me, either," she said. "But with everything that's already happened between us, it's hard for me not to want to ask what it is you expect from me, before . . . we go further with this." *Oh, Father O'Flaherty, I hope you're looking down on us now. Please, guide his answer!*

"I will never ask you to convert. I know your faith means too much to you. If you were to change your mind about that, I'd be overjoyed, but I also admire your loyalty to your family and church. As you said once, it makes you *you*. The you I love deeply."

He hadn't said those words since she'd returned. He must have known the power they'd have to soften her. "I love you, too," she whispered, putting her hand on his and giving it a small squeeze.

Billy laughed. "It's absurd! If you were Protestant, I'd have proposed the moment you stepped into the May Fair. But because you're Catholic, and both of us have important families whom we love, and *should* love, we have to torture ourselves before the real fun can begin."

"It is rather medieval, isn't it?" Though her words were calm and even, her mind was a mess—he'd sort of proposed. He *did* want to marry her.

"Except that in the Middle Ages, we wouldn't have this problem because Henry wouldn't have broken with the pope yet," he pointed out.

"Well that's one thing that would have been good about the Middle Ages," she said, and they both laughed.

Kick rocked herself up so that she was kneeling on the bed, and kissed Billy on the lips. "I want the real fun to begin."

Eyes closed, Billy murmured, "So do I."

"Then what's the problem?" she asked. "We keep our separate religions, and raise the children Catholic. It's a time-honored compromise in situations like ours. Two of your relations have done it," she said, referring to David and Sissy, and Derek and Ann. The issue of recusant and New World Catholics no longer seemed to be germane. This was just about her and Billy now.

He shook his head. "I can't agree to that," he said. "I'm going to be the Duke of Devonshire someday, and I want my heir to be Protestant, as has been the tradition for centuries. I've thought a great deal about this, Kick. I can't just turn my back on my own family and its position in

England because of the demands of your church. No matter how much I love you." England. There it was again.

Kick felt as if she were falling from a great precipice, grasping for a branch to hold on to. She said, the words painful to her, "What if we raised the girls Catholic and the boys Protestant?"

"What if we have no boys?" he countered.

"Look at my mother; I'm sure to have a few of both," she joked.

"What if they die in another one of these vile wars?"

She looked down at the bed. How could she make him see her side? There was so much she wanted to say, about the safety and wonder her own church made her feel, the closeness it helped her feel to her difficult family, the traditions she wanted to hand down to her own children. But she couldn't find the words. She hadn't been prepared for this conversation, not this morning.

"Kick," Billy said, taking her hands in his. Reluctantly, she met his eyes. "I know that England means a great deal to you, as it does to me. I know how you love it here, and that thrills me in my very bones. But we are a Protestant country. The war has made me want to defend England, and everything it stands for, in all that I do. It's important to me that our church doesn't answer to a pontiff who rules from another country. I don't want my children to answer to anyone but their king and their parents."

With a roiling sense of inevitability, she understood his position. She even admired him for it. How was it possible she should love him more for forcing her to make this impossible choice?

"You're not saying anything," Billy observed, worry starting to creep into his tone.

"It's a lot to think about," she said quietly.

"It's not like you to be so quiet," he said. "I don't want to lose you before I've had the opportunity to convince you."

"Convince me that betraying my family for yours is a good thing?" She couldn't help it. He had to hear how this felt for her.

"I do thoroughly understand what I'm asking you to do," he said, and the mournfulness of his tone made her believe him. "But I would ask you to think about what you'd *gain*."

She looked at him. His face was so hopeful, so handsome. It was the only face she'd ever wanted to dream about. The only one. For the first time in years, she pictured them with their children on the lawn of Chatsworth, the Marquess and Marchioness of Hartington. The children were running, happy, chasing each other around. There was indeed a great deal to gain.

"I will," she promised.

Billy put both hands on her face and gave her a long kiss. "Let's leave it there for now, shall we? I think we've made some progress, and you don't seem angry anymore."

"I'm not," she said. "Mostly."

"I'll take it," he said, stopping her from saying more with another kiss.

She wished she could feel soothed by the regular rock and chug of the train as it sped her back to London, her beloved green countryside blurring by, but she felt increasingly tense instead. If she wanted to marry Billy, to be with him fully in all the tempting ways that had occurred to her since that fateful afternoon in Maria Sieber's bed, if she wanted to stay in England the way she'd allowed herself to dream—as the future Duchess of Devonshire, a position and life she was convinced she would relish and be genuinely good at—she would have to agree to let all her children be baptized in another church. Billy would not be recognized as her husband by her own church, and so in its eyes she wouldn't be married at all but living in sin.

At least, that's the way her parents would see it. She didn't think Father O'Flaherty would, but he was gone. There was no way for him to convince Mother to see things differently. She'd be losing another daughter.

Kick felt guilty for even considering this agreement with Billy.

She grasped at the one thing that might be on her side: time. In the past, Billy had always pointed to the clarifying power of time, and now Kick hoped he was right. She was sure Billy wouldn't want to marry before the election in February, and in order to run he soon had to leave the Coldstream Guards, which meant that he wouldn't have to go to the front anytime soon. Surely another answer would present itself. She would pray ardently that it would.

When she wrote her next wave of letters home, she knew she had to mention Billy because her parents were likely to hear something from their other friends, or worse, from the gossip pages. But the last thing she wanted was their weighing in on the situation. So she tried to downplay it and reassure her mother that she was too good a Catholic to do anything that would imperil her soul. Even to Jack, she wrote of Billy, "Of course I know he would never give in about the religion and he knows I never would. It's all rather difficult as he is very, very fond of me and as long as I am about, he'll never marry. However much he loves me, I can easily understand his position."

In fact, she understood perfectly. She only wished she didn't understand so well.

CHAPTER 29

Joe Jr. arrived in London in the last week of September with rotten eggs and a box full of suckers, gum, and Mars bars, wanting nothing more than to get into the fight to prove he was as much a hero as his skinny little brother, who had once again been thrust into the spotlight. In the last few weeks, Jack had managed to save most of his crew after a Japanese torpedo hit their boat in the Pacific, using his prodigious and now-famous swimming skills to tow one of the injured men to shore in spite of his bad back. As if that weren't enough, he'd floated an SOS note into the ocean on a coconut, of all things, which against all odds made it to an Australian regiment, who did indeed rescue them. It had been all over the news, and Kick had become a hero by extension at the Hans Crescent. Once she knew her brother was all right, she couldn't help but laugh uproariously at the details. "A coconut?" she'd said to Dukie Wookie at the 400. "Even George Bernard Shaw couldn't have imagined something like that and made it believable!"

"If I didn't love him so much, I'd want to kill him," Joe Jr. said to Kick over a pint of ale at the Hans Crescent. Kick was fit to burst with happiness that afternoon, what with her brother in town, a date with Billy scheduled for the weekend, and Nancy Astor picking through the club's bar looking for boys from Virginia to cheer up, as she did periodically. Also, it was her favorite season in England—drizzly and cool one day, brilliantly blue and cold the next. She loved pedaling her bike through the streets with a scarf around her neck and yellow leaves falling on her head. Also, things felt back on promising and sturdy footing with Billy, who came to London every chance he got. Once, they'd met in Derbyshire and strolled the grounds of Chatsworth, and he'd lamented naughtily that with the girls' school in session at the house, there was really no way to accomplish the swimming *sans vêtements* he'd once alluded to before the war.

"Maybe you should just let Jack be president," Kick teased Joe Jr., "and you enjoy a nice louche life instead. I'll set you up in a castle."

"Lismore Castle?" Joe asked, referring to the Cavendish estate in Ireland.

"You never know," sang Kick.

After a short visit, Joe had to go with his squadron to Cornwall, where his planes would be helping the Royal Air Force patrol the coast. "It's coward's work," he'd told his sister before he left, "but I'm gonna parlay it into something real." Then he blew out of town as suddenly as he'd blown in, and life went on in the new usual way for Kick: a steady rotation of work, dinners, and after-hours dancing. At the end of the summer, she'd gotten into trouble with Scroggins for having too many friends over to the club and taking too many calls from her "damn suitors," and generally having too much of a social life outside the club. But she'd dropped hints to a few key friends that her boss was giving her difficulties, and two of the best had come to her rescue. Admiral Stark had told Scroggins in front of an entire room full of gin-rummy-playing captains and lieutenants that "Kick Kennedy, *John Fitzgerald Kennedy's sister* no less, is a national treasure, and d'you know how lucky you are to have her?" to a mortifying but also gratifying round of hooting applause led by Tim, of all people. And Lady Astor had written Scroggins about Anglo-American relations, "which are suffering terribly now, yes in part because of Kick's own father, but she seeks nothing but to remedy that. I advise you to let her steer her own course, for it will bring nothing but acclaim to your club and harmony to our allied men in uniform."

At the end of October, Joe got an assignment that brought him back to London. He joined Kick for dinner at the Savoy, courtesy of Bill Hearst, who'd been spending a lot of time at the Crescent while sending dispatches on the war back to his publisher father in San Francisco. Hearst liked Kick and was always trying to convince her to write more. "Wealth and writing can by very simpatico," he told her that night in the posh hotel restaurant. "They don't have to be at odds."

"You'd know better than anyone," she replied with a smile.

"Write me an insider story on the Hans Crescent," he suggested. "I bet you've gathered plenty of secrets there."

"I *am* the secret, Bill," she laughed. The truth was, she thought some-day she might go back to writing. She'd enjoyed her work on the *Times-Herald*, and was always threatening to write Nancy Astor's life story since the lady didn't bother keeping a diary herself that might someday be published. The project appealed to her. But she hardly had time for any-thing like that now.

"Your wit is wasted on the aristocracy, Kick," Bill said.

"What an American sentiment," she replied in her finest faux Cambridge-educated accent.

Bill and Kick and Joe Jr. were at a large table with Angie Laycock and her husband Robert, head of the highly trained and secret British Com-mandos, and Lady Virginia Sykes, who was about to have a baby any moment, though her husband was stationed abroad. "In case I go into labor," said Virginia, "I've brought my friend Pat with me. You know all about babies, don't you, Pat?" Virginia smiled at her friend Pat Wilson.

Joe was immediately intrigued by Pat, which was a bit awkward for Kick, since she knew of her brother's history with Virginia—they'd been caught kissing when she was a debutante before the war. No one brought up that old scrap of gossip, though, even in jest, and Virginia seemed quite content to become the mother of Lord Sykes's child. Pat Wilson was just Joe's type, which is to say she was married. It didn't hurt that she had big blue eyes under heavy lids and black lashes, dark hair, and lush red lips. Her second husband Robin Wilson had been with the British Army in Libya for more than two years. She had an easy way of being in her own skin, totally confident and relaxed. She was the opposite of ambitious, blond Inga, the epitome of Jack's type of off-limits woman—though Pat was foreign, like Inga; she was from Australia, which barely tinged her accent compared to Inga's more glamorous Danish pronunciations.

Kick listened as Joe uncoiled with this tempting stranger and talked about movies and Cornish pasties, and how happy he was to be with his sister. "We haven't been on an adventure, just us two, in almost five years," he said.

"Five years since Spain?" Kick exclaimed, allowing the champagne to make her a bit silly. "Impossible!"

"I love Spain," said Pat. "The people are so warm and friendly, and I think the food is the best in Europe."

"Don't let the French hear you say that," said Kick.

"Aw, the French can have their *petits gâteaux*," said Joe. "I'll take churros and chocolate any day."

Pat snickered behind red-tipped nails.

"What part of Spain were you in?" asked Joe, now focused totally on Pat. And off they went on a detailed discussion of Barcelona. The electricity between the two of them was unmistakable, sparking in everything from Pat's unbridled laughter to her brother's best behavior and liberal compliments. It made Kick miss Billy all the more, especially when she noticed that Joe and Pat disappeared into their own taxi at the end of the night, when the rest of them headed to the 400. Joe wouldn't miss out on his favorite nightclub for just anyone, and Kick found she was very jealous in that old familiar way. Once again, one of her brothers was having the sort of *real fun* she and Billy were waiting so bloody long to enjoy. She hated to wonder whether Billy already knew what he was missing. Worse, if he was enjoying it elsewhere, like Joe and Jack would have been in Billy's shoes. Somehow she doubted it. She'd learned well enough from watching her brothers and father that men couldn't keep that kind of behavior a secret for long. Still, she worried about what might be happening those cold nights in desolate Scotland when memories of her kisses might not be enough to keep him warm.

She tried to pray about these matters, to ask for guidance from Christ's mother Mary, but somehow she couldn't even admit in her prayers what she was really afraid of. Not to the virgin mother of God. She knew God saw her thoughts, and so she tried to avoid the thoughts altogether. All of this had the effect of making her feel removed from her faith for the first time. Instead, she prayed for Rosemary, that she might still recover and come home, get married, and be blessed with children of her own. She prayed for Rudi, wherever he was now. She prayed for her brothers, and Tim and the other boys in uniform, that they would return in one piece. She prayed last and most ardently for Billy, asking God to grant him his dearest wish to fight in the war, and then send him safely home.

❖ ❖ ❖

The next thing she knew, she was getting more and more correspondence from Billy's mother and sisters. They'd all be coming to a party she was throwing with Fiona Gore at Marie Bruce's apartment in a week's time. "Lizzy's never been to a party like the one you're likely to throw, so I don't want to hear about her being corrupted," Billy joked on the phone one night.

"You're sure you can't be there to defend her honor?"

"I wish more than anything that I could," he replied, "but I have to stay here." Kick knew better than to press the issue—Billy felt guilty enough about leaving the guards to run for a seat in Parliament; he didn't want to do anything but follow the rule book until he had to leave.

After a short pause, he said, "Speaking of sisters, I've been meaning to ask about your Rosemary. I'm so sorry I didn't inquire before."

This was an unexpected turn in conversation. Kick was touched, but wary. "She is in a hospital," Kick replied, not wanting to say more.

"Has the trouble I saw in her . . . worsened?"

"Not exactly," Kick said, calculating how much to reveal. *My parents couldn't stand that she was becoming a woman? That because of her problems she couldn't control herself around men like I can?* "But it took another turn. She started sneaking out of the convent where she was living, and the whole family was so worried, and . . ."

"You don't have to tell me if it's too distressing," Billy said. "It doesn't affect my feelings for you. I just wanted you to know that I remembered her, and care about her because she's part of your family."

"Thank you," Kick whispered, tears and phlegm making it hard to speak. She cleared her throat and said, "Well, my father thought it would be best if she took a rest in a hospital. And the doctors think it's best if her treatment isn't disturbed."

"I see," Billy said.

"I wish there was more to say," she added lamely. There was more, of course. The anger and mourning and frustration she felt, the fear. But now, on the phone, with so much at stake, was not the time to bring that up.

She could hear the hesitation crackle on the other end of the line before he said, "I hate the telephone, but I don't have any leave coming up soon, so I have to ask if you've given any more thought to what we discussed at Eastbourne?"

"I've thought of little else," she said, and it was true. No matter what she did during her full days, the questions about her and Billy were on a constant rotation in the back of her mind, often pushing through to the front.

"And?" He sounded a little afraid.

"Can I have a bit more time? The holidays are coming up, then the elections . . . We have some time, don't we?"

There was a pause before he replied, "Kick, I want so much to write to my *wife* at the end of my days here, call my *wife* on the phone at Churchdale or Eastbourne. I want to know that you're as safe as my sisters and sister-in-law. Maybe even with . . ." His voice trailed off.

"Babies hardly arrive overnight, you know," she said, seizing the opportunity to lighten the mood—though her heart had fluttered almost painfully every time he said the word *wife*.

He laughed. "No, I'd have nine glorious months to spoil you rotten. And not just with *things*, which are impossible to come by these days anyway, but with love and joy."

The phone's slick receiver was slippery in her sweaty hand. "And foot rubs, I hope. I've heard all my pregnant friends want is a good foot massage," she said, again trying to bring some levity.

"You'd want for no comfort," he said, his voice thick with emotion. "You'd have everything you needed."

If that were true, I'd say yes in a heartbeat, she thought.

❖ ❖ ❖

In the end, it was probably for the best that Billy couldn't come to her party, as playing hostess had her running around like a crazed person all through the night, especially when Joe arrived with his whole squadron, who'd all been out drinking before.

"You better behave, big brother," she said to Joe, who smelled of whiskey as he embraced her at the door to the apartment. Mercifully, he did. And in her prayers that night she thanked God for sending him with his men, because one of the young American soldiers saved the whole evening. Irving Berlin, a friend of Marie Bruce's, had put in a surprise appearance and performance at the party, and just as he finished a rousing "Puttin' On the Ritz" that had everyone on their feet, Elizabeth Cavendish's brand-new blue silk party dress caught on fire at the hem.

After a moment of loud exclamations from all corners of the room, one of Joe's men stamped it out with his well-shined boots, to more applause.

"Your party just went from excellent to legendary," said Irving with a smile at Kick, setting his black felt hat on his head. "Congratulations."

Kick was horrified, but when she reached the duchess and Elizabeth to ask if everyone was all right, she found them laughing. "It's just a dress," said the duchess reassuringly. "After a private performance by Mr. Berlin, how could anyone be upset about some fabric? We can make it into a tea-length dress with no problem." Elizabeth herself, suddenly the giggling center of five boys' attention, didn't seem bothered, either. *Well*, thought Kick, with enormous relief, *I'm glad it wasn't my mother and Jean's dress on fire!*

"You do lead a charmed life," Billy commented the next night on the phone, after hearing all about the evening from his breathless sister.

"I fear I'm more like a cat, with nine chances at recuperative luck, and steadily using up each one," she said.

Billy laughed. "Well, if anyone can get a tenth, it's you."

She nearly said, *I'd gladly lend one or two to Andrew, now that he's getting shipped to Italy*, but she stopped just before she opened her mouth. Billy had behaved so strangely when he heard the news of Andrew's assignment. He'd hardly been able to sit still at Boofie and Fiona's dinner, saying what rot it was that they were shipping off his brother, who was a new father with another child on the way. "It should have been me," he'd said morosely before getting blind drunk.

Though Kick had been extremely relieved that it hadn't been Billy who was called up, she had the uneasy sense that having to stay back and wait to do that thing he was so eager to do—*punish the Huns and show them what England really is*—might actually make him more recalcitrant on the subject of their marriage and religion. She hated to think that England and "everything it stands for," the very England she herself loved, might be the wedge to keep them apart.

"I love you," she said instead. It was the first time she'd said it before he had, and she meant it in every fiber of her body, but what she wanted most of all was to hear him say it back, to feel embraced by his words since he wasn't there to do it in person.

"I love you," he said, with an emphasis on the *you* that flooded her with such a wanton desire to kiss him, she thought about hopping on a train and surprising him that very night. Inga would do something like that. *But I'm not Inga*, she thought with as much reproach as regret.

❧ ❧ ❧

She had the mounting sense that Billy had enlisted his sisters and mother in helping Kick make up her mind about the matters they'd discussed at Eastbourne. The most significant sign of this campaign came shortly after Christmas. She'd had to spend Christmas itself at the Hans Crescent, making sure the boys, including Joe Jr., who'd made it to London for midnight mass, lived it up to Bing Crosby's Christmas tunes, and numerous performances by vulgar Santa Claus vaudeville acts, and dances with bands like the High Flyers. At last she got a few days off that coincided with the end of Billy's holiday leave, and she'd spent two glorious days with the Cavendish family at Churchdale Hall.

She'd arrived equipped with what passed for luxury gifts these days—two bottles of champagne, a box of Swiss chocolates for the duchess, cigars for the duke, and a pack of nylons and a brand-new lipstick each for Billy's sisters and Debo. Plus, a real present for Billy, which she planned on giving him in a private moment. The ladies received Kick's presents with exclamations of thanks and joy over tea and cookies in the drawing room, where a tall tree was trimmed with colorful glass orbs. The whole family was there, except Andrew, who hadn't gotten leave, and the duke, who'd escaped to his home studio to tie flies for his next fishing expedition. Kick wondered whether he'd be testing them in the bath that night. Everyone was lazily warming their feet by the fire and enjoying the twinkle of lights on the tree.

Then the duchess handed Kick a small black box that was festively tied with a red tartan ribbon. Kick almost said, *I can't accept this! I didn't get you anything of substance!* But the smile on the duchess's face made her realize that not to accept would be the height of rudeness.

Pregnant Debo shifted sleeping Emma in her arms and leaned forward to get a better look as Kick's trembling hands undid the ribbon and then lifted the top off the box. When Kick saw the delicate diamond-and-pearl cross pendant necklace glittering on the black velvet, she gasped, feeling guilty not just for her poor hostess gifts but also because the gift of a cross from Billy's Protestant mother felt . . . strange.

She looked from the duchess, who wore a face of bright expectation, to Billy, who wore the same, and gushed, "It's absolutely gorgeous."

Billy helped her fasten it under her hair, then everyone commenced oohing and aahing over its beauty and the way it complemented her creamy skin. Kick felt a bit better when she learned that Billy's parents had splurged on gifts for all the girls in the family, with Anne and Elizabeth each receiving golden bracelets, and Debo a ruby-and-diamond cross similar to Kick's.

Still, when she and Debo had a moment alone, Kick fingered the cross, which sat perfectly in the space between her collarbones, and whispered so that no one else could hear, "I can't believe this gift!"

"They want Billy to be happy," Debo said. "Now that I have little Emma, I can understand that. A mother's love is . . . well, I just want the world for Emma."

"I can't help but feel I'm wearing a Protestant cross, not a Catholic one."

Debo sighed. "That might be true, I must admit. Have you thought more about it? What about converting? We're not heathens, you know." Debo's voice was light, teasing. But she definitely wanted some sort of insight, and suddenly Kick felt wary of giving it to her, since she was now Billy's sister-in-law, the mother of his first niece and maybe soon nephew.

Kick laughed it off. "I know that, of course. I just . . . it's such a huge decision. I'll lose my own mother, to say nothing of my soul, if I convert."

Debo put a hand on her rounded belly and said, "Losing your mother would be terrible. But you'd gain a most wonderful mother-in-law."

Kick smiled but didn't say more. Debo's own mother, Muv, had made a choice to care for Unity at the expense of caring for her other daughters, and so Debo's affection for Andrew's mother had become more ardent, more loyal, than it might otherwise have been. But Kick was in a reverse position, with her own older sister gone.

"Do you like it? Mother's gift?" Billy asked much later that night, when they were alone in the drawing room with a fire and glasses of brandy. She was full of roast beef and potatoes and carrots and red wine, relaxing in Billy's childhood home. She wished the cross could be the pièce de résistance. And it was, in a way.

"How could I not love it?" she said, fingering the smooth pearls. "It's beautiful, and ever so thoughtful and generous."

"I still love the cuff links you gave me all those years ago," he said, "though there are fewer occasions to wear them these days."

"Those days will return," she said.

"I'm not so sure," he said. "I sometimes wonder if Chatsworth will ever be what it was in 1930. You should have seen it then. It was the stuff you read of in books."

"It can be again," she said firmly, squeezing his hand.

"The famous Kick optimism."

"Speaking of which, I want you to know it's my New Year's resolution to find a solution to our dilemma as soon as possible. That word, *wife*, you said on the phone, is still ringing in my ears."

Billy smiled and kissed her. "Good." He kissed her again. "And I love your gift this year," he said, patting the pocket where he kept his new handkerchiefs, one embroidered with his initials, the other with hers. "I'm sorry I couldn't get you more than stationery," he said, "but there's hardly any shopping by the base, and I like to be able to pick things out myself. And anyway, Mum was so excited about her gift, I wanted to let it have center stage."

"I love your gift," she said, because she did—the paper was so luxurious and velvety, with her name embossed at the top in a rich burgundy. "Paper like that is impossible to come by. Who'd you kill to get it?"

Billy waggled his eyebrows like a matinee movie villain, then put his hand behind her head and pulled her in for a long kiss that ended all conversation for the evening.

WINTER 1944

*T*wo things. All life—a life rich with laughter, tradition, conversation, celebrations, and even grief that made joy all the sweeter—now balanced precariously on the twin heads of two spinning tops.

War and love.

Love and war.

England was nearly ready for the promised invasion of France. Revenge. He couldn't wait, and he was ready. Gruelingly, his body had changed for it. His mind, too. In his dreams, he still heard the screams and saw the limbs in the matted leaves. Heard the tanks. Sometimes he'd wake up sweating but cold. Sometimes, still dreaming, he'd feel the Baby Austin roar to life beneath him and carry him away. Sometimes it flew, carried on the wind by winged horses.

Had we but world enough, and time . . .

He would never try to bed his love like Andrew Marvell, but he felt the poet's urgency. He couldn't help but feel selfish in this regard. He had pined for her so long, eschewing others. If he was going to war, he wanted to go to it a man, knowing what men knew of love. Real love. Since he'd become an adult in name only, there had been a few girls (fewer than he could count on one hand) who'd offered themselves to him, but he hadn't found true pleasure with them. The release was purely physical and left him empty. Like Marvell, he wanted to be the wooer. That was part of Kick's appeal. She didn't need him, or want him because he was William John Robert Cavendish, Marquess of Hartington. Unlike any other woman he knew, she could have anyone. There was real accomplishment in winning Kick. And there was love and backbone, too. He believed in his soul that if she loved him in return, if she agreed to be his, her vitality would make him keener, braver, tougher.

Love and war. War and love. If he could master them both, he could die complete. And if he didn't die . . . well, then, who knew what else was possible? He thought of his niece's tiny fingers coiled around his, the way her touch had sent an unexpected tremor through his chest. He'd never thought of himself much as a father, but his brother's child made him picture it. Made him want ten of her wrapping their fingers around his. He'd allowed himself to think enough about life after the war to know that he'd need something to replace the war in his heart and mind. Children. The smiling faces on the next generation of Cavendishes (and Kennedys, since God must be a comedian as much as a righter of wrongs) were the only images that could replace the one of him marching into enemy camps and enjoying their sniveling surrender.

But first there was love. No small task. He wanted Kick, and she would not simply give him what he wanted. He would have to be careful. Play his cards right.

> *But at my back I always hear*
> *Time's wingèd chariot hurrying near;*
> *And yonder all before us lie*
> *Deserts of vast eternity.*

PART 5

❖ ❖ ❖

WINTER 1944

CHAPTER 30

Kick prayed every night that the promising start of 1944 was a sign of more good things to come. Before the end of January she was ensconced in a London flat of her very own. After much convincing, her mother and father had finally agreed that sharing a room with strangers was not the best arrangement, and they would make a small contribution to help with rent, enough so that she could secure a lovely little place right near Marie Bruce's apartment. And Billy's mother had offered to equip it with napkins and tablecloths and sheets from Chatsworth. Imagine!

Kick wrote her mother about those, and the necklace she'd received for Christmas, then held her breath—so far, her mother hadn't said much about Billy, though Kick had been dropping hints all along, wondering each time what her mother would say. Finally, in reply to Kick's description of the Cavendishes' generosity, Rose had written, "It sounds as though Billy's family has embraced you with open arms, and I'm glad of that. Everyone needs a surrogate family while living abroad. But do be careful, Kathleen. I know how fond you are of Billy, and I don't want you to get hurt." Kick decided that this response was progress—no longer was Mother actively trying to keep her away from Billy. She appeared to be trusting Kick to make her own choices.

Perhaps best of all were the festive rendezvous that were becoming regular events at Pat Wilson's cottage at Crastock Farm. Kick, Joe Jr., and their friends congregated there on their days off, bringing with them whatever surprise goodies they could lay their hands on before catching the train: cured ham, a bottle of wine, bars of chocolate. Thanks to Pat's green thumb and excellent kitchen skills, even in the winter there were jars of pickled and preserved vegetables from her garden. One weekend, Debo impressed everyone with a spaghetti marinara made from Pat's jarred tomatoes. Kick consoled herself that even if she could barely boil an egg, at least she could keep everyone in candy bars sent from the States. (The box of sweets Joe had brought with him was long since devoured, but they were still working their way through a giant one Eunice and Pat had sent for Christmas.)

Since the house was just southwest of London, it was a perfect midpoint for many of her friends, with Billy stationed a little farther west in Alton, and Joe farther south in Dunkeswell. Kick called it Crash-Bang, because it quickly became the place where all her favorite people liked to crash—even more so than the nightclubs these days. There was a slightly different mix each time, and Kick enjoyed them all, though whenever Billy wasn't there, she always wished he was. Such was the case one cold day in January, when Bertrand and Kick lazed about with Sissy and David, who were visiting for the day with little Julian and Jane. The children chased a red rubber ball through the house while it drizzled outside.

"I fear Julian's tastes run more toward football than rugby," observed David.

"Don't be a snob, darling," said Sissy. "Rugby may be played by gentlemen, but it's a thug's sport. Football's a far more genteel game. No hands. No tackling."

"But it's actually played by thugs," David pointed out.

"Hence the snobbery," concluded Sissy.

"At least he's not waving a bat and declaring his interest in cricket," put in Kick. "Dullest game in the universe."

"No worse than American baseball," said Bertrand.

"Talk to me after you've seen the Red Sox play the Yankees," she replied.

The four of them had their feet up on ottomans and on each other, while Joe and Pat were "resting" and her children napped. The living room of the cottage was homey and well lit, with soft, comfortable sofas and shelves full of books and bric-a-brac from Pat's and Robin's travels. There were no portraits of imposing ancestors, but there were two small Picasso drawings hanging above an armchair.

"I fancy a cup of tea," said Sissy. "Anyone else?"

Everyone did, and Kick got up to help her. She'd been wanting to get Sissy alone. While her friend set the kettle on the hulking blue Aga, and Kick measured tea into the pot, she ventured, "Can I bend your ear about something?"

"Finally," said Sissy.

"Pardon?"

"This is about Billy, right?"

"You're not surprised."

"Kick, you're not fooling anyone. Not anymore."

"Well, I'm glad. *Finally.*"

"Wonderful! Have you two set a date?" Sissy was excited, but Kick could also hear the slight note of misgiving in her voice.

"I wish it were that simple," Kick sighed. "We seem to be at an impasse on the religion question."

"What question?" Sissy said, genuinely surprised.

"He's not asking me to convert," began Kick, "though I know that's what his parents would like."

"Out of the question," Sissy agreed with a firm shake of her head.

"But he's also made it clear that the children would have to be raised Protestant."

"Even the girls?" Sissy was incredulous, eyebrows raised. The kettle screeched, and she used a towel to hold the hot metal handle as she poured steaming water into the pot.

"Even the girls," Kick confirmed. "He said, what if we don't have boys? Or what if they die in another war? Then the estate would fall to the Catholic girls."

"And what would be so terrible about that? David's heir to the Harlech baronetcy, which is equally Protestant and frankly closed-minded about Catholics, and he's raising both our boys and girls Catholic."

Kick hadn't expected Sissy to be quite so vehement. Nor had she meant to question the arrangement Sissy and David had come to, but that was the way her friend seemed to be interpreting her queries. Eager to reassure her, Kick tried again. "David has been the utmost gentleman; I hope you don't think I'm saying anything less than that. I just wonder . . . was there ever a time he was in doubt about your arrangement? Was there anything you said that helped to sway him?"

Sissy shook her head. "He knew from the start that if he wanted me, those would be the terms. Plenty of dukes have done the same, you know. For heaven's sake, the king of England relinquished his crown to be with a divorcee. I know it's not exactly equivalent, but it's close enough. What compromise is Billy willing to make?"

"He's already willing to marry an untitled American. Of Irish descent," Kick said, appalled she was having to say the words out loud. Even Billy hadn't said them, but their truth was always hanging in the room.

"Et tu, Kick? *You*, of all people, are selling yourself short?"

"It's true, isn't it?" She felt suddenly bereft, and her chin trembled.

Sissy came to her side and put her arm around Kick's shoulder. "Oh, Kick. This must be terrible for you. But don't lose sight of what you *are*. You're a Kennedy, for heaven's sake! People all over the world know who you are. Who's heard of Billy outside our little island? It's not just because you're a Kennedy, it's because you're *you*. And I hate to be the one to say it, but even though you don't have a title, your millions are hardly worth nothing."

"Billy doesn't need money."

"All the great estates will need money after this war is over," Bertrand said. Suddenly, he was standing in the doorway to the kitchen. When the girls turned to look at him in surprise, he said with an incorrigible grin, "What? I was thirsty. And your lazy lout of a husband sent me down to see what was taking you so long."

"That's because he knows what's good for him," said Sissy to Bertrand in a jesting tone, but Kick heard her friend's double meaning, loud and clear.

"For what it's worth, Kick, I agree with Sissy. Why should you be the one to make all the sacrifices?"

"If I'd listened to your advice from thirty-nine," Kick said drily, "we wouldn't be having this conversation at all."

"Kind of tells you something, doesn't it?" Bertrand said, grinning again. Kick wanted to punch him. If he had been Jack, she would have.

"Don't listen to this sideshow Freud," Sissy said, grabbing hold of the tray with all the tea accoutrements. "Talk to Billy again."

So much for promising starts.

❖ ❖ ❖

Kick grieved the loss of Father O'Flaherty all the more in the following weeks. He would have known what she should do. When she prayed, she found herself praying directly to him instead of to God or the Virgin. *Father*, she'd address him from her knees at her bedside, or from a pew at St. Mary's, where she felt closest to him, *please guide me. Send me a sign, be my compass. Something, anything, that will show me the right course. I miss you so much.*

"You seem to lack the usual bounce in your step, Kick," observed Lord Halifax at the Hans Crescent. He and Lady Halifax were in England for a few weeks, meeting with Churchill and other officials before taking fresh intelligence back to the embassy in Washington.

"Have I?" Kick replied, bouncing a little jig in her worn brown work shoes. She was awaiting a new pair from her mother, who written that she'd seen some good ones at Bergdorf's.

Lord Halifax laughed and said, "Can you join me and Dorothy for lunch tomorrow?"

"I'd love that," she said, though she felt powerfully homesick at the sight of him. It was strange. Lord Halifax was English, but he reminded her of those days in Washington, DC, that had been far simpler than what she was facing in London. Thinking of Washington made her remember Patsy White—maybe she, an older, more experienced married woman who was totally removed from the situation with Billy, could offer some sage advice. She *had* once offered to act as a sounding board. Kick made a mental note to write to her American friend.

Over roast venison and potatoes at the Savoy, after they'd caught up on the Washington gossip, Lady Halifax said, "Now, Kick, you must tell us what's happening with Billy Hartington."

Recalling that in the past Lord and Lady Halifax had shown nothing but the utmost discretion, and also a philosophical approach to religion, Kick confessed the entire situation, trying to keep her voice as level and calm as possible. At the end, she said, "I just don't know what to do. It's all mixed up in my head—my mother, my father, his mother, his father, my religion, his religion, my heart. I don't know what to listen to. None of them agree."

"I suspect your father will forgive anything," offered Lord Halifax. "You are the absolute apple of his eye."

Kick blushed and felt tears rush to her eyes. "I hope so," she whispered.

"As for your mother," Lady Halifax said, "I don't know her very well, but I can't imagine not loving you no matter what. That's what a mother does—loves her children no matter what."

"I have no doubt of her love," Kick said quickly, but her mind turned to the closets of her childhood, and to all Rose's entreaties for Kick to remember who she was. "But she also believes very strongly in our family. And in the church. She would take it as the greatest insult and embarrassment if her . . ." *Oldest* daughter? Was that what she was now, with Rosemary gone? ". . . her first daughter to get married did so outside the church. And it could hurt Joe's and Jack's future careers as well."

At this, Lord Halifax laughed gently. "I think perhaps that might be a bit of Kennedy hubris, if you don't mind my saying so. From what I've gathered, the American public is more independent minded than your parents give them credit for. And while having their daughter marry a Protestant might hurt them with a certain very small contingent of Catholic voters in Boston, I suspect your father could find a way to use it to *win* more votes with those Brahmins he's been trying to best his whole life."

Kick hadn't considered this before, and a cool breeze of relief prickled her skin. What he said made perfect sense. And Daddy was a maestro with the press.

"And," added Lady Halifax, "isn't your oldest brother here in England? Why don't you ask him what he thinks directly?"

Kick nodded. "I will," she said, relieved to be taking advice like a dutiful child. "I can't tell you how much I appreciate this. I've needed . . . help."

In a motherly gesture that left Kick wrecked with longing, Lady Halifax brushed a lock of hair out of Kick's eyes and gently patted her cheek. "Of course you have, darling."

CHAPTER 31

By early February, Billy's race against Charlie White had become a national spectacle, with predictions that the decision of voters in West Derbyshire would shape future elections throughout England. Who would prevail? Billy Hartington, a Conservative who represented the old ways of landowners looking after their estates and people? Or White, a liberal who purported to represent change and greater independence for the workingman?

A pugnacious cobbler's son, White was to Kick a combative middle-aged man with small eyes and a perpetual snarl on his lips. Though the newspaper pictures were black and white, Kick could always make out the sunburnt ruddiness of his cheeks. His father had been the only non-Cavendish in hundreds of years to win the West Derbyshire seat, and Charlie had tried to reclaim it on the Labour ticket against Billy's uncle Henry in 1938 and lost. He wasn't even supposed to be running in this wartime by-election of 1944, but he had a big fat ax to grind, and he swung it at Billy and his family every chance he got. He regularly called Billy a deserter who wasn't doing his patriotic duty, going so far as to insinuate that Billy might in fact be a Fascist since he was "vaguely related" to Oswald Mosley. He repeatedly said that at twenty-six, "Baby Billy" had never known a day's honest work in his life. That last accusation had in-spired Robert Goodall, a farmer who was also running, to proclaim that Billy surely didn't know how to milk a cow, and how could a man who'd never milked a cow run a dairy county?

Kick had been so proud of Billy when he replied, with his character-istic calm, "Actually, Mr. Goodall, one of my favorite escapes as a child was to a farm right here in Derbyshire, where I milked my share of cows. *And* I learned to spread muck. Nothing so cleansing to the soul as moving manure around a farm." Kick was amazed at his wit and poise in front of the schoolrooms full of hostile mothers, fathers, and young wives whose sons and husbands were off dying abroad, and she loved him all the more in those moments. She wished she could be with him more on his campaign, but her duties at the Hans Crescent kept her frustrat-ingly away.

She wanted so much to help Billy that she'd rung her father in New York to ask his advice. "Have you heard what's happening to the Caven-dish family, Daddy? It's dreadful, and I just keep thinking that you'd have some ideas for how to help, so I had to call. The mail takes an age."

"Slow down, Kick," her father had said. "I'm glad you called. How are you? We treasure every one of your letters, and Mother's keeping them all, just as you asked."

"Is she there with you now?"

"No, she's out. Lunch, I think. Kick, it's marvelous to hear your voice."

In her mind, she could see her father's blue eyes smiling behind his glasses, and her heart was full of missing him. *Even now? Despite every-thing?*

"It's marvelous to hear yours, too, Daddy," she said.

Then, on the other end, he took a deep breath and said, "Well, your mother will have my head if I take too long on an international call, so let's get down to it. I have indeed read about Billy's battle with this man White. He sounds like a real piece of work."

"He's wretched."

"The first thing is not to let the voters or the press see that anyone on your side feels that way. If you sink to his level, you'll only get stuck in the quagmire."

"Oh, the Cavendishes are too proud to let it show that White's getting to them. And Billy's impatient with all the false accusations, but he calmly answers each one. I mean, really—the idea that he might be a Fascist, just because Debo's sister is married to Oswald! It's absurd."

"Politics is worse than absurd, darling; it's unfair and soul crushing."

"Don't say that, Daddy. Not you, of all people. Don't you still want Joe to be president?"

"Of course I do, but I also want him to know the risks. Kick, I'm afraid I can't help much from where I'm sitting now. The best I can do is put in a few calls with my contacts in London, but Churchill's already written a public letter supporting Billy. How much good would it do to have a lesser-known official do the same?"

Kick sighed. "I suppose you're right."

"The best thing you can do for Billy is support him." Then, after a pause, he added, "You really do love him, don't you?"

The pure, tender kindness in his voice was so rare, she felt comfortable telling him the truth. "I'm afraid I do."

"Is he going to convert?"

"No."

Joe was silent a moment, then he said, "Well now, *this* I can do some asking about. A few priests and even a cardinal owe me a favor or two, and of course the pope remembers us fondly. I can't have my oldest girl so miserable, can I?"

Oldest girl. So he was the one to say it first.

"You think there might be some sort of loophole in the church?" she asked, her heart lurching with happiness.

"If there is, darling girl, I'll find it."

"I want to hug you right now!"

Joe laughed. "So do I."

"And please don't tell Mother."

"She'll have to know at some point. And your mother's not a fan of loopholes, you know."

"I know. But . . . one thing at a time."

"You've become very wise," her father observed, and her heart once again pitched in her chest.

❖-❖-❖

Ironically, she had Charlie White's success to thank for securing a week off from work to help Billy in Derbyshire. Admiral Stark, Lady Astor, and the Duchess of Devonshire had all written Scroggins to explain how indispensable Kick would be to the Cavendish family in this trying time when the very future of England was in the balance. Plus, her twenty-fourth birthday was close to election day, and it was the informal policy at the Hans Crescent to let the girls have some extra time off around their birthdays. "No more days off for the rest of the month when you return," her boss snarled when he agreed to give her the week. "And stay out of the papers."

Scroggins needn't have worried. Billy's parents asked that Kick go incognito, posing as a local girl. After some joking with Billy about what pseudonym she should choose—Elizabeth True Door? The Honorable Jane Grey? Mary Luther?—she chose the name Rosemary. It was strange even to her, but the name was a comfort. A reminder of what she'd lost, but also of the freedom she might still gain.

Rosemary Tong wore a plain brown dress, old shoes, and a borrowed orange kerchief around her head. Her first day on the trail, she and Billy's sister Elizabeth knocked on hundreds of doors and passed out countless flyers that read "A vote for Hartington is a vote for Churchill." At the start, it had been thrilling to be so unrecognized, to be able to tell housewives and farmhands that Billy was the right choice for them and their country.

But as the day wore on and she heard the same questions over and over—"Thanks, lass, but what can a dandy aristocrat do for me? What does he know of my troubles?" and "What's a Yankee girl doing helping a Tory? You lot threw off the yoke hundreds of years ago"—she began to feel her feet ache and her spirit dampen. She got the sense that most of the people she answered viewed her words skeptically. No matter how much she assured people that Billy was a *progressive* Conservative who wanted to make real and tangible changes for the hardworking people in his county, who planned to go back and fight in the war as soon as the election was over, who was absolutely *not* a Nazi, she sensed that she was fighting a losing battle. *Poor Billy*, she thought. *And Poor Daddy*, was her immediate next thought, for he must have felt the same about those terrible late-summer days of 1939 when all that he deeply believed went on the chopping block.

In the afternoon, she went to hear the duchess speak at a church, before going to hear Billy and Charlie at the town hall. What should have been a little regional election had garnered so much attention that *Time* magazine and a few other American publications were covering all the final speeches. The duchess stood on the sparse altar with late-afternoon light raining down from the stained glass windows, wearing a simple gray suit and hat. Beaming a welcoming smile at the pews full of local women, she began, "And to think that when many of us were girls, we weren't even allowed to vote. The women of West Derbyshire have come a long way in that time, in no small part because of meetings like this one, where concerned people come together to rationally discuss their differences. That is what I hope to offer you today. Calm, rational answers to your questions about this election." Kick was impressed. With astounding grace given the circumstances, Billy's mother delivered exactly what she promised, and Kick could feel the machinations of scores of female minds grinding over to her side.

The men's speeches were not so tame.

The town hall was standing room only, and reporters and photographers jostled for the best shots of the two main candidates. Billy wore his Coldstream Guards uniform, and White wore an ill-fitting navy suit. First, Billy took the stage, to a respectable round of applause. Then, when it was White's turn, the room filled with cheers and whistles. A few even chanted "Char-lie! Char-lie!" Billy towered over White, kept his hands behind his back, and wore a look of benign calm that Kick knew had taken herculean strength to plaster on.

White spoke first, and began, "You've all noticed, I'm sure, that my esteemed rival is wearing his captain's uniform tonight, no doubt to remind you all that *no matter what happens on the seventeenth, he'll go to the front.* But I'd like to remind my friends here tonight that we don't know what he'll really do, because he's a Cavendish. And Cavendishes have been breaking promises to the good people of West Derbyshire for generations."

Billy's smile never faltered.

If only Mother and Daddy could see him now, she thought. *They'd know by his smile that he could be one of us.*

❖ ❖ ❖

"It's criminal," Kick said to Billy's mother at the end of another long day, which had seen Billy standing for hours upon hours in the back of an open lorry, waving at townspeople and stopping to speak and answer questions. Now it was late, and the family had gathered at Churchdale Hall, famished and exhausted, to eat a cold supper of sandwiches and preserved vegetables. "White is so full of empty promises and hot air, I keep wishing he'd just float away," Kick added.

The duchess shook her head and raised her eyes to heaven. "It's tragic that people are so unhappy they actually believe him."

Kick felt an arm suddenly around her, and looked up to see Billy beside her. She'd never seen him look so pale, with purple shadows under his eyes. "Thank you for being here, darling," he said. "Though I'd rather you see me on a winning streak."

Kick slid her arm around his waist and leaned on him sympathetically. "Would it be to hokey to say you'll always be a winner to me?"

"Yes," he sighed. "But I'll take it."

The duke joined them, brandishing a cheese and pickle sandwich. "I just don't understand what the devil these people want."

Billy snapped. "Haven't you been listening?" he yelled at his father. "They *don't* want *us*, they don't want the Cavendishes. They are done with lords and ladies having it all. I represent everything they want but can't have in the system as they know it. So they're going to elect change. And I can't say I blame them, since it's by and large *their* men who are in fact fighting and dying at the front. And our lot who got us into this mess in the first place." There was a blaze in Billy's eyes Kick had never seen before. Though his words were about the election, she could tell his mind was somewhere else.

"They don't see that the change will come at a great cost?" his father pressed. "To the dignity of them all? To have a man like White—"

"I can't talk more about this tonight," Billy cut in, punctuating his words by slicing the air with his hands.

The duke pursed his lips and stalked off to the library, and the duchess drew in a short, sharp breath. "Of course, Billy. You should rest."

The people of West Derbyshire did indeed elect change, by a landslide. Sixteen thousand votes to eleven thousand. In Billy's concession speech, which he delivered in an even voice just barely tinged with the bitterness Kick knew burned in his heart, he told the voters, "I shall now return to the Coldstream Guards to fight—and perhaps die—for you." He avoided eye contact with everyone, even Kick, and refused comments to the noisy reporters clamoring outside. Instead, he ducked into his family's black Packard and receded into the night.

The next morning at Churchdale Hall, he knocked on Kick's door. The breakfast tray hadn't yet arrived, and she thought it was the maid coming with it, so when Billy slipped in and shut the door gently behind him, she instinctively pulled the sheet up to her shoulders, though she was wearing a long-sleeved flannel nightgown.

Billy sat on the edge of the bed, and Kick felt a tug of desire that began at the base of her body, close to the fine cotton sheets. "Surely we're beyond that?" he asked with a smirk. So. He was returning to himself.

Kick dropped the covers with a relieved sigh. "Especially since this night-dress is far more modest than all my ball gowns ever were," she agreed.

"How I miss those days of no obligations," he said.

Kick put her hand on Billy's and said, "Let's get away for a few days. Crash-Bang is exactly what you need. Friends, laughter, music. Would your parents let us abscond with a few bottles of the good stuff?"

"I think my parents are planning something special for your birthday tomorrow."

"Could we celebrate it today, maybe at lunch? We could be at Pat's for cocktails."

Billy looked up at the ceiling, then at her, and said, "You're right. I'll see what I can do. I knew there was a good reason for me to disturb you this morning."

"Why *did* you disturb me?"

"Because last night I didn't want to see or talk to anyone, and when I woke up this morning, the first and only person I wanted to see was you."

Kick rocked forward onto her knees and kissed him on the lips. "I'm so glad," she whispered.

Billy must really have wanted to get out of Derbyshire, because in no time, a birthday lunch buffet had been arranged in the dining room, complete with fresh flowers and a banner that read "Happy Birthday Kick" in ribbon woven through burlap.

"I'm sorry there's no ice cream," said the duchess to Kick as they all sipped champagne. "I know how much you love it. We were going to make it for tomorrow, but to be honest, I'm glad you thought to get Billy away for a few days."

"I'm so relieved you approve," said Kick, realizing how relaxed and at home she'd begun to feel with Billy's mother.

The duchess glanced across the room, where the duke was frowning over his coupe by himself. "It will be good for everyone, I think," added the duchess. Then, with a suddenly nervous expression, she said, "Kick, I hope you won't feel I'm overstepping, but I have a suggestion."

Kick raised her eyebrows in anticipation.

"We have an old family friend who is an Anglican monk. Ted Talbot. He's a wonderful man, and he said he'd be very glad to speak with you about Anglicanism and Catholicism. I believe they have a great deal in common. I promise that he will not pressure you, but only . . . chat. Answer any questions you might have. I know how seriously you take your faith, and I want you to know I take it seriously as well."

Kick felt like she was standing on a rocking boat.

The duchess went on, "Billy loves you, Kick. And we have all come to think of you as a member of the family. I just . . . want to help."

"Thank you," said Kick. Taking a deep breath to steady herself, she said, "I think it is high time I do ask some questions." But in her heart, she was hoping for the loophole her father had mentioned.

"Marvelous," said the duchess.

At her birthday lunch, everyone stuffed themselves with a quintessentially English meal of roast lamb with mint sauce, potatoes, strawberry trifle, and a cheese course with the creamiest wedges Kick had ever sampled. "All from a farm up the road," the duchess said with pride.

"I milked the cow myself," Billy said wryly, and everyone laughed, even his father. Kick loved him so much for that comment, the self-deprecating humor meant to set everyone at ease. He did drink too much of his favorite gardener's ale, which the butler brought to him at lunch in a special pint glass while the rest of them drank Burgundy, but Kick didn't mind—how could she? If anyone was entitled to a little oblivion that day, it was Billy Hartington.

Then, Kick was thrilled and also embarrassed when a silver tray of wrapped presents was set before her. In her family, birthdays weren't celebrated with such fanfare, likely because there were eleven of them in the family, and there always seemed to be some birthday or other to celebrate, and half of her siblings and often her parents weren't in the same house on the day anyway.

Anne and Elizabeth gave her a few of the latest swing records. Billy's mother gave her pearl earrings (to match the cross from Christmas, Kick had to assume), and when it came time for Kick to open the duke's heavy rectangular present, the duchess warned in a light tone, "I had nothing to do with this one."

Kick cocked an eyebrow and said, "Now I'm *extremely* curious." She tried to look the duke in the eye, but he was taking advantage of the relaxed luncheon atmosphere to smoke a pipe, which absorbed his attention. Everyone else seemed to be a little nervous; the room was completely silent. She glanced at Billy, and he shrugged.

She carefully peeled off the thick, crisp brown paper and saw a leather-bound Book of Common Prayer. There seemed to be no other appropriate response but laughter. "Thank you, Duke," she chirped, springing up from her seat and bounding around the table to give Billy's father a spontaneous kiss on the cheek, which produced a brief round of applause.

Billy's father, now looking up at Kick because she was standing and he was still sitting, said with a levity that for the first time made her see the resemblance between him and his oldest son, "Have to start somewhere, *Rosemary Tong.*"

"Indeed," she said with a nod, feeling a chill at the duke's use of her sister's name to address her. She realized then that posing as a nobody, a nobody with her sister's name, had been a test: Could she set aside her own identity for the sake of the Cavendish family? For the first time in her life, she felt queasy at having passed a social test with such flying colors. Tapping the heavy volume in her arms, she added, "I shall enjoy this light reading."

Billy took her hand and stopped her as she headed back to her own seat, and said quietly, "I'll give you my gift later."

Billy leaned on Kick and slept the entire train ride to Crastock Farm and woke up in an excellent mood. The evening had the makings of a great night. Joe Jr. was already there, unshaven and unwound, as were Boofie and Fiona, and Sissy with her two children, who were playing with blocks and dolls in the nursery with Pat's three. David was bringing Bertrand with him on the seven o'clock train.

Kick hugged her brother and said, "What a wonderful surprise. How long have you been here?"

"Since yesterday," he replied with a toothy grin that bespoke a happiness she hadn't seen in him for years.

"You seem so . . . *content*," she observed.

"Love will do that to you," he said. "I finally understand that."

"*Love*, dear brother?"

"And I don't care who knows it," he said. "I even love her little monkeys."

"I'm glad," she said. And she was. Now was not the time to bring up husbands at war, or different religions. Now was the time for Sancerre and more of the delicious cheese they'd brought with them from Churchdale Hall. Now was not even the time for her birthday present from Billy, it appeared, since he'd already begun on the first bottle of wine. *Well, this is what we came for. I can be invisible a little longer.*

CHAPTER 32

While Billy was sleeping in the next morning, Kick woke much earlier than she would have liked, her mind reeling with questions and doubts about everything that had happened in the past five days. At last, her desperation to pee drove her out from beneath the pile of blankets and duvets on her bed. Then, needing coffee or tea, she padded down into the kitchen in wool stockings, with two wool sweaters over her wool dress. She was still cold and saw her breath as little puffs of smoke in the damp morning air. She was surprised to find her brother already sitting at the rough kitchen table with a steaming cup of coffee and yesterday's newspaper.

He looked up and his face brightened. "My little sister, the birthday girl? Up before the birds?"

"I couldn't sleep," she muttered. Peering down at the hot milky liquid in his cup, she observed, "You know how to make coffee? I'm impressed."

"You don't?"

"On an American stove I do, but those things are terrifying," she said, gesturing with an accusatory finger at the Aga.

Joe chuckled and stood up, and went to work filling a metal espresso maker with fresh water and coffee grounds, then setting it on one of the large flat rings. "See? Simple," he said.

"Let's see if it tastes good," she said.

"Always the challenger," said Joe with a smile. "How's Billy? You came down here to rescue him from the vagaries of the election?"

Kick shook her head. "It was terrible, Joe. Charlie White was a bully and a beast. The voters deserve what they get from him."

"That doesn't sound like my charitable little sister."

"Charitable?" Kick laughed. "You have me confused with Eunice."

"All right, 'charitable' wasn't the right word." He searched for the right one. "Optimistic, then. Positive. Upbeat."

Kick looked down at her small hands and felt her eyes go hot with tears. "Yeah, well, that girl's done a lot of growing up."

"Maybe," Joe said slowly, "but I'd hate to see her lost altogether." The coffeemaker whistled its finish, and he combined it with some milk in her cup, then handed it to her.

She took her first sip as they sat down and exclaimed, "You make *excellent* coffee, Brother Joe. I had no idea."

"Yeah, well, some of us have grown up in other ways."

"You're practically a father," she observed, recalling the sweet way he'd wrestled and kicked balls with Pat's three children, then carted them off to bed over his shoulders, to their shrieking amusement.

"I always liked being the oldest brother," he said, "so being a father feels kind of natural."

"You *do* seem like a natural," she agreed.

He let a few quiet seconds go by, and then he asked, "What's bugging you, sis?"

Recalling Bertrand's words from five years before, *If there was ever a time for bald honesty, this is it*, Kick asked Joe, "Would it trouble you greatly if I married Billy? I mean, what would you think of me? Would you hate me forever for hurting your political career, betraying the family name, and raising Protestant children?"

"Oh, is *that* all?" he asked jokingly. When she didn't laugh, he gave her a little punch on the arm and said, "Need some whiskey in that coffee?"

"You were the one who asked me what's wrong."

"I did. Okay, I'll be serious. Because this is serious, you're right." He paused, then said, "So, it sounds like Billy's told you his terms? He won't convert or agree to raise the children Catholic?"

Kick nodded. "But he isn't asking me to convert."

"That's something," Joe agreed.

"Daddy said he'd check for a loophole, but . . ."

"You're not optimistic?"

She shook her head miserably. "And yesterday, the duchess suggested I talk to an Anglican monk. She means well, but . . . what could he possibly tell me to set my mind at ease? That God still loves me? I'm not worried about God, I'm worried about Mother!"

"You know, I have to admit I'm impressed that Billy's sticking to his guns. He's a lot less of a namby-pamby than he was before the war."

"Joe!"

"Well, he is."

"This is not helpful."

"And I've seen the way he is with you. He's crazy about you, sis. That's not easy to come by, especially when you're a man who could marry the future queen of England. He could have anyone, and he wants you."

"That *is* flattering, I must admit."

"But the same's true for you, kid. You could've had Peter Grace or any one of Jack's or my rich Catholic friends that would make Mom and Dad happy. But you want Billy. That says something about how much you two love each other."

"I've never heard you sound so wise, and . . . *sentimental*," Kick said.

"You can thank our hostess for that," he said, his eyes traveling up the stairs to where Pat was still asleep. "And getting stuck in Jack's big black shadow has mangled my manhood, which might explain why I'm going all girlie on you."

"I like this girlier Joe," she said, holding up her cup and taking an appreciative sip. "He makes great coffee."

He shrugged. "There has to be a benefit somewhere."

"So . . . you don't sound mad at the prospect of my marrying Billy on those terms."

"It wouldn't be my first choice for you," he admitted. "But when have any of us gotten to choose a fate for anyone but ourselves? And even then, the road's a long and hard one."

She didn't feel like pointing out that their father had chosen Rosemary's fate—and that if she was being completely honest, she didn't want to suffer a similar future: the thwarted, dutiful life. And maybe a tiny part of her, too, wanted to show her parents that they couldn't control all nine of them.

"And," Joe went on, "I'm thinking about asking Pat to divorce Robin and marry me, so I'm hardly one to talk, am I?"

"You are?!"

"I've been with countless women in my life, and not one has ever made me feel the way Pat does. That has to mean something."

"It does." Kick nodded vigorously. "It absolutely does."

"In short, I'll stand by you, especially if it means I can get my charitable sister back," he said with a smirk.

Kick threw her arms around her brother and nearly knocked over her coffee. "I love you, Joe."

Hugging her tightly in return, Joe said, "So do I, little sister. And if *we* can't stand by each other, who the heck will?"

❧ ❧ ❧

Billy gave her his birthday gift in the afternoon. They were alone for once in the living room, sitting shoulder to shoulder on the floor with a fire going and one of her new records on the gramophone. Without any ceremony, he pulled a small black box out of his pocket and set it gently on her lap. "Happy birthday," he said.

Inside the box was a glittering eternity ring with small diamonds that went all the way around in a golden channel setting. "Billy," she breathed, "it's beautiful."

"The election at least afforded me a few minutes to shop," he said, plucking the ring out of its velvet slot and holding it between him and Kick.

She offered him her right hand, but he took her left and slid the band on her ring finger. "I hope," he said in a low voice, "that this ring can be more than a birthday present."

"Billy, I . . ." she began, but he put his index finger on her lips to stop her.

"I know you have more to think about, and I respect that," he said. "But as you think, I want you to consider the fact that I'll be rejoining the guards this week, and the invasion of France is coming soon. We don't have much time, and what I want more than anything on this earth is to be your husband."

"Whatever happened to not wanting me to give everything up in case you die?" she asked, referring to that long-ago conversation at Blenheim.

"That was rubbish, I realize now," he said. "I was afraid then, of so many things. Maybe it's selfishness, or growing up. I'm not sure it matters."

Kick thought of Gabrielle and Pedro, and the Spanish girl's wish that her fiancé would make her pregnant before he went off to fight. Kick was stunned to realize she wanted precisely the same thing.

She kissed Billy, then said, "My father said he would ask about loopholes that might allow me to stay in the good graces of the church if I marry you."

"Kick, I want you to know that I do realize what I'm asking of you," Billy said.

This time, Kick put her finger to his lips, and said, "Let's not talk more about it now. I promise to think and pray about nothing else. I even agreed to meet with your mother's friend, this Father Talbot."

Billy smiled. "He's a good man."

"So I've been told," she replied.

"Thank you," he said.

They kissed again, the delicate ring making it newly awkward for them to interlace their fingers as they usually did when they lost themselves in the little bit of passion they were allowed.

❖ ❖ ❖

Patsy White's reply letter came to her the morning she was set to meet Father Talbot, and she read one section many times on her train north to Yorkshire:

> *I always thought you were too good for my lout of a brother, so I'm glad you've followed your true heart and found love with Billy. What a shame it would be to extinguish that flame, when you've both burned for each other so long. As far as advice from a "mature married woman whose opinion I trust" (Was that just a kind way of saying I'm old?) what I'll say is this: When you're married, your husband becomes your world. You won't depend on your childhood family in the same way. So it's essential that you feel that the life he offers you, in all regards, is what you want. You are strong and independent, Kick. Even rebellious, when you want to be. If any woman is brave enough to follow her heart, it's you.*

She recited that last line like an incantation when she met Father Talbot at the Community of the Resurrection monastery, which was a large, stone Victorian building with Tudor details, like its peaked roof. It was surrounded by that lush English grass that felt pillowy soft under her feet and never seemed to get brown. When she knocked on the rectory door as instructed, she was shown into a simple, oak-paneled office by a very young monk with a limping, jerky way of walking that make Kick wonder if he'd seen battle, or if his disability had kept him from having to fight. He asked her to sit and said that Father Talbot would be with her very soon.

She sat in a large wooden chair and looked around at the sparsely decorated room. On the wall to the left of the large desk was a simple bronze cross and a calendar, and a small unframed canvas with a still life of some apples sitting on a shiny, dark table. As she waited, Kick wondered whether she was following her heart or betraying her family. Then she wondered whether there was a difference. Running her right index finger over her lower lip, she felt how ragged it had become from the biting she hadn't even realized she was doing.

Soon Father Talbot arrived, followed by a teenage girl in a long-sleeved, floor-length maid's uniform, carrying a tray with a pot of tea and two cups.

"I'm terribly sorry to have made you wait, Miss Kennedy," said Father Talbot, and she stood and the two of them shook hands.

"I've hardly waited at all," Kick reassured him as she tried to figure out what sort of man and priest he would be. She'd been able to tell right away that Father O'Flaherty was kind and generous. Father Talbot, considerably shorter and balder, and a bit plump beneath his black robes, had a ready smile that crinkled the skin around his eyes. But there was something rigid about him, his firm handshake and the way he held his robes as he sat and then smoothed them out and allowed the maid to serve him his tea, reminding her, "No sugar, Agatha."

"Yes, sir," the girl said, and Kick got the feeling that Agatha knew perfectly well how he took his tea, and yet he likely told her every time as if he doubted she'd get it right. "Miss, how do you like yours?"

"Just milk, Agatha. Thank you so much," Kick replied.

Once the tea had been served and pleasantries about the weather and her train ride north were exchanged, Father Talbot set his cup in front of him on the saucer with a resolute clink, and said to Kick, "Now, Miss Kennedy, Moucher Cavendish tells me we have serious matters to discuss."

Kick still couldn't believe she was doing this. She tried to think of Billy's face in the hopes it might relax her, but nothing could undo her knotted stomach now. "I'm not entirely sure how much the duchess explained," Kick began, "but I suppose the matter is rather simple, even though it's causing me great distress. I am, as you know, an American and

Catholic. Of Irish descent. And Billy is what *he* is. And he also would prefer that all our children, even the girls, be raised in the Church of England."

Father Talbot nodded, and said, "I feel for you, my dear. Even five years ago, it was easier for our churches to find a middle ground for mixed marriages. But as I'm sure you know, the Vatican has made it increasingly difficult for Protestants to marry Catholics. They have made it an all-or-nothing proposition for the Catholic by demanding that he or she marry another Catholic or be excommunicated from the church."

"Only temporarily," Kick pointed out drily. *Until the Protestant spouse dies and the Catholic is free to rejoin the church.*

"You don't want to live in an earthly limbo, I'm sure," said Father Talbot. "No young wife wants to start her married life under a cloud like that."

Kick swallowed and nodded.

"How do you feel about these restrictions?" he asked her. No one had asked her that before. How unexpected that Father Talbot should be the one to do it.

"To be honest, I feel that no one is on the side of the couple. Both of us feel we must give up something essential in order to be together, and how is *that* a sunshiny way to start a life together?" Kick surprised herself with the vehemence of her own words.

"I understand completely," Father Talbot replied, and he really did seem to. His sympathetically wrinkled brows said it as much as his tone. "But, then, why are you here?"

"Because I love him," she said, her heart speeding up. "And I want to be with him. But . . . I don't want to disappoint my parents."

"Ah," said Father Talbot. "Are your parents the sticking point here, more so than your church?"

"It's not just my parents," Kick said, the words tumbling out in a rush, "but everything my parents stand for. I'm not a Cavendish, but I'm a Kennedy. My father has worked so hard for everything he's earned in his life, for the name he's made for our family. He's made mistakes, yes, and believe me, I understand those mistakes better than anyone might know, but I can't help but feel real allegiance to our family. I don't want to embarrass them."

"Of course you don't," the monk replied soothingly. He let a few seconds tick by before he said, "You say that both sides here are asking you to give up something essential in order to get married, but that isn't strictly true. Your church and family would ask you to give up *Billy*. And that does seem unfair. But the Church of England makes no demands on one of their flock marrying a Catholic. The Protestant is free to make their own decisions about their married life. Of course, we prefer that he or she marries and produces more Protestants, but that is not a *requirement* of our church as it is of yours. It may be a requirement of Billy's family, but not of his church."

"Are you trying to make me angry with Billy and his family?"

"*Are* you angry with Billy or his family?"

She rotated the eternity ring, which she hadn't worn to work or anywhere else public yet because she wasn't ready for those questions, on her finger. "No," she replied. "I don't want to be angry with anyone. I want to be happy. I just want everyone to be happy."

"Sometimes that's impossible," he said with a sad smile.

"Then why am I here?"

"You tell me."

Kick drew in a long, deep breath. *You are strong and independent, Kick. Even rebellious when you want to be.* "What would conversion entail, exactly?" she finally asked.

She and Father Talbot talked for three hours that day, and three more the following day. His parting words to her were, "Don't decide anything now, Kathleen. Give everything we discussed some time to settle in your mind. Pray on it, and ask God for guidance. And remember that your job is to have your own relationship with God. Only your own. Your mother, father, and brothers and sisters have to find their own ways to be with God."

When Kick got on the train back to London, she clung to the hope that her father could find a loophole somewhere, anywhere, because all the options she had discussed with Father Talbot filled her with dread. She knew, in that same place she knew how fiercely she loved Billy, that she could not convert. Leaving the Catholic Church would be the worst possible thing she could do to her family. The best of the terrible choices was a registry wedding—if she could get Billy to agree to that. It wasn't a grand way to get married, but who was having grand weddings these days anyway? She probably wouldn't even be able to get enough material for a floor-length gown. And it would at least demonstrate to the world that she wasn't willing to betray her family by pledging her life and children to Billy inside a Protestant church; it would be clear she had drawn some line, and he had made some compromise. As Father Talbot had said, "The symbolism of that gesture would be clear." But still, a loophole in Catholic doctrine would be far better.

The only thing that was clear to her, as her train sped back to the English capital, was that she'd gone too far down this path to turn back now.

CHAPTER 33

"I'm sorry, kid," her dad said over the fuzzier-than-usual phone line. "I've spoken to every priest and cardinal who's ever shown any affection for the Kennedy family, and I'm afraid no exceptions can be made."

Kick sank down into one of her hard wooden kitchen chairs, but her legs continued to shake. She'd been counting on this, the exception that could—*would*—be made for her, because of her family. And there it went, *poof*, like a cloud of smoke.

"Kick? Are you there?" her father shouted.

"I'm here," she said quietly.

"I know this must be a terrible disappointment. You'd have made a terrific Duchess of Devonshire."

"That's not the reason I want to marry him," she said.

"I know it's hard to believe now, but there are other men out there who will be better for you, sweetheart. Who you'll love just as much."

Kick shook her head, though she knew her father couldn't see it. It surprised her that she wasn't crying. Instead she felt numb, weightless. She could scarcely feel her feet on the ground.

Next came a letter sent rush air service from her mother that surprised her with its compassion, the extent to which Rose understood how much she wanted Billy. She told Kick how sorry she was that she couldn't have her heart's desire. Like her father, though, she assured Kick that her heart would mend, and implored her to come home soon. "My darling Kick. Let me help. Let the Florida sunshine and the comforts of your church and family embrace you." Kick couldn't sleep for days on end, and went through her routines at the Red Cross in a barely cognizant state. She began to wish for John White's back rubs, of all things. Anything to get some decent sleep so she could think clearly.

Billy hadn't been able to get any leave time since the election, so she hadn't seen him in weeks. He invited her to come up to Yorkshire, where he was temporarily stationed, and stay with his cousin Jean Ogilvy, now Lloyd. By the time she got there, Kick was spoiling for a fight.

There were things that needed to be said. She hardly knew where to start. He showed up for dinner the first night with lobsters and champagne for everyone, but Kick had little appetite for the treats. During dinner, as Jean and her husband and Billy talked about "the old days" like they were long gone, not just five years ago and on their way back once the Germans were vanquished, Kick finally exclaimed, "You sound like a lot of grannies! We'll dance again. If not to the Big Apple, then to whatever's the next big thing. We've been dancing throughout this whole ordeal, haven't we?"

"That may be," conceded Jean's husband David. "But I doubt it'll be the same."

Billy nodded. "I don't think the dukes of Devonshire will live in Chatsworth the way my grandfather and his ancestors did, that's for certain."

Kick was at the end of her patience—for all of it. She'd had enough of bad news, for herself and Billy and England. "None of us here has a crystal ball. All we have is what history tells us," she said, glad to be able to use Billy's precious history against him for once. "And England's risen from worse than this in the past."

"From your mouth to God's ears," Billy said, though she could tell he didn't believe it.

At last, they were alone. After brandies in the kitchen, Jean and David retired upstairs at a much later hour than Kick had expected, and she muttered, "At least our friends with children go to bed earlier."

Billy laughed and put his arms around her. "You've seemed rather . . . on edge all night." Her back was up against the kitchen counter. She wondered if Billy knew he'd pinned her there. Normally she'd have enjoyed the position, but not tonight.

Enough. Securing her palms on the wooden surface behind her, she said, "I spoke with Father Talbot. He was a wonderful, kind man and very learned, but . . . I can't get married in a Protestant church. It would be too much for my family. It goes against too much of what I believe to be true and sacred."

"All right," said Billy, his voice even despite the fact that she could tell she'd taken him off guard.

"That's not a problem?" she demanded.

"I'm not sure yet," he said. "What else did you and Father Talbot talk about?" He released her and took a step back.

"The children, you mean? The future little dukes of Devonshire and their sisters? Who will never live at Chatsworth?"

"There's no need to be hostile, darling."

"Why not?" she exploded. "You're asking me to give up so much."

"I know, and I'm sorry."

"You're *sorry*? *That's it?*"

Billy stepped toward her and took her hands in his. "Kick, we balance each other so well. You are fiery and alive, and I am reserved and . . ."

"Stubborn," she concluded for him.

"I prefer *persistent*," he said, obviously hoping to lighten the mood.

She was *not* going to let him do this to her, not right now. "To make matters worse, my father says there are no loopholes. Which means that the Catholic Church will say I'm endangering my soul by marrying you. And my mother will believe it."

"Do *you* believe you'd be endangering your soul by marrying me?"

She didn't. Not as long as she believed there might be more priests like

Father O'Flaherty on earth. But she did not want to lose that bargaining chip yet, so she challenged him. "I'd feel a lot better about my soul if I knew my future husband was willing to compromise on some aspect of this mess, to show everyone who's watching us that *he* doesn't want to endanger my soul."

"Is our marriage really about everyone who's watching?"

"How can it not be, Billy? You stand for everything your class of people admires. It's why you want your children to be Protestant. You *are* England. But I stand for everything my people admire, too, which is why if I'm going to raise my children Protestant, I want to show in some way that I didn't give in on everything that was important to me."

Billy was silent for a moment, and he frowned as he thought. He put his hands behind his back and opened his mouth to speak, then closed it again. He went to the table and chairs near the window, whose eyelet curtains were closed. He sat and invited her to do the same. She did, recognizing that sitting, he didn't tower over her so completely. He arranged his chair so that they were face-to-face and their knees touched. He folded his hands between his legs and looked at her. She wove her fingers together the same way she did at church, self-consciously aware of the eternity ring on her left hand, and tried to ignore the sparks she felt running up her legs at the touch of his knees.

"You're right," he said. "I can see absolutely why you feel the way you do, about our respective positions in relation to 'my people,' as you called them, as well as *your* people. I'm sorry I didn't see it that way before."

"Thank you," she said. "So you see that I cannot marry you before the world in a Protestant church?"

"I suppose I do. But what does that leave us?"

"The registry office. We can have a legal, but not religious, ceremony."

Billy did not break eye contact this time, and searched her determined face. At last he said, "I hadn't thought of that before."

"Father Talbot was the one who suggested it," Kick countered. "And you did say he was a wise man."

"I did," he admitted grimly.

"So . . . ?" she asked.

"I'd like to think about it," he said.

There wasn't a name for the dance they were doing. It was torture, though. She wanted nothing more than to lollygag with him before a fire, take romantic walks, and peel off every layer of his guards uniform, throwing each piece on the floor, one by one. She envisioned each of these movements in painful detail while he was away the next day. At the same time, she wanted to shout at him that he was putting her in the worst possible position. And there was also the fear that surged through her whole body in waves throughout the day: *What if I lose him—again?*

But he showed up the next night at Jean's, as promised, with another set of lobsters.

"This is getting ridiculous, Billy," laughed Jean as she happily put an enormous pot of water on the stove to boil.

He also had an announcement: "My regiment's been called up. I finally get to go back."

He sounded so happy about it. Kick's stomach contracted painfully, as it had on that train ride from Cannes. But hadn't she been ashamed and disappointed in John White for *not* wanting to go?

While Jean cooked, Billy took Kick by the hand and led her into the back garden, where an early-spring twilight beamed pink rays through the branches of tall oak trees. He kissed her there, fully on the mouth, and she leaned up on her tiptoes so she could wind her fingers into his hair and feel the firmness of his long body against hers. They kissed like that for a long time, and as a host of images and sensations flashed through her mind, all of Kick's answers became clear. It was like praying. After a while they were interrupted by Jean's voice strained through the waning light. "All right, lovebirds! Time for dinner!"

Jean and David retired early that night, as soon as the last dish was dried. When they were gone, Billy poured himself and Kick two glasses of the champagne left over from their meal, and they went to sit on the sofa in the drawing room. They sat at each end of the three-seater, facing each other, not yet touching.

He sipped, then asked, "If I agree to the registry wedding, would it make things easier with your parents?"

"I hope so," she said. "As much as it's possible anyway. My mother's not likely to make anything easy. But someday I hope she'll see that I did the best I could with the choices I had."

"Would it help if I wrote to her myself, to explain the situation from my side? I don't want the burden to be entirely on you," he said, his eyes in wide earnest. "You're already giving so much. I cannot say that enough, Kick. I do understand."

"And I understand that if you go back to France to fight for what you believe in, you must do that with a pureness of spirit," she said, "without having given in on this issue that for you is synonymous with England. I wish I didn't love that about you, but I do. Ironically, you have my father and brothers to thank for it."

Billy's relieved and surprised smile nearly broke her heart. "Then I shall thank them, many times over," he promised. Then he moved to the middle seat of the couch and set his glass down on the nearby table.

He looked down at her left hand and used his index finger and thumb to twist the eternity ring on her slim finger. He looked up at her and said, "So, I agree to the registry wedding. Does that mean . . . ?"

"Yes," she whispered.

He laughed then, a splendid and loud and thankful laugh.

"Shhhhhh," she said. "You'll wake Jean and David."

He rocked back on the couch and pulled her on top of him, and they kissed even more fervently than they had in the garden before dinner. Then he said, very quietly, "I'm the happiest man in England, thanks to you."

"And I'm the happiest woman in England *and* America," she countered, and despite everything that had gone before and was still to come, she knew it was the truth.

❦ ❦ ❦

No sooner had she and Billy each sent their letters of announcement and explanation to Rose and Joe Kennedy than the campaign began.

The first was a telegram from her mother:

AM IN BED SICK WITH THE NEWS FATHER KELLER
VISITS ME DAILY TO PRAY WITH ME FOR YOU TO
CHANGE YOUR MIND THINK KATHLEEN THINK AND
PRAY REMEMBER WHO YOU ARE

Next came a letter from Eunice:

*Have you any idea what you've done? What this is going to do? I
can't believe you'd be so selfish.*

So much for Eunice being the charitable one, Kick thought.
And Bobby:

*Mother's in a tizzy. And I'm in shock, I have to admit. I never
thought you'd go this far. Are you sure you've thought it through? I've
always admired your independent spirit, but maybe this is taking it
too far?*

And even Teddy:

*If there is anything you can do to make this better, please, Sister
Kick, please do it. Everyone's miserable, Mother's checked herself into a
hospital she feels so poorly.*

And on and on. She didn't hear from Jack or Joe Jr. right away. With
each new communication from her other siblings, she replayed her last
conversation with Joe, in which he'd said he'd stand by her, and hoped
that when she saw him again, he'd make good on that promise. Jack's silence felt more ominous. She'd written repeatedly, asking his advice for
months, and told herself the problem was that her letters took too long to
get to the Pacific theater, where he was stationed, but surely he'd gotten

them by now. And he must have gotten her short plea for help by telegram. Why hadn't he replied yet?

Meanwhile, spring brought the color back to London. Daffodils, then tulips and cherry trees, in fluffy waves of yellow, then white and pink and red. And Billy's mother and sisters rushed to London to take her to lunch and shopping for china and crystal. They showered her with congratulations and warm hugs of relief and welcome. "You've made us all so happy," the duchess said after kissing Kick on each of her cheeks, twice. "*All* of us," she further emphasized. "Eddy, too. He sends his love as well."

Kick went to mass every chance she could, always trying to get to St. Mary's to feel closer to her favorite priest and the kind of church she felt she belonged to—a more tolerant one, which valued goodness over rules. She no longer prayed for guidance but for peace and joy. *Holy Virgin, please help Mother and Daddy and my brothers and sisters to see how happy I am to be marrying Billy, and what a wonderful life we will lead that I want so much for them to be part of. Vacations at Lismore Castle in Ireland, hunts at Chatsworth, and a brood of grandchildren and cousins with funny little accents who will want to know and love their mother's side of the family. Help them see there is no impediment to our continuing to love each other.*

And also, on her darker days: *Please God, allow me to find bliss in my marriage despite my sins. I am not perfect, but I want to lead a virtuous life. Help me to be content, and good. If I can be happy, I will know I have your grace.*

She finally saw Joe Jr. at Crash-Bang on a day off from work. He took her on a glorious footpath through hedgerows and pastures with cows and sheep grazing on the long, whispering grasses. They walked awhile, then took a seat at the top of a slope where they could see a patchwork of small farms spread out like a green quilt before them.

"I believe congratulations are in order," Joe said, smiling broadly at her. He looked so handsome, so relaxed and content.

"Daddy couldn't find any loopholes, though, so the registry office it'll be," she said, still nervous, though her brother appeared nothing but happy for her.

"I know," he said.

"You do?"

"I've gotten a crate of letters and telegrams begging me to talk some sense into you."

"You did? And you didn't tell me?"

"Have I ever been able to talk any sense into you?" he teased.

"No one has," she sighed. "They think that's my problem."

"Well, some of us think it's your strength."

Tears flooded her eyes. "Thank you," she whispered hoarsely.

He bumped her shoulder with his. "I mean it. I wish I had half your courage."

Not trusting herself to speak, she rested her head against his arm and tried to enjoy the view.

❖ ❖ ❖

She and Billy decided that to minimize the publicity that was bound to follow their announcement, it was best to have the shortest possible engagement and get married right away—"And anyway," Billy added with unconcealed lust in his voice, "I'm tired of waiting, aren't you?"

"Very," she had replied. "We've waited years."

In a little less than a week, before they told the papers, Kick quit her job, much to the sneering relief of Scroggins, and packed up her little flat with all the borrowed linens and other collected knickknacks that would now comprise her trousseau, since nothing was coming from America. Occasionally, she sat and cried, longing for her mother and sisters. She was getting married! She'd already given up her cherished childhood fantasy of a long white dress, fabulous flowers, and luxurious reception and honeymoon. It turned out those trappings were infinitesimally less important than family. Rose and Rosie, Eunice, Pat, and Jean—they were supposed to be with her, fussing and reminiscing, and giggling about her future happiness! When she thought of Rosemary especially, alone somewhere like Kick was, she cried all the more.

As one of those fits was starting and she was telling herself to get on with the packing and organizing, there was a knock on her apartment door. She was surprised to see Sissy and Debo with their brood of little children. And Debo herself was practically bursting with the new baby, due any moment now.

"We came to help," said Sissy. Seeing Kick's red-rimmed eyes, she added, "And it looks like we got here just in time!" Kick fell into her friend's embrace and sobbed as Debo efficiently ushered the confused children into the sparse room, opened a tapestry bag that held jacks and soft rabbits and a few other diversions, and then went to hug Kick herself, which was so difficult to do given her enormous belly that it made both of them laugh.

"Thank you both for coming," said Kick, hiccupping now between laughter and tears.

"Darling," Sissy cooed, rubbing Kick's back, "tell us what's wrong."

"I miss my family," she said, feeling the sobs gather again like a storm in her chest.

"Of course you do," said Debo, sliding down into a chair at the table. "They should be here."

Sissy went to make some tea, and after a few deep breaths, Kick said, "Of course they *can't* be here because of the war and all—"

"Kick," interrupted Debo firmly, "there's no need to pretend with us. We know you're not talking about the Atlantic Ocean or the Germans."

"Have they written at all?" asked Sissy gently.

"Nothing I'd want to share with you," admitted Kick.

But Sissy frowned and said, "I'm sorry. No one should be unhappy about starting a new life with a wonderful man." Kick was so touched by this, she burst into tears again.

Sissy actually laughed, and sat down next to her friend. "I didn't think *that* was such a dangerous thing to say."

Sissy's fine features blurred in Kick's watery eyes. "It's just that I wish, I wish . . ." she gasped.

Debo reached over and put her hand on Kick's. "We know. You don't have to say more."

"Please don't tell Billy," Kick whispered.

"Welcome to being a wife," said Sissy.

"Exactly." Debo grinned slyly, and despite her pregnancy-plumped face, she looked exactly like the party girl of eighteen Kick had colluded with six years ago.

Towheaded Julian wandered over to them and said to Sissy, "May I have a biscuit, Mummy?" Then, catching a glimpse of Kick's red face, he asked in such a proper manner that Kick blushed at the absurdity of the moment, "Are you all right, Miss Kennedy?"

Sissy intervened. "She won't be Miss Kennedy much longer, Julian. You'd better start to practice calling her Marchioness."

Safely back in the territory of etiquette, Julian gave Kick a little bow and said, "I hope you feel better, Marchioness." Clearly bewildered, he took a handful of digestive biscuits and rejoined the other children.

Kick and Sissy and Debo dissolved into hysterical laughter, an absolute balm on her soul. Her friends' visit also proved essential for her housewarming preparations, as they were able to advise her on the sorts of items that would be most useful in her post-honeymoon life in a hotel in Alton near Billy's regiment. Debo said, "I've never been so bored as I've been as an army wife, so bring plenty to read."

Sissy removed the nicer dresses from the packed trunks, saying, "Leave those in storage. There won't be anywhere to wear them in Alton, and while you honeymoon at Compton Place, well, I'm sure Billy won't want you wearing much of anything," and again Sissy and Debo exchanged amused looks.

"Sissy!" Kick said, embarrassed but also flushed with anticipation.

"She'll likely have to dress for dinner once," Debo pointed out. "Duke and Duchess might pop by for supper."

"Actually, speaking of . . . all that," Kick said, hardly able to believe she was asking, "do you know anywhere I might be able to buy some satin sheets?"

Sissy grinned and said, "They cost more than gold at Harrods because of the fabric restrictions, but I have a set to give you. Consider it a gift. David prefers cotton."

In the evening post the next day, a brown paper parcel arrived, and inside was Kick's very own set of freshly washed yellow satin sheets that smelled like sunshine and dried lavender, and a note in Sissy's hand that read, "A marchioness <u>should</u> sleep on satin sheets. <u>Enjoy</u> them."

In the same post was a short note from the duchess saying that earlier in the day, Debo had delivered Peregrine Cavendish safely into the world. "It appears our family is growing and growing, and I couldn't be happier," she concluded.

Kick put the note between the pages of the Book of Common Prayer and packed it to take with her into her new life.

CHAPTER 34

As soon as Kick and Billy announced the engagement on May 4, the press devoured them. It was worse than either of them had predicted, with reporters taking their tea and meals on the pavement outside all their homes as they waited for one of them to exit, and calling the Cavendish family secretary at all hours of the day and night, begging for a comment. They even had the poor taste to call Debo right after the birth of her child. Billy, staying in the house his family had rented in Easton for the reception, called Kick and said crabbily, "I don't dare say anything over the phone for fear it's being monitored." No one in the family could leave their homes without being attacked by cameras and pencil-at-the-ready reporters. Kick assumed it was happening to her parents and siblings, too, though they also made no comment. All Kick knew of her scattered family was their worrying silence, and the fact that her mother was in a hospital in Boston.

Kick hunkered down in Marie Bruce's apartment, allowing her mother's friend to fuss over her and steadfastly *not* mention Rose or any other Kennedy, for that matter. Instead, Marie focused her energy on making sure Kick had a beautiful if last-minute wedding dress, which she insisted was a gift—and the milkman's, it turned out, since she convinced him to give her a few of his fabric coupons when she didn't have enough, promising to repay him with just as many of those plus some coveted bottles of wine when her next allotment came in. It was a knee-length dress made of a very fine crepe in the palest of pinks, reminding Kick of the peonies that bloomed in Hyannis Port in the early summer. Marie also wrapped up a box of brand-new lingerie she'd originally ordered for herself, and gave it to Kick over tea the afternoon before her wedding. "I can't accept this," Kick said, embarrassed by the charity as well as the unexpected frills and ties on the undergarments.

"I insist," Marie replied firmly. "A young bride needs to feel seductive. It puts some of the power back in your hands."

And she made sure Kick had a cake to serve to her guests. Because of the restrictions on sugar, even Claridge's, whom Marie convinced to bake it, had to assemble it without frosting. But it would be chocolate, and that was a real consolation, to Kick's mind.

At last the morning arrived. Kick stood before Marie in the dress that had come off the sewing machine mere hours before, with drops of Vol de Nuit on her wrists and behind her knees. Her mother had bought it for her annually since that first trip to Guerlain.

"You're a vision," said Marie, dabbing tears out of her eyes. They embraced, and Kick pretended for a moment that the other woman was Rose.

Then Joe Jr. bounded into the apartment looking very smart in a dark wool suit and tie, and exclaimed with open arms, "Where's the bride?" with such enthusiasm, Kick felt her heart soar.

Ducking into a taxi, the three of them sped to the Chelsea Register Office.

"Have you heard from Jack?" asked Kick.

"No, and I cabled him the other day and told him he was a bastard," Joe said.

"I'm glad I could provide you with another excuse to malign him," Kick said.

"Yes, I appreciate that," Joe replied. "He's become Dad's whipping boy, and it's sad. But let's not talk about sad things today. Let's think about Debo's new baby, and champagne in a few hours, and how pretty you look, and how you'll become a marchioness today. Little Kathleen Kennedy of Boston, a marchioness! It's quite a coup, little sister."

"Oh, Joe, don't be vulgar," said Marie, but Kick could tell she was amused by her brother's bragging.

"Kick loves vulgarity," whispered Joe. "It's one of her best-kept secrets."

He prattled on the whole ride, and Kick loved him for it.

In its staid redbrick way, the Chelsea Register Office was a reassuring building even if it wasn't Brompton Oratory or Westminster Abbey—maybe, Kick thought, *because* it was neither the Oratory nor Westminster. It was *their* place, hers and Billy's, and she was suddenly happy about the uniqueness of it, the way it said, *We made our own choice.*

"Ready?" Joe asked her with his most open and exultant expression, his hand on the door of the taxi as the reporters swarmed the black car.

She closed her eyes and pictured Billy in her mind and saw his smile at the May Fair nearly a year ago when she'd returned. "Yes," she said. And her brother opened the door.

As the flashbulbs popped and the reporters shouted—"Miss Kennedy! Is there a Protestant priest inside?" "A Catholic?" "Did your parents call to congratulate you this morning?"—Joe put his arm protectively around her, and they ran from the taxi, up the steps, and into the building, which was mercifully free of the press. In fact, with all the neatly dressed people going about their quiet business, no one would ever know there was a tempest outside.

A giddy Anne Cavendish stopped Kick in the hall and said, "You look absolutely beautiful! I've been sent to whisk you away so Billy can't see you till you walk into the room. You should see *him*, by the way. A nervous wreck! I've never seen him so emotional about anything."

"I hope that's a good sign!" Kick said, following this girl who would soon be her sister-in-law to a whitewashed room only big enough for a desk and two chairs. She wondered what it was used for. Joe went to check on Billy, and Marie to check on the flowers.

"Of course it's a good sign," Anne reassured her. "I didn't mean to worry you, only to let you know that he is rather overcome."

Kick longed to see him. It had been three whole days since she'd laid eyes on him. Anne chattered on about something to do with their parents, but Kick couldn't focus on a single word. She was sweating. She hoped she didn't stain her delicate dress!

Soon, though, Joe knocked and put his head around the door and declared, "Showtime!"

He handed her a bouquet of the pink camellias from Chatsworth that the duchess had brought down for the occasion. Kick put her nose to them and breathed in the sweet, springtime scent of her future home. She felt honored that Billy's mother had wanted her to carry them toward him that day.

Jutting out his elbow, Joe offered Kick his arm, and the two of them followed Anne down the hall to a room only a little larger than the one they had been in, equally unornamented except for the proudly displayed Union Jack, and a few vases of pink carnations and camellias blooming cheerfully around the room.

Kick had thought that when she was finally in the room with Billy, she would look to him right away and their gazes would be romantically locked for the rest of the ceremony, but she found herself feeling suddenly and deeply shy. So instead of raising her eyes to the front of the room where Billy stood in his uniform waiting for her, she made grateful eye contact with her new family and old friends—Elizabeth, the duke and duchess, Anne, Nancy and Waldorf Astor, Debo, Sissy, David—and smiled with a slightly bowed, embarrassed head.

A man at an upright piano in the corner played the most famous bars of Beethoven's "Ode to Joy" for Kick's short walk from the door to Billy on her brother's arm. At last, she looked up at him, and his smile—that same smile she'd loved even when she feared she'd forgotten it, that smile she'd changed her whole life for—made everything else disappear. Their short ceremony was like an intimate prayer. *I, Kathleen Agnes Kennedy, take you, William John Robert Cavendish, to be my wedded husband . . . I, William John Robert Cavendish, take you, Kathleen Agnes Kennedy . . . in sickness and in health, as long as we both shall live.* When he slid the eternity ring onto her finger, it looked new again. She gave him a golden band that clinked against hers when they kissed to seal their promises to each other. When their small audience cheered, Kick was startled to remember they were not alone.

At the reception in the Easton town house, where two hundred guests gathered to wish them their best and enjoy the chocolate cake, Kick found that all she wanted to do was leave and be truly alone with her husband. *Her husband!* Even though this party was *for* them and *about* them, it didn't feel nearly as merry and gay as any of their evenings at the 400. For Kick, the highlight of the tedious hours was the moment when the duke took her aside and said, just, "Thank you."

"Thank *you*, Duke," she replied, and when he smiled, she knew that he understood she was talking about much more than the party or the sparkling bracelet, a Cavendish heirloom, he had given her as a wedding present.

At last Billy came to her side, put a warm hand on the small of her back, and whispered in her ear, "Come with me."

Lacing her fingers through his—her husband's fingers, she thought with a shiver of pure happiness—she followed him out of the drawing room, up the stairs, and into the bedroom where he must have been staying these past few nights, judging from the men's grooming materials on the vanity.

He shut the door, then scooped her into his arms and laid her down on the bed. Her whole body hummed with desire; even her toes were curled with it. He gently lowered his body onto hers and began to kiss her. First on the lips, and then her jaw, and neck, and even the tender space below her ears—what a revelation that such a small bit of skin could be sensitive enough to make the rest of her convulse with pleasure. She reciprocated, at last able to touch and kiss him the way she had dreamed so many times. His body was heavier on hers than she'd imagined, but she wasn't afraid of *his* desire, even though she'd thought she might be when it came to it. When she felt him press against her, she moved her legs so that her knees were on either side of him, and she could feel him, the beginning of what it would be like to be fully one with him, and there was no fear, no hesitance, only an intense, resonant craving.

Unexpectedly, Billy groaned roughly and then pulled away, rolling onto his side, and put one hand on her feverish belly.

"What?" she asked, genuinely confused.

"Not here," he said. "Not the first time, with all those people downstairs wondering where we are."

"Oh, them? I'd forgotten all about them," she said, and they both laughed, but with a note of dread that they *did* have to face them once more.

It was another several hours before their train arrived in Eastbourne. They walked in the twilight to Compton Place, where a romantic meal with another bottle of champagne was waiting for them in the dining room, which they completely ignored in favor of retangling themselves as they had been earlier, and then as they never had before.

❖ ❖ ❖

Sissy had been right. Kick wore very little real clothing in the next few days, and instead was extremely grateful for Marie Bruce's generous stash of lingerie, not that she ever wore any single piece for long, as Billy became hilariously adept at untying, unsnapping, unhooking, and flinging away. Still, she wore every item and discovered that satin sheets felt even better, more shivery and supple, on her legs sliding toward his than she'd dreamed. She hadn't felt this good and strong in her own body since she was a child glorying in the surf at Hyannis Port.

They ate strawberries in bed and read bits of their favorite poetry and novels to each other, letting newspapers stack up outside their unopened door. When they did leave the room, it was to take long walks in the orchards or laze on chaises among the copious spring flowers in the gardens. Once they walked on the beach, getting themselves ice-cream cones and eating them even though the wind whipped their hair and made them freezing cold. It was fun to get warm again.

They did initially accept the post into their little bubble, but it was a mistake they didn't repeat, for among the plentiful notes of congratulation were envelopes full of vitriol, mainly for Kick. The worst of them were from strangers, Catholic matrons from Boston to Dublin. *Whore! You little Judas. How could you do this to your mother?* Other letters, from people she knew, were more tempered in their outrage, but she felt them just as sharply.

While Billy went through his own stack of missives, lying with her on the bed, she began to sniff back tears.

"Darling, what is it?" he asked, suddenly alert and sitting up.

She handed him one of the letters.

"This is abhorrent," he said.

She nodded. "The thing is, *this,*" she said, crumpling one of the letters, "doesn't bother me as much as knowing my mother agrees. I still haven't heard from her. She's gone down to a spa in Virginia, and she hasn't even said hello, or . . . or . . . *anything.* I'd rather her get angry with me, and say *something.*"

Billy kissed her on the cheek, then disappeared for a few hours that afternoon while she bathed and got some fresh air. The next day, the disagreeable mail had been tidied away, and all Billy said of it was, "Let *me* deal with the letters, since it's my fault they're arriving at all." And two cables arrived. The first was from Jack, and it read:

SORRY FOR THE RADIO SILENCE YOU'LL ALWAYS BE
MY KICK GIVE ONE TO BILLY FOR ME I SAW YOU
FIRST LOVE JACK

She laughed till she cried, and pressed the telegram to her chest. Billy was pouring himself a whiskey and looking rather pleased with himself, and she asked, "Did you have anything to do with this?"

He shrugged. "Your brother loves you, Kick. I don't think he realized how much you were suffering."

She hugged him tightly and felt slightly more relaxed.

A few hours later, another cable arrived from her father.

```
WITH YOUR FAITH IN GOD YOU CAN'T MAKE A
MISTAKE REMEMBER YOU ARE STILL AND ALWAYS
WILL BE TOPS WITH ME
```

"And this?" she asked Billy, showing him the second wonderful telegram.

He shook his head. "Much as I'd like to take responsibility, I can't in this case."

It must have been Joe, she thought, and her chest filled with relief and love for her oldest brother. She would try once more with her mother.

Kissing Billy on the cheek, she said, "See you at dinner? I have a letter to write."

"Of course," he said.

After saying a rosary in the quiet of her own room, which she hadn't visited since her arrival, and lighting a candle to the Virgin, Kick sat down to write to Rose. She told her mother how much she hoped she had regained her health, and took pains to reassure her. "You did your duty as a Roman Catholic mother. You have not failed, there was nothing lacking in my religious education." And she stated again, as she had many times before, that she herself was still a Catholic, and would continue to be one. Billy didn't want it any other way. She would pray, and hoped her mother would pray, that the church would change its views of marriages like hers. *I love him, Mother, and I know you love me. And I love you. Please let your love guide you to know how I feel, and why I've done what I've done.*

She felt better for having written it, and sent it with the evening post, telling herself as the butler took it away that it was the best she could do and every word was true. God, she felt certain, would forgive her.

It was time to enjoy the rest of her honeymoon.

❖ ❖ ❖

The following week found Kick and Billy in the little town of Alton southwest of London, where his regiment was once again stationed. They knew he'd be sent to the front soon, and so Kick tried to make sure every moment they shared as newlyweds would be like a page in a book Billy could turn to when he'd gone. It was no mean feat, since their suite of rooms at the Swan Hotel amounted to little more than the single bedroom they'd spent so much time in at Compton Place, and they were far enough away from London to make all their favorite social rituals impossible.

"Well," she'd said when they first surveyed the tiny quarters, "good thing we've been practicing living small." She wondered idly where the Greek vase from her mother had gone.

Billy laughed and pulled her to the bed. "We don't need any other furniture, do we?"

When he wasn't with the guards, they went on bike rides and ate picnics, napped in the long grasses of summer meadows. She shopped for his favorite lemon-cream biscuits and whiskey and even discovered a bottled local ale that met his standards, kept vases of fresh flowers in their rooms, and dreamed up new ways to please him in the evenings when he returned. They visited with Boofie and Fiona, and David and Sissy, and went to Crash-Bang one weekend and had a marvelous time with Joe and Pat.

"How's it feel to be a marchioness?" Joe asked her.

"Like nothing," Kick replied. "I haven't assumed any duties yet."

"You just wait," Billy said threateningly. "Mum's giving you an adjustment period, but she'll be sending the lists soon."

"Well, tell her I can't wait," Kick replied. Because she couldn't. People like the Irish bellboy at the Swan treated her with an almost absurd level of respect, *Marchioness* this and *Marchioness* that, but it all felt very abstract. Half the time she didn't even respond when they addressed her that way, since she was so used to responding to *Miss Kennedy*. She longed to *do* something—and initially, she hoped that something might start with a baby, but then her period arrived. Billy had said with a naughty grin, "We'll just have to try harder."

In a moment by themselves at Crash-Bang, Joe Jr. said to Kick, "I got a letter from Mother. She's back to buying you clothes at Bergdorf's, so you must be forgiven."

So Kick's earnest letter from Eastbourne must have had some effect. But still. "Marie Bruce told me she'd heard from Mother, too," Kick said, "and that she was in good health. I just wish she'd write to *me*."

"She will," Joe reassured her. "Give her some time."

Kick sighed. She'd begun to grow numb to it all. The happiness she was experiencing with Billy tempered every other feeling, made all that sadness and loss feel somehow irrelevant. The ocean between her and the rest of her family helped, she had to admit.

"What about you?" Kick changed the subject. "By the looks of things, you and Pat are closer than ever."

Joe laughed in a chagrined way. "I can't explain it," he said. "After all the other girls, why should a married mother of three kids make my heart triple its former size?"

"Maybe it's because of the children?" Kick mused. "The little ones adore you, and you like being adored."

"I'll take that as a compliment," he said. They were both quiet for a few minutes, then Joe went on, "I hope I'll finally get my opportunity to show everyone what I'm really worth on this second tour of duty."

"You don't have to prove anything to me, Joe. Nor to Pat. I hope you know that."

"I do," Joe said. "I have something to prove to myself, though."

"Don't go doing something stupid just to be a hero," she said, her voice becoming wet and thick with emotion, "because I don't know what I'd do without you." She wanted to say the same thing to Billy, since he was so eager to get to France, but she didn't dare. She knew he'd hear such a warning as sacrilegious, since his primary quarrel wasn't with his brother, as was Joe's—no, Billy's fight was a sacred one for king and country.

"Don't you want to be proud of both your big brothers?" Joe asked.

"I *am* proud of you both."

Joe shook his head. "All right, I want you to be *more* proud of me. Is that so terrible?"

Kick laughed. "I'll tell you a secret," she said. "I already am."

For just a second, Kick saw Joe's eyes go watery. Then he coughed and used the back of his hand to rub his eye. "You don't have to flatter me, little sister."

"I'm serious. I don't think I've properly thanked you for everything." *Everything* hardly covered it. Joe Jr. had been there for her when no one else in the family had. And he'd been amazingly humble about it, too. She'd learned the other day, from Debo, that her brother had even stood up to Billy's father before the wedding when he'd asked Joe to get Kick to sign some paper saying she'd raise the children Protestant. "You even told the Duke of bloody Devonshire where to put his pen," she said to him now, slyly. "That took some guts, big brother, guts and backbone."

"Well, Billy's father needed to know you're a woman of your word."

"You're a good man, Joe. Better than you give yourself credit for. There's more than one way to be a hero."

This time he cleared his throat and stood up. "Enough of this sissy talk," he declared. "Time to find the monkeys and teach them some American football."

CHAPTER 35

Billy was called up on June 13. He was to leave for France early on the fifteenth.

"I've been expecting it every day," he said to her as they lay naked in their rumpled bed at the Swan. "But it always felt so distant, almost like it could never happen. How could anything disturb *this*? It's like we've been living in a brilliant dream."

Kick trailed her fingers slowly up and down his arm. Her ear was resting precisely over his heart, and she could hear how erratic its beat had become since he'd begun thinking about this again.

"I'll miss you so much," she said, not trusting the strangled tears in her throat, the heat squeezing her eyes. The last thing Billy needed was a weeping wife. *Wife*, she thought again, the word still giving her a zing of pleasure.

Putting his large, warm hands under her arms, he gently pulled her up so he could gaze at her face. He didn't look so boyish anymore, though he ought to have looked even younger with his hair tousled and his pale chest and shoulders showing. The sadnesses of the past few years had given him the finest of lines around his eyes and lips. She kissed him so she wouldn't have to look at him any longer. It was too painful.

"You make me so happy," he murmured as they kissed more, arms and legs tangling in that way that was becoming more and more familiar, though every time they came together, it was a little different, and she always looked forward to finding out how it would be the next time. That night as they moved together, she sensed him getting a bit lost, his heart and body speeding up but never evening out. Closing her eyes and twisting her fingers into his hair, she allowed herself to go with him, wherever it was he was going, and found that she didn't lag behind but caught up, and when they reached the end, it was together, and she forgot for one blissful second where it was they'd started. She opened her mouth to tell him how happy he made her, but he'd fallen asleep with his arms still around her and she didn't have the heart to wake him.

❖ ❖ ❖

The fifteenth found Kick at Marie Bruce's apartment in London, collapsed in a puddle of tears.

"Poor darling," Marie cooed, wrapping Kick in an afghan and handing her a cup of tea. "The war will be over soon, and he'll be back, and you can start again. Think how wonderful it will be to be reunited."

Kick cried and hicupped and tried to smile, then slept for three hours that afternoon. Later, Fiona practically forced her into the taxi to come to Ciro's with her and Boofie, saying, "No use acting like someone's dead. Carry on like the rest of us."

"Even when someone *is* dead," added Boofie a bit drunkenly. "It's the English way."

And so began what Kick came to think of as her third life in London. While she carried on doing many of the things she had always enjoyed—dining with friends, weekending at Crash-Bang, and renewing her charity work in the form of corresponding and meeting with the duchess about beginning her duties as marchioness—everything was done under threat of the German doodlebugs, which served as constant reminders of the dangers Billy was in overseas. Bug was a good name for them. Like jet-propelled wasps, they buzzed over London, and everyone who heard them girded themselves for their bite. They weren't even piloted by humans, which added to their insect-like character.

Though the press denigrated the missiles as Göring's last-gasp offensive after the embarrassment of June 6 at Normandy, the bugs "get under my skin," Bertrand quipped at the 400 one night. The death toll was mounting, and important buildings like the Guards Chapel were completely gutted. Marie Bruce began chewing her nails. "I haven't done this since the Blitz," she said. Kick gave her a manicure with her best red Chanel varnish. "If this doesn't keep you from biting, nothing will," she told her friend, though Kick's lips were ragged and bloody from her own nervous habit.

Billy wrote her, worrying over *her* safety, but she always assured him she was fine. Nothing, not even a doodlebug, was going to keep her from that reunion Marie Bruce had helped her envision, which was the only thing to prod her out of bed some mornings. He also wrote of the hearty, thankful greetings he and his men received as they marched north. The Allies were winning, and Kick began to put real faith in the image of herself and Billy on the lawn at Chatsworth—though not, she felt with a startling sense of grief at the onset of her second married period—with her belly rounded with joy. *Soon*, she told herself. *We'll just have to try harder*, she thought with a smile, remembering Billy's words.

Another hopeful sign was the beginning of correspondence directly from her mother, starting with one of her roundup letters consisting of news about all the family, addressed to Lady Hartington in Rose's own hand. Though the letter contained no congratulations to Kick on her marriage, nor even a recognition of it beyond her changed name, Kick felt a deep sense of relief at this discreet opening of the door.

The day after she received the letter, she went to Brompton Oratory, her mother's old favorite, and offered up two rosaries of thanks. She'd continued to attend mass as much as she had before marrying Billy, but she still could not get used to sitting in the pew while the other congregants rose to receive the body of Christ. She felt the lack of this Communion in her soul, as much as she felt Billy's absence in her heart and body. Lying alone between cool cotton sheets, she wondered whether she was doomed to always feel something missing in her life, if that was the price she would have to pay for her independence.

❦ ❦ ❦

Work proved the only salve, just as it had at St. Mary's when she was a girl and at the *Times-Herald* when she was not much older. Throughout the summer, Kick and the duchess attended agricultural fairs and flower shows in Derbyshire and organized teas and luncheons to raise money for a variety of war-related causes. Inspired by Lord Halifax's son Richard, who'd lost his legs in Syria and now got on remarkably well with wooden limbs, Kick asked if she could begin a charity for veteran amputees, and the duchess said that was precisely the sort of thing she hoped Kick would come up with. "And *after* the war," the duchess added in a heavy tone, "if there ever is an after the war, we can think about arts and culture again, as we did before."

"I remember those days well," said Kick.

"As do I," the older woman replied wistfully.

Even the duke took notice of Kick's industriousness. After reading his morning post over breakfast at Eastbourne one morning, he turned to her and said, "I've just read a letter from the prosthetics surgeon at the hospital, and he says you have a good head on your shoulders."

At the end of July, Kick sponsored her first carnival. In a neat print on the blue program, it read, "Red Cross & St. John Carnival, *Under the Patronage of the Marchioness of Hartington*," which gave her a thrill. She sent her parents a copy and hoped that seeing her name so printed would remind them of how far they'd all come in the world. The day itself was considerably less posh than her name on the program. It had rained earlier in the week, so everyone had to wear wellies because of the mud, and the day was hot. She couldn't even imagine dancing when the Derby Home Guard Band took the stage. But when the premier farmer in the region, a handsome, graying man of middle age, offered her his hand and said, "It's a shame what happened to Billy in the election. But perhaps if he'd married you first, he'd've won," she was happy to oblige.

In a rare telephone conversation with Billy, she relayed some of the summer events in a mad rush, and he'd laughed till he coughed. "So, you're finding out that the life of a marchioness isn't so grand after all. I wasn't joking when I told the crowd I knew how to spread muck."

"What, judging cows and pets isn't grand? I relish my newfound power," she said with a cackle.

"I miss you so much," he groaned, reminding her of the low tones he used when they were in bed, and making her want him so much, she had to sit down.

"I'm not sure why this is occurring to me now," she said, clutching the phone, "but I want to tell you how happy you make me. On our last night together you told me I make you happy, but you fell asleep before I could explain just how perfect and wonderful *you* are, and how *perfectly happy* I am to be your wife."

Billy cleared his throat, and she could tell he was struggling to contain his emotions. "I hope to be home very soon, darling."

"Hurry," she whispered.

"I shall," he replied. "I don't think it will be long now."

❧ ❧ ❧

On a stifling morning in the second week of August, which was at least mercifully free of doodlebugs, Kick was breakfasting with the duke and duchess in a town house they'd hired in London so that the duke could attend to some business. They were companionably reading the papers and drinking tea, and Kick was looking forward to meeting Debo later in the day and then having dinner with Marie Bruce.

There was a firm rap at the front door, and soon after the butler showed a uniformed Royal Air Force officer into the room, announcing him as Officer James Woodman. He was older than Billy or Joe, and he walked with a slight limp. His right hand and cheek were scarred from a burn. He stood stiffly in the dining room, though the duke quickly asked if he would like to sit and have a cup of tea.

"Thank you, sir," the man replied with a respectful bow, before taking the seat the butler arranged for him.

Kick's heart thudded in her ears. This could not be good. This stranger had come with news, and her whole body was afire with dread and longing to know what it was. The duchess also appeared stricken with fear, her posture rigid, her eyes wide.

Before his tea arrived, Officer James Woodman said, "I know you want me to get right to it." He looked squarely at Kick now, and she felt sure her heart stopped for a moment. "Marchioness, your brother Joseph Kennedy died yesterday doing a great service to his country and ours. He will go down as one of the heroes of this war for his bravery and leadership. All his men loved him. He died trying to destroy one of the bases for those blasted doodlebugs."

All eyes were now on Kick. She felt as though she might throw up. She stared at her fine porcelain teacup. *Joe!* Her pillar of strength and protector, whom she'd only just gotten to know. Dead.

"Darling Kick," said the duchess, getting up to crouch beside Kick's chair and take her hands in hers. "I'm so sorry. Words are . . . *inadequate.* Please, just tell us what you need."

Kick turned to face Billy's mother and felt the first tears come. She opened her mouth to ask Officer James Woodman if her parents also knew, but she could barely utter anything. "Do my . . ."

Amazingly, the duke knew what to ask. "Have her parents and family in America gotten the news?"

"They have," the officer replied with a nod.

"Excuse me," Kick whispered, standing up and muttering a hasty thanks to Officer Woodman before running from the room and up the stairs to the bedroom where she'd slept fitfully the night before, wishing for Billy. With the door closed, she curled up in the bed, held on to one of the pillows, and sobbed.

When she emerged a few hours later, she knew with a clarity she hadn't felt in a long time what she needed to do. She found the duchess writing letters at a desk in the library, and said, "I have to go to America, to comfort my parents. There are things only I can tell them about Joe's last days on this earth, and I just don't want you to think . . . I'm so worried about Billy, but I feel I must go."

The duchess put a reassuring hand on Kick's arm and said, "Of course. You must."

After one businesslike conversation with her father's personal secretary, who assured Kick that her parents desperately wanted her home but were too overcome with grief to be on the phone, it was arranged that Kick would fly to Boston on an army transport plane. Exhausted, she slept most of the way on the overnight flight, but she was painfully awake for the last hour, feeling her body wind itself tighter and tighter with every mile that brought her closer to the family she had not seen in more than a year. In a cold sweat, she picked her lips till they bled.

After stepping on weak legs from the plane to the ground, blinking back the white light of the Boston morning, she saw Jack. Scrawny, tan, straw-haired Jack, in a white linen shirt and wrinkled khaki pants. She was so relieved to see him—just him—standing there waving his arms over his head in big swooping arcs, as if she might not recognize him, that she broke into a run and launched herself at him with a laughing-crying embrace. Nothing else—not his initial silence about her marriage, nor the letters he'd never replied to—mattered as much as his body standing there waiting for her at that very moment.

"Kick!" he said.

"Stick!" she said.

They didn't dance this time, but shouted rhymes at each other till they were hoarse. This time he didn't end it with a cough, but with an admiring "Marriage suits you, sis. You look great."

"I'm not sure why," she said. "I've been crying for three days."

"Mom always said water was good for the skin," he quipped, putting his arm around her and steering her home.

CHAPTER 36

"Mother!" Kick said, strangling the rising emotion in her throat. Rose looked terrible, with no makeup or jewelry on, wearing only an oriental housecoat that swamped her frame, for she was thin to the point of gauntness and her eyes had sunken in so much that they looked bruised. Kick rushed to her and put her arms gently around her for fear of breaking her, but she was surprised at the strength of her mother's return embrace.

"Mother, I've missed you so much," said Kick.

"We've missed you, too, Kathleen," Rose said, her voice smaller than it used to be, like a child's. "I've set some new clothes out for you on your bed."

"Thank you," Kick said, not knowing what else to say.

"I'm going to rest," Rose said. "I'll see you at dinner."

"All right," Kick replied, her heart wringing itself dry in her chest.

Teddy and Jean at least tackled her with hugs, then tears, and Bobby, who'd suddenly become a man with broad shoulders and a reddish beard he hadn't bothered shaving that morning, hung in the background and waited for his turn to hug her affectionately but casually. "Hey, sis. I kept all the stuff I read in the papers about your wedding. It's in your room."

"Thank you, Bobby," she replied, touched by this unexpected gesture.

"That was sweet of you. I have gifts for everyone as well." Then she looked around the Hyannis Port living room and asked, "Where are Pat and Eunice? Daddy?"

"Pat's over at the McDonnells', and I'm not sure where Euny is," Bobby replied. Jack had already made himself scarce. "And Dad . . . well, we haven't seen much of him."

On her way to her childhood room, Kick saw Eunice sitting on the bed in her own room, reading. Kick leaned her head in. "Hi," she said, not sure why her sister hadn't come down to greet her. Had she really not forgiven her for marrying Billy? Even Mother had come down.

But the red eyes that looked up at Kick told her that her younger sister was lost again, as she had been after Rosemary's disappearance. "And then there were six," Eunice said drily.

"Six? Shouldn't it be seven?"

"You aren't staying, are you?" she asked bitterly.

Kick stepped into the room. "Please, Eunice, forgive me. Someday . . . someday when you find someone of your own, I hope you'll understand."

"You haven't been here. *You're* the one who doesn't understand."

"Eunice, please, for Joe's sake."

Her sister laughed and shook her head. "Of course you'd say that." Then she fastened her eyes back on her book.

I have a lot of work to do here, Kick thought miserably. *Help me, Joe. Please.*

Everything Mother had left for her on the bed was perfect. The many pairs of nylons, the silk and gabardine dresses, the new lipsticks and nail varnish, and even the fresh bottle of Vol de Nuit. Everything she might have picked for herself as a new marchioness but couldn't find on the barren shelves of Harrods or Selfridges. She fingered the hem of a trim violet day dress and felt a bottomless gratitude for her mother. When she picked up one of the dresses, she saw lying beneath it a peachy lingerie ensemble, more modest than what Marie Bruce had given her, but worlds more suggestive than anything her mother would have given her before. She'd thought of everything. Of course.

Kick had just sat down at the little desk in her room to write Billy and let him know she'd arrived safely and wished so much he was there with her, when she heard her father at her door. "Kick?" he said.

She turned and saw him, and wanted to burst into tears again at the sight. Like her mother, he'd lost a great deal of weight and his skin looked sallow. Behind his glasses his eyes were puffy and red.

She rushed to hug him, and he held her a long time. "I'm so glad you're here," he said into her hair. "With you here, I feel I might be able to bear it."

"I couldn't be anywhere else," she said.

Dinner was a cookout on the porch, and everyone came and went between the beach and the table, alternately eating and swimming as they'd done for years. The white clapboard house with the black shutters was the same as ever, and it felt right to be carrying on as they always had, even though Kick was aware that each of them was performing for the others, acting out the parts that had been assigned to them at birth. At least, she and her siblings were. Her parents were silent, mostly watching their children eat and toss baseballs and towel off.

When the sun began to set, Kick felt very sleepy and realized it was after midnight in England, and she hadn't slept well for days. "I'm tired," she said to no one in particular. "Good night."

Bobby and her father wished her a good night, and she headed into the house, annoyed that she'd acquired two mosquito bites on her arm. Typical of a night spent out of doors on the Cape. Some things never changed, even when everything else had.

❖ ❖ ❖

The following morning began a week's worth of exhausting activity. Jack went to the hospital in Boston for surgery on his back, which left Bobby and Eunice to beat the drum of summer fun. After a few days, Kick wondered whether she'd really ever thought this schedule of swimming, sailing, tennis, and hiking was enjoyable. Once she decided to stick to golf and swimming, she was better off, and she focused on championing her brothers and sisters in their more athletic pursuits. Eunice seemed the most determined to bleed her deep reservoir of grief into sweat and salt, even winning a race in her new sailboat. Once she fell down on the tennis court, slipping and skinning her knee on the damp grass, and Kick ran to her and asked if she was all right. "Fine!" her younger sister sang, picking herself up and winning the match despite the crimson trickle running down her skinny leg.

While their mother prayed at St. Xavier every day, their father cheered his children on as loudly and enthusiastically as he always had. There were times, when Kick stood beside him, whistling and hollering and clapping, that she felt utterly one with him in joy and pride in her family. "Kennedys are champions," her father said to Eunice when she won her race. "Thanks for reminding everyone today, kid."

Other times, though, especially at night when she prepared for bed, Kick felt close to tears all over again. She would kneel by her bed and pray with clenched hands, *Holy Virgin, hear my prayer. Send Billy home soon so that we can begin our own family. I might not be able to teach our children my faith, but I can teach them about being a Kennedy, which you have shown me is more than just mass on Sundays and all the sacraments. And please give my love to Joe. Tell him I miss him every minute. Even though he had his own doubts about reaching the pearly gates, I am certain he's with you now.*

Toward the end of her first week back, Kick finally got up the courage to go to St. Francis Xavier with her mother for the early-morning mass she'd been attending every day. When Rose came downstairs looking a bit healthier, clean and wearing a fresh summer dress—though still in a mourning navy—Kick, also just bathed and made-up, was waiting for her on the sofa. "Where are you off to?" her mother asked in surprise.

"I thought I'd come with you," said Kick. "If you don't mind." She held her breath, because she wasn't sure if her mother *would* mind being seen in church with her outcast daughter who couldn't even receive Communion.

But Rose nodded and held the house door open for Kick.

Seated beside her mother in the wooden pews beneath the bracingly white arches that formed the nave, Kick felt acutely aware of her changed circumstances. The church itself was the same, but the azure blue of the wall behind the altar, and the lapis in the paintings of God and St. Francis Xavier that Kick had always found so soothing, reminding her of the nearby beaches, failed to comfort her. The pew felt hard beneath her rear and her knees. The coastal air gave her a chill, and she wished she'd thought to bring an extra sweater.

The short sermon that morning seemed tailor-made for Rose. And why not, since she and her daughter were two of only eleven congregants present that morning—and since Rose had been attending daily, surely Father Keller knew he ought to speak directly to his most loyal patron. It was based on a passage from James: "Blessed is a man who perseveres under trial; for once he has been approved, he will receive the crown of life which the Lord has promised to those who love him."

"Although recent events might make us doubt it," the priest said, "the Lord does not give us more trials than we can bear. There is a reason for every loss, just as there is for every triumph. Our reward in heaven, the crown that James speaks of, is sometimes hard to remember. It's not an easy reward to work toward, for it is not made of gold and diamonds and pearls. So God in his wisdom gives us smaller rewards here on earth, to remind us that he is watching over us. To keep us on the right path." Rose broke from her posture of prayer to put her hand on Kick's, and though she didn't look at her daughter, she squeezed her hand before folding her fingers and palms together once more. This small act of affection felt like a mug of hot chocolate on a cold morning, sending a rush of heat and comfort throughout her body.

The next day, Kick played golf with Jack, whose back was much better after the surgery. They returned cheerful only to find Bobby waiting for them nervously in the front yard, hands stuffed into his chino pockets as he paced the lawn. "A letter arrived today," he explained. "Joe must have written it . . . before . . . anyway, it arrived today. His last letter. Dad's taking it pretty hard."

Lips pressed together, Jack nodded and looked up at the house with a private dread. Inside, everything was quiet except for the sound of their father weeping behind the door of his study, the occasional murmur of Rose's voice, and once a strong, bitter version of their father's voice saying, "It's over. Nothing will ever be as good again."

❖ ❖ ❖

The first person Joe Sr. asked for was Kick. She'd been preparing to attend mass again with her mother, but Rose told her to visit her father instead. "It's your calling this morning," her mother insisted.

Kick found her father wrapped in a blanket with an untouched cup of coffee on his desk, staring out the open window at the foggy beach as drizzly air blew in.

"It's cold, Daddy," she said gently. "Want me to close the window?"

"There's a pile of blankets over there," he said without looking at her or the blankets, which were indeed stacked on a chaise against the wall. She wrapped herself in a pink afghan knitted by her grandmother Fitzgerald, and sat down. She noticed there was a carafe of coffee and a clean cup, so she poured herself one, more because she wanted the heat than anything else.

The two of them sat in silence awhile before Joe turned to her and said, "Tell me about Pat Wilson, and the children. Tell me what he was like with them. And in London with his buddies. Help me"—here his voice thickened, but he went on—"see what his last days were like. I want to feel that I was there with him."

"Daddy, he was very, very happy," she said, finding her own voice to be completely clear. It was good to feel needed in this way, and she managed to keep her composure even though she occasionally teared up when she was describing some silly thing Joe had done with Pat's children, or the way he'd stuck up for her with Billy's parents. She spent a few hours a day with her father like that, until he began asking for repeat stories, and then one day he didn't ask for her at all.

Jack said to Kick one afternoon, "I've been thinking that all of us have stories about Joe, like the ones you're telling Dad. We should write them down and put them in a book."

"Another bestseller?" Kick asked wryly.

"Nah, just for the family," he said.

"That's a marvelous idea," she said. In fact, she'd already begun her part by writing down some of the stories she'd told her father in her notebook. "Mother and Daddy will especially like it, I think, since . . ." She was never quite sure how to say *his body was never recovered*. Her brother, their son, had exploded in the sky, leaving nothing behind. A book would be a tangible reminder of him.

"Yeah, I know," Jack said.

The first week of September, as the younger siblings drifted off to school and the usual preparations were made to close the Hyannis Port house for the winter, Kick planned to follow her parents to New York City, see some friends, then fly home to England. She missed her English friends, even the duke and especially the duchess, and she longed to renew her life there, the shape it had begun to take around her new position as marchioness. Here in America she felt adrift. She nearly left after Labor Day, but sensed that her parents still needed her.

Their last night in Hyannis Port, Kick and her parents and Jack and Bobby and Eunice ate dinner and then enjoyed a last swim. The sun had almost disappeared on the horizon, and the sky was a blaze of orange and red. A few stars twinkled in the blue above. Kick had taken a walk by herself down the beach, talking to Billy in her mind—a new and comforting habit. She found herself talking to him a great deal in bed at night. It was the only antidote for the sharp ache she felt there, when she allowed herself to linger over the memory of his touch.

Just as she was laughing with him in her imagination about some long-ago prank at Cambridge, Kick looked up to see Jack sitting on the sand, his arms wrapped around his knees, staring into the distance as the tide came closer. Not far behind him, their father got up from the table and went to the edge of the porch. Putting his hands on the white rails, he leaned forward and looked long and hard at his son. Now his oldest son, just as Kick was now his oldest daughter.

Poor Jack, she thought. And then, with an ironic laugh to herself: *Debo's mother should go into business as a fortune-teller.*

CHAPTER 37

For a week, Kick was glad she'd come to New York. She lunched, shopped, danced at the Cotton Club, saw a few shows, and visited every single room at the Met. In a letter to Billy, she wrote:

> *The city has an energy and vitality to it that I'd forgotten. Or perhaps it's new, the result of the depression lifting and the war giving everyone a sense of purpose. I wish so much that you were here to see it with me! I think you'd enjoy it thoroughly, though likely we'd have to escape every afternoon to take a break from all the noise and bustle. What a shame. Whatever <u>would</u> we do with our time?*

She also worked on her part of Joe's book and wrote copious letters to friends in England, including a long one to the duchess with ideas for fall and winter events in Derbyshire.

It had been a month since Joe Jr.'s death, and her sorrow had begun to clear like a mist chased away by the sun. Some mornings she still woke in a thick fog, but she was able to grope around and find her way. She found that if she thought of her future with Billy, she could feel genuinely happy and excited about what was to come.

One gloriously blue September morning a few days before her departure for England, she went to Bonwit Teller for a last shop. She'd been amazed at how much clothing there was in the stores in New York. It was therapeutic to see so much bounty, and she purchased surprises for Marie Bruce, Debo, Sissy, Elizabeth, Anne, and her other friends who deserved a respite from wartime austerity.

At noon, she met Eunice for lunch, but her sister wore a mask of worry and wrung her hands at her waist.

"Daddy wants you to come and see him before lunch," she told Kick.

Kick's heart sped up, in that lurching way it had when Officer James Woodman had come to the Cavendishes' place in London. "What is it, Euny?" Kick demanded.

"I . . . I'm not sure," her sister replied. "Daddy just said to come right away."

Kick wasn't sure whether she believed her sister or not, but the Waldorf was only a few blocks away, so she stalked off in that direction. The traffic was at its midday peak, and she had to wait at every corner for cars and taxis and horse-drawn carriages to make their honking way through the intersection before she could cross. She kept telling herself that this had nothing to do with Billy.

But when Kick stood in the entrance of her father's opulent suite with the bright sunshine pouring into the room from the picture windows behind him, making him look for all the world like the angel Gabriel, she knew. His arms like wings were open, and she rushed into them and felt herself enfolded in their embrace just as everything went black.

❖ ❖ ❖

The accounts of Billy's relentless bravery and inspiring leadership only made it worse, though her family must have thought it would do the opposite from the way they kept slipping clippings and cables under her locked door. The way he'd slept in trenches with his men, and insisted they drink their rum and whiskey out of glasses, saying, "This is war, men, not the end of the world. Remember your women back home." The way he'd listened to them talk about their hopes and dreams for after the war, with an earnest nod and a supportive word. The way he'd told them to buck up and march on after they'd lost a quarter of their number in the successful capture of Beverloo, then how the very next day he'd gone on ahead to scout the area for the capture of Heppen, which got him shot in the heart by a sniper. *In the heart*, Kick kept saying to herself. *His heart, his magnificent, tender English heart.*

There she'd been telling her daredevil brother not to do anything stupid—not that any of those entreaties had worked, either—when Billy was practically daring the Germans to shoot him by wearing his white officer's mackintosh all over France and Belgium. She blamed Churchill for sending the English boys in too soon in 1940 and sowing in them the seeds of revenge, she blamed Charlie White for calling Billy a coward, she blamed God for making her love him, she blamed herself for not marrying him sooner. Maybe if things had been different, if she hadn't been such a ditherer, the future would have been different. He might have won the election, he might not have gone back to the fighting, she might have gotten pregnant. *Might, might, might . . .*

She didn't want to see anyone. People knocked on her door when they heard her crying again, which was how they knew she wasn't asleep in the darkened room. Her mother asked if she wanted to go to church. Eunice asked if she could just sit with her awhile. Jack asked if she wanted to forget her troubles. "No!" she shouted, once hurling a pillow at the door for emphasis. When her father asked if there was anything he could do, anyone he could ring for her, she answered "Patsy White," because she could think of no one else in America who understood and respected what Billy had meant to her, even though she knew her father didn't like Patsy much.

Hours later, there was a tentative knock on the door and Patsy's voice called, "Kick? It's me."

"Is anyone with you?" she asked.

"No."

Kick unlatched the door and let Patsy in. Her old friend was carrying a tray piled high with all kinds of food. It all looked disgusting, even her favorite candy bars.

Patsy set about opening the curtains, letting in a late-afternoon light that blinded Kick, sending her back to the bed to pull sheets over her eyes. Then she opened a window to let in some fresh air. Kick assumed it smelled wretched in there, but she hardly cared. Her nose was stuffed solid from all the crying.

Then her friend sat on the bed and put a gentle hand on Kick's leg. "I can't even imagine how hurt and angry and sad you must feel. Losing Joe was bad enough, but this . . . it's too much."

Kick sat up and nodded, her face crumpling once more. This time she sobbed into Patsy's shirt, and took some small comfort in feeling a friend's arms around her.

After a while, Patsy said, "John already wants to know if he might have a second chance," and Kick burst out laughing, though it hurt her ribs, which felt bruised.

Then Patsy added, "I told him I didn't think anyone could ever hold a candle to Billy, though."

Kick shook her head.

"What does your heart tell you now, Kick? What would make your burden just a little lighter? I'll help you with whatever it is."

"I want to go home," Kick said, remembering that when she'd told the duchess she wanted to see her parents after Joe's death, she had not used the word *home*. It had been deliberate, just as her use of it now was.

Pat nodded, and said, "All right."

Knowing that she would soon be back in England buoyed Kick. Patsy and her father made phone calls and sent cables while she finally took a long bath and choked down a small apple and some bread with a creamy, salty butter. She hadn't had butter in months, and this little pat must have cost a fortune, but her parents had obviously decided it was worth its weight in gold if Kick would eat it.

"It's all set," her father told her that evening. "You'll leave in two days for Quebec, and a British plane will fly you to London. Tonight we dine at the Ritz, then Charlie Parker is supposed to be playing at Minton's later, and I'm sure I can get us in."

A night out was the last thing she wanted, but she didn't see any choice now that she'd emerged. She'd come back to help her family because of Joe, and that tour of duty wasn't yet over. If Billy could push onward after losing so many men, she could go to dinner with her family. *Buck up*, she told herself. With the help of some makeup and a glitzy dress, she took Patsy's arm and headed out into the bright lights of Manhattan. Everyone engaged her in conversation, Jack and Eunice and the friends her father had invited along, but no one mentioned Billy, and she didn't bring him up, either.

The next morning, her mother came to her after breakfast dressed in a fine red suit with brown kid gloves and a hat with black feathers and netting. Kick picked at the eggs and toast that were delivered to her room while Patsy showered. On top of the grief, she was also hungover after the whiskey and smoke at Minton's.

Her mother perched on one of the other chairs, and said, "Come to mass with me, Kathleen. You'll be able to receive Communion again, and that will be such a balm on your soul. I'm sure of it. The church helped me so much after Joe's death."

"I can't, Mother," Kick said, a sob rising into her throat and nearly choking her. "I still feel married to Billy. It wouldn't be right."

Rose pressed her red lips into a thin line and studied her daughter. Kick's heart was exhausted from the effort it had put forth in the last few days, but still it tightened as she stood her ground.

"I want to, Mother, believe me," Kick said, hoping to soften the stony look on Rose's face with a plea for understanding, "and I will. Just . . . not now."

Patsy burst into the room wearing a bathrobe, toweling off her hair and saying, "Mmmm, breakfast. I'm famished."

She stopped cold, seeing Kick and her mother sitting in silence, and whispered, "I'm so sorry," and turned to go back to the bedroom.

Rose stood and put out her hand, and said, "No, Patsy, have some breakfast. There's no reason for me to stay."

And she left.

Rose's last words to Kick before she left on the plane for Quebec were "Don't wait too long."

❖ ❖ ❖

Billy's final letter to her, written five days before he was killed, might have crossed paths with her own letter to him over the ocean that separated them. She received it weeks after he'd written it, though, since it had gone to her Cape address, then was forwarded to New York, then back across the Atlantic to Churchdale Hall. He wrote of "the permanent lump in my throat," and how he longed for her to be there with him because it was "an experience which few can have and which I would love to share with you." Just as she'd written to him about wishing *he* was with *her* in New York. His was clearly the finer wish. And now she wished more than anything that his had been granted, even if it had landed her in the mud of Belgium. At least she would have been by his side.

This posthumous letter slayed her the way Joe Jr.'s had their father, and she understood in the very marrow of her bones his outburst that the best of everything was over now.

Billy's parents and sisters, and Debo and Marie and Sissy and Nancy Astor, were one with her in their sorrow. They knew what an excellent man Billy had been, and how much he and Kick had loved each other. They also understood, as her own family couldn't, what Kick had given up to be his—things she couldn't simply pick back up again, like gloves left at a party. She spent hour upon hour with them, usually not even speaking. Sometimes crying together, sometimes reading one of Billy's books aloud or quietly in companionable silence, sometimes riding horses or sharing a cup of his favorite ale. The frenetic energy of Hyannis Port was a distant memory, and she was relieved.

One idle Wednesday in October she took the train down to Crastock Farm and saw Pat Wilson for the first time since before Joe's death. The ride was soothing, shuttling her through the brick outskirts of the city, then into verdant pastures with their quintessential hedgerows and stone cottages, the ones that had withstood centuries of wreck and repair.

When Kick arrived, she and her friend hugged and then shared a quiet lunch in Pat's kitchen. The children were at school, and there weren't any other visitors, so the house felt unusually empty, but Pat assured Kick that this was the case only rarely, as she entertained as many houseguests as ever.

"I find I don't much like being alone," said Pat, "so even though it's not the same as when Joe was here with me, I still want to have people near. Sometimes I even have fun. Joe made me love life again, and I feel it would be a great disservice to him to go back to the way I was before."

"I envy you your perspective," said Kick. Billy's loss had begun to feel like a numbness in her heart, as if it was in danger of becoming what John White had once described Dr. Freeman's patients becoming after his surgeries. *Oh, Rosie, I miss you, too. How I wish we could eat sweets and laugh again.*

"It'll come, in time," said Pat. "It will take you longer. You and Billy weren't married for long, but you were *together* for years. Part of each other's lives and in each other's blood. That's not an easy thing to get over."

Kick nodded. "Any advice on *how*?"

"Well, I have the farm and the children to keep me busy. What can you lay your hands on that might distract you?"

"Not the work of a marchioness," she said bitterly. That dream was gone, too. Andrew and Debo were now the Marquess and Marchioness of Hartington. "But," she went on, "I have an appointment next week with Scroggins, of all people."

Pat laughed. "Maybe a little rough treatment will do you good."

"I hope so," said Kick.

When she stepped into the bar of the Hans Crescent, the first person she laid eyes on was Tim. He saw her, too, and immediately stood up and went to her with a glad smile and a kiss on the cheek.

"Tim! What are you doing here? I thought you'd left in the summer," she exclaimed. Seeing him was so unexpected, she smiled—and meant it.

"Just finished my second tour," he replied. "So I'm enjoying some R and R at my favorite watering hole. Come on, I'll get you a drink."

By then other men and some of the girls who'd been there since Kick's time had seen her and were shouting, "Kick!" "Nice to see you!" and even, "Our patron saint is back!" There was a lot of hugging and hand shaking and laughing, and Kick began to feel the tiniest fissure of . . . something . . . warm and good . . . in her heart. Then a girl from Memphis who didn't know her well because she'd started work just as Kick was getting ready to leave said, starry-eyed, "I heard you got married?"

Those of the company who knew what had happened stopped talking and laughing to stare coldly at the girl, who winced, suddenly understanding. "She married a hero, is who she married," said Tim, with a smile at Kick. "She's got two hero brothers and a hero husband, which is more than most of us will be able to say in our lives."

For the first time, this reference to Joe and Billy did not make her want to run from the room in tears.

She swallowed and said, "Thanks, Tim, but I'm sure everyone here has a story a lot like mine."

"I doubt that very much, Kick," said Tim, handing her the half-pint of ale and clinking his glass to hers.

After her drink, she and Scroggins decided that the best position for her would be a senior one where she could give high-ranking officers tours of the clubs and the city, since even Scroggins had to admit, "No American knows this ruined place better than you do."

Kick stepped out into the cooling twilight. There were still no streetlights as there had been during those enchanted prewar nights when it seemed as though fairies lit her way to adventure. And now, around every corner she was sure she saw Billy's ghost. But this haunting made London even more itself to her, the capital of her greatest joys and now her greatest sorrow.

Wrapping her coat more tightly around her body, Kick renewed the promise she'd made in the fall of 1939: she would be here when the lights came back on. And longer, she knew now. Much longer. It would be worth whatever it cost.

ACKNOWLEDGMENTS

This is a debut novel so it's A Very Big Deal, but it's hardly my first novel, and so it's tempting to use this space to thank everyone who's ever helped me get to this point. But I don't want a hook to drag me offstage, so I'll keep it to those who had a hand in this book. To everyone else since I started writing in fifth grade: please know I'm deeply, soulfully grateful for your love and support.

First I want to thank my mom and dad, who have been unwavering in their belief that I am a writer, and that this was The Book. Mom, thank you for reading every single draft I've ever written, and being honest about them! Dad, it's always meant the world to me that you thought of my writing as the real thing. And thank you (thank you, thank you!) to the friends who gave their time and mental energy to reading the many drafts and iterations of Kick's story, and for offering such insightful feedback, sometimes at the eleventh hour: Cheryl Pappas, Dana Christensen, Danielle Fodor, Diana Renn, Erin Moore, Johanna Lane, Kate Bullard, Kip Wilson, Laura White, Lori Hess, Nancy Varela, Radha Pathak, Shannon Marshall, and Shannon Smith. Peter Su and Juli Sylvia, thank you for your visual acumen. Thanks, too, to my Weston mom tribe, for the playdates and encouragement—you really did help me get the job done.

I'm very grateful to Penn Whaling, who first encouraged me to write this book, saying I ought to try writing against type (you were right!), and to Ann Rittenberg, whose guidance on an earlier draft helped me reframe

Kick's story to make it bigger than I'd originally imagined. And thank you to fellow writers Josh Weil and Alisa Libby, who gave me exactly the advice I needed, exactly when I needed the courage to write what needed to be written.

A number of people helped in the research aspects of this book, foremost among them the wonderful librarians of the JFK library, especially Abbey Malangone and Laurie Austin, who helped me locate various boxes pertaining to Kick, and rolled up their sleeves to search for a few needles in the haystack. Thanks to Chris Paquin, Jacqueline Cox, James Towe, Jessica Maier, Katharina Wilkins, Mike Majors, Russell Anderson, Sarah Williamson, and Todd Smith, who answered important questions about cars, soap, morning suits, Trinity College, and other historical details.

Thank you to my editor, Kate Seaver—I couldn't be happier that you fell in love with this story! It is the best kind of fun making this book together. Claire Zion, I'm very grateful for your wisdom on everything from fried chicken to pen names. Angelina Krahn, thank you for checking all the nitty-gritty details. Ivan Held, Christine Ball, Jeanne-Marie Hudson, and Craig Burke: I feel like I won the lottery getting to be one of your writers; thank you for inviting me onto the team. Connie Gabbert and Kelly Lipovich, thank you for making the book so gorgeous! No small thanks to Fareeda Bullert, Jin Yu, Diana M. Franco, Danielle Kier, Heather Connor, and Sarah Blumenstock for all your work getting this book into the hands of readers.

Last but never least, thank you to my agent, Margaret O'Connor. You believed in me and my book when we needed it most, and it's not an exaggeration to say you changed my life. And we can laugh and talk about food and pets and movies, too! How lucky am I?

On that note, I want to say more broadly that I feel blessed to have such amazingly thoughtful and talented women as friends, family, readers, fact-checkers, and hand-holders. You mean more to me than I can express in a thousand pages like these. Thank you. You're totally my beautiful dream.

AUTHOR'S NOTE

Allow me to save you the rush to Google and fill you in on the last four years of Kick's impossibly short life (or, if you've already gone to the Wikipedia page, allow me to elaborate). Kick was indeed in England when the lights came back on, as she made it her permanent home. On that island, far from the expectations of her family, she was able to live freely and be fully herself—and to fall in love again.

In many ways, she made the same agonizing decision a second time when she chose Peter Wentworth-Fitzwilliam, the 8th Earl Fitzwilliam, as her lover. Like Billy, Peter was a Protestant. Worse, though, he was still married to Olive "Obby" Plunket when he and Kick became involved. When the Kennedys learned of their relationship, and of Peter's plan to divorce Obby and marry Kick, Rose flew all the way to London to camp out in Kick's town house and regale her with threats of eternal damnation—to say nothing of a final excommunication from the Kennedy family—should she proceed with her plan.

Readers of *The Kennedy Debutante* will not be surprised, I think, that Kick was undeterred by her mother's pleas. She followed her heart.

On May 13, 1948—four years and one week after her marriage to Billy—Kick stepped into a plane with Peter en route to Cannes from Paris, having arrived in that city safely from London. The couple had two purposes in France: to take a first holiday together, and also to meet with Kick's father in the hopes of convincing him to accept her new love. They never made it. Their little plane hit a terrible storm that jostled it horribly in the air and then sent it crashing into the Cévennes mountains, where all four passengers died instantly. Kick was only twenty-eight years old.

Her family mourned her, of course, but as they did with Rosemary, they relegated Kick's memory and rebellion to the past. She wasn't forgotten, however: Some close to Jack said that the lovely Jacqueline Bouvier reminded him of his sister, and Bobby named his first daughter Kathleen Hartington Kennedy. Then Bobby's namesake RFK Jr. named one of his daughters Kathleen, and that Kathleen goes by the nickname Kick today. That young Kick was recently a guest on an episode of the Smithsonian Channel's series *Million Dollar American Princesses*, on which her great-aunt, the original Kick Kennedy, was profiled.

In fact, it was a TV show something like that one that led me to Kick's story. At the height of the *Downton Abbey* frenzy (a show I relished till the end), PBS aired a series called *Secrets of the Manor House*, and *Downton*'s Highclere Castle was the marquee estate of the show. Chatsworth got its own episode, devoted to its long history, and a few minutes were dedicated to the fact that for a tiny fraction of its five-century life, Kick Kennedy would have someday inherited the house as the Duchess of Devonshire. Instead, Chatsworth fell into the worthy hands of her friend Deborah Mitford, whose long and complicated marriage to Andrew Cavendish allowed her to become one of the most revered duchesses in England, a writer, and a superlative estate mistress. If you visit Chatsworth today and revel in its majesty and preservation, you have Debo to thank.

Watching "Secrets of Chatsworth," I became entranced by Kick's story, but it was a few years until I began researching and writing about her in earnest, and the result is this novel. I read as much as I could about Kick, and for me as a first-time writer of historical fiction, there was just enough material to help me see the shape of her story, while also leaving me plenty of space to imagine how she must have felt about events.

Serendipitously, I live close to the John F. Kennedy Presidential Library in Boston, where the knowledgeable librarians helped me find all the material on Kick they had. It was a real treat to be able to hold in my hands the precious few of Kick's letters, diaries, and scrapbooks that have been preserved. From these, I took a handful of quotes, which have been used in the text of the novel. (See the following section for more details on the quotes.) Most of the letters and telegrams in this novel are fiction. Her diary was not confessional, betraying little of her true feelings about people and events; but to see what and whom she did mention, and with what frequency, was certainly illuminating. Letters are always performances, and I read Kick's missives to family and friends wondering what play she was staging for them.

When I first started this novel, the only two people to have written books about Kick were Lynne McTaggart in her 1983 biography, *Kathleen Kennedy: Her Life and Times*, and Robert DeMaria in his 1999 biographical novel, *That Kennedy Girl*. I read parts of both of these, though I took the advice of my novelist friends and mentors and read just enough to guide me, but not overly determine my story. Barbara Leaming's and Paula Byrne's 2016 biographies of Kick came out when I was nearly finished with my manuscript (*Kick Kennedy: The Charmed Life and Tragic Death of the Favorite Kennedy Daughter*, and *Kick: The True Story of JFK's Sister and the Heir to Chatsworth*, respectively), and I read pieces of Leaming's uniquely constructed book to check a few facts. I'm thrilled that the fourth Kennedy child has lately been getting the attention she so deserves—and surely would have relished.

I leaned heavily on Will Swift's excellent *The Kennedys Amidst the Gathering Storm: A Thousand Days in London, 1938–1940* for a better understanding of how Joe's ambassadorship fit with the lead-up to World War II, and how those years in London affected not just Kick but also Rose and the whole Kennedy brood. On that subject, I suspect many readers familiar with Joe Sr.'s foibles will have read my passages about his helping the Jewish refugees with surprise, since in other arenas he was a noted anti-Semite. In response, I can only say that people are complicated; my research revealed Joe to be much more interesting than simply an anti-Jewish isolationist, and he did try to help Jewish people out of Germany. In my view, it's the role of fiction to mine the paradoxes of characters like Joe, not oversimplify them. Along similar lines, I am frequently asked about Rosemary, who really did disappear from the family for close to two decades, her locations and circumstances shrouded in mystery. In fact, though she was cared for first at Craig House in New York, she spent most of the rest of her long life at St. Coletta in Jefferson, Wisconsin. The first time Rose saw her oldest daughter after the lobotomy was 1962, and in 1968 Eunice founded the Special Olympics in her sister's honor.

I am also grateful that Debo was a writer and memoirist, as I found passages of her memoir *Wait for Me!* to be extremely helpful (especially for that anecdote about the duke and his method for testing flies!). Parts of Catherine Bailey's *Black Diamonds: The Rise and Fall of an English Dynasty*, and my friend Michele Turk's *Blood, Sweat and Tears: An Oral History of the American Red Cross*, were also illuminating, as was a well-remembered 1983 *Vanity Fair* piece, "The Kennedy Kick" by Peter Collier and David Horowitz. I dipped in and out of Barbara A. Perry's biography of Rose Kennedy (*Rose Kennedy: The Life and Times of a Political Matriarch*), Kate Clifford Larson's and Elizabeth Koehler-Pentacoff's biographies of Rosemary (*Rosemary: The Hidden Kennedy Daughter* and *The Missing Kennedy: Rosemary Kennedy and the Secret Bonds of Four Women*, respectively), as well as Doris Kearns Goodwin's *The Fitzgeralds and the Kennedys: An American Saga* and Laurence Leamer's *The Kennedy Women: The Saga of an American Family*. And, of course, there is Google. What did writers of historical fiction do before they could Google "songs 1939" or "movies 1943" and instantly have the answer? I feel lucky to be writing about the past in the Information Age.

Although all the real people I used as characters in *The Kennedy Debutante* behave in ways that I made up, only two important characters are wholly fictional: Bertrand and Father O'Flaherty. Having been raised a

Catholic myself, I know there are nurturing, forward-thinking priests in the world. Given Kick's decisions about her life and religion, I like to imagine there really was for her a religious authority like Father O'Flaherty who could give her hope for a better future. And while Bertrand might not be real, the deep and lasting friendships Kick formed in England were very real indeed. Real and transformative, as great friendships are.

MORE DETAILS ABOUT THE QUOTES

One of the things I learned while researching this novel is that quotes are surprisingly slippery. For instance, in biographies and profiles of the Kennedys, one of the most quoted telegrams from Joe Sr. to Kick is the one he sent after her wedding to Billy: WITH YOUR FAITH IN GOD YOU CAN'T MAKE A MISTAKE REMEMBER YOU ARE STILL AND ALWAYS WILL BE TOPS WITH ME. Lynne McTaggart seems to have been the first to use it, but because the telegram itself has been taken out of public circulation—and believe me, I looked for it!—all subsequent writers can only cite her citation, or one of the subsequent writers, like Doris Kearns Goodwin, who quote her. To further complicate matters, among the books I read, the rules for citation varied widely with publisher and year of publication, so some of the original sources were tough to find.

Since this is a novel and not a biography, there aren't any footnotes or endnotes, but I thought I would highlight a few of my direct quotes in case readers are curious. I couldn't resist using two of Billy's tantalizing telegrams to Kick, which are pasted right into one of her scrapbooks: LETTER JUST ARRIVED WONDERFUL NEWS GET LEAVE JUNE 22 LONGING TO SEE YOU WRITING LOVE BILLY HARTINGTON. And also: REACH LONDON 7.15 SATURDAY STAYING AT MAYFAIR CAN YOU KEEP SUNDAY FREE BILLY. Moreover, there was "a permanent lump" in Billy's throat at the end of the war, and he really did write that he wanted to share the experience with Kick—it's all there in a letter he wrote to her just before he was killed. There was a lump in *my* throat when I read those lines. I couldn't think of better words than Billy's own, so of course I used them.

It was also fun to play with quotes here and there. When Bertrand says he should start taking bets on when Kick and Billy will announce their engagement, I was actually putting Kick's words in his mouth: in a letter dated July 14, 1943, to "Dearest Little Kennedys," she wrote that there is "heavy betting on when we are going to announce it." I also had to employ Jack's melodramatic line, used to counsel Kick against marrying Billy, that he has "come to the reluctant conclusion that it has come time to write the obituary of the British Empire."

I integrated about twenty short quotes from my sources, all of which I tried to weave in as I did the real-life events in the book—with imagination. My guiding light was the "beautiful dream" quote that opens *The Kennedy Debutante*, from a letter Kick wrote to her father in 1939, which she herself echoes so movingly when she writes in her 1943 diary of her first day back in London that "it all seems like a dream from which I shall awaken very soon."

THE
KENNEDY
DEBUTANTE

❖ ❖ ❖

KERRI MAHER

INTERVIEW WITH KERRI MAHER

1. Did the Kennedy family know you were writing the book?

Since I was writing a novel and not a biography, I did not contact the family; however, I did speak at length with the librarians at the John F. Kennedy Presidential Library, whom I believe are in touch with members of the family, though I have no idea if any of the librarians mentioned my project. Similarly, I contacted the archive at Chatsworth to ask a few questions, but I do not know if my project reached the ears of the current Duke of Devonshire.

2. How much of the book is fiction and how much is real?

This is a great question that's very hard to answer because it's impossible to quantify, and I don't think anyone wants me to go through the book scene by scene and explain what I made up and what I didn't! In my Author's Note, I talk a bit about direct quotes I took from certain irresistible letters and telegrams, but mostly the correspondence is fiction. Having read real letters written by Billy and Kick, I tried to capture their voices in my made-up epistles and telegrams (what a fun precursor to texting those were!).

Historical events like Kristallnacht, the Epsom Derby, and the Kennedy family attendance at the Pope's coronation are all "true," meaning they actually happened—but I wrote the scenes in the book from my imagination. Knowing what I did about the characters in the scene, I asked myself how they might actually have behaved and reacted to the event, and I wrote according to my writerly intuition.

Likewise, many small events and character traits are also "true" (like Bobby hiding Kick's left shoes and Rose keeping track of her children's weight and eating habits on index cards), but again, I used them where they were useful in the novel to build character and suspense.

Sometimes I deviated entirely from what is supposedly "true." For instance, according to most biographers and Kennedy scholars, Kick and Bill met at a garden party at Buckingham Palace during the 1938 season. But I liked the idea of them meeting at the 400 Club better—it's a sexier setting, and since I was writing a novel, it enabled me to show the chemistry between them right off the bat. And anyway, since Kick wasn't exactly keeping a record of her clandestine visits to the famed London nightclub, who's to say they *didn't* meet there first?

3. What was it like to write about America's most famous family?

I was so nervous! In fact, I spent at least a year avoiding writing the book altogether even though I had a file on my computer called "Kick Kennedy" that I kept opening and adding links and other ideas to. But I thought, "Who am I to write about the Kennedys?!" I told myself I was just some writer—who wasn't even a Kennedy aficionado—with five unpublished novels in her attic. Plus, I'd never tried to write novel-length historical fiction before.

Kick's story called out to me in a way that no other story ever had, though. She and I also had some important things in common that drew me to her and helped me understand her plight: I, too, was raised Catholic (Irish and Italian on my mother's side), and I had lived in London when I was about her age and loved the city and country just as much as she did.

Even when I made the decision to research and write the book in earnest, I was nervous, throwing all kinds of obstacles in my own way: *How can you write about JFK, one of America's most famous presidents, as a young man? Will the Kennedys get mad at you? What would Kick say?*

In the midst of this doubt, two writer friends from opposite corners of my life both asked me the same essential question: "But Kerri, this is *your* book, isn't it?"

Well, yes. Yes it was. And armed with that certainty, I was able to shove aside my doubts and write the book.

4. How long did it take you to write the book? What was your process?

It was six years from getting the idea to publication, but the actual research and writing took about three years, including a major rewrite. When I drafted the first version of the book, I thought it might be a young adult novel, and so I focused only on the eighteen-month period when Kick lives in London before the war breaks out, when she is still a teenager. But the book didn't come out as a YA novel, and my early readers indicated I should probably write the full story of Kick and Billy—which meant writing the next five years of her life! So it was back to the drawing board for me. Parts one and two of the novel you're holding in your hands are actually a wildly condensed version of the first draft of the book, which was itself a 450-page novel!

It turned out that even though I'd never written a historical novel before, the process of writing *The Kennedy Debutante* lit up parts of my brain that hadn't been inspired since college—and I loved it. Back then, I really enjoyed researching and writing English and art history papers in which I could explore real people and events, characters and subjects, and stitch them together with my own ideas and interpretations. Writing historical fiction felt much the same.

Before *The Kennedy Debutante*, I was entirely a "pantser" writer—I wrote without a plan, entirely by the seat of my pants. Penning

historical fiction made me into a "plotter" writer who needed an outline before starting a draft in order to organize all my notes, ideas,
and the timeline. Ironically, I found my outline incredibly liberating!

**5. What kind of research did you do on Kick and the Kennedy
family? Did anything surprise you?**

My favorite part of the research for the book was going to the John F.
Kennedy Library in Boston and spending a glorious day in the sun-filled
reading rooms, paging through the boxes of materials they had on Kick.
The librarians there were extremely helpful. I also really enjoyed reading
the many passages from and full books about the Kennedys that I discuss
in the Author's Note. The third type of research I did was online. I
would Google places like the 400 in London and music or movies of the
time. I'd listen to a few songs or watch a video clip to get a feel for the
atmosphere, then go back to my scene.

I was most surprised by the profound tragedies that befell the
Kennedys in the period I wrote about. Prior to this book, I wasn't
what you might call a "Kennedy watcher"—I knew about them, of
course, but in a casual way, and most of what I knew was from Jack's
election forward. So it was a real eye-opener to discover that in less
than five years at the start of the 1940s, the family endured Joe Sr.'s
political failure, Rosemary's botched lobotomy, Joe Jr.'s death, and
Kick's marriage to Billy and subsequent widowhood. You hear about
"the Kennedy curse," but for me it was an abstraction until I did my
research and really tried to understand what those events must have
felt like for the people involved.

And here was one laugh-out-loud surprise: Rose Kennedy was a
bargain lover! There was the most hilarious detail in one of the round-
robin letters she wrote to the family in 1943: "I have never seen such
crowds in New York City, especially at Bergdorf's where they seem to
be buying those expensive shoes at $20 a pair." This might seem small,

especially when I was writing a book set during World War II, for goodness' sake, but it really is the little details like this that bring a character alive to a writer—and then to a reader.

6. What about Billy Hartington and his family?

As with the Kennedys, it was the little details that brought the Cavendishes to life for me, like reading in Deborah Mitford's memoir *Wait for Me* about the Duke of Devonshire testing his hand-tied flies in the bathtub. I think maybe I was less surprised overall by the Cavendish family only because I didn't have any expectations of Billy and his family going in. That said, as I learned about Billy, the sheer force of his affection for Kick began to surprise and delight me. For a handsome, extremely eligible aristocrat to carry a torch for someone during three years of total separation says a great deal about the depth of his feeling (remember, these are the days of expensive and rare long-distance phone calls, and letters that take weeks to reach the recipients). Writers often become protective of their characters, and so when it came time for Kick to renounce her family and church to marry Billy, I was comforted by the steadfastness of his love for her.

7. World War II–era fiction is hugely popular. Why do you think people are so drawn to stories set during this time?

It must be because we're still discovering and imagining untold stories from that time. The war has proven to be incredibly versatile as a backdrop, as an integrated setting, and as a driver of action—much as the Middle Ages has, or ancient Rome. We're *still* writing about the Middle Ages and ancient Rome, and I think we always will.

I never set out to write a book set during World War II. I wanted to write a book about Kick Kennedy, and I would have been happy writing about her no matter when she'd lived. Also, at first, I did my best to avoid the war, setting my first draft entirely in the period before it started. But once I delved into the early 1940s, I was in deep.

Understanding the political and social situations in England and America in 1938 and '39 that led to the war was key for me—it gave me a way into the material that was quite different from the many wonderful movies and books I'd consumed about the war that took place on the continent of Europe. And then. . . . Well, how could I resist the music and fashion of the period, and discovering real-life bands like the Flying Yanks, or the life of Red Cross girls stationed abroad, and the dramatic cultural shifts that were taking place even among the wealthiest of families? The idea that a girl like Kick Kennedy wouldn't have been able to get enough fabric for a full-length wedding dress or enough sugar for a frosted cake is interesting to me as a writer. Historical details like that help me put pressure on a character; you know a girl *really* wants to marry a particular guy if all the trappings of her long-dreamed-of wedding aren't available *and* her family refuses to be present.

8. What are you working on next?

I am writing a biographical novel about Grace Kelly, from her early days as an acting student in New York until the end of her life. I was raised on old movies, with Hitchcock being one of my mother's favorites; *Rear Window* has always occupied a nascent corner of my imagination, so I feel truly lucky to be writing this novel! Though Grace's life has some important things in common with Kick's—complicated family dynamics, glamorous lifestyles, Irish Catholic upbringings, expatriating to Europe by marriage—Grace is a different subject altogether. She was an ambitious artist and career woman in the housewifely postwar years, but since I am writing about her as an adult woman, married with children, I also get to delve into the often-conflicting dynamics of her home and professional lives. I am excited to explore her often misunderstood life with readers.

QUESTIONS FOR DISCUSSION

1. In these days of Facebook and FaceTime, it is hard to imagine a love like Kick and Billy's, which endures four years of their being separated by an ocean and a war, with infrequent letters and telegrams their only means of communication. Why do you think their love survives that distance of time and space?

2. Kick often struggles with the relationship between her internal desires and her external image. Where do the internal and external meet for her? Where are they most different? How does Billy deal with the same struggle?

3. Family, religion, and class are powerful forces in Kick's life. How does she use them to her advantage? In what cases do they undermine her desire for an independent life?

4. Kick makes a number of observations about the differences between her own life and upbringing, and the expectations of her new milieu, English society. How does she use these differences to her advantage? Which ones does she try to minimize?

5. Have you ever been thrown into a new social scene and felt that you had to perform? How did it make you feel? What did you do?

6. Kick has to make a painful decision between her family and her love. Do you think you would make the same choice?

7. In what ways are Kick's years in England before the war like a "beautiful dream," as she described them in the letter she wrote to her father in 1939? Does the dream continue when she returns *during* the war?

8. Jack, Joe Jr., and Billy all fight valiantly in World War II, but how are their attitudes toward the war different from one another's? What do they have in common? What seems to be each man's primary objective?

9. Kick and her English friends tend to "Keep Calm and Carry On"—or maybe "Party On" is a better description. Why do you think that is possible for them? Do you think the modern sensibility about war would produce the same result today?

10. Kick often envies her older brothers for their independence and freedoms. In what ways have young women today transcended those gender roles? In what ways are they still present?

11. Many women have to reconcile personal desires with the constraints of family and society. What do you think of Kick's strategy? Do you think she would take the same approach today?

12. How does the Kennedy family as portrayed in the book fit with your own picture of the family? What surprises you?

13. The Kennedy women invest a great deal of time, effort, and money in fashion. What role does fashion play for them?

14. Jack tells John White, "There is Saturday night, and there is Sunday morning. Never the twain shall meet." Do you think Kick agrees?

15. How does the portrayal of Jack as a young man fit or not fit with your image of him as JFK, the man who—as Debo's mother correctly predicted—became president of the United States?

16. "Some lives are short," Kick writes to Father O'Flaherty from Washington, DC, "and I increasingly feel that it's essential to live the life it's in one's soul to live." In addition to the premature death of Kick's friend George Mead, what do you think prompts this revelation? Do you think Kick lives the life it's in her soul to live? Why is she so conflicted about her soul?

LOOK FOR
THE GIRL IN WHITE GLOVES,
KERRI MAHER'S NEW NOVEL
ABOUT GRACE KELLY,
COMING FROM BERKLEY IN EARLY 2020.

Author photo by Peter Su

Kerri Maher is also the author of *This Is Not a Writing Manual: Notes for the Young Writer in the Real World* under the name Kerri Majors. She holds an MFA from Columbia University and founded YARN, an award-winning literary journal of short-form YA writing. A writing professor for many years, she now writes full time and lives with her daughter in Massachusetts, where apple picking and long walks in the woods are especially fine.

CONNECT ONLINE

kerrimaher.com
facebook.com/kerrimaherwriter
twitter.com/kerrimaherbooks
instagram.com/kerrimaherwriter

Ready to find
your next great read?

Let us help.

Visit prh.com/nextread

Penguin
Random
House